You Were Gone

You Were Gone

TIM WEAVER

PENGUIN BOOKS

PENGUIN BOOKS

UK | USA | Canada | Ireland | Australia
India | New Zealand | South Africa

Penguin Books is part of the Penguin Random House group of companies
whose addresses can be found at global.penguinrandomhouse.com.

Published in Penguin Books 2018
001

Copyright © Tim Weaver, 2018

The moral right of the author has been asserted

Set in 13.5/16 pt Garamond MT Std
Typeset by Jouve (UK), Milton Keynes
Printed in Great Britain by Clays Ltd, St Ives plc

A CIP catalogue record for this book is available from the British Library

HARDBACK ISBN: 978–0–718–18900–6
TRADE PAPERBACK ISBN: 978–0–718–18901–3

www.greenpenguin.co.uk

For Sharlé

Day One

I

After it was all over, they let me watch the footage of her entering the police station. She seemed small, almost curved, in her green raincoat and dark court shoes, as if her spine was arched or she was in pain. The quality of the surveillance film was poor, the frame rate set low, which made it disorientating, a series of jerky movements played out against the stillness of the station's front desk.

She paused at the entrance, holding the main door ajar so that light leaked in across the tiled floor and seemed to bleach one side of her face. The faded colours of the film didn't help, reducing blacks to greys and everything else to pastels, and even when she let the door go again and it snapped shut behind her, her features remained indistinct. Her gaze was a shadowy blob, her blonde hair appeared grey. I couldn't see anything of the slight freckling that passed from one cheek to the other, crossing the bridge of her nose, nor the blue and green flash of her eyes. Under the glare of the camera, she may as well have been just another visitor to a police station.

A stranger, nothing else.

Once she let the door go, she headed across the room to the front desk. On the timecode in the corner I could see it was just before 8 a.m. An officer was standing behind the counter, engaged in conversation with someone else, a kid in his teens with a black eye and bloodied cheek. The woman waited patiently behind the teenager until the desk officer told her to take a seat. She did so reluctantly, her head down, her feet barely seeming to carry her to a bank of chairs.

Ten minutes passed. The angle of the camera made it hard

to see her, her head bowed, her hands knotted together in her lap, but then, after the desk officer finished with the teenager and told him to take a seat, she beckoned the woman back to the counter. I met the desk officer when I turned up at the station in the hours after: she had short black hair flecked with grey and a scar high on her left cheek, but on the film I couldn't see the detail in either.

The woman stopped at the counter.

The desk officer bent slightly, so that her head was level with the woman's, and even though the film's frame rate was low and it didn't record her lip movements in real time, I could still tell what she'd asked the woman.

'*You all right, love?*'

The woman didn't respond immediately. Instead, she reached into the pocket of her coat and started looking for something. It began as a slow movement, but then became more frantic when she couldn't find what she was looking for. She checked one pocket, then another, and in the third she found what she was after.

As she unfolded the piece of paper, she finally responded to the officer.

'*Hello.*'

I couldn't tell what the woman said after that, the frame rate making it all but impossible to follow the patterns of her mouth, but she shifted position and, because the camera was fixed to the wall about a foot and a half above her, I could see more of her, could see there was just a single line on the piece of paper. Under the pale rinse of the room's strip lights, her hair definitely looked blonde now, not grey, and it had been tied into a loose ponytail. Despite that, it was messy and unkempt, stray strands everywhere, at her collar, across her face, and even within the confines of the film, the way it twitched and jarred between frames, it was easy to tell that she was agitated.

Finally, her eyes met the officer's and the woman held up the piece of paper and started to talk. I could see the teenager look up from his mobile phone, as if sparked into life by what the woman was saying. They told me afterwards that the woman had been crying, that it had been difficult to understand what she'd been talking about, that her voice, the things she'd been saying, had been hard to process. I watched the desk officer lean towards her, holding a hand up, telling the woman to calm down. She paused, her body swaying slightly, her shoulders moving up and down, and gestured to the piece of paper again.

This time I could read her lips clearly.

'Find him.'

2

The call came on 28 December.

I'd spent Christmas with my daughter, Annabel, in her house in south Devon. She was twenty-nine and lived within sight of a lake at the edge of Buckfastleigh with her thirteen-year-old sister Olivia. I'd only known the two of them for five years – before that, I'd had no idea I was even a father – and although, biologically, Olivia wasn't mine, her parents were gone and I looked out for her just the same. Liv had now gone past the point of believing that an old man with a white beard came down the chimney with a sackful of pre-sents, but she was still a kid, and kids always made Christmas more fun. We opened gifts, we watched old movies and played even older board games, we ate and drank and chased Annabel's dog across a Dartmoor flecked in frost, and then I curled up with them in the evenings on the sofa and real-ized how little I missed London. It was where I lived, where my work was, but it was also where my home stood – empty even when I was inside it. It had been that way, and felt like that, every day for eight years, ever since my wife Derryn had died.

The morning of the call, I woke early and went for a run, following the lanes to the west of the house as they gently rose towards the heart of the moors. It was cold, the trees skeletal, the hedgerows thinned out by winter, ice gathered in slim sheets – like panes of glass – on the country roads. After four miles, I hit a reservoir, a bridge crossing it from one side to the other. Close by, cows grazed in the grass, hemmed in by wire fences, and I could see a farmer and his dog, way off in the distance, the early-morning light winking in the windows of a tractor. I carried on for a while until I reached a narrow road set upon a hill with views across a valley of green and brown fields, all perfectly stitched together. Breathless, I paused there and took in the view.

That was when my phone started ringing.

I had it strapped to my arm, the mobile mapping my route, and I awkwardly tried to release it, first from the headphones I had plugged in, then from the pouch it was secured inside. When I finally got it out, I could see it was a central London number, and guessed it was someone who needed my help, somebody whose loved one had gone missing. Very briefly, I toyed with the idea of not answering it at all, of protecting my time off, this time alone with a daughter I'd only known for a fraction of my life, and was still getting to know. But then reality hit. The missing were my ballast. In the time since Derryn had died, they'd been my lifeblood, the only way I could breathe properly. This break would have to end and, sooner or later, I'd have to return to London, to the work that had become my anchor.

'David Raker.'

'Mr Raker, my name's Detective Sergeant Cathrine Field.'

Thrown for a moment, I tried to recall if I'd come across Field before, or had ever heard anyone mention her name.

'How can I help you?'

'It's a bit of a weird one, really,' Field responded, and then paused. 'We've had someone walk into the station here at Charing Cross this morning. She seems quite confused.' Another pause. 'Or maybe she's not confused. I don't know, to be honest.'

'Okay,' I said, unsure where this was going.

'She doesn't have anything on her – no phone, no ID. The only thing she brought with her is a scrap of paper. It's got your name on it.'

I looked out at the view, my body beginning to cool down, the sweat freezing against my skin. My website was only basic, little more than an overview and a contact form, but it listed my email address and a phone number.

'I expect she found me online,' I said.

'Maybe,' Field replied. She cleared her throat, the line drifting a little.

'So are you saying she wants my help?'

'I'm not sure what she wants.'

'What do you mean?'

'She says she knows you.'

'Knows me how?'

Field cleared her throat for a second time. 'She says she's your wife.'

I frowned. 'My *wife*?'

'That's what she says.'

'No,' I said. 'No, my wife has been dead for eight years.'

'Since 2009,' Field replied. 'I know, I just read that online.'

I waited for her to continue, to say something else, to tell me this was a joke at my expense, some bad-taste prank. But she didn't. Instead, she said something worse.

'This woman, she says her name's Derryn Raker.'

'What?'

'Derryn Alexandra Raker.'

'No,' I said. 'No way. She's lying.'

'She seems pretty convinced about it.'

'It's not Derryn. Derryn's dead.'

'Yeah, well, that's the other thing she said,' Field replied, her voice even, hard to interpret or analyse. 'She tells me she's really sorry for what she's put you through – but now she wants to explain everything.'

3

I didn't get back into London until after four thirty, and by the time I arrived at Charing Cross the city was dark, its streets frozen. I felt numb as I climbed the steps, unsure of myself, angry, dazed. The phone call had created a hollow in my chest and I'd spent four hours on the motorway trying to close it up, trying to talk myself down.

It wasn't Derryn.

It wasn't my wife.

I'd buried her eight years ago. I'd been with her at the hospital when they told us she had breast cancer. I'd sat with her when she was going through chemotherapy. I'd been there, holding her hand the first time, the second, the third when she told me she couldn't carry on with it, because it wasn't working and she was tired, so tired, of all the medicine and the sickness and the hospital visits. She'd sat with me on the edge of the bed, in the house that we'd shared, as I'd cried, as we'd both cried. She was the one that started me along the path to finding missing people, sitting there in a chair on our back deck, telling me it was a perfect fit for who I was. She was the one they'd carried out of the house on a stretcher on the morning only one of us woke up.

The woman wasn't Derryn.

And yet, as I crossed the tiled floors of the station to where the front desk was, I couldn't quite let go of the idea that I wanted it to be. That somehow, for some reason, it really had been a lie; the past eight years had been a mistake, some sort of deception at my expense. I'd never loved another woman like I'd loved Derryn, and the women I'd met since her death, who I'd dated and tried to love the same way, had eventually fallen away because of it. What if it *was* her? Did that mean I was sick? Delusional?

'Yes, sir?'

The desk officer was looking inquisitively at me.

'I'm David Raker.'

The surname instantly registered with her and she told me to take a seat. A couple of minutes later, DS Catherine Field emerged from a security door beside the desk. She waved me over. I got up, my legs weaker than they should have been, my heart beating hard against my ribs, and we shook hands. She was in her thirties with sandy hair, clipped at the arc of her forehead and falling against her shoulders, and had grey eyes that matched the colour of her trouser-suit, the jacket buttoned up at the front.

She led me into a long corridor. I could hear telephones and the hum of conversation. Through a window, I glimpsed an office, a whiteboard with notes in blue and green pen, and a map of central London, pinned with pictures and Post-its.

At the end, we moved through a second security door, and as Field held it open for me she spoke: 'Thanks for getting here so quickly. I know this is . . .'

She faded out.

I'd told her on the phone that it wasn't Derryn. I told her everything I'd already told myself, except I'd left out the parts about wanting it to be her, much less the moments where I actually believed it might be. Closing my eyes for a second, I tried to clear my head. I needed to be lucid. When I faced this woman, when I tried to find out why she'd pretended to be Derryn, I needed my emotions pushed all the way back.

Field came to a halt in front of another office that – except for an interview room – was exactly the same as the first. There was a small Christmas tree on a desk in the corner, tinsel snaking through its fake branches, and a few token baubles hanging from filing cabinets and the corner of the whiteboard. Beyond that was the interview room, its door slightly ajar.

People in the office glanced at me, plain-clothes officers in the middle of phone calls or working at computers. I heard warm air being pumped out of a heating unit above my head, could feel it against my face. The longer I stood there, the more the heat started to create a haze behind my eyes, a blur, a fog that made me feel unsteady on my feet and vaguely disquieted: except it wasn't the heat that was getting to me, and it wasn't the detectives staring in my direction – it was the woman inside the interview room.

I could just see the slant of her back and some of her hair. Her legs were tucked in under a table, most of her face was obscured by the door, and the clothes she was wearing – a red jumper and a pair of pale grey tracksuit trousers – didn't fit. I doubted if they were the clothes she had turned up in. Those had probably been bagged as evidence and replacements provided by the police. She'd had no ID on her, couldn't remember her address when asked, and she'd been in a distressed state, so the minute Field met her, she'd have treated the woman like a crime scene: kidnapping, imprisonment, being held against her will – Field would have considered all of them. That made her clothes evidence, her skin, her nails. They would have used an Early Evidence Kit too if there were signs of sexual assault or rape. They would have been through the database looking for the woman, for a history, searching under the name she'd given them for any record she may have had, or connections to anyone. The only person they would have found was me. Derryn had never got as much as a speeding ticket, but I was different: I'd been arrested before, cautioned, interviewed about cases I'd worked and people I'd gone looking for. If Field was searching for a lead right off the bat, she'd have got it, and when I glanced at her, I saw the confirmation: my entry on the database had rung alarm bells, and now I wasn't just here assisting.

I was a potential suspect.

4

I looked at Field and said, 'My wife is dead.'

I wasn't sure if it was an effort to convince her or myself.

Field glanced at me. 'She died of cancer, right?'

'Right.'

'Breast cancer.'

'Yes.'

'And this was in 2009?'

I nodded.

'Yeah,' Field said, 'like I said, I found that online.'

She might have found it on a database somewhere, but more likely she'd got the details from the Internet. I'd never sought out notoriety, never given a single interview, but it hadn't stopped journalists from camping outside my door in the aftermath of some of my most publicized cases. And now the results of that were out there on websites: insects frozen in amber that I could never cut out or dislodge.

We looked at each other for a moment.

'You don't believe me?' I said.

'About what?'

'You don't believe my wife is dead?'

'It seems to be a matter of public record.'

I eyed her, trying to understand her meaning.

'You think I disseminated a lie?'

'No,' Field said, 'that's not what I said.'

'That's what it sounded like.'

'Don't get paranoid, Mr Raker.'

'It's not paranoia,' I said. 'I know what you're thinking. I understand why. I know it's your job to look at it from this angle. But I watched my wife die slowly over the course of two and a half years, and I didn't imagine that, or make it up. I sat beside her in the hospital and slept next to her at night, and when she decided that she'd had enough, when she finally died, it took everything from me. It took *everything*.' I turned to Field again and cleared my throat, trying to keep my emotions in check. 'I don't know who this woman is, or why she's doing this – but the one thing I can tell you for certain is that it's not Derryn.'

It was hard to tell if any of that had made any difference, because Field simply nodded again, her eyes on the interview suite, and said, 'I told her what you said to me on the phone earlier – you know, that she's lying about who she is – and she says you must be confused.'

'I'm not confused.'

'She also mentioned that she'd been missing.'

That stopped me.

'Missing where?'

'She didn't say, but that's one of the other reasons we have to get involved. She told us she's your wife, she mentioned that she's been missing for eight years, and she says she's not going to say anything else until she's seen you.' Field already had a pad; now she removed a pencil. 'She only wants to talk to you.'

There was a moment's silence, the lull filled with the sound of phone calls and conversations from the office. Eventually, Field said, 'You have a daughter, right?'

'Yes. Annabel.'

'Derryn wasn't her mother?'

She eyed me. She was clearly asking if I'd ever cheated on my wife.

'No,' I said. 'I never knew a thing about Annabel until her mother finally told me about her five years ago. Her mother and I, we went out for a year when we were both seventeen, before I left for university, and we split up – amicably – before

I went. She was already pregnant by then, but she chose not to tell me. I married Derryn not knowing I was a father, and Derryn never met Annabel before she died.'

Field nodded. 'Good to know.'

I looked towards the interview room again.

'We're not going to let you talk to her.'

I turned to Field. 'What?'

'Even though that's what she's requested, we can't do that. You can probably appreciate why. We need to fully understand her reasons for being here, and putting the two of you in the same room before we even know what those reasons are . . . Well, that's not going to happen.' Again, she was underlining what I already knew.

I was a potential suspect.

She gestured for me to follow her and took me into an adjacent room where a bank of monitors was lined up on a desk. From the doorway I could see the image of the woman on one of the screens, and the closer I got, the shakier I started to feel: I was swaying, my heart hammering so hard, I could hear its echoes in my ears. It wasn't hot in the room but I was sweating all the same – across my brow, along my top lip.

'Take a seat and put on the headphones,' Field said.

I leaned in towards the monitor, trying to get a better look at her, at her face, and as I did, everything seemed to still. I pulled a chair out, sat, and realized Field was watching me, not her. Almost on cue, the woman half-turned in the direction of the camera, her eyes on the door, and I saw her properly for the first time.

No. No way.

'Mr Raker?'

I glanced at Field, then back to the monitor.

'She . . .' The words stuck in my throat.

'She what?' Field asked.

'She looks just like Derryn.'

5

I watched through the feed, headphones on. Behind me, the door was ajar, a uniformed officer stationed just outside, but I was barely even aware of him. I was barely aware of anything. All I could focus on was the image on the monitor: Field, and the woman facing her across the desk.

Derryn.

I closed my eyes, denying it was her – over and over again – as Field explained to the woman that she couldn't let her see me until they'd figured out what was going on. 'David will be made aware of what you tell me, though,' Field assured her, and when I opened my eyes again, the woman was frowning, as if struggling to understand – or trying to work something out.

She looked around the interview room for a second, and then her gaze lodged on the camera. It was just above her eyeline, but it was obvious that she hadn't realized it was there until now. The picture had been zoomed in slightly, the feed creating a crisp, clear image of her. As I looked at her, it was like we were in the same room for a moment, across the same table, breathing the same air.

'Can David see me?' she asked Field. I listened to her voice for the first time, replayed it in my head, tried to recall if it was the same voice I'd listened to every day for the sixteen years Derryn and I were together. But I wasn't sure. It had been too long. And as I realized that, as I realized I could no longer remember my wife's voice, I felt a crushing sense of loss: dizzy with it, shamed.

'Tell him I just want him to take me home.'

'Take you home where, Derryn?'

Derryn.

I snapped back into the moment. *It's not her.* I looked at Field on the monitor. *Don't call her Derryn. That's not her name.*

'It's me, sweetheart,' the woman said, and this time she talked directly into the camera. 'D, it's me.'

D. That was what Derryn used to call me.

No. I realized I was shaking my head. *It's not her.*

'It's me,' the woman repeated.

I glanced at Field. She was watching the woman.

'It's me,' she said again, more softly, more defeated.

'No,' I muttered, the word so quiet, it barely formed in my mouth. I wanted to tear through the walls and ask her who she really was, and why she was pretending to be Derryn, but my head was just static, ringing like the impact of an explosion.

'David says you're not his wife,' Field said.

She glanced at Field. 'What?'

'He says you're not his wife.'

Tears instantly welled in the woman's eyes. 'Why would he say that?' she said. 'I've come back to him. Please just let me explain to him what happened.'

I was shaking my head again.

'*Please.*'

'He says you aren't Derryn,' Field repeated.

'I am.' She made a sound like she'd been winded. 'I *am.*'

I closed my eyes again.

Derryn's dead. She's been dead for eight years.

'All right,' Field said.

When I finally opened my eyes, the woman was leaning forward at the table, her fingers spread out in front of her, as if she were trying to reach for the door.

It wasn't Derryn, I knew it in my bones, but it was still hard to process the striking physical similarities between them: their eyes were so alike; the woman's hair was the same colour and cut into the same style as Derryn's had been; they were an almost identical size – same height, weight, build – and their faces were the same shape. But it wasn't her. If I struggled to remember Derryn's voice, I didn't struggle to remember her face. I'd seen it in photographs, over and over again, for eight years. As much as I wanted to pretend that I would never forget her mannerisms, the timbre of her voice, the way she expressed herself, the truth was, time had rubbed some of those things away. The minutiae that I promised myself I'd never forget, I stopped remembering as often, and sometimes didn't think of at all. But her face had never dimmed. I'd buried her, and I'd mourned her, and I'd felt every moment of it. I knew in every part of me that I hadn't mourned a lie, just as clearly as I saw the minor differences in this woman's face; the cracks in the fiction. Her physical similarity to Derryn *was* staggering – but it wasn't exact. Not quite.

'Please just tell David to come and get me.'

I tuned back in.

'Can you tell him to come and get me?' she asked Field again.

So if you're not Derryn, who are you?

'You know it's me, D.'

She was looking at the camera again.

Why the hell are you doing this?

Field said, 'I asked you where you lived earlier, do you recall that?'

'Yes,' the woman replied.

'You said you couldn't remember.'

The woman looked at Field blankly.

'Do you remember now?'

'I live with David,' she said, as if it were another trick.

'So what's your address?'

'My address?'

'Yes. Where's the house you share with David?'

'Forty Aintree Drive.'

She knows where I live. It wouldn't be impossible to find my

17

address, but it would be hard: I deliberately kept it out of the public domain.

'He says you don't live with him,' Field said.

'I do.' She looked into the camera again. 'Of course I do. I'm his wife.'

I glanced at Field, who was looking at the woman.

Stop this now. She's ill.

'You told us earlier that you were missing,' Field said.

'Did I?'

'For almost eight years.'

The woman frowned. 'I don't think I said that.'

'You did.'

'I'm sure I didn't.'

'You did. But you say you're living with David. So how is that missing?'

'It's not,' she responded. 'I said we got separated, not that I was missing.'

'You and David got separated?'

'Yes. Perhaps that's where the confusion comes from.'

'Where did you get separated?'

'At the pharmacy.'

I saw Field's gaze drift to the woman's right arm. Just inside the sleeve of the jumper she was wearing, almost hidden from view, was evidence of bandaging, the gauze dotted with blobs of blood. I hadn't noticed it until now. Field must have seen it already.

'You were going to get your arm looked at?' she asked.

'Yes.'

'How did you cut it?'

'Oh, it was a silly mistake. D was concerned and told me we needed to get it seen to, so he drove me to the pharmacy. He parked up and told me to go and show it to someone.'

This is insane.

'What pharmacy was this?' Field asked her.

'I, uh . . .' She paused. 'I'm not sure what its name is.'

'Do you remember where it was?'

'No.'

'Not the street necessarily, just the general area.'

The woman shook her head again. 'No.'

Field continued making notes in silence. The woman looked between her and the camera as if she didn't understand the silence, or why Field might be having doubts.

'Okay,' Field said. 'Let's go back to the start.'

The woman nodded.

'Can you give me your date of birth?'

'Yes,' the woman said, 'I was born in Guildford on the 3rd of March 1975.' She glanced at the camera, and I knew why: all the details were correct.

'When did you first move to London?'

'End of August, beginning of September 1993, when I was eighteen. I moved to London to study Nursing at South Bank, and then did a postgrad at King's College.'

This was Derryn's history. I remembered her graduation ceremony at the Royal Festival Hall. We were living in a flat in Holloway at the time.

'And how did you end up here today?'

'I came by train.'

'From where?'

'Woolwich Arsenal.'

'South-east London?'

The woman shrugged.

'You look confused,' Field said.

'I don't know London that well. What's east, what's west, all of that.'

Field tapped her pencil against her pad. 'You live with David but you don't know London?'

'No,' the woman replied innocently. 'Not really.'

'But Ealing *is* in London.'

'Ealing?'

'Where you and David live.'

'Oh,' the woman said. 'Oh, right.'

'So why would you go to a pharmacy in Woolwich?'

'Why wouldn't I?'

'Because it's on the opposite side of the city to where you say you live.'

This time, the woman didn't respond.

'Did you know it was on the opposite side of the city?'

'I, uh . . .' The woman halted. I felt relief start to wash through me. Whatever the motivation for this, it was starting to fall apart.

'What do you do for a living?' Field said, changing tack.

'I'm a senior nurse,' the woman said.

'So why did you need a pharmacist?'

'What do you mean?'

'I mean, couldn't you have just treated that cut on your arm yourself? You presumably know how to treat wounds?'

'Yes, of course I do,' she said, but didn't answer the question. Instead, she leaned forward at the table. 'I'll feel so safe once I'm back with David.'

Silence in the room.

Field looked between her and the camera, as if some unspoken message had passed through the wiring, through the walls, from one room to the next.

'What do you mean, "safe"?' Field asked.

The woman didn't move.

'You said you'd feel safe once you were back with David.'

A shrug. 'David's my husband.'

'He's says he's not.'

'Why would he say that?'

'Because he says his wife died eight years ago.'

But she was already shaking her head. 'No. No, that's not

20

right.' She looked to the camera. 'Why is he doing this? You said you would always keep me safe, D.'

'What do you mean, "safe"?' Field repeated. She'd come forward on her chair. 'Are you saying you felt *unsafe* before this? Who was making you feel unsafe?'

'It's just a figure of speech,' the woman said.

Field didn't seem convinced. 'Did someone try to hurt you?'

The woman saw that Field was looking at her arm again. 'Oh,' she said. 'It was just an accident. It wasn't his fault. He didn't mean it.'

Even from here, I could sense the air in the room change.

'I was just being stupid.'

I leaned away from the monitor, repulsed, knowing where this was headed.

'Did David do that to you?' Field asked.

'It wasn't his fault,' she said again, almost robotically. 'He didn't mean to.'

'Did he cut you with a knife?'

The woman looked down at the table and started shaking her head. 'I don't want to talk about it,' she said, her voice quiet, and linked her fingers across her lap.

'So you were going to get it looked at today?'

'Yes. That was why David took me to the pharmacy.'

'Why didn't you treat it yourself?'

'Because it's hard dressing your own wounds.'

'So why not go to a doctor or A&E instead of a pharmacy?'

'I don't know,' she said. 'David just said to me that a pharmacist would be the best place to start, and I trusted him. So he dropped me off outside and said he'd wait for me in the car.'

'Why didn't he go in with you?'

'I don't know. You'd have to ask him.'

'And you got separated from David?' Field pressed.

'Yes.'

'How?'

'Just as I was about to go in, I looked back at the car and saw a traffic warden speaking to David. They were arguing. So I wandered a little closer to see what was happening and, as I did, I saw David start to pull the car out of the space, and then he drove off and left me.' She looked at her hands, flat on the table. 'I waited for a while, and then started to walk down the road in the direction I saw David go. But I couldn't see him anywhere – and he never came back.' Tears began pooling in the woman's eyes again. 'I don't understand,' she said to Field, her voice breaking up. 'Why doesn't David remember that?'

Field's head dropped, eyeing her notes. Eventually, she said, 'Why not just go straight back to your house?'

The woman wiped at her eyes.

'I wanted to,' she replied.

'You could have got the Tube out to Ealing.'

Except she doesn't know where Ealing is.

'I don't ride the Underground much,' the woman said, still dabbing her eyes with a finger. 'I've only been on it a few times. I'm not confident on it. But when David drove off, I didn't know what else to do, so I went to the nearest station and the man there helped me buy a ticket to Charing Cross.'

'Why Charing Cross?'

The woman screwed up her face again, as if pained. 'Please,' she said quietly, 'I just want David to take me home. He knows that I get sick if I'm out too long.'

'What do you mean, "sick"?' Field asked her.

But the woman had started to sob. For the first time, I felt a stir of sympathy for her. She was like a lost child. I didn't know who she was and why she was pretending to be Derryn, but it was obvious that she was ill – and not physically.

'I don't know why this is happening to me,' she said, tears starting to fill her eyes again. 'David's my husband. We've been married for twenty-two years.'

We were married for fourteen years. It would have been twenty-two if Derryn had still been alive.

'I started living with him at nineteen,' the woman said, and broke into a smile. 'Ask him about our first flat in Holloway. He'll remember that. It was so small, but we loved it. We used to live directly behind an old cinema.'

The cinema wasn't there any more, so how could she know? I started to wonder if Derryn had had a sister she hadn't told me about, some close relative – a cousin perhaps – who looked a little like her. But that would have meant that she'd deliberately lied to me for the entire time that we were together and that her family had done the same, that they were all in on some secret that they'd decided to keep back from me, and I knew that wasn't the case. I'd got on so well with her parents, and when her brother was home I'd got on well with him too, it was just none of them was around to ask now: her parents had died within a year of each other in the late nineties, and her brother had been killed in Basra in 2004 when an IED went off under his truck. There were no nieces, no nephews, no cousins. It had just been her and me.

'David says you're not Derryn,' Field told her.

'I don't understand why he's doing this to –'

But then she stopped; and a second later something sparked in her face, as if a light had snapped on.

'Wait,' she said, 'he's had these moments before.'

Field leaned closer. 'Moments?'

'These moments of denial.' She turned to the camera again, her lips pressed together; saddened. 'He's needed medical help before. He must be confused again. That's why he drove off and left me there. It's come back.'

'What's come back?'

'He had a nervous breakdown.'

'This is bullshit,' I said into the monitor, but the only

reaction I got was from the officer at the door, who turned and looked in at me.

'You're saying David's ill?' Field asked.

'He might try to deny it,' the woman replied, 'or might have forgotten entirely. But it's his sickness talking. It's returned.' She put a hand to her mouth and started to cry properly. 'Please don't let it be this,' she whimpered, her words barely audible now. 'Please don't let his mind have gone again.'

6

'I'm not sick,' I said, my words lost in the silence of the room.

Onscreen, the woman blinked, saying nothing else, her eyes wet, her face pale, and then Field came forward at the table, a deep frown on her face. She glanced at the notes she'd made. 'David says his wife died of breast cancer in 2009.'

'It's his sickness,' the woman told Field. 'It must be.'

No. No, it's not a sickness, it's the truth.

Field, pencil poised above her pad, glanced at the camera, as if waiting for an answer. *What?* I thought, looking back at her. *Are you seriously asking me this?* I glanced over my shoulder, towards the door, anger humming beneath my skin. I didn't want to be in here, in this cramped, overheated room, listening to all of these lies on headphones. I wanted to be inside that interview suite. I wanted to know what the hell was going on.

'Everything that happened,' the woman said, 'it just destroyed him.'

I stared Field down as she looked at the camera again, even though I didn't blame her for any of this: she was only asking the same questions I'd asked myself. Across the table from her, the woman sniffed, wiping her nose with a crumpled tissue, and as the audio feed became quiet, I closed my eyes and repeated what I knew to be true: *On 26 November 2009, I woke up and Derryn was lying next to me in bed. She'd died in her sleep. I was due to take her to the hospice that day, because the doctor said she only had a week, maybe two at the most.* I opened my eyes again. I felt tears coming. I tried to blink them away, tried to find some measure of control. *She was so ill I didn't know what to do for her. I couldn't make her comfortable. She was in so much pain, it was . . . I was just . . . I . . .*

'David says his wife died in 2009.'

My thoughts fell away as Field started speaking again.

'That's not what happened,' the woman said in a low voice. She gathered herself for a few seconds longer and, more controlled now, looked across the table at Field: 'I was diagnosed for the first time in March 2007. I went through chemotherapy and it was successful – *really* successful – and I was given the all clear in October that year. After that, David moved to the States, to LA. The paper wanted him to cover the run-up to the election, first from the West Coast and then from Washington. He didn't want to go, and the paper said he didn't have to, but then I told him I would quit my job at the hospital and come with him, so I flew out to join him in November. I'd always wanted to go to America, especially Los Angeles. I'd barely been further than Europe.'

I realized I was holding my breath.

All of this was true.

'We lived in Santa Monica,' she went on, turning in her chair and looking up at the camera, as if she knew I was watching. 'David will remember that. That place we rented just off Wilshire Boulevard, D?' She glanced at Field. 'It was a couple of blocks from the clinic that I worked in. It took me time to adjust to LA, but I loved it eventually.'

Field looked sideways at the camera. I'd given her a brief history of my marriage, of the time Derryn and I had spent abroad – and this was it. This was what I'd told her – *more* than what I'd told her. The woman knew everything.

'How do you know all of that?' Field asked the woman, echoing my thoughts.

'Because I was there.'

'David says you can't have been.'

'Because I'm not his wife?'

26

'Right.'

'This is crazy,' she replied. 'He knows I was. I came out to the States with him and we loved it. We were so happy. Then, in March 2008, the cancer came back a second time.' She paused, swallowed; looked at Field. 'I got my treatment in America for that, because the oncologist where I worked – Leon Singer, a man who went on to become a great friend of ours – pulled some strings and did the treatment for virtually nothing – and, again, I beat it. We moved to Washington in late September, early October, so that David could cover the elections from there, and then – after the elections were over – we moved back home to the UK, in late November.'

Silence.

Field looked sideways at the camera again and I saw conflict in her eyes, a mirror image of how she'd looked in the moments before leaving me to go into the interview suite. There were clear signs of doubt now as she started to wonder if it was the woman telling the truth, not me.

'The cancer came back in April 2009,' the woman said softly, looking down at the table, the fingers of one hand gripped at the edge of it. 'It had spread. Things were a lot worse this time. I didn't know if I could go through another round of treatment. I told D I wasn't sure I could face it. I was so tired.' She looked up, tears glistening in her eyes. 'He kept saying I should do it, over and over: "You should do it, you should do it." We sat in the bedroom, on the edge of the bed, and he took my hand and he begged me to do it. It wasn't that I didn't want to live, it was just I was so tired of it all. The doctors, the hospital visits, the sickness, the recovery, the constant fear that it would come back again. It had hollowed me out. I loved David more than anything in the world, but I was so tired.' She wiped at an eye. 'So I started it, but then I changed my mind. I told him I loved him, but I couldn't go through it all again. I just couldn't do it.'

27

I could hardly rip my gaze away from the woman. How was this possible? I looked at her in the monitor, my throat tremoring. How the hell did she know all of this? There was no way she should have been able to recite this stuff. Most of it had been private conversations.

Unless she'd known Derryn somehow.

Onscreen, she turned and looked up at me.

'See?' she said. 'It's me, D. It's Derryn. It's time to take me home again.'

I tried not to cry. I tried not to let her get to me. However she was doing this, I didn't want it to work. I knew she wasn't the woman I loved – I could see that, I could feel it – and yet I couldn't stop myself. She looked enough like Derryn, seemed to speak enough like her – she knew everything we'd done together; the things we'd said – that finally, reluctantly, it became too much: I felt a tear break from my eye.

'I know why he thinks I died,' she said.

'Because he's sick again?' Field asked, a hint of scepticism lingering in her voice.

'Yes. Even now, he can still get confused sometimes.'

'About what?'

'About everything. I didn't die. It's true, I stopped the treatment for a short time, but then I started it again when I saw how it was destroying him, just like he wanted me to. And it worked this time. It really worked. The cancer hasn't come back.'

'He says that's not true,' Field said.

'It is.'

I felt more tears falling.

'After that third time, after I told him I wasn't going to carry on with the treatment, that I couldn't face any more of it, he had a breakdown – and by the time I started the chemo again it was too late. I thought I would be saving us both, but he was already too far gone. He was already in treatment

28

himself by that time and spent the next fifteen months being seen at St Augustine's. Do you know where that is?'

'No,' Field replied.

'It's on the river,' the woman said.

'The river? Do you mean the Thames?'

'Yes. About a mile from where the planes take off.'

There was only one airport by the Thames: London City.

I shook my head, trying to clear my eyes, impotent in front of the monitor, unable to affect the direction or flow of the conversation. *She doesn't know the name of the river or the name of the airport*, I wanted to tell Field. *How can you trust her?*

'He saw a doctor there.'

'A doctor?'

'Yes. Erik McMillan. Erik with a *k*.'

The scepticism was gone now: the naming of the hospital, the doctor – Field's doubts were back and they were absolutely real.

'Over time, it got so bad that he stopped recognizing me. He kept telling me that I wasn't his wife, that his wife had died. I begged him to stop it, tried to tell him I'd decided to have the treatment after all and it had worked, but he wouldn't have it.'

'You're lying,' I said, my fingernails digging into the desk.

'He kept saying I was dead.'

I stared at Field, willed her to hear me. *She's lying. It's all lies.*

'David's records will still be at St Augustine's,' she said to Field, 'so you'll be able to see I'm not making this up.' She looked at the camera again, her head tilted to one side as if she could actually see me; as if she felt sorry for who I'd become. 'He had his breakdown, and he stopped recognizing me. When I was around him, he would say I wasn't his wife, I wasn't Derryn. He would say I was an impostor. He wouldn't sleep in the same bed as me. He used to scream at me sometimes, asking me who I was and what I was doing in his home. It was only after working with Dr McMillan that he got better.'

None of this is true.

'All of it's true,' she said, as if she'd actually heard me, and then she repeated herself more forcefully, 'all of it's true. In the years since his treatment, ninety-nine per cent of the time he's been fine. But, occasionally, he has lapses. Occasionally, he'll still have these terrible, hurtful moments. I walk into a room sometimes and he goes a little crazy. He starts shouting and screaming at me for no reason.'

She held up her bandaged wrist.

This was who I'd become, according to her.

This was her evidence.

'Sometimes he still says I'm not Derryn.'

7

Field took me to an interview suite.

It was large and cold, the walls plain, the heating yet to kick in. She got a uniformed constable to make me a coffee and then asked if I was okay to wait. I could have walked away and gone home, I wasn't under arrest, but there seemed little point. I needed to find out who this woman was, why she was lying, and how she knew so much about my life with Derryn – and the best way for me to do that was by quizzing Field.

As I waited, I tried to get my thinking straight.

If the woman genuinely believed that she was Derryn, for whatever reason, that suggested some kind of mental health problem. It was possible the woman had spent all, or part, of the eight years that she claimed to have been living with me being treated at a facility somewhere. It was possible it had been St Augustine's, the place she'd mentioned to Field, and this was why she'd brought it up. Or it could be much simpler than that: she could be a liar and all her lies were to serve some other purpose. For now, I couldn't imagine what.

There was so much about her that I found disconcerting, and not just the fact that her resemblance to Derryn was genuine and striking. Grief had turned the memories of my wife into a sort of photograph album, individual moments pinned in my mind; clear snapshots of occasions and the way the two of us had felt about them. After so long, I didn't recall where every freckle on Derryn's cheeks had been; rather, what I remembered of our marriage were things like the two of us going to Brighton one summer and laughing so hard

31

that Derryn accidentally snorted candyfloss up her nose. I remembered, as a journalist, working all night on a story about corruption in the Home Office and thinking it was so important, then meeting Derryn for breakfast the next morning and finding out that she'd had four children die in A&E overnight. Seeing the anguish on her face, I realized my story didn't matter at all, not compared to that, and even now I could recall the sadness of that breakfast, like a prickle in my skin. I had no memory of what she looked like that morning, though she would have been in her uniform and probably had her hair up, but I'd never forget the way it felt, the sadness of it, the helplessness that came with knowing I could do nothing to comfort her.

When I'd looked at the woman in the interview suite, I'd seen an echo of my wife. It was why, at first, my legs had almost given way, why my heart had felt like it was escaping my chest. But it wasn't her. I'd seen the differences physically – they were minor, but they were there in the lips, in the shape of the nose, in the jaw – but I'd *felt* them too. None of the memories of my wife reverberated back to me when I heard the woman speak; I didn't feel the tingle in my skin, the unspoken, automatic charge of electricity that Derryn and I had shared for the sixteen years we'd been together. And that, as much as the physical disparities, was why I knew. That was why I knew I'd shared nothing with this woman – not a single memory; nothing like that day in Brighton, or the heartache of that breakfast. I knew it in my blood.

So who was she?

She knew about conversations Derryn and I had had, the pet name my wife had given me, the things I'd said in private. She knew all about Derryn's illness, when it had happened and where, even the name of Leon Singer, the oncologist we'd become friends with in the US. The account that she gave of our time in America, Derryn's work at the

Santa Monica clinic, the way – four months after we got back to the UK – the cancer returned for a third time and I begged her to go through the chemo again, it was all true. And if she knew that much, it was a fair bet that she knew more.

Perturbed, I checked my watch.

I'd been inside the room almost an hour. The constable came back and offered me a second cup of coffee, which I accepted, and as he walked away, I removed my phone and put in a search for St Augustine's.

The official website was conventional, just a huge photograph of the front of the hospital building – stark, white, modern. On the left of the homepage was a series of links – *Home*, *What We Do*, *Foundation*, *History*, *Support Us* and *Contact* – but nothing had been optimized for mobile and none of the links worked.

A few moments later, Field entered.

'Well, this is a bit of a mess,' she said, and handed me a coffee.

'Only if you actually believe what she's telling you.'

Field didn't respond.

'*Do* you believe what she's telling you?'

Field pulled the chair out from under the table, its legs making a dull scratching sound on the carpet.

'All I know for sure is that one of you is lying to me.'

8

She placed her jacket on the back of the chair and sat down, retrieving her notebook and pencil. I tried to get a sense of what she'd written while she'd been interviewing the woman, but could only make out a few words: *account, illness.*

She took a deep breath.

'It's not Derryn,' I said.

'Does she look like Derryn?'

She waited for my response, eyeing me.

'Does she look like Derryn?' she repeated.

'There are some obvious similarities.'

'But, to your mind, not enough?'

'No.'

'She's adamant she's your wife.'

She looked up again, her grey eyes like wet pebbles. Under the pale glow of the strip lights, the clip in her hair – a plain metal V – glinted slightly as she shifted position in the seat. She watched me for a second, tapping her pencil against the pad.

'Her story doesn't stack up,' I said. 'You know it doesn't.'

Field didn't say anything.

'She goes all the way out to Woolwich to try and find a pharmacy, *then* comes into Charing Cross because she wants the police to call me? Why choose this police station? Why bother involving you at all? I mean, wouldn't it have been easier for her to have just gone back to the home we apparently share? Except, of course, she can't because she doesn't know where Ealing is – in fact, she doesn't know London at all.'

Field leaned back, crossing her arms.

'Should I be worried that you're silent?'

'I'm maintaining an open mind,' she said.

'You really think she's telling the truth?'

'I think she might be ill.'

'Well, you've got that right.'

'Physically ill, I mean.'

'What, you *really* believe that she can't be outside for longer than a few hours or she'll get sick?' I shook my head. 'She's not physically ill.'

'I was talking about the cut on her arm,' Field replied firmly. 'I've had a doctor examine her: it's deep, it's infected, and she's running a temperature. She says she's been feeling light-headed. The doctor says all of that could have come into play.'

'So – what? – the infection's to blame for this delusion?'

'That's not what I said at all.'

'Even if you're right, even if the cut's bad, why not go to a doctor, rather than a pharmacist? And why not go straight from there to a police station in south-east London?'

'She says she *did* try to find a police station out that way, but then she walked to Woolwich Arsenal, noticed the Charing Cross train, and something sparked.'

'"Something sparked"?'

'She said she remembered finding some notes you'd left at the house once, and the words "Charing Cross" had been written on them.'

'Are you kidding me?'

'You're saying that's not correct?'

'What do you think?' I paused, looking at Field. 'Come on, surely you can see how crazy this sounds?'

'She told me it was' – she checked her notes – '"a spontaneous action".'

'What was?'

'Getting the train to Charing Cross.'

'And you're buying that?'

'I'm not *buying* anything. I'm trying to get to the truth.'

The subtext was obvious. The woman was carrying an injury and she'd implied that I'd put it there. Field had asked her if it was a knife injury, but either way it was a deep, infected wound, and that was ringing alarm bells. The woman's refusal to apportion blame to me, the deference in many of her answers, the way she spoke about me – in Field's experience, in my experience too, they were all warning signs. So Field had to make certain I wasn't a threat in this instance – a kidnapper, an abuser, a rapist. She needed to find out who the woman was, why she felt she should use the police as a first port of call, and why she didn't know where our house was located. She needed to find out why the woman had come to Charing Cross and not gone to a police station somewhere closer to Woolwich – and then why the woman was even *in* the Woolwich area in the first place. There were simply too many questions now for Field to dismiss it all out of hand.

As for me, I needed to try and get on top of my emotions, because I didn't want her thinking that I really was the type of man who scared women; worse, one who was violent and abusive to them.

'Does she have any ID on her?' I asked.

'No. She says she has some at home.'

'At *my* home, you mean?'

'That's the obvious assumption, isn't it?'

'Does she have a mobile phone?'

'No.'

'So no ID and no mobile phone?'

Field could hear the cynicism in my words.

'That's pretty convenient, don't you think?'

'How's that?'

'You don't think it's odd that she doesn't have a mobile

phone? Everyone has a mobile phone. This way, she's not making any calls and she's not sending any texts.'

'So?'

'So she doesn't have a contract, there's no paperwork with her name on it, and there's no way to track her movements and prove what she's saying – *and* we can't see who she's contacting.'

'You wouldn't be privy to that information anyway,' Field said coolly. 'Or, at least, not professionally, and not legally.'

It was a dig – at the fact I wasn't a police officer, and at the way she imagined I went about solving cases.

'Is she even on the system?' I asked.

'What do you mean?'

'I mean, is there a Derryn Raker on the system somewhere?'

A long pause. 'No.'

'So she hasn't got an NI number, but she works as a nurse?'

Field didn't say anything.

'That makes zero sense, and you know it.' I waited for a response, didn't get one, so pushed on: 'Have you taken her prints?'

Field smirked this time. 'Are you leading this investigation now?'

'I'm just asking.'

'Yes, we took her prints.'

'And?'

'And they're a dead end.'

'So which hospital does she say she works at now?'

'Queen Elizabeth.'

Field gave me a blank look but I knew exactly what she was thinking: Queen Elizabeth was in Woolwich. That might explain why the woman was in the area.

'Have you phoned them?' I asked. 'Or the people she works with?'

'I'm waiting on a call back.'

I smiled to myself.

'It's Christmas, David. Medical staff are stretched and most of the people in admin roles are at home with their families.'

'Right. So there's no easy way of backing up her story is what we're saying.' I paused, rubbing my eye. 'Did she have any cash or cards on her?'

'Your point being?'

'How did she afford the train to Charing Cross?'

Field seemed to be weighing up whether to respond.

'No cards,' she said eventually.

'So she teleported here from Woolwich?'

'No, she had twenty-two pounds on her in change.'

'No ID, no cards, no phone, no confirmation from the hospital yet that she's even an employee there.' I looked across the table at Field but she had her head down, making indecipherable notes. 'Nothing here feels right. You know it too.'

She eyed me. 'How does she know so much about you?'

'I've genuinely no idea.'

'All the stuff she's saying, it checks out.'

'In what sense?'

'Well, she knew about the flat you had in Holloway, she knows about your wife's illness. You said that was all correct. She seemed to know a hell of a lot about your life in America. I was talking with her in there and it seemed . . .' But she didn't continue.

'Seemed what? She's not my wife, okay? That woman in there, she's a fantasist, or she's ill, or she's just a pathological liar. She's not Derryn.' I leaned back in my chair. 'Come to my house. It's all there. I've got the death certificate. I've got the receipts from the funeral director in the attic somewhere. It'll take about ten minutes for me to show you it all.'

'What about this breakdown she says you had?'

I frowned. 'Surely you don't believe that as well?'

'You're saying it never happened?'

'That's exactly what I'm saying.'

'You don't remember it?'

I let out an exasperated breath. 'Don't remember it? Why would I remember something that never even happened? Whatever she's told you in there, it's lies. I never spent fifteen months being treated at a hospital, let alone one I've never even heard of until today. I try to spend as little time as I can in hospitals. What she's saying is insane. She's delusional. And the worst bit is, you're actually willing to believe her.'

Field went to speak, then stopped.

'What?' I asked.

'I called this doctor she says treated you at St Augustine's. Erik McMillan.'

She studied me.

'And?'

Field leaned towards me. 'And he backed up everything she said.'

9

'That's impossible.'

'McMillan said you'd deny it.'

'I'm denying it because it didn't happen.'

'He said the denial, the belief it never happened, is part of your condition. He said you had depression, anxiety. You had headaches. He said you went through a period of blacking out frequently.'

'That's bullshit,' I said. 'I've never blacked out in my life.'

But then I stopped.

I'd just lied to her, automatically, instinctively: I *had* blacked out once, three years ago – and, judging by her face, either Field knew all about it, or she knew enough.

She tapped a pencil to her notes. 'We've put in a request for your medical records, and I'll be speaking to your GP, Dr Jhadav, once we get the relevant sign-off. But is there anything else that might help us in the meantime?'

'You getting all this from McMillan?'

'All of what?'

'Depression, anxiety, blackouts – is he feeding you all of this? My medical records are protected. He's breaking the law by discussing them with you.'

'He wasn't discussing them.'

'That's not what it sounds like –'

'He was talking about some of the initial challenges we might face in trying to deal with someone who has the type of condition you do.'

'I don't *have* a condition.'

'Okay,' she said softly, holding up a hand to me as if trying to reason with a child. 'Okay, that's fine.'

And then I realized what she was doing. It was a clever piece of bait that I'd been too emotional to see coming: either I'd get angry, lose focus and behave like the man McMillan had painted me as, or I'd try to explain my way out of these lies by giving her some of my medical history. Ultimately, she was more interested in the second one than the first, but both would tell a story of who I was.

'Look,' I said, trying to draw the ire from my voice, 'I haven't seen Jhadav for a year – maybe more. I had one blackout. It was the case I was working. I was tired and I was stressed. That's it. That's all it was. So, yes, I blacked out once and I get a few headaches, but that's not the same thing as having a complete breakdown, is it?'

'Were you ever prescribed anything?'

'I got prescribed Cipralex, but never took it.'

'That's for depression, right?'

'But, like I said, I never took it.'

'Why?'

'Because I don't take pills I don't need to.'

Field paused for a moment, staring at her pad.

'So everyone's lying except you?' she said.

'Not everyone, no.'

'Just the woman in there and this Dr McMillan at St Augustine's?'

'Yes.'

'What happens when your medical records turn up and your treatment at St Augustine's is in there?'

'What happens when they turn up and it's not?'

She looked up at me. 'I saw you in there.'

'Where?'

'In front of those monitors. You looked shocked, disorientated. You reacted like she was actually your wife.'

'So? What does that prove?'

'But you take my point, right? She looks enough like your wife that you thought it might actually *be* her, even if it was only for a moment. She knows all about you, even about the things the two of you talked about in private. She *says* she's Derryn Raker, she *looks* like Derryn Raker, and now you're telling me you've had problems with depression and stress –'

'I didn't have problems with depression –'

'– and you've had blackouts and headaches, and a doctor – Dr McMillan, a doctor of some renown from what I've been able to find out about him – tells me you were so sick they had to treat you as an inpatient. He says you have something called Capgras delusion. It's –'

'I don't need to know what it is.'

'It's a condition where people believe that a husband, a wife, a child, someone close to them, has been replaced by an exact duplicate.' She paused, looked at me. 'An impostor.'

'Are you serious?'

'He tells me it can sometimes be brought on from head trauma.'

'I've never even met this guy.'

'Have you suffered head trauma in the past? Did you ever suffer any before that, in your days as a journalist? I read that you worked in Iraq, that you went to Afghanistan. You were in South Africa during the elections –'

'It doesn't matter.'

'It does if it's relevant –'

'It's not relevant if it's not true.'

She didn't come back at me this time, just stared.

'It's not her,' I said again, trying to sound as calm as I could.

'Okay,' Field responded. 'It's not her.'

There was no cynicism in her voice, no judgement, but it was clear I hadn't done enough to convince her. I looked at her wedding ring and said, 'You're married, right?'

She frowned. 'That really *is* irrelevant.'

'Imagine if your partner had been dead for eight years and then all of a sudden someone who looks like them turns up out of the blue, pretending to *be* them. How do you think you would feel? Do you think you would have walked into that room earlier today and *not* reacted?' I stopped, the anger starting to hum in my veins again. 'I reacted to her because, yes, she *does* look like Derryn. Not exactly the same, but very similar. And yes, she seems to know a lot of stuff that she shouldn't. But do you know why I was really in tears watching that?' I paused again, looking at Field. 'It's because I buried my wife. I watched her die slowly and painfully over a long period of time, and I couldn't do a single thing to stop it. And I've spent every day of the past eight years crawling through the darkest hole imaginable trying to get out the other side. And now I'm finally here, now I've finally managed to get my life back into some sort of order, this woman appears out of nowhere and razes everything to the fucking ground.'

Field's face remained blank.

When I saw I was going to get no response from her, I said, 'Can I go now?'

'It's your right to do that.'

I got to my feet, looking at Field, at the room I'd been sitting in for hours. I'd been with my daughter this morning. I'd been happy, maybe the happiest I'd been in years. And now all of that was rubble. It was just this.

'One thing,' Field said.

I returned my gaze to her.

'I know the instinct to play detective is probably running hot right now, but I need you to steer clear of her. I'm not going to sit here and read you the rulebook, because I think you're pretty familiar with it already, but I'm asking you not to make things complicated.' She paused, watching me for a moment. 'Is that clear enough?'

'She and this doctor are lying.'

'Regardless, I can ask you nicely like this, or I can go and get something signed and make it shiny and official – but I'm sure I don't need to go to all that trouble, do I, Mr Raker?'

Mr Raker now, not David.

'I want you to remain contactable,' she said.

I didn't reply.

'Mr Raker?'

'Fine,' I said. 'I'll wait for your call.'

'You do that.'

Except, after a day of lies, I'd just told her another one.

IO

The woman left thirty minutes later.

A taxi pulled up at the station entrance, beside a female police officer who had come out to speak to the driver. The night was calm so I could hear snatches of conversation, and managed to pick up that they were putting the woman into sheltered accommodation for the evening. The officer was giving the driver directions.

I took a couple of steps closer, trying to hear where exactly the hostel was located, but I was still too far away to get it all, and then the woman finally appeared and I was forced to retreat into the shadows again. I watched as she got into the back seat, the officer returning to the station, and the taxi pulled away.

It got to the end of the street and stopped, its brake lights flashing red against the night. But it didn't make a turn. It just idled there at the junction. I waited for it to go, to disappear out of sight, but it just stayed where it was.

Something's wrong.

A few seconds later, the woman's door opened. Automatically, I took a couple of steps forward, trying to understand what was going on. She got out again, and I saw the driver gesturing at her, turned in his seat. But whatever it was he was trying to say, she wasn't listening. Instead, she headed in the direction of the police station. I retreated, conscious of being seen by her, and waited for her to take the steps back up to the entrance. Maybe she'd forgotten something. Maybe something had spooked her.

Instead, she bypassed the police station completely.

I was half shadowed by four elm trees, marking the end of Agar Street. When she got a little closer to me, I crossed the Strand, the night air suddenly filled with light and noise – engines and horns and sirens, Christmas decorations hanging from street lamps and blinking in shop windows. As I watched her, she headed to her right, in the direction of Trafalgar Square.

Where was she going?

As she walked, she glanced behind her, and then dug around in her coat pockets and removed a scrap of paper – a Post-it note. She read it, slipped it back inside her jacket, then removed a digital watch and checked that.

She picked up her pace.

I tried not to let the utter surreality of this moment – of following a person who looked like someone I'd loved and lost and mourned – distract me from tailing her but it was hard. As I crossed the road again, back to her side of the street, I had a weird moment of déjà vu, a second where it felt like I'd done this before in a past life – the one I'd shared with Derryn. Had we ever been on the Strand together? Was it the Christmas lights that had set me off? Or had there been a time when I'd been hurrying to catch up with her somewhere? I couldn't remember, and when I fell into line behind the woman, sixty feet back, I forced the thoughts from my head entirely.

This wasn't Derryn.

She kept going, head down, hands in her pockets, but just as I thought she was about to cross the road to Trafalgar Square, she surprised me and headed down into the Tube. I held back for a second, confused, conscious of being spotted, and watched her disappear into the bowels of the earth. Where was she getting the Underground to? Waterloo? Was she heading back to Woolwich, where she claimed I'd dropped her outside a pharmacy and then driven off?

If she was, this wasn't the route she'd used this morning, and getting the Tube there was going to take longer than the mainline. There was something else too: she'd told Field she didn't like the Underground. She said she rarely used it.

It had been another lie.

I picked up the pace and, inside, saw her on the far side of the concourse at a ticket machine. She was feeding coins into it, the Post-it note in her hand again. She made for the barriers. The station was busy, so it was easy to remain hidden, but then she surprised me again: instead of heading south to Waterloo, she made for the northbound platform on the Northern line.

I tried to work out what was happening, where she might be going, and fifteen minutes later I found out: she exited at Chalk Farm. Once she got back to the surface, she paused, and took out the Post-it note again. I was behind the barriers, still too far away to see it in any detail, but it looked like it was entirely covered with writing. Was it directions? Instructions? Briefly, she checked her watch again, then moved out into the night.

She crossed Haverstock Hill and went north along a narrow road walled in by a succession of faceless offices and warehouses. I dropped back, her silhouette passing in and out of the lights as the street curved around to the left. When she came back into view, she'd changed direction again, cutting between a community centre – a paint-peeled relic from the seventies – and an ugly red-brick building which appeared to be the first in a zigzag of identical five-storey flats. Beyond them were a tower block and a deserted children's play park.

I headed around the park and came to a halt. She took the staircase belonging to the second five-storey building, the steps spiralling up the side in a concrete corkscrew, and on the fifth floor made her way along the walkway. It was open, exposed to the elements, and as a sudden gust of wind ripped in, she pulled up the collar on her coat and dipped her chin, then came to a stop two flats from the end.

She stood there for a moment, checking the Post-it note yet again, staring at it, as if it might come alive in her hands – and then she placed a hand to the door and pushed. It swung open.

The door had been unlatched.

As she disappeared inside, I tried to figure out what the hell was going on. Why had she come here? Who did the flat belong to? I thought about heading up there, confronting her, trying to get her to tell me why she was doing this, but as the door shut behind her, I forced myself to stay where I was. If I stormed up there, it might scare her – especially because she'd realize that she'd been followed – and that would only harden Field's position, perhaps confirm her worst fears about me. I didn't want to end up in handcuffs, arrested, my opportunity to find out the truth about this woman gone. I didn't need some court order hemming me in either. Field's warning to me, about getting something shiny and official signed off, was a test. At its crassest, it may even have been another piece of bait. She wanted to see if I would take it; if I might be that kidnapper, or that abuser, the person who'd slashed the woman's arm in a fit of rage, and scared her enough not to talk about it.

I wasn't going to play into her hands.

I took note of the address and headed back to the Tube, starting a search on the way. Without an actual name for the woman – not the name she believed she shared with my wife – directory enquiries was basically worthless to me, so I switched tack: I went to my Contacts, scrolled through the list of names and called a man named Spike, an old source of mine from my newspaper days. I often used him to do background checks for me, had used him for other, less legitimate things too, and while I didn't pretend what he did for me was legal – or particularly ethical – I accepted his help because sometimes it was the only way to get quick answers. I didn't know his real name, I didn't know where he lived, all I knew was that he was Russian and that when he was done helping me, I'd drop his money off in a locker at a north London sports centre.

'David,' he said once he'd picked up. 'How's things?'

'Good, Spike – you?'

'Can't complain,' he said, his Eastern European accent heavily anglicized now. 'You got something fun for me?'

'I need to run a background check.'

'Okay. What's the name?'

'Erik McMillan.' I spelt it out for him. 'I need absolutely everything you can get on him. He's a doctor, a psychiatrist at St Augustine's – it's a unit out in Thamesmead. Start with who he is: personal details, marriage status, that sort of thing, and where he lives; and then anything else you find out beyond that will be a bonus.'

'You want his phone records?'

I thought about it – but not for long.

He was playing dirty. I was going to have to as well.

'Yeah,' I said, 'if you can get them, do it.'

When I was done with Spike, I called St Augustine's. I hit an automated message with options to be connected to various people in different departments, but none of them was Erik McMillan and the bored-sounding voice on the recording said that the public-facing parts of the hospital were doing truncated hours because of Christmas. I checked my watch, saw it was seven forty-five, and thought about leaving a message. The recording said that, if I did, someone at St Augustine's would call me back as soon as possible. I hung up instead. I needed to cool off first, and it would be better to get hold of the background check on McMillan before making any approach. By calling him now, speaking to him,

49

I was playing into Field's hands again, and immediately giving McMillan an advantage; all I could fight with at the moment was anger. That would make me sloppy.

Worse, my emotional state would make me easy to manipulate.

I needed to be clear-headed, I needed time to think, but – even as I told myself that – it was hard to let the anger go. On the train home, again and again I tried to imagine who the woman was, how she knew so much, what her endgame was, and what McMillan's part in all of this might be. If the woman had been a patient at St Augustine's then that explained their connection, but it didn't explain why he would tell the police he'd treated me for fifteen months. If Field found out he was lying to her, which would happen eventually, he risked his job, his reputation, even his freedom, which seemed an insane risk to take for someone in his position.

Unless he was confident he could prove everything.

And that meant one of two things: either his lies could be backed up somehow, making them more convincing than I'd feared – or he was telling the truth.

And, if that was the case, I really was sick.

11

Except for the watery yellow glow of the security light at the front, my house was completely dark. It was a three-bedroomed bungalow, unusual for this part of the city, which Derryn and I had signed the contract on the year before we'd moved to the States. We'd only lived in it for nine months before the move, and for just eleven after we got back to the UK, and once she was gone, what had seemed such a perfect size before – such an ideal place to start the family we'd always wanted – suddenly felt too big; it was empty, almost paralysingly so. Because of that, for over a year I was unable to sleep in the bed we'd shared, barely able to set foot in our bedroom, choosing to fall asleep on the sofa instead, in front of the TV night after night. Since then, I'd moved beyond those moments, but it still felt like a home I'd always been alone in, a place that Derryn had never had the chance to enjoy; and because of that, I was never really sure if I liked it in a way a home was supposed to be liked. If a home was a castle, some sort of bastion, a place to seek refuge, this place had failed.

I turned on the lamp in the hallway and then the Christmas lights. They exploded into life outside, wrapped in diagonal lines along the guttering and the downpipes. This time of year tended to hurt: Derryn had loved Christmas, the decorations, the trees, the festivities. The lights had been chosen by her and, every year since she'd passed, I'd put them up as a way to remember that, as a simple way to touch a small part of who she'd been. I watched them as they winked red and yellow and blue, pink, purple, but somehow the colour, the joy, didn't feel like it belonged here after today. I reached down and switched them off, pushed the door closed and stood in the silence of the hallway, listening to the muted tick of the central heating.

As I did, I felt the same fears start to surface again.

In quiet moments alone since my blackout, since the headaches had started, I'd sometimes considered the idea that I might be ill. It never seemed impossible to me that it might be the reason I'd been so incapable of moving beyond Derryn's death for so long; that I might be falling apart, being destroyed somehow, cell by cell – quietly, slowly, over months and years – without even knowing. Those worries were ones I'd carried with me for a long time now. Some kind of illness may have been the reason I couldn't sustain other relationships, why I felt so restless all the time, and why I found it so hard to settle inside these walls. It may even have been the reason that I felt such a powerful connection to missing people and why I'd gone to such lengths to track them down. I was obsessed about saving them – sometimes, *often*, dangerously so – and while all of me railed against the suggestion that I'd spent fifteen months in an institution and didn't remember any of it – that I was suffering from a psychological condition where I refused to recognize or accept that my wife was alive and well – the idea of a sickness, one that was more subtle and masked, was much harder to expel. Its claws were already in me.

Through the window at the side of the house, I could see into next door's living room, my neighbours Andrew and Nicola sitting beside one another on the sofa, watching something on TV, a wine bottle on the table in front of them. I hardly knew them, had barely spoken to them in the entire three years they'd been living a few feet away, but as I looked at them now, I felt totally alone and besieged by jealousy. I knew why, I knew the reasons, and I knew none of this was their fault. They hadn't brought that woman to the police. They hadn't caused my blackouts or my headaches. I was driven by a compulsion I'd never been able to articulate, and which controlled me during cases, and none of that was down to them. But it hurt me to look at them, just as it hurt me to watch someone pretending to be my wife. And that was exactly what made me so vulnerable: I pretended I was clad in armour, I made my enemies believe I couldn't be bruised, or threatened, or scared. But I could. I could be broken.

And the way to do it was so simple.

All they had to do was use Derryn.

Do you remember the day we first met? I do. It was a Tuesday morning in March and the sun was streaming in, casting strobes of light from every window. I looked around at all the faces and everybody's skin had this ethereal glow, like something had caught light inside them. It had been a long winter, I suppose, so maybe the burst of bright sunlight just looked odd and out of place for a moment; or maybe it was you. The way you were. The way you could walk into a room and light it up.

That's not an exaggeration, by the way.

I might have romanticized the sunlight thing, the ethereal glow and all of that stuff, but I'm not overplaying this. Honestly. It was your eyes, the way you greeted people, the way you eventually greeted me. You know how some people don't smile from their eyes? Over the years, you must have seen that a lot in your job. I mean, you can see their face moving, you can see muscles and cartilage and whatever else shifting and changing, but you know it's not an emotional reaction to something — not an act of joy or spontaneity — because there's no light in their eyes when they don't mean it. But when you smiled, it was different. When you smiled, it genuinely came from somewhere good.

There's this book I've always loved — I've read it over and over again — called Garden Apex. *In it, the author describes people like that who don't smile from their eyes. She says their eyes are like caves carved out of a granite cliff. I suppose she means that everything you see on that cliff face is resolute and unyielding — sometimes impossible to break or chip away at, even over a whole lifetime — while the caves are so inaccessible and so difficult to see into that there's absolutely no hint of what lies beyond, what secrets may be hiding within, so you're never sure* if the cliff and the caves are dangerous. Anyway, I love that description because I've met so many people like that. On certain days, I'll even admit to looking in the mirror and seeing someone like that staring back. But you were never one of those people. You were never like me.

You always had that light in your eyes.

And, I suppose, that was one of the reasons I was drawn to you. I remember watching you work your way around the room, going from bed to bed, smiling at people, and the closer you got to me, the more nervous I became. I didn't want to say the wrong thing. I didn't want to be just another patient.

I wanted you to like me.

'Good morning,' you said.

'Morning.'

'How are you feeling today?'

I shrugged. 'Sore.'

'Well, you're in the right place.' You smiled and then leaned down and started raising my bed up, the silence filled with the high-pitched squeal of the mechanism. 'I'm one of the nurses on duty today, so I'll be looking after you.'

'Okay,' I said. 'That's good.'

'Is there anything I can get you?'

'No,' I said, and glanced at your badge.

You were a senior nurse.

You were called Derryn.

'What a beautiful name,' I said.

'Thank you,' you replied, and then you smiled again, and if I'd had any doubts before, they were gone after that. From that moment, I knew for sure.

You were someone very special.

12

For a long time after my father died, the cottage he'd lived in in south Devon had remained empty, except for when I'd drive down a couple of times a year to check on it. Those were the days before I knew Annabel and the first years after Derryn had passed on, so I never had a reason to be there. There was a short period, after a case I'd worked had almost cost me my life, when I did spend some time there recovering, but mostly I never went unless I had to. The house was just another repository for bad memories, a reminder of the people I'd lost, until – at the end of 2014 – a man called Bryan Kennedy became my tenant.

Kennedy wasn't his real name, even though that was the name in the passport I'd organized for him. We never used his real name any more because, as far as the rest of the world was concerned, that man had died three years ago. It had taken some getting used to on both our parts, but I pushed for us to use 'Kennedy', even in conversations with one another, because then it would feel less unusual. As I was making dinner, he called.

I toyed with the idea of letting it go to voicemail. I felt tired, overwhelmed, way out to sea with no sign of the shore and no idea of where I was heading. But then I realized that, if anyone understood that sensation, it would be Kennedy. If I told him about the woman, about the lies she was trying to sell, he would believe me – instantly, without question – because, like me, he'd had to watch a person die who he loved deeply, perhaps above all others, and when she did, he found out the same thing as I had: you couldn't lie about the people you loved – and no one could replace them.

'How's things?' I asked.

'You know: same old, same old.'

I'd last spoken to him on Christmas Eve, calling him because I knew he'd be alone, and at this time of year, that was hard. Kennedy had been a cop once; now he worked on a fishing trawler. That was maybe even harder for him, so when we'd spoken, I'd let him talk for an hour about his days at the Met, and about working over Christmas.

'Have you had a good break?'

'It's been all right,' he said. 'Back to work on Saturday. Got to work Sunday too. Don't know what the point of going out New Year's Eve is but I'll be back in time for the huge party I'm hosting.'

I smiled; it felt unnatural, as if I'd forgotten how to do it. It hadn't even been a day since I'd left Annabel and Olivia, but it felt like months.

'Oh, didn't I tell you?' he went on. 'I'm throwing a party in the front room. Women, booze, drugs. It's fancy dress, so I'm going as a leprechaun.'

I smiled again. 'Well, it's important to stay true to your roots.'

'Exactly.' He stopped, and I heard him take a drink of something. He'd been off the booze for three years, so I imagined it was tea. 'Weather's supposed to be shite next week. There's a storm coming and we're going to get four weeks of rain in a day, so I guess I'll be home in front of the TV for a change.'

'I hope you've got some movies on tape.'

'It feels like I've watched them all.'

Kennedy didn't have the Internet at the cottage. He didn't have a mobile phone or a driving licence or credit cards either. I paid for the electricity and gas and water, and then he gave me the cash when the bills came. His passport was his only ID and that was there solely to aid him in a quick escape, should he need it. We never spoke about the reasons why we'd ended up here, the decisions he'd made, but both of us could still feel the echoes of them: the blackout I'd suffered had been during the course of trying to help him; my headaches had started then too. Kennedy's daughter, Leanne, had been murdered, a case he'd been leading had spiralled completely out of control, and in the aftermath he'd suffered a heart attack and nearly died.

The scars ran deep for both of us.

Eventually, he said, 'So what have you been up to?'

'I got back to London today.'

'How come? I thought you were staying with Annabel until the new year?'

'I was. But something's come up.'

'Are the girls all right?'

'Oh, it's not them. They're fine, don't worry. Liv's a proper teenager now.'

Kennedy made a noise down the phone, a breath that said he remembered those days. 'That's what happens,' he said, and a hint of sorrow crept into his voice. 'They learn to walk – and the next minute they're taller than you and they're leaving home . . .' He faded out, the line quiet for a moment. 'So why *are* you back?'

'Can I ask you a question?' I said in response.

'Yeah.'

'Did you ever have any dealings with a Catherine Field?'

A pause. 'Who?'

'She's a DS in Charing Cross CID.'

'No, not that I remember. Why?'

'She just came up in relation to something.'

'You in trouble, Raker?'

Yes. I just don't know how much.

'No,' I said.

'But you're working a case?'

58

'Maybe the beginnings of one.'

I thought of the woman, and then of Erik McMillan.

'You ever heard of St Augustine's?'

'Is that the hospital?'

'Yeah,' I said, surprised. 'So you know it?'

'Not well,' he said, 'but I've been there. Once.'

'When was that?'

'Probably ten, eleven years ago. A seventeen-year-old girl turned up in the water at Shadwell Basin.' Kennedy paused. 'Anyway,' he said, his Irish accent fainter now, 'long story short, I went to the hospital to chat to a patient there who had lived with her for a while to see if he knew anything. He didn't. It was a waste of time, really. He'd been reprogrammed by then.'

'Reprogrammed?'

'You know, rehabilitated or whatever.'

'Did you meet a doctor called McMillan?'

'I don't think so, no.'

'Anything else you remember?'

'About what?'

'About your trip there.'

'Yeah,' he said, but then the rest of his sentence fell away. I wondered for a moment if it was because he didn't actually have anything else to say, and he was just looking for a way to keep me on the line. Other than the father and son he spent his days with on the trawler, he was alone, so I knew he enjoyed these calls. He'd loved being a detective. Now he could only get a taste of it when we talked.

'It's just a weird place,' he said finally.

'St Augustine's?'

'Yeah.'

'In what way's it weird?'

'Well, you know what it used to be, right?'

'"Used to be"? No.'

'It was a quarantine centre. If you had leprosy, typhoid, tuberculosis, smallpox – anything like that – you got shipped off there, even if you didn't want to. It's why they built it in Thamesmead: the way they designed it, there's only one way in and one way out, and that's along a single stretch of road. Before things changed in the sixties, people would just get dropped off there, the gate would get locked, the doors would be bolted, and no one would ever see them again. Also,' Kennedy said, 'only half of it's open.'

'What do you mean?'

'They only use half the site.'

I frowned. 'Really?'

'Yeah. One half of it hadn't been used in decades, so they closed the whole place down for a couple of years in the early eighties with the idea that they'd restore the entire thing. But by the time they'd done all the rebuilding work on the existing half, they realized all these protected birds had started nesting in the other, shittier side. Anyway, it's too late now: it's been designated a nature reserve.'

'So one half just sits there deteriorating?'

'That's what I mean,' Kennedy said. 'It feels *weird*. You're standing in this ultra-modern hospital, looking out the window at the other half of the site, and it's broken and rundown; it's overrun by trees and grass, weeds, birdshit everywhere. That place . . .' His words fell away for a moment. 'It's like there's something wrong with it.'

13

After dinner, I zeroed in on Erik McMillan.

Spike was already on the case, putting together a background check for me, but I couldn't wait and do nothing – I needed to fight back – so I returned to Google and started doing a basic search. Field had told me that McMillan was a doctor with a good reputation and it didn't take me long to realize she wasn't joking. He'd published acclaimed research, had written books on the subject of psychiatry and had won countless awards, and to top it all off he was a huge campaigner, raising hundreds of thousands of pounds for mental health charities. Understandably, he was well respected and extremely well liked.

In his late forties and photogenic, he was also attractive, his side-parted black hair perfectly arranged, his beard exact, his choice of glasses – a bright red – adding an unorthodox twist to his appearance. People called him innovative and principled. They said that he was caring.

So why had he lied to the police about me?

I returned to the St Augustine's website and cycled through the links that had failed to work on my phone at the station. *Contact* and *Support Us* were self-explanatory, and *Foundation* just detailed the work of the hospital's fundraising arm, Asclepius – the Greek god of healing – and featured a series of photographs of staff members and patients at various events. McMillan, with his red glasses, was in a couple of them. I tried to imagine what he might have to gain from lying about me, and what his connection might be to the woman who claimed to be my wife, but I was still struggling to see the link. After that, I went looking for a home address. I couldn't find one. It was possible he was ex-directory, or he didn't have a landline, or maybe Erik wasn't even his given name. It would be in the paperwork Spike sent me, so I moved on.

Under the *History* tab, I found a dry, concise account of the hospital since it opened its doors in 1901. They'd downplayed its history as a quarantine centre in the bio, and a series of images – maps of the site from various points in history, including an up-to-date satellite photograph – showed that it was built right on the edge of the Thames. I thought of how the woman had told Field the hospital was close to London City Airport, but it was at least a mile and a half away, north of Thamesmere lake. There were two housing estates on either flank, a newer one to the west and a much older one immediately to the east, built right on the fringes of the nature reserve. If it hadn't have been for the security fences, boxing the entire St Augustine's site in, it would have looked like an innocuous industrial site from above.

I moved on to the *What We Do* tab.

The hospital described itself as providing 'medium-secure inpatient services for adults with mental health illnesses and/or personality disorders'. That meant it wasn't quite Broadmoor or Ashworth, but the people being treated had almost certainly committed an offence, and were most likely a risk to themselves and the public. Under a subheading titled *Who are we?*, there were photos of the management team, seven in all, three men and four women. McMillan was second from the top, his job title listed as Clinical Director. He had opted against the glasses this time.

There were no answers on the hospital website, and McMillan didn't seem to have any social media accounts, so I shifted my attention back to the woman, to the job she said she had, and to the flat at Chalk Farm.

I dialled the Queen Elizabeth Hospital in Woolwich.

Even though I knew, if the woman even worked there at all, that she wasn't going to be on shift tonight, I pretended I was trying to locate a nurse.

'What's their name?' the woman on the switchboard asked.

'Derryn Raker.'

I heard my voice splinter, my words catching, and felt a swell of emotion: panic, and sadness, and anger.

'I can't see anybody of that name on our lists,' the operator said.

'Nothing at all?'

'No, nothing.'

I thanked her and put the phone down, realizing I'd been holding my breath. The woman had lied about her place of work, which meant she'd probably lied about plenty of other things too. I wasn't sure if that made it better or worse. Field might start to see that I was telling the truth – because she'd almost certainly got the news from the Queen Elizabeth herself by now – but that didn't answer the question of why the woman was pretending to be Derryn. It didn't reveal how she knew so much about me, or what her aim was. Was she trying to confuse me? Unsettle me? Throw suspicion on me?

I turned my attention to the flat in Chalk Farm.

It took two minutes on the Land Registry website to find out that the flat was owned by an Adam Reinsart. I'd never heard of him before and was pretty certain he hadn't been a friend or work colleague of Derryn's. Instead, when I put his name into Google I discovered that he ran a series of successful north London restaurants and – because of that, as well as his involvement with local food banks – his name had frequently featured in the pages of the *Hampstead & Highgate Express*.

Again, just like with McMillan, I couldn't find any connection between him and the woman. I didn't know her real name, which didn't help, but I couldn't see her picture or description in any of the stories about Reinsart or any of the photographs of him – and there were a lot of photographs: in front of his latest restaurant; at Camden Lock as part of an anti-graffiti campaign; dressed in pink, at the start of a fun run; with his wife, who – like Reinsart – was in her sixties – and then with the female manager of his best-known restaurant, XYZ, in Belsize Park. Lots of women, but not the one I was after.

I put his name into the phone book. There was only one A. Reinsart in that part of the city and he lived at the top of Highgate Hill.

I went to the bedroom, dug through my drawers and found a prepaid mobile, then brought it back to the living room. I was going to need to lie to him in order to get him to talk to me, and I didn't want the Met going through his phone records – if it ever came to that – and finding my number on his bill.

A woman answered. 'Hello?'

'Mrs Reinsart?'

'Yes.'

'I'm calling from the Metropolitan Police. Is your husband home, please?'

'Uh, yes. The *police*? Is everything all right?'

'Everything's fine.'

'Oh,' she said, 'oh, okay,' and I heard her place the phone down. In the silence that followed, I felt bad for lying to her, but this was the quickest and most efficient way to get answers. My identity – who I was and what I did – had to remain hidden from her for the same reasons I hadn't marched up to the door of the flat and demanded the woman let me in. It would just raise more suspicions about me, and would edge me closer to a pair of handcuffs.

'Hello?'

'Mr Reinsart?'

'Yes,' he said. 'What's this about?'

He had a South African accent.

'Mr Reinsart, I'm calling from the Metropolitan Police, but I assure you, there's nothing to worry about, and you're not in any trouble. I was just hoping you could help us with our enquiries. Am I correct in saying you own a flat at 2 Sovereign House in Chalk Farm?'

'Yes,' he replied. 'Yes, that's right.'

'Flat number 99?'

'Yes. Is everything okay with it?'

'Everything's fine, sir. We're investigating a crime that took place nearby and I was hoping to get in touch with the person who is currently renting the flat from you but we haven't been able to speak to them. No one is answering the door.'

'I'm not surprised,' he said.

'Why's that, sir?'

'Well, because there's no one living there at the moment.'

I paused: surprised, confused. 'The flat's empty?'

'My last tenant moved out at the end of November, and the new one isn't due to move in until January. Uh . . .' I heard the sound of pages being turned. 'The, uh, the 6th of January.'

'Does anyone else have keys?'

'Sure. The rental agency will have a couple.'

'Which agency are you using?'

'Hammond's on Highgate Road.'

'Anyone else?'

'No, no one else has keys.'

I could tell by his voice that he was getting suspicious, that the cogs were beginning to turn. I tried not to let him affect my own reasoning, and focused on how the woman hadn't had a set of keys either. So was that why the door was off the latch? Had *she* left it like that? Could she have been living rough there?

'What was the name of your last tenant, Mr Reinsart?'

'Mark Wissich.'

'Did he live alone?'

'Yes.'

'Do you know where he lives now?'

'He emigrated to Australia at the end of November.'

I'd been writing Wissich's name down, but now put a line through it.

'And your new tenant? What's their name?'

'Uh . . .' Pages being turned. 'Kevin Eggers.'

'But he doesn't have a key yet?'

'No,' Reinsart said. 'He'll pick them up from Hammond's on the 6th of January.'

Even if the woman *was* living rough in the flat, how could she possibly have found out that it was empty? She'd told Field she lived with me, but appeared to have connections to Woolwich, and both of those places were at least ten miles away from Chalk Farm, so it seemed highly unlikely she'd just stumbled across an unoccupied, unlocked flat in a completely different part of the city.

I thanked Reinsart and hung up.

It was after 10 p.m., and much too late to call Hammond's, so I tried to figure out where I went next. As I did, my gaze stopped on a drawer in the sideboard, one I hadn't looked inside for a long time. I got up, went across to it and slowly slid it open.

It was full of old video-camera tapes.

I hadn't thought about them in a couple of years, and I hadn't watched them in even longer.

They were all home movies of Derryn.

14

I selected two at random.

The first was recorded on a skiing holiday we'd taken to the Austrian Alps in February 2002. In the footage, we weren't out on the slopes; instead, Derryn was walking ahead of me, through the local village, looking over her shoulder and smiling as I filmed us approaching the restaurant we were eating in. The village was beautiful, utterly picturesque, its rows of timber buildings dwarfed by grey folds in vast, snow-streaked mountains.

I asked her what she was going to have for dinner.

My voice sounded different, stronger somehow, my words crackling slightly as my mouth drifted close to the microphone. Derryn smiled again at me, looking into the lens of the camera. She always hated being filmed.

'Glühwein,' she replied.

'For starters?'

'Starters, mains and dessert.'

She flicked me a V sign, not bothering to turn around this time, and then doing so eventually, her face outlined by the blue hood of the ski jacket she was wearing. I paused the film, studying her, looking for things that I could see were different from the woman claiming to be her – the eyes, the shape of her jaw, the teeth. Derryn had chipped one of her central incisors on the edge of a surfboard during a trip we'd made to Cape Town one year, and while it had been repaired, the chip itself had remained a different shade of white. It was a small thing, a tiny defect that most people wouldn't even notice, but it was a thing I remembered with absolute clarity now I saw it again, and I didn't recall the woman having the same imperfection, though it would have been hard to see, even on an HD feed. She definitely didn't have the same colour eyes or the same lips either – not quite – nor the same chin, and she didn't speak like Derryn was speaking here. She hadn't emphasized the same words.

Because she isn't my wife.

I said it over and over to myself, trying to settle the turbulence in my head, and then carried on watching. I'd taken the camera out on the slopes the next day, keeping it in a backpack, and, with the wind roaring in the microphone, I'd filmed the two of us descending into the valley. On the TV, I watched Derryn weave a series of perfect turns, so smooth and capable on the snow that she was soon far ahead of me, like a blob of ink on an alabaster wall.

The film cut away again, to later on, the two of us in the ski lift, heading back up the angle of the slope, people like ants below our dangling feet. She was filming this time.

'Are you scared?' she said. 'Admit it, you're scared.'

Onscreen, I smiled. In the living room, I smiled too.

'Ooooh yeah,' I told her. 'I'm absolutely terrified.'

'We've made a bet, right?'

'Right.'

'Room service for the person who gets down the slope fastest.'

'Room service? I thought the bet was one euro.'

'You always *were* tight with money, Raker.'

That made me smile again onscreen, my whole face lighting up. I hardly recognized the person I was watching. It had been so long since I'd smiled like that. It wasn't even a reaction to her comment, really, a jokey, throwaway line she always used whenever money came up. Instead, it was a reflection of who we were at the time and who we'd been all the way up until the end. It was a reaction that spoke so eloquently of our marriage, its comfort, without a single word being uttered.

My phone started ringing.

I was so hypnotized by what I was seeing, it took me a couple of seconds to register the sound. When I did, I hurriedly paused the video, picked up my mobile and looked at the number.

Tanya Rye, one of Derryn's best friends.

They'd been at nursing college together. I hadn't spoken to her in months – maybe even a year – but I'd left a message for her while I was waiting for the woman in the shadows outside Charing Cross police station. I'd been confused at the time, completely knocked off balance, and I'd needed somewhere to go for reassurance.

'Hey, Tanya,' I said, trying to sound relaxed.

My eyes were still fixed on the TV; on the frozen image of Derryn.

'David *Raker*,' she replied, clearly surprised that I'd left her a message.

'Thanks for calling back. How are you?'

'I'm fine. I hope it's not too late?'

'No,' I said. 'No, not at all. I'm sorry it's been so long.'

'It's fine. I mean, it's lovely to hear from you.'

'How are you? How are Mick and the kids?'

'Yeah, we're all good, thank you.'

'That's great.'

I asked Tanya a little more about her husband, about their kids, about where she was working these days, and then said, 'Listen, I've been going back over a few things.'

'Okay.'

'Would you mind if I asked you a couple of questions?'

'Sure.'

'About Derryn.'

'Oh. Okay.'

I cleared my throat.

'You, um . . .' I stopped. 'You remember the funeral?'

'Yes. Yes, of course I do. What's up?'

'Do you remember anything unusual about it?'

'Unusual? Unusual how?'

Unusual like I imagined the whole thing, or there was no body in the coffin, or Derryn told you to play along with whatever I said because I was ill.

'Unusual how?' Tanya repeated.

'The, um . . .' *The funeral definitely took place, right?*

'David?'

'Do you remember where we held it?' It wasn't the question I wanted to ask, but I couldn't ask that because it made me sound utterly insane.

'Yes,' Tanya said. 'The funeral was in Holloway. What did you mean by "unusual" earlier?'

'I was just, uh . . .' I ground to a halt again.

'No,' she responded, starting to sound concerned. 'No, I don't remember anything unusual. It was a terrible day, I know that.' A pause. 'Is everything okay, David? Is there anything I can do to help?'

'It's fine,' I said, trying to sound unruffled.

'Are you sure?'

'Yes. Everything's fine. I just . . .' I faded out.

'Just what?'

'When was the last time you saw her?'

A long pause this time.

'Are you sure everything's all right, David?'

'Fine,' I said again. 'Honestly. I just have some questions. Some things I need to square off.'

'Okay,' she said, but didn't continue.

'So when was the last time you saw her, do you think?'

'I don't know. A few days before she died, maybe.'

'And you and Mick popped by a lot after the funeral, right?'

70

'Of course we did. You were our friend – *are* our friend.'

'I seemed okay? I mean, other than the obvious.'

'What do you mean, "okay"?'

I mean, was I sick? In denial? Was I grieving for an empty box? Did I really have a condition where I believed Derryn had been replaced by some kind of twin?

And was everyone in on it but me?

'I know I was grieving,' I said, 'but was Derryn actually . . .'

I stopped. *Was Derryn actually what?*

Dead? Was I really going to ask her that?

I stared at the television screen, at Derryn's face. I knew Tanya best of any of Derryn's friends, and she was probably going to be the most patient and least judgemental of anyone I might think to call. Yet alarm bells had already started going off in her head, so how could I phone around anyone else – people I didn't know as well and wouldn't cut me as much slack – and ask them these kinds of questions?

'It doesn't matter,' I said finally.

'Are you sure?'

'Absolutely,' and I started to wrap the conversation up.

Tanya said she'd call me sometime soon, that I should come over for dinner with her and her husband, but afterwards, as I sat alone in the silence of the living room, all I could think about was how I must have sounded to her; how the lies being told about me, and about my wife, had got into my bloodstream, lodged so deep that I'd become irrational.

I turned back to the television, studying Derryn's face, and then ejected the first tape and slid in the second. I could see that this video was from much later on. A date in the corner read 25 December 2008.

The Christmas before she died.

She didn't know that then; neither of us did. We'd just got back from the US in the November, and she wouldn't find out that the cancer had come back until the following April, so as I filmed her in the kitchen of our house – the house that we'd barely had a chance to live in – she was dancing around in front of the oven, a party hat on, checking on the meat. She had no idea she was on video, her shoulders swaying from side to side, the radio playing Christmas songs from the worktop.

'Ho, ho, ho,' I said from behind the camera.

Derryn looked around and broke into a huge smile.

'How long have you been there?' she asked.

'Long enough.'

'If you filmed me dancing, there *will* be beatings,' she said, and came towards me, mock-threatening me with a baster. 'You didn't record me dancing, did you, D?'

D. My heart started to hurt.

'No,' I said onscreen.

'Liar.'

'Wait, was that dancing you were doing?'

'Ha ha, very funny.'

I came further into the room and put the camera down on the worktop, then grabbed her by the shoulders and brought her into my chest. She pretended to try and wriggle free but eventually gave up and, although we weren't perfectly framed and I hadn't left the camera at an ideal angle, it was good enough. I shuffled us both around to face the lens and told her to wave to the camera.

'Merry Christmas, dance fans,' I said.

She gently slapped my stomach. I kissed the top of her head. And alone in the dark of the living room, as I watched it play out nine years on, I started to cry.

15

Just before midnight, something woke me.

I'd been sleeping lightly, despite feeling exhausted, and as I lay there, I'd been aware of noises from inside the house: the tick of the central heating; the hum of the fridge in the kitchen; a vent in the en suite that snapped open and closed whenever the wind picked up. But the noise I heard wasn't any of those.

I sat up in bed, tossed back the duvet and grabbed a T-shirt. Slipping it on, I went to the bedroom door and looked along the hallway. The house was dark: my office was on the left, the spare bedroom was to the right, and at the end was the living room. There was a cloakroom off that, in a narrow cove between the living room and the kitchen, and an amber pool was coming from it, cast through its small window by next door's security light.

I checked the spare room and office and then moved through to the living room. To my right was the TV cabinet, sofas and a back door, leading out on to the rear deck. In front of me were the sideboard and the dining table, one of the chairs askew where I'd not pushed it back under. My notes were spread out on top – I'd been too drained to tidy them before bed – and my laptop was still charging.

I padded through to the kitchen, went to the sink and poured myself a glass of water, trying to see what had set off the security light. Our row of houses backed on to a footpath that ran north to south, and about five minutes' walk away was a giant swathe of allotments. That would occasionally bring animals in – field mice, shrews, badgers, most often foxes – with the braver ones straying beyond the sheds and vegetable patches to the gardens and driveways along here. Often, in the days after Derryn died, I'd sit at the kitchen window in the early hours of the morning, or at the side door looking out at the drive – unable to sleep, the grief like a knot in my throat – and watch the same fox returning, trying the same tricks to get into the same bins.

But there was no fox this time. No cats, no dogs. The spaces between my house and Andrew and Nicola's were empty, two driveways side by side, garages next to one another, our metal bins upright, our cars untouched, their interiors dark.

I finished the water, placed the glass in the sink, and went to check that I'd definitely locked the side door. Halfway across the kitchen floor, I stopped again.

The door handle was all the way down.

I walked over and yanked it back up, resetting it. It had been stiff for a while, in need of some oil. The door was still locked, the slide bolts all in place; it was just the handle. I tried to remember if I'd used the side door at any point during the day, or since I'd got back from Chalk Farm. Could I have left the handle like that before I'd gone to Annabel's for Christmas?

Or had someone been trying it from the outside?

I looked out to the driveway again, then out of the front window, over the lawn, towards the street. Everything was quiet. The parked cars were all ones I recognized. The same internal lights were on in exactly the same houses as always: people who didn't sleep much, shift workers, a young couple a few doors down who'd just had twin boys. The gates to my driveway were both closed, the latch still in place. When I returned to the side door and looked the other way, down towards the rear, I could see the gate connecting the driveway to the back garden was locked up safely.

A few seconds later, the security light snapped off.

I was tired and drained, and I didn't want to add paranoid to the list. I didn't want to be sick – at my strongest, believed profoundly that I wasn't – but moments like this, standing alone in the dark of my house at midnight wondering if I'd left the door handle down, didn't help. So I made my way back along the hallway, taking a long breath as I went, trying to relax myself, then climbed back beneath the covers.

That was when I saw it.

In the space between the two curtains, where I hadn't quite pulled them shut, the window had fogged up. I could see traces of the decking, of furniture, but they were only vague – grey hints, angles and shapes. It was what was on the outside of the window that had got my attention.

Something was drawn in the condensation.

It was a heart.

16

I got out of bed and went to the window.

The garden was quiet, the skeletal bushes closest to me shifting stiffly in the faint breeze. Further out, it was harder to see anything, the rest of the lawn shrouded in shadow, the only source of light the pale glow from a street lamp out on the path beyond the fence at the bottom of the garden. Down there, built into the furthest panel to the right, was a door: access to the path. I kept it bolted from this side, but it was too dark to see if it was still locked; too dark to see if the door was open.

Too dark to see anything but the heart.

I grabbed some clothes, hopping into some old tracksuit bottoms, a hoodie, a pair of trainers, a warm coat. When I was dressed, I looked again at the window.

The image was starting to fade.

Someone must have breathed on the glass in order to create the fog, but – when I stepped in closer – there was no hint of a smear, no trace of grease from a fingertip.

Nerves scattered across my back and along my arms, into my neck, as I moved to the rear doors, unlocking them and heading out on to the deck. It was icy, slippery underfoot, the wood creaking as I moved across it and then down the steps, on to the grass. The lawn was hard, already glistening with frost, the skies clear, the air bitter. I switched on the torch I'd brought with me, then directed it towards the corner fence panel, at the door there: everything between sparkled, as if dusted with glitter.

The door was still closed, but something was missing

from it: a sign that normally hung from a notch in the wood, three-quarters of the way up. I'd bought it for Derryn the year we moved into the house, because she'd always loved being outside, had a flair for landscaping, and knew more about flowers than I ever could have learned. The sign said, THIS IS THE EXIT IF YOU DON'T LIKE GARDENING.

Now it wasn't there.

My pulse quickened. Sweeping the torch left and right, searching the shadows that remained in the garden, I found nothing – no one waiting for me, no one hiding – and moved forward again, inching towards the door. The further away from the house I got, the more the temperature plummeted and the harder the frost became. It sounded more like glass beneath my feet, cracking and fracturing. When I got to the door, I snapped across the slide lock and opened it towards me.

Where the hell was Derryn's sign?

It wasn't near the door, in the grass, or on the ground any-where nearby. Had I taken it off for some reason and forgotten to put it back up? Had I mistakenly left it in the house some-where or out in the garage? Why would I do that? Why would I forget it?

Maybe because they're right.

Maybe because I'm sick.

I shook the thoughts from my head, refusing to accept any of them, but as I did, I found myself glancing back in the direction of the house, looking for the heart symbol on the bedroom window, trying to reassure myself that it had def-initely been there. It had disappeared now, or at least I couldn't see it any more. Was it because I was too far away? Or was it because it had never been there in the first place? I'd been tired as I'd wandered through the house. Was it pos-sible I'd imagined it?

I squeezed my eyes shut.

No, I hadn't. It was real.

All of this is real.

A sound – out on the footpath.

I opened my eyes again, pinging back into focus, and moved through the doorway, out on to the narrow lane. There was nothing to my left. I couldn't see the allotments from here, but because of the street lamp I could see enough: the path was empty, a lonely avenue of trees and identical fences.

In the other direction – south, towards the Tube station – the pathway was darker, more opaque. When the wind picked up and the fir trees lining the left-hand side moved, it seemed like the whole night was coming alive: branches shifted, pine needles fluttered, the trees rolled and lurched and shivered. And it was only when everything settled again, when the breeze had washed through and the stillness of the night had returned, that I saw it.

A sliver of white, stark against the blackness.

'Hello?' I said, my voice betraying me.

I took a step forward, then another, and then stopped, my heart hammering in my chest. I tried to use the torch, to spread the light further, to reveal what was waiting for me, but it made little difference.

'Hello?' I said again, my tone stronger and clearer, even though I felt none of that poise.

I took another step forward.

There was nothing there now – no sliver of white, no hint of colour. All I could see was blackness, a swirl of shadows so impervious it could have been a wall.

'Hello?' I repeated, moving forward again.

I swung the torch, trying to get a better angle on what was out there, but if it was a person, they were too far away, the beam not strong enough to reach them. I listened for footsteps, for a sign they were making a break for it – stones kicking up, spitting against the garden fences – but there was nothing. Instead, there was just the faint hum of the traffic nearby.

I carried on south – further and further along the path, further and further into the dark, the cold, the silence – but there was no one there, no hint of anyone or anything. It was as if I'd imagined it.

I stopped again.

Had I imagined it?

I thought about the heart symbol on the window. I thought about the door without Derryn's sign on it. Now this. Another soft breeze began to roll through, coming from the north, and as the trees erupted into life again, I pushed on, passing under a ceiling of tangled branches, past endless back gates – on and on until, finally, I came to a halt.

I was following nothing, no one.

I was out here alone.

Turning around, I headed back to the house.

There was no evidence of the heart now, no hint it had even been drawn there. I stood motionless, the torch at my side, and stared at my own reflection. I didn't like what looked back. It was the person I always saw when I was at my lowest – pale, eroded, hunted.

I moved from room to room in the house, trying to find Derryn's sign, opening drawers, searching boxes, and then marched up the driveway and unlocked the garage. I pulled the door up on its runners, the hinges wheezing, and looked around. I didn't expect to find the sign because I felt absolutely certain I'd never removed it – I'd had no reason to, and I had no memory of doing it.

But I was wrong.

It was sitting with some tools on the workbench.

#0509

In the days after we first met, you asked me if there was anyone special in my life. I felt, by that point, we'd really hit it off. Our conversations were always natural and interesting, not filled with the bland patter you had to deal with from some of your other patients. With them, you'd be forced to talk about the weather, ask rehearsed questions about their family, whether they were coming in during visiting hours or not, that sort of thing – but with us it was more profound than that, almost immediately. I'm not saying we talked about politics or religion or philosophy, although we may have, but when we talked, we learned things about each other, important things; I was able to build a picture of you, and you of me, and what we had just grew out of it naturally and elegantly.

'So is there?' you asked.

'Is there what?' I replied, but I was smiling.

'Is there someone special in your life?'

I shrugged.

'Are you too shy to tell me?' you said.

'No.'

You were changing the dressing on my head. I watched you work: you were always slightly slower than the other nurses, but you were meticulous and gentle.

'There was someone once,' I said finally.

'Sounds like it could be a sad story.'

'Yes,' I said, 'it is.'

We ended up talking about something else after that – the saddest films we'd ever watched – and you didn't ask me again. For the rest of the day, I felt confused, because you not asking either meant you didn't want to get into a conversation about my past – and you weren't as interested as you'd made out – or you wanted me to make the next step now you knew that I was single. I didn't want to misread the signs, but at the same time, whenever I thought of asking you to go for a drink with me, my heart would skip a beat.

So, on my last morning on the ward, while you were sitting there next to me, perched on the edge of the bed, changing my dressing, I said, 'Her name was Nora.'

You looked up. 'Sorry?'

'My sad story.'

You just frowned at me.

'My sad story,' I said again.

'I don't follow.'

'You asked me if there was someone special in my life.'

You made an 'oh' with your mouth.

'There was,' I said.

'Nora.'

'Yes.'

'And what happened to Nora?'

I shrugged. 'She cheated on me.'

'I'm sorry to hear that.'

I remember looking at you then. Did you really mean that you were sorry, that you simply felt sad for me and that was the end of it? Or were you secretly pleased that things hadn't worked out with Nora because it meant I was available?

'She wasn't the woman I thought she was.'

You just nodded.

'She lied to me.'

This time, you looked up, your expression difficult to read.

'She was seeing someone else.'

'I'm sorry to hear that,' you repeated.

'Life moves on, I guess.'

'That's what they say.'

I wondered what you meant by that.

'What about you?' I said.

You finished the bandaging, not responding, applying tape to the top of the gauze, before ensuring all sides of the dressing were properly secure. You then stood, still saying nothing, and began to gather up some torn wrappers, the roll of tape.

'What about you?' I asked again.

'The doctor should be around shortly,' you replied. 'He'll ask some questions, make sure everything's all right, and then you'll finally be able to escape this place.'

You smiled at me, but this time I hardly noticed.

Instead, I blurted out, 'You don't wear a wedding ring.'

It was the wrong thing to say, and I knew it instantly. It sounded crass and insensitive, like I was somehow putting the blame on you for not being married. I didn't mean that at all, but it was too late to do anything about it. The words had escaped, they'd been spoken, and now I had to deal with the fallout.

'Sorry,' I said. 'That came out wrong.'

'It's okay.'

'Can you forgive me?'

You smiled again. 'There's nothing to forgive.'

Day Two

17

My phone woke me.

It was still dark outside, the window completely misted up with cold. I rolled over, sheets twisted around my body, and scooped my mobile off the bedside cabinet. It was Annabel.

'Hey, sweetheart,' I said, unravelling myself from the blankets. 'Is everything all right?'

'Have you been online this morning?'

I sat up. 'It's not even seven yet.'

'I know,' Annabel said. 'But I think you should go to *FeedMe*.'

FeedMe was the UK's biggest online news site, a mix of serious reporting, influential campaigns and salacious gossip.

'Why, what's up?'

'Do you ever read that "Crime and Punishment" blog they do?'

'Sometimes.'

'Well, they've posted a story about you.'

I felt my fatigue instantly drop away. '*What?*'

'I don't know what it means,' she said.

'Crime and Punishment' was a twice-weekly column written by an anonymous ex-copper. Despite the size of *FeedMe*, the column had existed in relative obscurity until a couple of years ago when it began reporting on a high-profile murder investigation, quoting sources inside the Met on things that all turned out to be true, and stealing a march on the national media in the process. I went through to the living room, grabbed my laptop off the table, and brought it back to bed, wedging the phone between my ear and shoulder.

'You don't know what it means?' I said to Annabel, puzzled by her choice of words but then I clicked on the latest 'Crime and Punishment' column and found my answer in the last paragraph.

And, finally, a weird story from the Met. Sources at Charing Cross tell me that a woman walked into the police station there early yesterday morning and told detectives that she's been missing for eight years. The officer leading the investigation, DS Catherine Field, declined to comment, but I'm hearing the missing woman gave her name as Derryn Raker, the wife of investigator David Raker. Never heard of him? That's because he keeps a deliberately low profile, but Raker has ended up front and centre – much to the chagrin of the police – of some of the biggest cases of recent years, including the hunt for the Body Snatcher, the disappearance of Met chief superintendent Leonard Franks and the baffling discovery of The Lost Man. Despite that, until now, Raker has managed to remain relatively unknown to the wider public, even while he continued to make enemies in police forces up and down the country. One Met detective I called said Raker was 'an amateur and a liar', and another labelled him as 'a danger to himself and to the public'. Either way, I don't imagine this latest twist in his story will help his cause much with the police *or* with the media: he told the world his wife had died of breast cancer in November 2009.

'What's going on?' Annabel said.

I didn't reply as I tried to work out how this had got into the media so soon, and who might have put it there. Below the last paragraph was a picture of the woman, taken against a bland backdrop. Her eyes were wide, her skin pale. There was a look of mild confusion to her, her hair a mess, a coiled tangle of strands at her cheeks, framing an expression that seemed almost childlike. If the intention was to make her seem vulnerable, it had worked. If it was to get her noticed, that had worked as well.

It was impossible to identify the location, but it could easily have been a police interview room. Could Field have put this story out into the wild? Could one of the officers she shared a station with? The woman at the front desk? The PC who'd stood guard as I'd watched the interview on the monitors? I reread the anonymous quotes from the Met detectives at the end of the article and realized it could have been anyone. There were things I loathed in the piece – suggestions I'd deliberately lied, that I'd sought cases out purely for the publicity they might bring – but it had hit on one, incontrovertible truth: there were plenty of people at the Met who knew me, hated me, and would take pleasure in feeding my name to the sharks in the media. A few journalists had tried to write about me before and had failed to get anything to stick. I'd managed to avoid the limelight then, deliberately so, despite the impact of my cases. But this felt different.

'What's going on?' Annabel repeated.

I'd almost forgotten she was on the line.

'Nothing,' I said decisively. 'This woman's mentally ill.'

'You've met her?'

'Yesterday. That's why I had to come back to London.'

'Why is she saying these things? Why is she saying she's Derryn?'

'I don't know.'

There was a long pause.

'The pictures you've shown me of Derryn . . .' Annabel said hesitantly.

'I know what you're going to say.'

'She looks just like her.'

'She doesn't. Her mouth, her eyes, the way she holds herself – it's not the same.'

'But it's close enough.'

'I'll call you back in a second,' I said, and retreated to the living room. I'd left my notes out on the table the previous night, and somewhere among them was Field's business card.

She answered on the third ring.

'CID.'

'It's David Raker. What's going on?'

'What are you talking about?'

'There's a story in "Crime and Punishment" this morning.'

'About?'

'Take a guess. So was it you?'

'Was *what* me?'

'Did you give them the story?'

'No,' she said. 'We haven't put any information out.'

'Well, if it's not you, then it's someone else at the Met – or it's her.'

'It's 7 a.m., Mr Raker.'

'So?'

'So I've only been in work for ten minutes. I've barely got to my desk. Why don't you calm down and give me an hour to take a look at the column and then I'll have –'

'This isn't just another case to me. This is my life.'

'I understand that.'

'*Do* you? For the last couple of years I'd almost managed to find some sort of peace – and now my life is plastered all over the Internet.'

'I can't control the media, Mr Raker.'

'She's *lying*.'

'Calm down.'

'Everything's a lie.'

I thought of the previous night – the sound that had woken me, the heart on the window, the sign in the garage, and then what I thought I'd seen out on the path. *Or hadn't seen*. Was it the woman who was lying to the cops, or was it me? Was I starting to imagine things now?

I hung up and reread the article again. At best, I came out of this looking like I was confused, or sick. At worst, I was a con artist who'd invented a harrowing lie about a wife dying from cancer. And then there were the eight missing years mentioned in the article, something that the woman had already denied she'd ever said when quizzed by Field. She'd told Field she'd got lost, not that she was missing, but none of that mattered now. The eight years, the distortion of the truth, was out there, on the web, and now it would lead to obvious questions among readers. What if I was the reason she'd spent so long unaccounted for? What if I'd kept her locked up? As I thought of that, I thought of something else: was it possible that the woman had given *FeedMe* the story herself? Or maybe Erik McMillan had? Was this their attempt to now fully shift the narrative away from themselves and on to me? All it had taken was two hundred words on a website to create the idea of me as a suspect.

I called Annabel back, hoping her voice might calm me, but she sounded upset and her sentences were clipped. Did she, like Field, mistrust me now? I'd only known my daughter for five years, our lives before that built on a deception that had deliberately kept us apart. It was hardly any time at all. She'd seen a version of me, but not all of me: I kept the worst of my work back from her because I didn't want her to experience the effect it had on me, and because I vowed never to drag her into the orbit of my cases. So I *had* lied to her on occasion, or at least sidestepped the truth, but I'd always done it for what I thought were the right reasons. She didn't need to hear about the bodies I'd found, or the killers I'd sat across the table from. She didn't need to hear the truth about people: that sometimes there was no light in them at all. But maybe she was starting to remember those moments when I'd stopped short of telling her everything, when I'd hesitated. Maybe what I was telling her now about the woman felt like the times before when I'd stopped short of giving her the truth about my work.

'I don't think this woman was missing,' I said to her. I tried to sound unequivocal.

'Okay.'

'I mean it, sweetheart. This woman . . .' My words dropped away and I rubbed at my eyes, a distant thump starting to pound behind them. 'This woman, she looks like Derryn and she does seem to know the things we did together . . . but it's not her.'

'What sort of things?'

'Just information,' I replied, and then stopped before adding hesitantly, 'and some other, private things.'

'Like what?'

'Dates, places we lived, things we shared.'

'So she knows all that *and* she looks like her?'

'It's not Derryn.'

'How can they look the same?'

I closed my eyes, trying to seek solace in the darkness.

'Why is she saying these things? What's in it for her?'

'I don't know,' I said, 'but I'm trying to find out.'

Silence.

'It's the truth. You're my daughter. I wouldn't lie to you about this.'

'I know,' she said. 'I trust you.'

But there was a tremor in her voice as she said those last three words – and it made me wonder whether, this time, it wasn't me who was lying.

It was Annabel.

18

I made myself some breakfast, but couldn't stomach it. Pushing my plate aside I went back to 'Crime and Punishment', reading it over and over again until it stopped meaning anything. The more times I read it, the angrier I got. I knew my anger was dangerous, something that would only get in the way, so I closed the browser and tried to douse my frustration.

Think.

Retrieving the prepaid mobile, I found the number for Hammond's, the rental agency that Adam Reinsart used for the flat in Chalk Farm, and gave them a call. The woman who picked up put me on hold while she connected me to a guy called Gavin, who she said looked after the property. When she'd asked for my name, I said I was from the Met. Sooner or later, I knew all of this deceit would catch up with me – that someone, most likely a cop, would retrospectively connect the calls – but at the moment I hardly cared. Someone – maybe more than one person – was trying to destroy my life, and all I wanted now was the reason why. I needed to talk to the woman. I needed to talk to Erik McMillan. I needed to look them in the eyes. This was just one small step towards it.

Gavin finally picked up. 'Hello?'

I went through exactly the same routine as the previous evening with Reinsart, and then asked, 'So, there's definitely no one living in the flat?'

'No,' he said, 'not until the 6th of January.'

'Because we've got witnesses that say there is.'

A confused pause.

'Gavin?'

'There shouldn't be. Here at Hammond's, we pride our-selves on –'

'Would anyone else there know anything?' I said, cutting off his sales pitch.

'No. I handle that property.' I could hear the shrill sound of phones in the background; voices. 'If there's been a break-in, I should probably go and take a look, shouldn't I?'

'No, it's fine, sir,' I said. 'Leave it to us. You have two sets of keys at the office, is that correct?'

'Yes.'

'I might need to come by at some point and pick a set up.'

'Sure,' he said. 'That's fine.'

I thanked him and hung up.

I looked at my notes, at the address for the flat, which I'd underlined a couple of times the previous night, and thought about paying the woman a visit. And then, almost instantly, I dismissed it. There were even more compelling reasons than yesterday not to go to Chalk Farm this morning. The *FeedMe* article was out there, people were looking at it, forming opinions about me, and Field had told me to steer clear of the woman. Being seen at the flat confronting her, the potential for raised voices, accusations, tears – none of it would help me if they thought I'd genuinely harmed the woman in some way.

My phone burst into life.

I looked at the unknown number on the display and tried to imagine what type of person would call me this early in the morning, during Christmas week. In the aftermath of the article there was really only one answer.

'Hello?' I said, picking up.

'Mr Raker?'

'Speaking.'

'It's Connor McCaskell from the *Daily* –'

I hung up.

Shit.

The media weren't hanging around.

Getting to my feet, I tried to clear my head, and then happened to glance along the hallway, in the direction of the bedrooms. Immediately, I thought of something.

Derryn's death certificate.

I'd forgotten to get it the night before.

The loft access was via a hatch halfway down the hallway. Reaching up, I grabbed the handle, flipped it down, and a three-section ladder began sliding out. I extended it, set it against the carpet and climbed up. The ladder creaked, its metal joints whining, and then the musty smell of the loft greeted me.

The loft was about half the length of the house, and narrow: everything I'd put up here, I'd had to stack to one side in order to allow access. Most of the stuff was in boxes, my handwriting in black marker pen on the sides, the boxes all identical because I'd bought them in bulk and spent an entire weekend sorting everything into order. That had been about seven years ago – a year after Derryn had died – and had been the first time I'd felt strong enough to tackle what she'd left behind: her clothes, jewellery, keepsakes, photographs. There were tons of books too, all boxed up, as she'd been a massive reader, but she'd never wanted to give any of them away, so – during our marriage – the deal I'd managed to cut with her had always been that her least favourite novels stayed up here. The rest were on shelves in the spare room. I could have got rid of them after her death, or left them at the door of a charity shop somewhere, but the books – even the ones up here that she didn't love as much – were a memory; a reminder of who she'd been.

I couldn't remember exactly where I'd left the death certificate, or any of the paperwork from the funeral, so I started going through the boxes one by one, lifting them off the stack and setting them down on the floor. I used my pen-knife to cut along their tops, through lines of packing tape that had become brittle over time. Under the stark glow of the loft's only light bulb, I found clothes that still held the scent of her perfume, photos of her childhood, of her parents, of her brother in Iraq. I tried not to linger on any of them, not because I didn't want to, but because I didn't want to lose focus.

It took a while but, eventually, I got to the one I was after, *Important Docs* written on the side. This was where I'd kept the death certificate, the receipts, the brochure from the cemetery where Derryn had chosen her plot. This was evidence in black and white that I'd lost her, laid her to rest, and that she really had been gone eight years. When I'd put them in here, I'd never wanted to see any of it again, to read it, to even touch it. Basically, I'd been burying it.

Now I was digging it all up again.

I cut along the packing tape.

Inside, box files were stacked on one side, manila folders – secured with elastic bands – on the other. I turned the files, trying to read the spines, and dust swirled in front of my eyes, the smell of old paper carrying up to me. It wasn't just Derryn in here, it was both of us: there were documents from our house move, copies of visa applications for the States, nursing manuals, pay slips, contracts and insurance forms. I took out each of the box files, unable to remember which of them I'd put the certificate in. I had to go through them one by one, sifting through reams of paper. Finally, I found what I was looking for: a file with *Derryn Estate* on it. I looked at my handwriting, the colour of the ink faded, and then opened it up.

My heart stopped.

Everything was gone.

19

There was no death certificate.

No legal letters, no official record that Derryn had died or that she'd had a funeral, no will, no proof that I'd ever laid her to rest. All of it was missing.

I brought the box file closer but it was no illusion: it was empty. I had no documents to help back up the statements I'd made to Field; none of the paperwork that I promised to deliver to her, or the evidence I was going to use to halt the lies. It was all gone.

Or it was never here in the first place.

I ignored the nagging voice in my head and started going through the other files again, emptying them out on to the floor, frantic, desperate. I dropped to my knees, swiping things aside, tossing them away. When I couldn't find the certificate, I returned to the other cardboard boxes, unloading them, ripping open new folders, poring over sheets of paper, clothes, photos, things I hadn't even thought about once in all the time they'd been here. By the time I'd gone through everything, my head was banging and my eyes felt like they were on fire. The light bulb swung gently as a faint breeze passed through the loft space, light scattering and re-forming, scattering and re-forming – and every time it did, my headache became worse.

Someone's been inside my house.

I searched for obvious signs of a disturbance, images from the night before flashing through my head. The heart on the window. The hint of white in the dark that could have been a face. I'd unstacked the boxes, opened them up before setting them aside. It was a mess. There was no way to tell now if someone had left a trace of themselves; I'd trampled over evidence that might have been left in the wake of a break-in. Now everything was spread around me like the aftermath of an explosion.

I stopped, drained by hours of searching, and glanced down at a pile of books inches away from my feet. I'd emptied them out of a box in an act of desperation. Even if none of these had been her favourites, Derryn would have been horrified by the way I'd treated them, discarded them, their covers turned, a couple of them torn. But then my eye was drawn to one on top, its pages browned and corners curled.

No One Can See the Crows at Night by Eva Gainridge.

The sight of it gave me pause. Gainridge had been Derryn's favourite writer. Her books shouldn't have been up here. I picked it up, examining the front: the image was of a crow sitting on a branch, its beak black except for the tip, which was stained with blood; in its eyes, ringed a faint grey, was the reflection of a Normandy cemetery, rows of pale crosses fading into the distance. I began to go through the rest of the pile, trying to see if there were any other Gainridge novels here. There weren't. The rest were downstairs, on the shelves in the spare room. Derryn had devoured every single thing the author had written, reading and rereading her work until the covers began to slough away and the spines began to fracture. *No One Can See the Crows at Night* had been her favourite. When she was still alive, she hadn't kept her copy of that on the shelves in the spare room, she'd kept it next to her bed. So why was it up here now?

I lingered on the question for a second longer and then snapped out of it. *What the hell difference does it make?* In the context of what had happened here, of the missing death certificate – and the possibility that I was either crazy or had been robbed – a misplaced book was staggeringly irrelevant.

But then I started reading the back of the book.

No One Can See the Crows at Night is Eva Gainridge's 1975 debut, a remarkable and powerful story of loss, set in the aftermath of the Second World War.

When Caroline welcomes home her husband William, scarred by his experiences on the battlefields of northern France, she starts to realize something is very different about him. It's not just his flashbacks or the way he wakes up at night sobbing and screaming. It's not the way this previously placid man now scares her with his temper and seems unable to hold even the most basic of conversations. It's that Caroline genuinely believes the man who came home from the war isn't William. It's someone else entirely.

He's an impostor.

An impostor.

I thought of what Field had said to me after speaking with Erik McMillan: *He says you have something called Capgras delusion. It's a condition where people believe a husband, a wife, a child, has been replaced by an exact duplicate.*

I'd always been aware of *No One Can See the Crows at Night*, although I'd never read it myself, because I'd seen it so often on Derryn's bedside cabinet. She'd told me it was set after the Second World War. She'd told me it was about a marriage. But I'd never bothered to find out any more than that. If Derryn had described the story in any detail, I'd forgotten it. If I'd ever read the synopsis before, it hadn't stuck. Now, though, I saw my reflection.

This story was my story.

And as that hit home, as I wondered again why this book was up here, I started to flick through it. On the first page was a stamp in red ink: four letters, or maybe a set of initials. *PCCL*. I kept going, trying to think straight, but there were no other stamps, no dedications, no notes in the margins or things underlined. Then something fluttered out from between the pages.

I bent down and picked it up. It was a square piece of paper, three inches on all sides, almost certainly from the type of memo block people kept on desks. One side of it was blank. On the other was a handwritten message.

The ink had faded, but I could still read it.

And, as I did, it felt like my ribs had clamped shut.

Derryn:

Thank you for our special time together x

20

I stared at the message, stunned.

The longer I looked, the more nauseous I felt.

There was one, immediately obvious interpretation of what it meant, but I could barely bring myself to form the thought, let alone seriously consider it. The idea that Derryn had kept a previous relationship secret from me, one she'd never told me about at any point, was bad enough; much worse was the idea that she'd had an affair, something illicit, a relationship she'd kept buried in the background of our marriage.

No, I thought. *No way. There's no way in hell that ever happened.* As my grip tightened, I slid the paper back inside the novel, hiding it deep within the pages.

Think.

I headed for the ladder, my legs barely carrying me.

Back in the hallway, I made an immediate beeline for the spare room, for the bookcases in there. One of them was packed with files, missing persons cases I'd worked and put to bed; the other housed the rest of Derryn's books, crammed in tight, vertically, horizontally, filling every inch of the shelves, and stacked two deep.

I found all her Eva Gainridge novels, their spines lined, and pulled them out. Among them was a copy of *No One Can See the Crows at Night*. The moment I had my hands on it, I could recall her reading this version. It was a newer edition than the one I'd found in the loft, in hardback instead of paperback, and had a different cover: a man stood in a doorway, cast into silhouette by the eaves of a house, with an ominous line of crows on the guttering. Beneath Gainridge's name and the title of the book, it said '30th Anniversary Edition'.

So the edition I'd found in the loft wasn't the copy I remembered her reading, which – combined with the note inside – *had* to mean that someone had given it to her. I thought about the message again, the choice of words. Who would give her a gift like that? What did they mean by 'special time together'? Who would be familiar enough with her to know she loved Eva Gainridge? Did the fact that she'd relegated it to the loft mean that she didn't like this person and, by association, hadn't ever appreciated the gift?

I found some instant comfort in the idea, but then it began to crumble again as the same doubts returned: *what if the reason it was in the loft was because she was trying to hide it from me?* Even if it was true, and I absolutely believed – in every part of me – that it wasn't, and that Derryn had never cheated on me, it was just a distraction. It barely mattered at this point. For now, what mattered was the death certificate.

What mattered was that someone had stolen it.

I drank two mugs of coffee in the kitchen, looking out at the frost-flecked driveway. Ordering another copy of the certificate from the register office was one possible route, but it was Christmas week and everything was shut down until the new year, and anyway I wasn't even sure if that was the most immediate issue. My house had been broken into. Things had been stolen from me. A woman was lying to the police about who she was, and a doctor was lying to them about my mental health. When I tried to still my thoughts, all I could feel was a repetitive thudding, a series of gunshots behind my eyes.

The minute I tried to ignore the pain, something else filled the gap: the same insidious thoughts, thriving like weeds – that there wasn't a death certificate, no proof that Derryn had died, because she hadn't, because she was still alive; and if I went to the cemetery, to her headstone, beneath me would be nothing, just endless earth.

I pushed all of it back, as far into the darkness of my mind as it would go, and my eyes returned to Derryn's copy of the Gainridge novel. There was no description on the rear of the jacket, not like the version in the loft, because this one was a hardback. Instead, there was a short extract.

'Who are you?' she said to him.

'I'm your husband.'

'No. No, you aren't. I don't know who you are.'

He was absolutely still except for his eyes, as green as dragon scales, which moved around the room, stopping on the walls, on the exits, the shelves, the furniture, as if he could hear someone calling his name but didn't know where from.

'You aren't my husband.'

'I am, Caroline. You've lost your mind.'

'No,' she said. 'In my heart, I know you're not him.'

I thought of the previous night, of following the glimpse of something – someone – into the darkness of the alleyway and finding nothing, no one, not even a hint. Was I really seeing things? The idea I'd hallucinated, that I might have suffered some acute lapse of perspective, didn't tally with how I was feeling physically this morning, despite my headache, but I couldn't deny things were stacking up. Either I was correct, and someone was toying with me, or I was so sick I had no concept of it any more. Like the woman in the book, I believed in my heart that that wasn't true. But now, in order to convince myself and do the same to the police, I had to prove it. And I could only really see one way of doing that.

I had to do what I'd promised myself I wouldn't.

I had to go to the source of the lie.

#0633

The doctor came around an hour after you left my bedside for the final time, just as you said he would. He was a disinterested Asian man in his fifties with an accent I could barely follow. I listened to virtually nothing he was saying, except when he finally told me I could go, and then I got up and headed out of the cramped, sterile room I'd been in for three days, and into the corridor where the nurses' station was located. You weren't there.

'Is Derryn around?' I asked one of the nurses.

She looked up. 'I'm sorry?'

'Derryn. Is she around?' The nurse looked at me properly this time, as if I'd said something offensive. 'I just wanted to thank her again for her care,' I added.

'She's on a break at the moment.'

'When will she be back?'

'Not for another hour.'

I walked out of the ward, wondering where you would spend your lunch break. In a staffroom somewhere? Outside in one of the insipid green spaces? The hospital was like a maze, so trying to track you down would have been impossible. I did a quick circuit of the immediate area, and – when I couldn't find you – returned to the doors of the ward and waited. Fifteen minutes passed. Twenty. Forty. An hour.

You finally returned after seventy-five minutes, reading what looked like medical notes. You didn't notice me until you were almost at the doors of the ward, your fingers already on your security card, ready to buzz yourself in. I took a step forward – into your field of vision – and you stopped, looking up at me.

'Oh,' you said. 'Hello again.'

I swallowed, my response catching in my throat. I actually felt nervous. 'Hello,' I managed.

We looked at each other for a moment.

'Is everything all right?'

'Yes,' I said, and held up a hand. 'Yes, sorry.'

Why was my mouth so dry?

'I just wanted to say thank you.'

You frowned. 'For what?'

'For the care you've given me.'

You broke into a smile: that wonderful, luminescent smile. 'Oh,' you said. 'That's very sweet of you. Thank you. I was just doing my job – but I appreciate it.'

I glanced at your ring finger again.

There was still no ring.

'I didn't mean to offend you earlier.'

You frowned again. 'What do you mean?'

'With my comment about you not wearing a wedding ring.'

You looked at me blankly.

It had only been a couple of hours since we talked but you clearly had no recollection of our conversation. Had you already forgiven me and forgotten my mistake? Or had what we'd discussed really not stuck with you at all? Had it meant that little to you? I'd told you about Nora but I'd never got to hear anything from you in return. I'd never got to find out whether there was someone in your past, in your life, who'd hurt you like Nora hurt me. I didn't know – yet – why a person like you wasn't married.

'Well, I'd better be going,' you said.

Almost immediately, the doors to the ward buzzed open and a male nurse emerged, and you and he started talking about something – a patient, a case. You looked back at me, smiled again, and said, 'I hope your recovery goes well. I really appreciate what you said. We don't often get people making that kind of effort.'

Any frustration I might have felt for you vanished instantly. You didn't remember the specifics of our conversation about the wedding ring, about Nora, but it hardly seemed to matter now. Your smile, the way you spoke to me, the way you looked me in the eyes, was like a magnet: I wanted to reach out and touch you; I wanted to feel my fingers on your skin.

'Goodbye, Derryn,' I said after you were gone, watching you through a small glass panel in the door as you walked away, giving instructions to the male nurse.

Goodbye.

But only for now.

21

The wind ghosted across the playground at the front of the Chalk Farm flat as I made my way up the stairwell. I could hear the swings squeaking as they rocked back and forth, saw a roundabout turning gently in the breeze, and then the walls closed in around the stairs and all I could see was foot-thick concrete, wet with leaking water.

I kept an eye out for cameras, just in case, but I didn't expect there to be any on the stairs or out on the walkways where the flats were. Any cameras would be at ground level, in the streets that circled this part of Chalk Farm, and I'd been careful to avoid as many as possible on the walk from the Tube. I'd thought about going to Hammond's to pick up a key, but had then decided against it: it would have been easier and less stressful than the alternative – breaking in, if she wasn't there – but my visit would be remembered by Gavin, the agent who looked after the flat, and by the cameras they probably had inside the shop. If the police went through the footage in the coming weeks, they'd place me there, Gavin would tell them I'd pretended to be a cop, and it would become a lot harder to paint myself as a victim.

So, instead, as soon as I'd left the Tube station, I'd flipped up the hood on my top, tilted the peak on the baseball cap I was wearing and, whenever a camera came into view, dropped my gaze to the floor. It wasn't foolproof but it made it tricky to ID me easily if I kept my head low, and I knew – from experience – that all I'd need, in order to push back at any future allegations from the Met, was for there to be enough doubt about who I was.

At the fifth floor, the building opened up again and, below me, a vague grey in the morning fog, I saw the roundabout was still on a listless rotation and a gang of kids had gathered. Their cigarettes flickered orange in the dull light and they were laughing about something. Conscious of being seen, even five floors up, I took a step closer to the flats, and hurried down to the end. At the penultimate door, I stopped. It was the same one I'd seen the woman go into.

I flipped down my hood and knocked twice.

As I waited, I could hear my heart in my ears. What was I going to say to her when she answered? How was I going to prove she was lying? But my knocking went unanswered, a third time too. The door was peeling and old, its frame warped, rotten, smeared with mud and grime. I knocked again, harder.

Nothing.

I felt around in my coat pocket for a packet of sterile gloves – lifted from a pile I always kept at home – and then paused. However careful I was, I was going to leave trace evidence behind. Skin flakes. Fibres. Hair. Fragments of who I was. Maybe that wouldn't matter if the Met had no idea the woman had come to the flat, but if they ended up here, it would matter a lot. If they matched one skin or hair sample to me, they would know I'd accessed the property. Worse, they might begin to believe I'd genuinely come here to hurt the woman.

I took an automatic step back.

First, she'd appeared out of nowhere claiming to be my wife. Then a doctor had lied on her behalf, telling police I'd had to be committed. Then someone had snuck into my house and stolen paperwork from me that would have helped prove my story. What if this was the next part? What if that person expected me to come here?

What if this was a trap?

I continued pulling the gloves on, but more slowly now, still undecided about what to do. The door had no handle, just a basic Yale cylinder lock, so the only way to check that it was secure was by laying a hand on it.

I pushed, but it didn't budge.

So are you going in or not?

Looking along the walkway, all the way back to the stair-well, and then the other way, to the flat after this one – the last on this floor – I saw there were no windows on any of the flats, just doors. Each one was a different colour; only some had numbers.

I was tempted to knock on the neighbouring flats, to see if they'd seen or heard anything, but doing that presented the same problems as with Gavin at Hammond's: they'd remember me. I could dump a prepaid mobile where it would never be found; it was harder to defend yourself when an eyewitness could pick you out in a line-up.

I waited for a moment, checked I was still alone, got out my picks and set to work on the Yale lock. It was simple, and didn't take long.

I gave the door a gentle shove.

It juddered briefly against the frame and then, slowly, arced away from me, into the flat. As the door swung back towards me again, I stopped it with a gloved hand.

Staying where I was, I took in the interior.

A hallway ran from front to back, all the way through to the kitchen, and I could see the outline of cupboards, the edges of a laminate worktop, and a small window made from ridged glass that showed nothing but vague squares of light from adjacent buildings. There were three further doors in the flat: the one nearest to me looked like it went into a living room – I could see the edges of an empty TV stand – and the next must have been the bedroom, because the last one was a bathroom.

I hesitated for a moment longer, then slowly started moving inside. The whole place felt airless. An extractor fan, high up above the kitchen worktops, rumbled softly, and somewhere else wind was escaping in, the sound like a child's whimper.

'Hello?' I said quietly.

In the living room there were the ghostly shapes of photo frames still visible on the walls and the impressions of furniture embedded in the carpet, and just one curtainless window: its view was of the nearby tower block, shrouded in fog.

The bedroom was also empty and, in the bathroom, modern and newly installed, one of the taps was dripping. I moved through to the kitchen. There was nothing in any of the cupboards, the shelves entirely empty.

No one was living in the flat.

If the woman had spent time here, it had only been temporary. There was no evidence of clothes, of food, no smell of cooking, or perfume. If she was returning day after day, as part of some routine, it seemed unlikely she wouldn't have been seen and heard. The flats were packed in so tightly. The walls were thin. Standing in the kitchen, I could hear the TV from next door – and not just a vague hum but actual words being spoken. Using saucepans and frying pans in here, turning lights on and off, walking around, all of that would have registered with a neighbour, and I just didn't get the sense that that was what the woman would want. If it was, why fail to mention this place to Field? She'd talked about Woolwich, but never here, a property in a district ten miles from the train station she'd used and the pharmacy she claimed to have been left at.

So why had she come to the flat last night?

I returned to the walkway, clicking the door shut behind me, and peeled off the gloves. Pulling up my hood again, I looked out over the edge – to the ashen city, the mist, the people, and then to a car moving into the estate. It was a grey Volvo. I watched as it nosed its way into one of the parking bays reserved for residents and, as it did, something instinctive kicked in, a low-level alarm: somehow I just knew it didn't belong here. A few seconds later, both the passenger and driver's side doors swung open. I stayed there, looking over the rail: I didn't recognize the man getting out of the passenger side. But I recognized the driver.

Shit.

It was Field.

I didn't have time to think about why she was here – I just needed to get out without her seeing me. I headed for the stairwell, keeping back from the edge of the walkway in case she looked up from the parking bay. At the stairs, I paused, listening for footsteps. I couldn't hear any – just the incessant leak of dripping water.

I took two steps at a time down to the fourth floor, listened, and then did the same down to the third. At the second, I heard them: Field and a male voice.

Darting into the second-floor walkway, I sidestepped immediately to my left, where I knew there would be a ridged cove under the steps, created as the stairwell spiralled upwards, because it was exactly the same on the fifth. It was the only place to hide – the walkways were absolutely straight up and down otherwise.

' . . . shitty weather.'

It was the man speaking.

'You working New Year?' he asked.

'Not if I can help it,' Field replied. 'Although Mike said he's bringing his mum around for dinner, so I might try and wangle some overtime.'

The man laughed. 'I forgot about your mad mother-in-law.'

And then they were past me, heading up towards the third floor. I waited, counting footsteps in my head, and when I thought they must be close to the fifth-floor walkway, I moved back to the stairwell and made for the ground floor.

As I exited, I kept my head down, more conscious than ever of being caught on film, and finally emerged on to Chalk Farm Road. I headed straight for the Tube. I'd made it out without being caught, but that did little to settle my nerves: Field knew about the flat – which meant the woman must have told her about it since last night.

And now I was starting to worry that I was right.

Maybe I really had walked into a trap.

22

A few minutes after I got home, Spike called: he had the background I'd asked for on Erik McMillan. I grabbed my laptop from the bedroom and sat down at the living-room table.

'There's a lot of info,' Spike said. 'His phone records – mobile and landline – are there, and I've tried to attach a name and address to every number he's called, or received a call from.'

'Brilliant. Thanks, Spike.'

'I've sent it all as a PDF.'

'Okay,' I said, seeing that the email was already waiting for me.

I hung up and dragged the PDF attachment on to the desktop. It was almost fifty pages long, the bulk of it made up of McMillan's phone records. What was obvious, even at a quick glance, was that his home landline had gone the way of most people's: he paid the line rental because he wanted the Internet, but he hardly used it to make any phone calls. Across the six months I was looking at, McMillan had made, on average, ten calls a month from his home and received about the same. On the other hand, his mobile phone statements for the same period ran to forty pages.

I set those aside and moved on.

McMillan lived in a huge detached house in Kew, between the botanical gardens and the National Archives. When I went to Street View in Google, I found out just how big: it went back about eighty feet, with another sixty-odd foot of garden beyond that, and was built on three floors. On a satellite shot, it looked like his was the biggest house, not only on the road but in the entire zigzag of homes that existed between the Thames and the South Circular. The front was red brick, with white render around the doors and windows, but at the side it was sand-coloured London stock brick. There was also an unusual extension there that looked like some sort of converted chimney stack: it was tall and quite narrow, but had a series of long windows dotted all the way up it.

According to mortgage statements, and an insurance policy that McMillan had renegotiated back in April, he had a daughter who was twenty-one. I found her online quickly: she was studying Medicine up in Edinburgh. That meant he'd been in a relationship once, but while the house seemed ridiculously big for just one person, I couldn't find any evidence that he was sharing it with anyone at the moment, so if he'd been married, or attached, I got the sense that he wasn't any more. I wondered if he'd retained the property in some kind of settlement, but from the documents Spike had sent me, there was nothing to suggest that. I made a note to chase it down.

I worked my way through another insurance policy that McMillan had taken out and gathered a few more personal details and, elsewhere, saw that he'd listed the value of his house as £2.2 million. On a mortgage application, he'd noted his yearly salary as £108,329. None of that was especially interesting: I already knew the house was big, and as the Clinical Director at a London psychiatric unit, he was always going to be on good money.

Eventually, I ended up back at his mobile phone records.

I methodically worked through the numbers he'd called, as well as the ones that had called him, seeing if I recognized any of the people he'd been in touch with, or the home addresses that were registered to them. I didn't. Once I was certain of that, I began entering the names into a document of my own, alphabetically listing them so it would be easier to come back to afterwards. It took patience: the first time I checked the clock, I realized I'd been going for over an hour; the second, almost two. By the time I was finally done, when I went through to the kitchen to make myself a coffee, the sky had already begun to alter, fading as the day slowly burnt out.

Back in the half-light of the living room, I went through the names again, drawing connections where I could back to McMillan. Most appeared to be friends or people he worked with. As I'd already found out, he didn't do social media himself, but that didn't mean he didn't appear on his friends' Facebook, Twitter and Instagram feeds, and – on occasion – his daughter's too. None of the photos I found rang any alarm bells, though: McMillan wasn't trying to hide, the things he was doing – going out for meals, drinking at pubs, social events, charity dinners – were prosaic and normal. He was always smartly dressed, his black hair showing no signs of grey, his trademark red glasses staying on for some pictures and removed for others. On one friend's Instagram page, I found a group shot, some sort of university reunion, everyone's names listed below, which allowed me to tick off a whole raft of people that McMillan was in regular contact with.

By the time I was done, there was only one anomaly: a call made to McMillan the previous day, not long before I'd arrived at Charing Cross police station.

It was from a landline: an 0208 number. In Spike's notes, he'd assigned no address to the landline, just a road. Cavanagh Avenue. When I looked it up, I saw it was at the south-west edge of Plumstead Common. I paused there for a moment, considering something else: Plumstead Common was less than a mile from Woolwich, where the woman claimed to have come from, and about two and a half miles from Thamesmead, where St Augustine's was located. Could that be relevant?

I wondered why Spike might not have followed this number up properly. Maybe it was an oversight. Maybe he'd forgotten to run it down. He was normally reliable, meticulous and precise, but tracking names and addresses was tedious work, even if you were being paid for it, so it wasn't impossible that this was an error.

Unless it wasn't an error at all.

I went to Street View.

Cavanagh Avenue was a small cul-de-sac just off Plumstead Common Road, and snaked south from the bottom edge of the hundred-acre park. It didn't take me long to find out the reason Spike hadn't written down a name or a house number for the landline: it didn't belong to a home or a business.

It belonged to a phone box.

Someone had called McMillan from a payphone.

It was on the corner of Cavanagh Avenue, on the other side of the street from the park. The cul-de-sac was mostly small terraced houses – two windows at the top, a single window and a door at the bottom – but on the corner, where the phone box was located, and where Cavanagh Avenue became Plumstead Common Road, there were a series of businesses, their windows obscured behind red metal cages: a grocery store-cum-off licence, a Polish deli, a Bangladeshi takeaway and a newsagent.

Why had someone called McMillan from here?

It was rare that people chose to use phone boxes now – mobile phones were relatively inexpensive, calls either free with a contract or a matter of pence on a pay as you go. In fact, the main – perhaps only – reason to use a phone box these days was if you were keen not to be identified. The person who'd got in touch with Erik McMillan evidently didn't want the call traced back to them. But just because the call came from a phone box, it didn't mean the caller couldn't be ID'd.

There just needed to be a camera nearby.

A moment later, the doorbell rang.

Surprised, I turned at the living-room table and tried to look along the hallway to the front door. I wasn't expecting visitors and I rarely, if ever, gave out my address – which made this what? The postman? Someone selling something?

Or a journalist?

On edge now, I got up from the table and made my way to the front door. There were two figures standing behind the frosted glass: one, I realized quickly, was Field; the other was the man I'd seen her with in Chalk Farm. They spotted me straight away – my shape in the hallway – as I moved slowly towards them, trying to imagine why they might have come all the way out here. But, in the end, I could only really think of one reason.

Something had happened.

And, whatever it was, it led back to me.

23

I unlocked the front door, my head still humming.

If they simply had more questions – straightforward ones, standard queries that needed to be ticked off a list – Field could have just picked up the phone. So she was here for something else. Had she seen me at the flat in Chalk Farm? I'd been careful, so it was unlikely, but it didn't mean I hadn't walked into a trap, or was about to.

Or maybe it wasn't that at all.

Maybe she'd come here because I'd told her the day before that I had all the evidence I would ever need at home and I could prove the woman's deceit instantly. Except I couldn't – not any more. Because I'd told her my evidence was the death certificate. And now I had no idea where that was.

I pulled the door open.

Field was dressed in the same dark blue skirt-suit and pale raincoat I'd seen her in at the flat in Chalk Farm. The man next to her was in his mid thirties, but his black hair had begun to grey and so had an untidy beard he'd allowed to creep towards the top of his cheeks. He had a blue RSI bandage on his right wrist and a phone in his other hand.

I hadn't met him yesterday at the station but I recognized him instantly as the person Field had been with at the flat. And by the way he was studying me, blue eyes narrowed, I knew he'd already made up his mind about me.

'Mr Raker,' Field said. 'This is Detective Constable Gary Kent.'

He nodded, still watching me closely.

'Do you think we could come in?'

I backed away from the door. Field wiped her feet on the mat, but Kent just walked straight through to the living room, his boots leaving muddy imprints on the floorboards. There were going to be bigger battles to fight, but it annoyed me nonetheless. I watched him as he leaned in to look at photographs of Derryn.

'Do you want something to drink?' I said to Field.

'No, we're fine, thank you.'

She followed me through to the living room where Kent had now picked up a picture of Derryn and me, taken at Imperial Beach in San Diego. Again, I felt irritated at the way he was systematically working his way along the sideboard, touching everything, minutely adjusting all their positions.

'Please don't touch those,' I said.

He stopped. 'Oh, I'm sorry,' he said, although his apology conveyed little in the way of actual contrition. He looked at me and then back to the photographs and shrugged.

I kept my eyes on Kent for a second and then directed Field to one of the sofas. She casually glanced around the living room herself, taking in the decor, the layout, the things I had on show: she was doing exactly the same thing as Kent – checking out the pictures of Derryn – but she was just doing it more subtly. Thankfully, I'd put my laptop and notepad away, as well as all the printouts I'd made from the PDF that Spike had sent me.

'So,' Field said, removing the same pad as the day before, 'early this morning, we went to talk to the woman claiming to be your wife. We arranged to drive over to the hostel we'd put her up in. From our side, the arrangements were pretty clear.'

I frowned. 'She wasn't there?'

'No, she wasn't,' Field responded, a bite to her voice now. 'Why?'

'That's what we're trying to find out.'

I eyed them both and, as I did, it dawned on me: *they can't find her.*

'She's disappeared?'

'The people at the hostel said she never turned up last night.'

I couldn't work out if I should be pleased or concerned. If the woman had stayed at the flat in Chalk Farm overnight, that explained why she hadn't been at the hostel – but it didn't explain why Field and Kent had gone to the flat, or how they had found a connection to it.

'Wasn't she supposed to show you some ID this morning?' I asked.

'That was one of the reasons we went to see her, yes.'

'The ID that she forgot to bring with her to Charing Cross?'

'Yes.'

'The ID that was supposed to prove who she was?'

Field sighed. 'Yes.'

'What about the hospital in Woolwich?'

'What about it?'

'Did you know she's not an employee there?'

Field glanced at Kent and then back to me: 'What did I tell you about playing detective, Mr Raker?' As I responded with silence, she sighed a second time and said, 'No, as far as we can tell, she isn't an employee at Queen Elizabeth Hospital.'

'As far as you can tell? She isn't. So she lied about that as well.'

'Well, we're still looking into it.'

'"Looking into it"? Come on, she's a liar.'

'We're looking into it,' Field said again, firmly.

I kept my expression neutral, but inside all I could feel was a flood of relief. Field had asked the woman for ID, for confirmation of her details, and she'd bolted. A single day of lies was all she'd been able to muster before the foundations started to creak, the walls cracked and the whole thing came down. It still didn't explain how she knew so much about me and about my marriage, it still didn't explain why someone had got into my house and stolen documents from me – but I would find out those answers; I'd seek them out once the dust had settled. For now, it was enough that I'd been proved right: the woman was a con artist, a fraud, a charlatan. She wasn't Derryn.

'Where were you last night?'

Kent this time.

He hadn't come over to the sofas. Instead, he was perched on the edge of the living-room table, so that I had to turn around to get a clear view of him.

'What?'

'Where were you last night?' he repeated. His accent wasn't strong, but it was local.

I glanced at Field. She was staring at me, her face a blank wall. When I returned my attention to Kent, he'd removed his own notebook.

'I was here,' I said. 'Why?'

He opened his notebook and flipped through the pages. 'Can anyone confirm that? Friends? Family? A girlfriend perhaps?' He looked up from his pad. 'Or a boyfriend?' It was hard to tell whether he'd delivered the last question as an insult or not, because his voice remained completely neutral.

'No,' I said. 'I was here alone.'

'You said you had a death certificate for Derryn?' Field asked.

'Yes,' I said to her.

'In your loft?'

'Yes.'

'Can you get it for us?'

I frowned again. 'What's going on?'

'Can you get it for us or not, Mr Raker?'

'I don't know where it is exactly.'

Field didn't seem surprised, just nodded and looked at

Kent. Any respite I'd felt before, any brief feeling of exoneration, was gone.

'The loft's full of boxes,' I said, uncertain where the words were taking me or how I might back them up. 'But it's up there. I'll find it and drop it in.'

'Mr Raker,' Kent said, and waited for me to turn on the sofa to face him. 'The woman claiming to be your wife called us last night, about an hour after she left the station. DS Field had left for the day, so I was the one that took the phone call.'

'And?'

'And she says you followed her.'

'What? No. No, I didn't follow her,' I said, and then stopped myself. I *had* followed her. I'd watched her all the way to the front door of the flat in Chalk Farm, the Post-it note in her hand. It had been instinct to deny I'd ever been there, instinct built off the back of having to deal with the woman's lies the day before. But I had followed her. I'd followed her there, and the cops would know it the second they pulled film off the local CCTV cameras.

'Mr Raker?'

I looked from Kent to Field, kidding myself that I didn't know where this was going. They were trying to work out why she wasn't at the hostel this morning, as arranged; why she'd never turned up there in the first place; why, after so vociferously telling Field about the death certificate, about proof I held that my wife had been dead for eight years, I wasn't making an immediate dash for my attic.

'Okay, yes,' I said. 'I *did* follow her.'

The two of them stared at me, unmoved.

'But I never talked to her. I never confronted her.'

Field rubbed a hand against her mouth, obviously suppressing a desperate urge to say something. She'd asked me to steer clear of the woman and I'd done completely the opposite. I must have made a mistake in tailing the woman, some tiny error that I hadn't accounted for. I didn't remember one, didn't even recall her looking in my general direction, at any stage, but how else would she have known I was there?

Field said, 'Where was it you followed her to, Mr Raker?'

It felt like a trick question, like they already knew the answer was the flat at Chalk Farm – after all, I'd seen them there myself this morning. And if they knew the answer was the flat, it meant that – at some point last night – the woman herself, or someone she knew, must have told the police that she'd gone there. The question was: *what* had they been told? What explanation had been given for her heading there first and not to the hostel? Whatever it was, it must have been the reason that Field and Kent had gone there this morning.

'Mr Raker?' Field said again.

'Chalk Farm.'

'I'm sorry?'

'I followed her to a flat in Chalk Farm.'

Field tried to act surprised: 'Chalk Farm?' she said, glancing at her notes. 'So you're saying you went to Chalk Farm last night?'

'Yes.'

'Why?'

'She got into the taxi you booked for her and then got out again before it had even left the road. I wanted to find out why. I wanted to find out where she was going. I thought she might go back to Woolwich, but she ended up in north London.'

'Why were you even waiting there?'

I didn't have an answer for that, or at least not one that would satisfy them, so I said nothing. It seemed to make things worse, my silence emboldening them both.

'Had you ever been to the flat in Chalk Farm before?' Field asked.

'Never.'

'Derryn didn't mention it to you?'

It was hard to tell if she meant Derryn my wife, or the woman who purported to be her. I said, 'No.'

'You never lived there?'

'No.'

'Never knew anyone who did?'

'*No.*'

'Because that flat is empty,' Field said.

I couldn't admit that I knew that already.

'Did you know that, Mr Raker?'

'No,' I lied.

'There's no tenant there at the moment.'

'So why did she go there?'

'All I know are the facts: she told DC Kent on the phone that she was at the address in Chalk Farm; DC Kent asked her why, but she wouldn't tell him. All she told him was that she thought you might be following her. DC Kent advised her to stay put, he drove out there to make sure she was all right, but by the time he got there, she was gone. DC Kent says that the woman sounded . . . *distressed* on the phone.'

I glanced at Kent. His expression had hardly moved but his eyes were the same as when he'd first entered the house: watchful of me, mistrustful.

'Why would she sound distressed, Mr Raker?'

The insinuation weighed heavy in Field's words, but I tried to head it off and turned to look at Kent: 'You said she called you from the flat? How did she do that?'

His face finally moved as he frowned.

'She doesn't have a mobile, right?' I looked at Field. 'Right?' She nodded.

'And if there's a landline at the flat, it's probably been dis-connected because no one is living there at the moment.' I made it sound like a guess, but I'd seen no phone in the flat earlier. 'Right?'

'She called from a prepaid mobile,' Field said.

'So she *does* have a mobile?'

Field shrugged. 'We can't trace ownership if it's prepaid.'

Which was exactly why I'd used one to call Adam Reinsart the previous night. I pressed her again: 'But you can see my point? She told you that she didn't have a phone.'

She didn't respond to that. Instead, she asked, 'What time did you follow her from, Mr Raker?'

'From when she left the station.'

It didn't seem like it was news to them, but they put plenty of emphasis on it by saying nothing. I'd followed her; now she'd disappeared.

A moment later, I heard a rustle from Kent's direction and saw that he was removing something from the inside pocket of his coat. It was a thin plastic package.

'We need to take a DNA sample from you,' he said, holding up the package.

'What are you talking about?'

'Are you saying you need me to explain what a DNA sample is?'

'Don't patronize me.'

'Mr Raker,' Field said, her voice quiet, firm. When I looked at her, there was a steel in her eyes that I hadn't seen before. 'Will you provide us with a DNA sample?'

'If you tell me why.'

They looked at each other. The room was filled only with the soft tick of a clock on the wall: one that Derryn had bought when we'd spent a weekend in Bristol.

Quietly, Field said, 'When we went to the flat this morning, we found something on the door.'

I thought of the peeling paint, all the dirt and grime I'd

123

seen at the bottom of the door frames on both sides – none of which I'd looked at closely.

Now I realized it hadn't all been dirt.

'What did you find?' I asked her evenly, but I thought I knew the answer and I was dreading it.

'We found some blood spatters,' she said.

24

'Blood spatters?'

Field nodded.

'And you think that blood's mine?'

'Or hers,' Kent said.

'You really think I would hurt her?'

Kent started opening up the DNA kit. Inside were a pair of gloves, two pots, and two samplers to take the swabs. He removed his coat and started to pull on the gloves: they were awkward and unyielding. He couldn't blow into them to loosen them up or he risked contamination, so while he tried to lever his fingers in, Field came forward on the sofa and said, 'We accessed the flat and searched it, and there didn't appear to be any sign of a disturbance. We're not accusing you of anything yet, but you will be well aware of how this process works. I have blood on the door frame at the flat. I've got a woman I can't locate. Now you're admitting you followed her home last night.'

'That blood isn't mine,' I said, and then became less certain. Was this another set-up? How would someone have got hold of my blood? 'It's not mine,' I repeated, although this time it was more for my benefit than theirs.

'Well, let's find out for sure,' Field replied.

Kent had the gloves on now, had set the pots down beside one another on the table, and had already removed one of the samplers from its plastic. I thought about the consequences of refusing to give them a sample. I didn't legally have to, I wasn't under arrest, but I was a suspect and that made any decision not to help them look problematic. I'd provided a DNA sample the one and only time I had been arrested properly, but that was seven years ago, it was a set-up, and no charges were brought, so it was likely the sample I gave had been destroyed.

'Are you ready?' Kent said.

I nodded and he came forward. I opened my mouth, felt the sampler against the inside of my cheek, and then felt the same thing again when he took a back-up swab. The second time he pressed much harder.

'Easy as that,' he said once it was over, but there was something in his voice, a cynicism, a distrust, that suggested he'd already made his mind up about what they were going to get back from the lab. As he sealed everything up, preserving the evidence, I watched him for a moment, trying to recollect if we'd crossed paths before on a case I'd worked. Was that the reason he didn't like me? Was he another detective I'd upset because I'd hunted around in the shadows of a failed case and found the answers he'd missed? It was possible, even if I didn't remember it. It was possible he might have been the person who'd given *FeedMe* the story about the woman. Or maybe he'd just heard conversations about me at the Met from friends and colleagues. I wasn't sure what was worse: at least if he'd seen my work first-hand, he might admit to its logic or proficiency; if he'd only heard about me, that would be something different, because no one at the Met was talking about how capable I was.

I returned my attention to Field.

She wasn't the same as Kent. If she'd heard about me, she'd chosen to ignore the whispers and judge me for my actions. I admired that, even if I knew I wasn't ingratiating myself with her. I'd been emotional yesterday, had lost my cool; I'd gone against her instructions by following the woman home; now I'd dealt with the subject of the death certificate, all my proof, with a vague wave of the hand.

'Is there anything else you want to tell us, Mr Raker?'

She watched me, her grey eyes like hard chunks of rock.

I thought before answering. Fleetingly, I even considered telling her that someone had been inside my house. But I couldn't decide, in the fraction of time I had, whether it would help or hinder me, so I just said, 'No, there's nothing else.'

'You said you don't know where that death certificate is?'

'No. Not exactly. I need to look for it.'

Those eyes lingered on me and then finally she nodded, looked past me to where Kent was gathering everything up, and stood, buttoning up her coat. It hadn't been a white Christmas, but it had been bitter for days, the ground frozen, the wind biting. Her expression made it look like she'd brought the weather inside.

'If you find that death certificate, it might be useful.'

'I agree,' I said.

It was the wrong choice of words, because her gaze stayed on me for a second too long, as if she understood the meaning of my response. Was she keeping something back from me? Did she and Kent know more than they were letting on?

'The registrar here in Ealing is in India for Christmas,' she said, looking away again, 'but she lands in London on Monday. It's a public holiday then, but we've spoken to her on the phone and, once she's back, she's agreed to open up the office for us. She says she'll find their copy of the certificate.'

Monday was three days away.

Even though I knew there was little chance that the register office had been broken into in the same way as my house – that their digital archives would be secure and off-limits – it didn't settle my nerves. Three days was a long time. In just under a day, a woman had turned my entire life upside down, someone had broken into my house, and I'd found a book with a message in it that I didn't understand; and I couldn't tell the police about any of it because I had no idea where it would end up taking me. Would I be better off telling Field? Would it absolve me of suspicion or increase my problems? Would it just dig me in deeper by somehow connecting me to the blood at the flat?

I didn't know, so I chose to say nothing.

'And if we don't get anywhere with the registrar,' Field went on, 'we can always chase down the funeral director. They tend to keep records. Do you remember which company you used?'

I did, because I'd already considered the idea myself, but I knew it wouldn't go anywhere: the company I used had gone out of business a couple of years after Derryn's death. Their records probably existed somewhere, had perhaps been donated to a genealogical or historical society, but it wouldn't be an easy lead to chase down. I told Field as much and then she just stared at me for a moment, as if the closure of a company was something else I might have had a hand in.

'I need you to undergo a medical assessment,' she said eventually.

'What?'

'An independent medical assessment.'

I shook my head. 'I told you, I'm not sick.'

'This woman's story, there are holes in it,' she went on, as if I'd said nothing at all. 'I'll admit that. It's our job to find out which parts of her story are true and which aren't. But I look at some of the things we're getting from you and I'm concerned, Mr Raker. They're inconsistent. Some of it doesn't add up.'

'I'm not *sick*.'

'I need to know how to proceed.'

Her response threw me for a moment, but then I got it: she didn't know whether to believe me, arrest me or hand me over to the hospital system. If it was the latter, if I really *was* sick, they needed specialist doctors, not police officers.

'You're going to take that assessment,' she said, and then headed for the door.

As I watched Field and Kent return to their car, I tried to make sense of everything I'd just found out. The lies, the half-truths, the things that didn't add up, the countless connections, but it was hard to even think straight. The only thing I knew for certain was that this was a map, a route taking me somewhere.

And it wasn't leading me anywhere good.

25

After Field and Kent were gone, I called Erik McMillan's mobile. It went straight to his voicemail: 'You've reached Erik McMillan. Please leave a message.'

'This is David Raker,' I said. 'Apparently, you know me, so I think you and I should talk.'

Next, I tried St Augustine's and, this time, got through to someone, rather than just an answerphone. They said McMillan was on holiday and wouldn't be back until the new year, and that they could either pass on a message to him or connect me to someone who worked for him.

'Tell him David Raker wants to speak to him,' I said.

'Does Dr McMillan have your number?'

I gave it to her.

A few moments later, my phone started ringing. On the display was a number I didn't recognize, but an area code I did: Kingsbridge, south Devon.

Kennedy.

He wasn't calling from the cottage. *Why?*

'It's me,' he said, as soon as I picked up.

'What's wrong?'

'Nothing,' he said, immediately trying to allay my fears. 'Nothing's wrong. It's just my day off today and I came into Kingsbridge, to the library, to use the Internet there and look at the news, and . . . and I just read about you.' He sounded shocked, confused. 'Did you know you're in that "Crime and Punishment" blog on *FeedMe*?'

'Oh,' I said, and allowed myself a moment of respite: I

thought he'd been compromised; that someone, somehow, might have seen through his new identity.

'What the hell's going on, Raker?'

I told him about being called into Charing Cross, about the woman, about the things she knew. I told him about Erik McMillan, about Field wanting me to take a medical assessment, and about how the woman had disappeared into thin air sometime last night, leaving behind some blood on a door frame.

'Shit,' Kennedy said.

'Yeah, that pretty much sums it up.'

'I saw her picture this morning.'

Her picture.

He meant the photo of the woman they'd used on *FeedMe*. What he didn't say was, *and she looks just like Derryn*. Kennedy hadn't known Derryn, had never met her, but I'd talked about her a lot in the time since we'd known each other, and he'd seen countless photos of her and been around me in those first few years when, some days, I wasn't even sure if I wanted to go on.

'I don't know what's happening,' I said, and I heard the desperation in my voice. I'd heard it a lot over the last twenty-four hours, and I'd tried to reel it back in as fast as possible when I'd been around Field or Kent. But with Kennedy, someone I trusted implicitly, I didn't have to pretend. I *did* feel desperate. The woman's similarity to Derryn was unquestionable, but that was all it was: a similarity. In fact, most people who looked at a clear photograph of Derryn and one of the woman, side by side, would be able to spot the physical differences. Yet that was just the problem: the only photograph of the woman currently in existence was the one that had run in 'Crime and Punishment' – and, in that, blurred and over-saturated, the woman could easily have passed for my wife.

'You know, one of my team caught a case a bit like this once.'

I tuned back in. 'What?'

'That's why I wanted to find a payphone and call you. I don't know if you realize, but there's actually a department at St Thomas's that deals with stuff like this, and looks into it – did you know that? Or maybe not *this* specifically, but twins, genetic similarities, all of that.'

'What are you talking about?'

'I'm talking about people who look alike but aren't related – they call them "twin strangers" over there.'

'Are you serious?'

'One hundred per cent. It's a thing. Google it.'

I pulled my laptop towards me and did as he asked. Inside a second, I saw that he was right: there was an entire department at St Thomas's dedicated to twin research and to the study of genetic and environmental traits. Their database had 12,000 names on it.

'There was a documentary about their work on Channel 4 last year,' Kennedy went on. 'You know, how they were also studying unrelated people who could pass as twins. Anyway, ten, twelve years ago, that was what we had in this case we landed, so we ended up speaking to one of the doctors there.'

I heard cars in the background, the muffled sound of conversations fading in and out as people passed his phone box.

'I guarantee you,' he said, 'if you had a clear picture of Derryn and you could find this woman and get the cops to take her to St Thomas's, those quacks there, they'd tear her story to shreds.'

' "Her story"?'

'This physical similarity she has to Derryn. Maybe it looks like they're the same, but they won't be. The software they use there, it's all maths-based, right? So they take a picture of these so-called doppelgängers, put them side by side and compare them, and the computer reveals all the things that aren't the same: measurements, colour, how much bigger or smaller the nose is, where the ears are, distances between prominent features, all that sort of thing.'

'Okay.'

'But the thing is, when you put a *human* in front of the same two people, and not the computer, it becomes less absolute. They studied this too. This is what the documentary was about. In this murder case, we had these two guys who everyone on my team, including me, thought were identical – most of us honestly believed they were twins – and then one of the doctors put them through the computer and showed us *hundreds* of disparities. It's because we don't see people the same way as a machine does. This doctor told us that humans may actually be inclined to look past things – even fairly big physical differences that the computer would deem significant – if a person closely mimics someone else's characteristics and traits. What I'm saying is, if you had a half-decent resemblance to another person – which this woman obviously does – but you absolutely nailed their gestures, their patterns of behaviour, qualities, traits, you could fool a lot of people. That's clearly what she's done.'

'And it helps that she can cite private conversations too.'

'Yeah, well, I don't have an explanation for that part. But I'm telling you, Raker: this is a bona fide branch of science. The cops will drop their trousers for these doctors if you can get them there.'

We were both quiet for a moment. If Kennedy was right, this could be a way of proving my side of the story – except I didn't have the woman, had no idea where she was, and didn't even have a decent photograph of her to use as a comparison against Derryn. Despite that, Kennedy's call had offered me a glimmer of hope.

'I appreciate this,' I said to him.

'I just thought you should know.' He paused. 'And for what it's worth, I believe you. If you've lost someone the way you did, you don't make up shite like this.'

We were both silent for a while.

Finally, the line crackling slightly, he said, 'Look, before you go, I know this sounds rich coming from me, the things I've done, the amount of times I've lost my head, but just . . .' He paused, cleared his throat. 'Just be careful, okay? You're emotional. I can hear it in your voice, and I understand why. I do. I get it. But when we're emotional, we do stupid things and make bad choices. I've been there. I've done it over and over. I mean, my life down here is testament to that, right? When we're grieving, or we're angry, or we're confused . . .' He stopped again and I heard him let out a long breath, exhaling into the mouthpiece. 'Ach, I don't know, I never *was* very good at pep talks.'

'I understand,' I said. 'The emotion will make me sloppy.'

'It will if you let it.'

Sometimes it was hard to square off the man Kennedy was now with the man he'd been when I first knew him. Being alone, living in isolation – it had given him a lot of time to think. It had given him a lot of time to change too.

'So what's next?' he asked.

'Next?' I looked down at the notes I'd made off the back of McMillan's phone records and zeroed in on the one I'd circled: the call from the payphone near Plumstead Common. 'Next, I'm going to try and get hold of some surveillance footage.'

I thanked Kennedy again and hung up, then grabbed my prepaid mobile and dialled the number for a man called Ewan Tasker. Task, like Spike, was an old source from my newspaper days. He'd worked for the Met and NCIS – a precursor to the National Crime Agency – and now he was semi-retired, doing part-time consultation work at Scotland Yard.

'Raker,' he said, picking up, recognizing the number of my prepaid.

'Hey, Task. How's things?'

'Pretty good, old friend.'

We talked for a while about things other than work, and then I steered us back to the point of my call: 'How easy would it be for you to source some footage for me?'

'Not very. But that doesn't mean I can't.'

'I'm looking for footage from any cameras close to a pay-phone on the corner of Cavanagh Avenue and Plumstead Common Road.'

'Are there definitely cameras nearby?'

'I don't know. That's what I was hoping you could find out for me.'

'What dates are you looking at?'

'Yesterday afternoon. The caller I want to identify made a phone call at four forty-five – so maybe an hour either side of that.'

'Anything else?'

'I was also hoping you could pull footage from any cameras close to the Winhelm Estate in Chalk Farm. I'm specifically looking for any around 2 Sovereign House, although I'm not sure how many working cameras are actually there. I'm after anything between 4 p.m. yesterday and 8 a.m. today.'

'This is going to take some time.'

'I know. I'd just appreciate anything you can do, Task.'

He didn't reply for a moment, seemed almost hesitant, and I figured out what was coming: 'Is this anything to do with that story on *FeedMe* today?'

Everyone's seen it.

'How did you guess?' I said.

'Are you okay?'

He sounded concerned.

'I'll be fine, Task.'

A second later, my main mobile came alive, buzzing across the table towards me. On the display was a central London number, but not one I recognized.

'I've got another call waiting.'

'I'll get back to you about the footage.'

I grabbed my other phone and pushed Answer.

'Hello?'

'David.' A man's voice: quiet, well spoken. 'It's been a while, but it sounds like you might need to see me again. It's Erik McMillan.'

#0635

Let me tell you the truth about Nora, Derryn.

My sad story.

I didn't tell you much about her on that last day in hospital, because I never really had the chance. But if I'd had the opportunity, I think you probably would have got everything from me. I doubt I would have been able to look you in the eyes and hold back. I would have told you about Nora and what she did to me. I would have told you about how it ended with her.

Once we really get to know each other, we can share these kinds of things, can't we? We can share the intricate, intimate details of our pasts – the full, gory details of our war stories. I'm sure we will tell each other everything.

For now, though, all you really need to know about Nora is that she was a cheat, a deceiver – as much as it pains me to say it. I mean, finding your partner in bed with someone else is such a cliché, isn't it? But that's exactly what happened to me. I got home early from work one day and heard voices coming from the bedroom, so I went to investigate and there she was: naked as the day she was born, half covered in bedsheets, on top of some guy that I'd never met before, with tattoos. He was big, maybe six two, six three, and as he gathered his clothes up, he gave me a look that said, 'Come on then, if you think you can take me.' I was so angry; so angry I could feel it going off like this siren behind my eyes.

But, to my eternal shame, I did nothing.

He walked past me, out of the bedroom, and I stood there – small, pathetic – and listened to him on the stairs, pausing at the bottom to zip up his trousers, and then the click of the front door. Nora got out of bed, sheet wrapped around her, almost bashful, as if I were some stranger who had just wandered in off the street.

'I'm sorry you had to see that,' she said.

Not sorry she was having an affair, not sorry for having sex with another man in our bed, just sorry I had to walk in on them. I remember the next bit so clearly: I didn't reply straight away, because the words wouldn't form. The anger was like this blockage at the top of my chest. Instead, I looked around that terrible little flat we were renting at the time, the leaks from the roof, industrial units out the back, a main road at the front, the air filled with the constant stench of varnish and polish from the nail salon below, and I thought, 'Is this it? Is this all I amount to? Is this all I'm worth?' I mean, back then, I never would have imagined I might get the chance to meet a woman like you. My only reference point at the time was Nora, who I'd given a room to when she was drinking too much, who I thought had grown to love me – but who had, instead, taken my kindness and ripped it to pieces.

'Why did you do this to me?' I asked her.

She shrugged.

I'm not sure she even knew.

I suppose that side of Nora was there all along, because our weaknesses are always humming close to the surface, aren't they? But either I didn't notice, or I chose not to look, until Nora's weakness – this perpetual search for destruction, in drink, in drugs, in sex – eventually got the better of her. I think, perhaps, in a weird way, she wanted me to find her that day. Or maybe it was much bigger than that: maybe it was some form of providence.

Because without her indiscretion, I never would have left her.

And if I'd never left her, I never would have met you.

26

I headed for the Tube. It was bitterly cold, the open skies already setting to work across Ealing Common as its grass started to bead with tiny, hardened flecks of frost.

The conversation with Erik McMillan had been short, his voice pronounced and calm. 'David?' he'd said, when I hadn't responded to him introducing himself. 'You called me, so am I right to assume you would like to meet again?'

'Again?' I said. 'We've never met.'

'We've met many times.'

'Except I don't remember any of them.'

A pause. 'I'm happy to explain the reasons why you think that.'

'It's because it's the truth.'

'You want answers. I understand that.'

I stopped myself from replying, even though I wanted to come back at him; any battle I fought on the phone was going to be a waste of time. He'd just bat everything off. What I needed to do was look him in the eye.

'Where would you like to meet?' he asked.

'I'm open to suggestions.'

'Well, I'll be at St Augustine's later.'

I delayed my response, trying to decide if it was some kind of ambush.

'David?'

'I thought you were supposed to be on holiday?'

'Until Wednesday, yes. I'm just having some days off over Christmas and New Year,' he said, 'that's all. The reason I suggested the hospital was because I thought it might be useful for you to see your file. I know this must be a very confusing time for you, but I really, genuinely want to help.'

Again, I chose not to respond.

'I'm out with some friends for an early dinner at the moment, but I can either see you later on tonight or first thing tomorrow morning.' He paused. I tried to listen for background noise to see whether he was lying to me about being out – but if he was in a restaurant, he was somewhere quiet. *Or he wasn't out with friends at all.* 'Which would suit you better, David?'

'Later,' I said.

'Shall we say around 9 p.m.? I'll have someone meet you at the front gate.'

Once I arrived at the Tube station, I found a bench while I waited for the next train, my thoughts switching from McMillan to my notes – to everything I'd compiled. I pored over them, refreshing my memory, arming myself against whatever McMillan had in store, and then wrote down a list of questions I hadn't squared away.

There were a lot.

Why did the woman have an infected cut on her arm? Had she really been in Woolwich trying to find a pharmacy? Why did she choose to go to Charing Cross police station? Why did she go to the Chalk Farm flat afterwards? Who did the blood on the door belong to? Did she use her own prepaid mobile to call Kent and tell him I was following her, or was it some-one else's? If it was someone else's, whose? I kept going, raising queries about my loft, the missing death certificate and the book I'd found in there, until – finally – I was saved from even more questions by the train pulling in. But not before I'd, once again, seen the through-line in all of this: the woman claimed that the pharmacy was in Woolwich; she said she worked at the Queen Elizabeth hospital nearby; and the call that had been made to McMillan's mobile yesterday had come from a payphone on Plumstead Common Road.

All three were close to St Augustine's – only a matter of miles away – and that put them close to where Erik McMillan worked.

As soon as I thought of that, on the spur of the moment, I changed plans and platforms: before going to the hospital, I was going to head south.

Fifteen minutes later, I got off the train at Kew and followed the eastern wall of the Gardens all the way up Kew Road. At the junction with the South Circular, I crossed and then went the long way round, so that I could approach from the direction of the river. There was a point to the diversion: if I came from the south, I wouldn't get a good view of McMillan's property until I was right next to it; if I came from the north, I could see it front on from a street away, scope it out, get a sense for the rhythms of the road. I wanted a good look at where he lived.

He wasn't in, but because it was Christmas, people were at home with their families, and as the house came fully into view – looking exactly like the version of it I'd seen online – I could see his immediate neighbours were all at home: fairy lights winked in the windows, tinsel glittered, illuminated reindeers stood on patches of grass in the gardens and, a few doors down, someone still had a SANTA – STOP HERE! sign hanging from the front door knocker.

McMillan's place was different.

There were no lights on at all.

Moving towards the house, I kept my eyes on his windows, looking for signs that he might actually be in, that he might be lying about being at a dinner, but the property was dark. I reached into my jacket for my picks – but then, any momentary buzz I might have felt about tearing into his life, his home, his secrets, soon died.

To the left, there was a box high up on the wall, adjacent to one of the second-floor windows: it was blinking on and off. The alarm I'd half expected, but there was a plate screwed to the front wall with the silhouette of a CCTV camera on it and the number of a security firm underneath. I couldn't see any cameras, and wondered if that was just a bluff, but the security firm were real, and his alarm would almost certainly be linked to their system. If it went off, and the code didn't get put in, they'd be turning up on his doorstep inside ten minutes. It was way too risky to attempt a break-in.

For now, his house would have to wait.

27

Eighty minutes later, I saw the hospital for the first time.

I approached it from the west, along the Thames Path. On the near side of the building, I could see a short road, illuminated by security lamps, leading from the hospital site, and then the hospital itself, modern and brightly lit; on the far side, it was almost completely dark, difficult to make out except for some high fencing. As I continued towards it, I remembered what Kennedy had said on the phone to me about St Augustine's being a difficult place to forget, and how it had been divided into two distinct halves.

He was right. The half closest to me was made up of five buildings, all angular except for one on the end – a cylinder – which appeared to house four lifts, side by side: I could see two of them moving up and down, the cylinder finished in a mix of glass and steel, so that the occupants of the lifts could look out at the river, and anyone outside could look in at them. The other four buildings were constructed in a succession of layers, different-sized rectangles laid one on top of the other, like a wedding cake gone awry. It shouldn't have worked, but it did: in the darkness, it was like a Cubist interpretation of a boat, a huge vessel about to push off. Maybe that was the point: now I was closer, I could see triangular flags on the roof which could only have been put there to look like sails.

But the half furthest away from me was different.

The closer I got, the more I could see. A gauzy white glow had bled across it from the hospital side, from the housing estate crammed in on the other side of the nature reserve as well, revealing a similarly sized chunk of land. Except, in this half, nature had taken control: trees and vines, weeds and wildflowers had all swamped the structures that had once contained this part of the former sanatorium. Even at this hour and deep into winter, I could hear wildlife: the squawk of Canada geese, the chirp of smaller birds like starlings, goldfinches, redwings. Trees, twisted and gnarled, had risen up and spread above the level of old buildings, some still intact, some hollowed out and half collapsed. Most of the walls – whatever their condition – were covered in greenery, thick and rampant, but I could see these buildings were made from London stock brick and, under the lights, and with the structures long abandoned, their yellow colour made them look sickly. Along the high fences were signs saying DANGER! KEEP OUT! and NO UNAUTHORIZED ENTRY.

I turned my attention back to the newer half and drew level with the entrance. Every night light was on here, lamps perched on top of the huge gate that segregated the approach road from the route into the hospital. Behind the first gate was a second, and beyond that was the hospital itself. Whether you came by foot or car, or tried to get here by boat, it wasn't important – there was only one way in and out.

On a wall adjacent to the gate was a buzzer. I pushed it and waited, reading the signs above the bell: EAST LONDON MENTAL HEALTH TRUST. ST AUGUSTINE'S HOSPITAL.

It took a couple of minutes and then a slot in the gate whipped across to show the face of a man in his early sixties, white-haired and dressed in a security uniform.

'Yes, pal?'

'I'm here to see Erik McMillan.'

He nodded. 'Mr Raker, is it?'

'Yes.'

'Dr McMillan says, "Welcome back." '

28

His office was on the top floor of Newton Block, a big building with west-facing views towards Beckton and the towers of Canary Wharf.

It seemed to take an age to get there. The interior of the hospital was a rabbit warren, corridor after corridor, all colour-coded in whites, pale greens and blues like a mainstream hospital, but sectioned off by secure doors, communal areas and suites with reinforced glass. The walls were a mix of plaster and brick, and I realized this half of the hospital – all the new buildings – had been built on the carcass of the original quarantine centre. It made me wonder how many untold stories were trapped beneath, how many echoes of the hospital's former existence, the conversations that had happened here, the arguments, and then – almost on cue – I heard someone shouting, unintelligible, strained; there was a howl, animal-like, that became a scream. Some nurses appeared from one door and crossed the corridor into another. After that, there was silence.

The route we took seemed to follow the entire north wall of the block, presumably avoiding the areas that were most high risk. A couple of times I tried to engage the guard in conversation, but on both occasions he shut me down almost straight away, and the further in we got, the more on edge I started to feel.

Why had I agreed to meet McMillan here?

There were more doors, each one opening and closing with an identical buzz, a flight of stairs, and then we were in the administration block, a dark space with an open-plan seating area and a series of offices in a vague circle around it. All the offices had night lighting on and were empty; everyone who worked in admin had gone home. Bright ceiling lights came on as we moved towards McMillan's office, the room slightly removed from the others and positioned in the corner, the door ajar, his job title stencilled across the middle in black: CLINICAL DIRECTOR.

The guard knocked twice and then pushed.

The door swung back to reveal a large room with windows most of the way around. McMillan was behind a desk directly in front of me. He was smiling.

'Hello, David,' he said calmly, warmly. 'It's nice to see you again.'

I just stared at him.

'You look like you've lost a little weight.'

This was a game, and he was playing along beautifully.

'Thank you, Clive,' he said to the security guard behind him. 'David will be fine with me here.'

'Are you sure, Dr McMillan?'

'Positive.'

The guard's eyes lingered on me, and then he left. I quickly took in the room. There was a line of cabinets and bookcases, and two sofas with a low table between them. On the walls were bright artwork and an old framed map of the hospital site. Through the windows, London sprawled, seeming to exist only as lights, thousands of them, the Thames a ribbon fringed by dots. To the right, between here and the housing estate, there was a huge block of darkness.

'How *are* you, David?'

McMillan was dressed in a blue checked shirt and mauve tie, his hair perfect, his beard neatly trimmed, its lines exact, as if it had been applied rather than grown. He wore his red glasses initially, but he took them off now, putting them down in front of him without ever taking his eyes off me.

'We're on first-name terms,' I said. 'Is that right?'

'Would you rather I *didn't* call you David any more?' he said, finally getting up and coming around the desk. His trousers were blue too, his brown brogues polished to a shine. 'I mean, if you'd rather we were more formal, I –'

'Enough bullshit.'

He just looked at me, clearly hurt.

'Why are you lying to the police about me?'

'Lying? You mean about your treatment?'

'There *was* no treatment.'

He frowned. 'It concerns me that you think that, David.'

'Why are you doing this?'

This time he flattened his lips, pressing them together so hard they bleached white. 'I'm not lying, David,' he said. 'What do you think I've lied about?'

'Why don't we start with "everything"?'

'And what have I said that you think is untrue?'

I studied him for a moment, watching for fractional slips, for a moment of proof – but there was nothing. He looked as if he felt sorry for me. I tried not to show him how much his reactions were throwing me: I'd expected the mask to slip quickly when I faced him down, but it hadn't slipped at all. He was professional, courteous; in his eyes, when he spoke to me, I saw genuine sorrow.

I hadn't prepared for this.

'That woman isn't my wife,' I said, my voice a little shakier than I wanted it to be. 'Before yesterday, I'd never met her in my life.'

'It's not surprising that you believe that.'

'I believe it because it's true.' I gathered myself again, trying to add some steel to what I was saying. 'I could give you fifty ways in which they're different.'

'I'm sure you could, David.'

He was talking to me like a child now, his tone gentle and patient.

'Was it you who gave *FeedMe* that story?'

'I'm not certain what you mean,' he said, puzzled.

This was going nowhere. I looked at the sofas, at the rest of his office, at a coffee percolator on top of one of the cabinets. There were bottles of water there. Looking at them made me realize my mouth was almost completely dry. It couldn't have been more than a couple of hours since I'd last drunk something, but it felt like days.

'Can I get you something?' he asked. 'I remember you liking a strong cup of coffee.' He took out a filter and fitted it to the machine. 'I'm happy to join you. Or there's water here if your taste for caffeine has fallen away in the time since I saw you last.'

'Just tell me why you're doing this.'

He poured some of the bottled water into the coffee machine and flicked a switch. 'David,' he said, turning to me, 'I'd really like to help you.'

'You can help me by telling the police the truth.'

'I did.'

'No, you didn't. You've never treated me.'

'I have,' he said, a harder edge to his voice now. 'I *have* treated you, David.' He returned to his desk, the percolator dripping, the air in the office already heavy with the smell of coffee, and picked up his glasses. The red frames were bright against the low light of the office, and as he sat again, he removed a handkerchief from his pocket and began cleaning the lenses. 'I think it's important,' he said, head down, focused on his task, 'that you and I are always one hundred per cent honest with each other.'

When he finally looked up, he placed his glasses on his face, and then instantly adjusted them with the knuckle of his forefinger, pushing them up the bridge of his nose.

Behind the lenses, his brown eyes appeared bigger, clearer, and I was close enough to see flecks of green in them, like dots of moss on a tree trunk. They were unusual; so much so that I felt sure I would have remembered them if we'd met before. He said, 'I know this is a confusing time for you. But, like I told you, let's always –'

'Why did you back up her story?'

'By "her", you mean Derryn?'

'No. Derryn is dead.'

'Why don't you take a seat? Please.'

I hesitated for a moment. Eventually, I pulled a chair out, seated myself on its edge and looked at him. He had a hand flat on a spiral notepad, the cover closed, a blue fountain pen attached to the binding.

'DS Field called me again this evening,' he said.

'To say what?'

'She's concerned.'

'Perhaps she'd be less concerned if you told her the truth.'

'That's what I've been doing.'

I took a long, audible breath.

McMillan said, 'I suggested to DS Field earlier that I could talk to you, that it may help you to see things more clearly. It was why I returned your call tonight. I felt it might be pertinent for us to meet again, because you clearly don't understand.'

'Really? What is it that I don't understand?'

He eyed me for a moment.

'You don't understand how dangerous you are.'

29

McMillan was watching me again, a habit of his I'd quickly picked up on, every silence like some minor therapy session where he would examine the tiny movements of my face.

'David?' he said. 'Are you listening to what I'm saying?'

'I'm dangerous?'

'You could be.' He studied me. 'Did you harm Derryn again?'

'"Again"? I've never harmed anyone.'

'Did you hurt Derryn?'

'She's not *Derryn.*'

He didn't move for a moment, still watching me, and then he nodded, almost glided on to his feet, and returned to the percolator. 'I discharged you from my care back in 2011,' he said, fiddling with the top of the machine, 'because you'd made terrific strides in your recovery. This belief of yours, that the Derryn you knew was dead, and the one that had remained behind for a while *after* was an impostor, a double, we worked through that. I'm not saying we got to a complete recovery, but we got to a point where I felt you were able to function on your own –'

'Stop.' I held up a hand to him. 'Just stop.'

He snapped the lid shut on the machine.

'Please just tell me why you're doing this.'

'That's what I'm trying to do, David.'

'Not this bullshit about me thinking she was dead when she wasn't. That's not what I mean. I don't need to hear any more about that, about how I'm sick, and I was treated at St Augustine's for fifteen months. It's lies. None of it adds up. I mean, if you're saying you'd finished treating me by 2011, if I'd made a recovery by then and accepted that Derryn was alive, where's she been for the last six years? Because she sure as hell hasn't been living with me, and it doesn't matter how many times that woman tells the police that she has, or that I drove her to some pharmacy in Woolwich yesterday, or that I'm in denial, or I'm sick, or whatever else – *none* of it is true. Nothing. She's a fantasist and the worst bit is, you're backing up her story. She should be the person you're trying to help.'

'It isn't a story, David. It's reality. This is *real*.'

'Then why isn't she living with me? I could go home tonight and ask my neighbours if I've been living with anyone and I'd bet all the money I have – every penny – that neither of them would have ever seen her at the house.'

'It would be a bet you'd lose, David. Derryn has been living at 40 Aintree Drive with you for –'

'She *hasn't*. She's not *living with me*. She's not my fucking wife!' I screamed the words at him, and as soon as they were out of my mouth I regretted them: this was exactly what he wanted. Whatever his reasons for doing this, my loss of control, my absolute denial that it was Derryn, all of it played into the idea that I was sick, that I couldn't – or wasn't able – to face the truth. I felt so angry it was like a vibration in my blood, in my muscles, in my cartilage, but I closed my eyes and tried to reel it back in. Once I had, very gently, I said, 'Why are you risking your career like this?'

'I'm not.'

'You could get struck off.'

'For wanting to help you?'

'You're not helping me, you're ruining my life.'

We could both hear it: the break in my voice, the last few words collapsing as they formed in my mouth. McMillan came a couple of steps closer to me, and his face took on the same look again, as if he felt genuinely sorry for me, for the fact that I couldn't recognize or deal with the truth. As I saw his expression, I thought of the conversation I'd had with Tanya Rye – of the ones I'd decided not to have afterwards with Derryn's other friends – and all the questions I'd tried to ask her returned to me, all the things I'd been unable to say out loud. Had Derryn died? Had the funeral ever taken place? Could I be so sick that I didn't even realize I was living with another person?

'*No*,' I said, the word out before I could rein it back in. It had been a reaction to the questions I'd been going through, the ones I'd never asked and was never going to. But as I looked at McMillan standing in front of the cabinets, I realized it had reinforced his position. Now I looked exactly as confused as he needed me to be.

He poured two cups of coffee.

'Black, no sugar, right?'

Again, his familiarity with me, his ease in my company, threw me, but I tried not to show it. He brought the drink over and placed it on the desk in front of me.

'You're emotional,' he said, 'I understand that.'

'Of *course* I'm emotional.'

He sat back down, taking a mouthful of his coffee.

'Did you have anything to do with Derryn going missing?' he said.

'She's not Derryn.'

'Okay.' He held up a hand. 'Okay.'

He took another long gulp and then placed the coffee down.

'Have you harmed the woman who says she's your wife?'

'Of course I haven't.'

'DS Field says they can't find her.'

I shrugged.

'You don't know where she is?'

'No. And why would I harm her, anyway?'

'Because you can be . . . unpredictable.'

I frowned. 'What the hell are you talking about?'

He opened both his hands out, trying to calm me down, and then came forward on his seat, elbows on the desk, the coffee sending strands of steam past his face. He was so close now I could smell the scent of his aftershave and the faint hint of mint on his breath.

'Among other things, you have a condition called Capgras delusion.'

I shook my head.

'Yes,' he said, his voice harder again, 'you do. I need you to listen, okay? You are suffering from something called Capgras delusion. It's a condition where you believe a loved one has been replaced by someone else: a lookalike, an impostor. The condition most often occurs in people with paranoid schizophrenia or dementia, but there's plenty of evidence to suggest that patients suffering from brain injuries are susceptible to it too. There have even been documented cases of migraines bringing it on for a time.' He stopped, saw me react: a confirmation that the word *migraines* had registered, meant something, had affected me in the time since he said I'd been here.

'Stop this,' I said.

'I have access to your medical records, David,' he said, 'through the hospital system. When DS Field got in touch, I went back and had a look at your history and, since I discharged you from my care back in 2011, you've been seen a number of times with head injuries. I can see your GP, Dr Jhadav, has noted that – since 2014 – you've been suffering from headaches and even experienced a blackout. We, in the psychiatric community, are still learning all the time about Capgras delusion, but what we *do* know is that it can be transient. It can come and go. And even if you'd been fine every day for the past six years, even if you'd been functioning completely normally, it wouldn't mean it couldn't come back. It doesn't mean it *hasn't* come back. It doesn't mean it's come alone this time either. If you're suffering headaches, if you're blacking out, if you refuse to recognize that your wife is alive and well and living in your house, it means these delusions about Derryn have returned. Worse, it could mean your illness hasn't just come back – it's come back in an even more aggressive form than before. You were diagnosed with PTSD three years ago. You might be suffering exhaustion as well, depression, any number of other things.'

All I could feel was a dull pounding behind my eye. It was making me feel nauseous. I felt frayed, on edge and boxed in, like I needed to scream.

'Let me help you,' he said softly.

I shook my head.

'You can trust me, David.'

I looked up at him. '*Trust* you?'

'My strong suspicion is that part of this cocktail of illnesses may be a delayed reaction to some of the things you saw and witnessed in your days as a journalist. You spent time in South Africa at a dangerous and traumatic point in that country's history; you were in Iraq and Afghanistan for a time; you told me you spent weeks bedded in with the police in major US cities and were seeing murders on an almost daily basis – all those things could have had an effect on you. And now history is repeating. In your job as an investigator, you're experiencing all those things again.'

He waited for me to say something.

'Let me help you,' he said again.

'So everyone just played along?'

'I'm sorry?'

'The funeral, the grave, the aftermath – everyone in my life, anyone who's ever met me – they all just played along with it. That's what you're saying, right? Because I've talked

154

to Derryn's friends and they remember the funeral, so the funeral clearly took place.'

McMillan grimaced. 'It's your sickness. You're hearing what you want to hear.'

I reached for my coffee, felt its warmth against my hands, and said, 'I've got a question for you.'

'Okay, that's good.' He smiled. He was clearly encouraged by something in my voice. I sounded calmer to him, more cooperative.

'Who called you yesterday afternoon?'

'What?'

'You received a call at four forty-five in the afternoon yesterday while I was on my way to a police station in Charing Cross. You may or may not know that the call was made from a payphone in Plumstead, but I'm betting you knew who the caller was.'

A flicker of something crossed his face.

'Uh, I'm not sure I underst—'

'You understand just fine.'

'Really, I've no idea what you're talking about.'

'It's on your phone bill.'

'If it is, I don't specifically remember any call.'

I smirked. 'You're a liar.'

'I can assure you, I'm not.'

I thought of the book I'd found in the loft: the copy of *No One Can See the Crows at Night* with the message inside. *Thank you for our special time together.*

'Did you know Derryn before she died?'

'She hasn't die—'

'Did you give her a book?'

'A book?'

'*No One Can See the Crows at Night.*'

His expression was benign, unchanged, but the colour had drained from him, pink rinsing out of his cheeks. He smiled, tried to act unconcerned, but finally I'd got to him and we both knew it – I just wasn't sure if it was the book that had done it, or me telling him I knew about the phone call. His eyes shifted from me, to the walls, the windows and out to the semi-lit staff area. The security guard was back at his post. We were entirely alone.

'You're confused,' he said quietly.

'Am I?'

'I've really no idea what you're talking about.'

'I don't believe you.'

'David, you're sick and you don't even know it.'

'I don't think I am.'

'Of course you don't. That's how it works.'

'So who was it who called you yesterday?'

This time I wasn't sure if he was genuinely puzzled or just pretending to be. Getting up from the desk, he said, 'When we spoke on the telephone, I promised you I'd show you your file. Would you like me to do that, David?'

I didn't move.

'David, would you like me to do that?'

If he had a file, I wanted to see it. If he didn't, I wanted to see him flounder. But I'd had him for a moment. He hadn't given me much in the way of a tell, but it was enough. So I stayed where I was, seated at the desk, drinking my coffee.

'David, would you like to see your file?'

'Did you give Derryn that book?' I repeated, ignoring his question entirely. 'Did you know her before she died?'

'I really don't know what –'

'Were you the one who gave it to her?'

'I've no idea what you're talking about.'

'Where's Derryn's death certificate?'

'*Death* certificate? She's not dead, David.'

'Stop *lying*.'

He came around the desk, almost standing over me. 'I'm

not a liar, David. Whether you choose to believe me or not, I'm trying to help you. You want to know what's going on, and I believe showing you your file is the best way for me to do that. I'll present to you some of the work I collated on our sessions, some of the proof that you really were in my care from the autumn of 2009 until the early part of 2011. All of us here just want to see you get better, and I'm sure Derryn would like –'

I launched myself at him, grabbing him by his collar and pushing him against the wall. He winced, hissing through his teeth as his back crunched against the hard surface. Rage was charging through my veins, it was humming in my blood, my bone marrow – I couldn't help it. I'd had enough. As I pinned him there, I felt the thump become more violent behind my eyes, the pressure building.

'Stop saying her name, or I'll . . .'

My words dropped away.

Somewhere, a door had just opened and closed.

I let go of McMillan's collar and looked out of the office, into the staff area. There was no sound of footsteps, but the ceiling lights at the other end, close to the doors in and out of the admin block, had come back on.

I glanced at McMillan. 'Who else is here?'

'No one,' he said, straightening up.

'So what was that noise?'

He frowned again. 'What noise?'

'Don't play games with me.'

'I'm not,' he said, holding up a hand. 'I swear.'

I studied him, but his face was a blank. When I looked back at the staff area, in the direction of the entrance, I saw a minor shift.

A shadow on the wall.

It was moving.

30

I went to the office doorway and looked out. More ceiling lights flickered into life above me. Apart from at the entrance and the low light of the offices, everywhere else on the floor – its edges and corners – was pitch black.

I glanced over my shoulder at McMillan. He had an expression which I'd seen today already, one of confusion and concern. 'David, what's going on here?'

'Do the guards do a rotation?'

'You seem agitated.'

'Do the guards do a *rotation*?'

'Sometimes, yes.'

'Stay here,' I said to him and left him by his desk.

I moved out of the office and into the hub of the admin block. More lights snapped into life above me. Working my way around, I checked under desks, in hiding places between cabinets, pushed open the doors of the other offices to see if anyone was inside. They weren't. By the time I was done, the entire floor was lit up.

'David?' McMillan called from his office.

'Stay there.'

I looked over at the main doors.

'This really needs to stop, David.'

'Shut up.'

I moved across to the doors and looked through the re-inforced glass panels. It was near-dark on the other side, the stairs that had brought me up dotted with low-power night lights. Next to the entrance was a release button. I pressed it, the door buzzed open, and as I stepped through to the landing, more lights sprang into life.

The staircase was empty.

At the bottom was the first of the security doors I'd have to pass through to get out of the hospital. There was no access, no way to open it, without the proper pass.

No one's here.

We're alone.

I rubbed at my eyes again, trying to settle the thump behind them, to clear it, and when I opened them, I felt off balance and my vision was smeared. What the hell was wrong with me? Was I hearing things now too? I gave myself a moment, drawing my perspective back, my sense of clarity, and then I slowly headed back to McMillan.

'What were you hoping to find?' he said.

'I thought I . . .'

I stopped in the doorway of his office, glancing over my shoulder.

'I'm worried about you, David.'

I ignored him.

'I'm worried about your state of mind,' he went on, 'about these headaches you have. I'm worried about the blackouts. At times of stress, all those things are big –'

'Why are you lying?'

'Stress could bring on more blackouts.'

'Why are you *lying*?'

'Why won't you let me help you?'

Suddenly, I felt light-headed.

'David?'

I swallowed, closed my eyes, trying to regain my balance.

'David?' McMillan said again.

I held up a hand, not wanting him to come any closer.

'Are you okay? Do you want some water?'

I lurched to my left, reaching out to the door frame for support – but where I thought the frame was, there was only space, and I fell sideways, missing it entirely.

I hit the floor hard.

I managed to roll over on to my back; was conscious long enough to see McMillan drop to his haunches beside me.

'I'm sorry, David,' he said.

Then the sound went.

And so did the light.

Day Three

31

I opened my eyes.

My head was throbbing so much it took me a second to focus, the pain forking across my nose, under my eyebrows and into my temples. I could see daylight off to my left, a block of it cutting through the gap between the curtains and spilling across my feet and legs. When I looked the other way, I heard the mattress creak as I shifted my weight, felt it soften beneath me, and saw the en suite, the dresser, the wardrobes.

I was at home, in my bedroom.

Confused, I slowly hauled myself up, still feeling woozy, a little nauseous, my head swirling like I was drunk. As I sat at the edge of the bed, I closed my eyes for a second, trying to think, and remembered McMillan's office. That was where I'd been.

That was where I'd blacked out.

I'm sorry, David.

McMillan's last words to me in the seconds before I lost consciousness. What did he mean? What was he sorry for? I thought of the coffee he'd made for us both. I'd been thirsty, my mouth bone dry. I'd taken the drink from him willingly.

Had he spiked it?

Something else resurfaced: the vague image of a red door. I didn't recognize it, had no idea where it was or why I'd retained it, but, as I tried to blink it away, it came back again, over and over, like a strobe. I tried to think where I might have seen it but then, finally, the image started to fade.

Unsteadily, I got to my feet and then had to halt for a moment as my head swam, another wave of nausea hitting me. Once that had passed, I shuffled across the carpet to the mirror and looked at myself: I was dressed in some pyjama bottoms I'd forgotten I even had and a white T-shirt I thought I'd thrown out. My hair was a mess, flattened to my skull on one side where I'd been sleeping. When I leaned in closer to the mirror, turning my head so I could see my face and neck clearly, there were no visible injuries. No marks on my skin, no lump on my skull where I'd fallen down, no bruising, no evidence of blood.

My head began swimming again.

I moved back to the bed and waited for it to pass. I looked at the bedside clock. Eleven fifty-seven – in the morning.

How the hell had I got home last night?

Had McMillan dropped me back?

Why would he drug me and then take me home?

I looked around the bedroom for my phone but couldn't see it anywhere. As I turned, I felt a sharp pain flare in my left shoulder. When I pressed fingers to the top of my arm, to the blade, everything was tender.

Impact injuries.

My left shoulder must have taken the weight of my fall.

Getting to my feet again, I went through to the en suite and ran the cold tap. As I splashed my face with water, a feeling shivered through me, a sense that something wasn't right – beyond waking up here, in my bed, and not on the floor of McMillan's office. But I couldn't interpret it, couldn't determine what it was exactly, and pretty soon all I could think about was taking a painkiller and finding a dressing gown or a jumper, anything to warm me up, because, despite the sun outside, the room was cold and I was chilled to the bone. I went to the drawers where I kept my sweaters and yanked the top one open.

It was empty.

I tried the next one down: the same. I tried the bottom

one and this time there were clothes inside – but they weren't mine. T-shirts and vest tops, folded neatly into a pile. A cardigan. A faded denim jacket. Six sets of leggings, each a different colour.

They all belonged to a woman.

I shoved the drawer closed and glanced towards the door and the hallway, as if the answers might be out there. What was going on? Why was there female clothing in here? Where were my sweaters, my underwear, my T-shirts? Moving across the bedroom to the wardrobe I yanked one of the doors open. Some of my clothes were inside this time – jeans, shirts, a jacket, pairs of shoes at the bottom – except, again, something wasn't right, and it took me a second to work out what.

They were my clothes, but they were old.

I hadn't worn any of these things in years; in fact, I was pretty sure I'd actually given the jacket away, and the rest had been in storage in the garage. On the left-hand side of the wardrobe the hangers were full of blouses, skirts, dresses, a long winter coat. More women's clothing.

I went to the bedside tables and checked the drawers. Empty. I went to the bathroom, opened the cabinet and looked inside. It was full of things that didn't belong to me. Roll-on deodorant. Hairspray. Face and body creams. Make-up.

What the hell was going on?

'David.'

I stood there, surprised, taken aback, staring at the bedroom door. The house fell silent again. I moved past the bed and went to the doorway, looking along the hall towards the living room. My feet were heavy against the carpet and everything above it – all my joints, tendons, muscles – suddenly felt like weights sinking to the bottom of the ocean. I could taste bile at the back of my mouth and smell sweat on my skin.

'Hello?' I said.

My voice was weak, hoarse. I cleared my throat.

'Hello?'

No response.

I began to feel ill again, queasy, in pain. Goosebumps scattered up my arms, across my shoulder blades and down the ridge of my spine. I was cold, disorientated. I could feel sickness on me like a fever. I was hearing things, maybe seeing things as well, and as I looked along the hallway, it felt like the walls were closing in on me. It felt like the ceiling had dropped a couple of feet, like the whole house had shrunk. My vision warped and compressed – and then, totally unexpectedly, tears filled my eyes.

What's wrong with me?

'David, lunch is ready.'

Her voice stopped me dead.

I could hardly move, the soles of my feet glued to the carpet, my fingers gripping the door frame so hard, my nails were making gouges in the wood.

'D,' she said again, 'lunch is ready.'

32

I moved into the hallway. The doors into the spare bedroom and my office were both closed, and – ahead of me, off the living room – I could see that the cloakroom door was shut too. It made the house feel dark and confined. As I passed the office, I stopped for a moment, gripping the door handle, wanting to open the house up and get some more light in. It was cold, the heating off – even though I ran it throughout the winter – but now I felt feverish and hot, and the sense of being enclosed didn't help.

The office door wouldn't open.

I tried it a second time, but it still didn't move, so I tried shoving it harder, tried putting a shoulder to it and pressing, rattled the handle over and over. There was no give. I'd never fitted a lock on it, because I never actually kept it closed – couldn't even remember a single time, in all my years in the house, when I'd chosen to shut the doors like this – so why were they closed now? I stepped across to the other side of the hallway, trying the handle on the spare bedroom door. That wouldn't yield either.

Neither door would budge.

I switched my attention back to the living room, my heart starting to race. I thought about what McMillan had said at the hospital, about the condition he claimed I had; I thought about Derryn's sign that I'd sworn I'd left hanging from the back gate, but which I'd actually left in the garage; I thought about seeing someone out in the darkness of the alley when, in reality, no one was there; and then this – waking up with no idea how I'd got home, no clothes in my drawers, doors that shouldn't be locked, and a woman in the kitchen, calling me for lunch, who sounded exactly like my dead wife.

Was this a hallucination?

I moved forward, McMillan's words like an echo behind the thump of my head: *If you're suffering headaches, if you're blacking out, if you refuse to recognize that your wife is alive and well, these are warning signs.* What if he hadn't drugged me?

What if I was in the middle of a breakdown?

At the door to the living room, I stopped again, looking left and right. The curtains had been drawn together most of the way, light cutting through in a thin block, just the same as in the bedroom. It was tidy, much tidier than I remembered leaving it; much tidier than I remembered it ever having been. It had been hoovered, dusted down. There was the smell of polish in the air, mixing with the scent of roasted meat and potatoes coming from the kitchen.

The living-room table had been set for two.

Two pairs of knives and forks. Two spoons. Two wine glasses. One bottle of red wine, already uncorked. A candle, unlit, and a present, in wrapping paper, next to one of the settings. On top of the present was a label, attached to a ribbon, with *D* on it.

'Here we go, then.'

She emerged from the kitchen. She was in a knee-length floral dress, a cardigan, and had her hair up in a bun. There was a light dusting of make-up on her cheeks, around her eyes, a hint of pale pink lipstick too. She was barefoot and smiling, and didn't look at me when she entered, as if this – her, me, this house, this dinner – was nothing out of the ordinary; just a wife cooking a meal for her husband.

She put a bowl of roast potatoes down and then returned to the kitchen. In my ears, my pulse was pounding so hard it was like my skin was vibrating. I watched her come back again with another bowl, this one segmented, each of its parts filled with a different type of vegetable. She looked up at me briefly, still smiling, but once she put the bowl down, a frown formed, as if she'd only just noted the confusion on my face.

'How are you feeling, sweetheart?'

I tried to speak, but the words wouldn't form.

'I know you're not feeling well,' she said, 'but it's so lovely to spend time with you like this. You're so busy with work that we don't often get the chance, do we?'

I looked at the table, steam rising off the food, then at the place settings, the glasses, the gift – wrapped and waiting for me.

'What are you doing here?' I said.

When my eyes returned to her, she'd come even closer, and I could detect Derryn's perfume. I would never forget the scent, because it had been on the clothes of hers I'd held in the months after she died. Once, a few months after the funeral, I suddenly started crying in the beauty section of a department store when I smelled it in the air.

'How did you get into my house?' I said.

'What?'

'How did I get home last night?'

Her expression was that of someone who thought this might be a joke that she just wasn't getting. From the kitchen, the timer on the oven sounded, beeping gently.

'That's the lamb,' she said.

'What are you doing? What's going on?'

'What does it look like?' she replied softly. 'I'm making you a meal. I've opened a bottle of wine and I've got you a little present for your birthday. It's not much – I know we're saving up for a new kitchen at the moment, but –'

'It's not my birthday.'

That seemed to throw her. 'Of course it is.'

'My birthday is in July.'

'I know,' she said, 'the 14th of July.'

169

'We're in December.'

A smile skirted her lips, waiting for the punchline that wasn't coming. 'Okay,' she said, waving me away, her gaze switching back to the table, to the food that was waiting. 'You win, funny man.'

'Win? What do you mean?'

She smiled again, her eyes flashing, even in the subdued light. 'I mean, I get it,' she said. 'You're in denial about your age, and that means ignoring your birthdays.'

She picked up the present and handed it to me.

'Open it,' she said.

I looked at the gift, then at her.

'Go on,' she said. 'Open it.'

Reluctantly, I took it from her, looking at her again, along the hallway towards the kitchen, breathing in the smell of the house for a second time. Was this what it had smelled like when she'd been alive? The smell of good food, of clean surfaces, of a house that was cherished?

'Open it,' she repeated.

I looked down at the present, at the ribbon, at the label with *D* on it – the handwriting clean and elegant, just as I remembered Derryn's being – and then tore the paper away. It was a book, a copy of *No One Can See the Crows at Night*, different from the one she'd always kept by her bed, different too from the one I'd found in the loft.

'You said you wanted to read it,' she said, smiling.

'No, I didn't.'

'Of course you did. You've been saying it for months. You said you liked the sound of the storyline.'

The spouse who might be a stranger.

The impostor.

'Where did you get this?'

'It doesn't matter,' she replied, winking. Was this all a game to her or did she actually have no idea what the significance of the book was? I'd never said I wanted to read it. I'd never told Derryn that. Except I had to stop myself: *this isn't Derryn.*

Is it?

She headed back into the kitchen.

As I stood there, I zeroed in on the wall clock, hung above the TV cabinet: the one Derryn had bought when we'd spent a weekend in Bristol. Painted on the face was a triskelion, a motif with three interlocking spirals. Beneath that, in panels at the bottom, were readouts for the day and month.

It said it was 14 July.

My birthday.

She returned with some Yorkshire puddings.

'There we go,' she said, setting them down.

'What the hell is going on?'

She glanced at me. 'What? Are you talking about the Yorkshires? Don't tell me that, now you're a year older, you've decided to start watching your weight?'

'How did you get in?'

A pause. 'Get in?'

'How did you get into the house?'

'Uh, I live here.'

She came around the table towards me.

'Are you . . .' She stopped, looked bewildered. 'Are you okay, D?'

She put a hand to my arm and I pulled away.

'David,' she said. 'Please. You're starting to worry me.'

'Has McMillan put you up to this?'

'McMillan?'

'Erik McMillan. Is he doing this?'

She didn't respond, and as I thought of McMillan, I thought about the coffee again. What had he put in it?

Was that how all of this seemed so real?

I looked around the living room. My head was agonizing, the pain like a ball of barbed wire behind my eyes, scratching and twisting and tearing. She reached out to me a second time and put her fingers on my arm, and I was so distracted that I didn't notice it to start with, and by the time I did, she'd come all the way in, sliding her arms around me. Suddenly, she was embracing me, her head just below my chin.

'What are you doing?' I said.

'I'm cuddling you.'

'No. I mean, what are you doing here?'

She looked up at me. 'Everything's all right.'

'No,' I said. 'No, it's –'

'Everything's all right,' she said again and gave me a gentle squeeze. 'You need to relax. Things have been stressful for you. But you're home now. You're with me.'

'How did I get back?'

She didn't answer.

'How did I get back from the hospital?'

'You weren't *at* any hospital,' she said.

'I was with McMillan.'

'No, sweetheart.'

'I was.'

'No, you were here. You've always been here.'

You've always been here.

I thought of the red door, my memory of it.

'Why can I remember a door?' I said.

'A door?'

'A red door. What does it mean?'

She didn't answer.

I could smell her perfume again, could smell the shampoo in her hair, felt her skin against mine, and my eyes began to well up. I didn't want to cry, wanted to push her away, wanted to blink and wake up and find myself at the end of a nightmare I'd finally dragged myself out of. But I didn't. I stood there, her arms around me, her face against the top of my chest, and it was like time had folded over, one point connecting to another:

the sensation of her against me – her physicality, the smell of her, her size and weight, her substance – took me all the way back, across eight long years of grief and mourning and agony. For a few seconds more, a part of me railed against the idea it could ever be her – I felt my teeth grit and my muscles tense, heard a voice telling me, *It's not her it's not her it's not her* – but then the fight started to fade, and the voice did too, and all that was left behind was the ache of my head, my body and my heart. She squeezed me again, told me she loved me, said it over and over, and this time I closed my eyes, raised my arms and took hold of her.

And just for a minute, I pretended.

I pretended she'd never died. I pretended my life had never changed that day, never cracked, never shattered into millions of pieces I was never able to put back together again. Just for a minute, I gave in and accepted what I was being told. I was sick. This was real.

This was my wife.

This was Derryn.

33

I followed her into the kitchen, waiting in the doorway as she flipped the oven open and, using a pair of gloves, slid the joint out on a roasting pan. It crackled and popped and the aroma of it began to disguise the smell of her perfume.

'Why are all the blinds shut?' I asked.

Through the frosted glass of the kitchen door, all I could see was light, sun arcing on to the driveway at the side of the house. As she set the roasting tray down, she said, 'I thought it would be better for you, especially because you've been having such terrible migraines. Keeping the house dark helps, plus it's more romantic.'

She flashed me a smile.

'Go and sit down,' she said. 'I'll sort this out.'

The pounding in my head was so bad now, white spots were flashing in front of my eyes, so I moved from the kitchen back into the living room, dragged a chair out from the table and collapsed into it. As I sat there, eyes closed, trying to make sense of it – of *any* of it – I listened to the house creak in the sunlight, to the low hum of the oven, a soft, repetitive timbre that slowly started to make me drift.

The further I drifted, the less I could hear.

Then there was silence.

When I woke up, I was on the sofa. My clothes felt damp, sweated through, my head was sore – no longer pounding; almost bruised – and the television was playing, the sound on mute. It was showing an old repeat of a British detective series.

Gingerly, I sat up and then looked towards the living-room table. It was still set, slices of lamb laid out on otherwise empty plates, and while the food was still piled into bowls in the centre, there was no steam coming from it. It was cold; none of it had been touched.

I got up, swaying for a moment. I heard the same low hum of the oven in the kitchen, and the sound of birds in the garden. And something else from the bedroom.

Sobbing.

I left the living room and headed down the hallway. The spare bedroom and office doors were still closed, and the air was starting to feel dry, the house airless. At the door to the bedroom, I found her sitting with her back to me on the edge of the bed. In a mirror directly across the room, I could see more of her, a reflection of a woman whose hair had begun escaping the bun, falling past her face in long, pale strands. Her face was red from tears, blotchy and raw, and her fingers were clutching a piece of kitchen towel, folded quarter-sized, which she'd been using as a tissue. She clocked my movement at the door and glanced over her shoulder. Her gaze stayed on me for a while, and then she dropped her head.

'What's the matter?' I said, feeling a pang of sympathy for her.

She looked at me again. The blue-green of her eyes flashed with more tears and I could see deep red blood vessels jagging out from her irises, like forks of lightning.

Quietly, she said, 'I don't want you to be ill.'

'I'm not ill.'

She just stared at me, as if to say, *Come on, be serious.* I thought about the clothes of hers I'd found in the wardrobe, the locked doors I couldn't open; I thought of sitting down at the table, blacking out and waking up on the sofa.

'Where are the rest of my clothes?' I said.

'What?'

'Where are the rest of my clothes?'

She was frowning again, using the kitchen towel to dab at her nose. When she saw that it was a genuine question, she pushed herself up off the bed and went to the wardrobe, opening it. Inside were the clothes – hers, mine – I'd found earlier. But now there were more: the hangers on my side were full up with shirts and trousers, jackets, sweaters, and all of them belonged to me.

I stepped further into the room. 'They weren't there before,' I said, and took another step, then another, opening up the chest of drawers. They were divided up: drawers for her, drawers for me, mine full of underwear and socks and running gear.

'What's going on?' I said.

'You're sick, D.'

I shook my head, eyes still on my clothes.

'You are. You're sick.'

I looked at her, then out at the room.

'I thought you'd got better, but you haven't.'

'I'm not sick.'

'Is this why you get so . . . so angry sometimes?'

'What are you talking about?'

'You don't need to be embarrassed. I can help you.' I could hear birds out in the garden. 'I love you, David. I've always loved you. I will always love you, but you know we can't go on like this. You asking me all these weird questions. "What am I doing? How did I get into the house? Where are my clothes?" Some days, it's not your fists that hurt me. It's your words that hurt more.'

I looked at her and, somewhere in the fuzz of my head, I remembered watching her on a monitor in Charing Cross police station when she'd implied I was violent.

'I've never hurt you.'

She didn't say anything.

'I've never hurt you,' I said again, and then caught myself: I was treating her as if she were my wife. I was talking to her like she was Derryn. I stayed where I was and studied her face, looking for the things that weren't the same, and I saw again all the differences – the subtle disparity in the colour of her eyes; the way her nose didn't run quite as straight as Derryn's; the thinness of her lips – and I said, 'You're not Derryn.'

She looked bereft.

'*You're* the one that's sick,' I said. 'Let me help you.'

She nodded, wiping at her eyes, her nose, looking around the bedroom at the pictures of Derryn and me, and then she started to cry again. I didn't know what to do.

Quietly, she said something.

'What was that?' I asked her.

I took a step closer.

'What did you say?'

She looked up at me.

I dropped to my haunches in front of her.

'I can help you,' I said again. 'Let me help you.'

She shook her head.

'I can.'

She shook her head a second time.

'No,' she said.

'Let me help you.'

'No. I don't even recognize you.'

My head began pounding again, the sensation so sharp and so sudden, I had to reach out for the bed, feel for it, and guide myself on to the mattress. I lay there, legs dangling off the side, trying to regain my composure, my sense of balance, my grip on reality. But none of it would come. If anything, I began to feel worse, the blackness behind my eyelids offering no comfort at all: my skull was on fire, front to back. It was swimming; I felt like I was on a boat being thumped by waves, far out into the ocean.

The sounds began to drift first.

I could hear her asking me if I was all right, over and over, her hand on my arm. I heard her telling me she would call an ambulance. I tried to respond, wasn't sure if I actually had, and then I heard her telling me she was going to phone 999.

The creak of the mattress as I slumped sideways.

The thump of her footsteps as she left the bedroom.

And then there was nothing.

#0701

After I left hospital, I didn't see you again for two weeks, but I thought about you all the time. I remembered that smile of yours. I remembered how, when I was still recovering on the ward, you'd bring me water in the morning and always pour the first cup for me. None of the other nurses did that. That was why everyone — all the patients, I mean — liked you the best, because you took care of the small things as well as the big stuff. You'd puff up our pillows, make sure we had enough blankets; you'd pretend to be a drill sergeant in order to get us to eat that terrible food; you'd come around at night and talk to us, every one of us, your voice soft and calming, especially when you were talking to me.

'How has your day been?' you'd say.

'It's better now you're here.'

You'd smile. 'You old charmer, you.'

I think you liked it when I said those things, even though you made light of them. Sometimes I felt sure you were looking at me when I didn't realize it. I'd turn and you'd look away, and every time you did, I felt myself drawn to you even more.

Two weeks after I was discharged, I needed to see you again. I just needed to speak to you, to hear your voice and see your face, so I returned to the hospital. I went in and was prepared to wait for you outside the ward, for however long it took, but as it turned out, I only had to wait ten minutes. It was like you knew I was there, like we were connected somehow. You were returning from lunch, eating a tuna sandwich out of a carton, checking your phone.

'Derryn,' I said.

You looked up from your mobile and it took a second for you to

*realize it was me. 'Oh,' you said, your mouth full. You looked slightly
embarrassed. 'Hello there.'*

'How are you?'

'I'm uh . . . Yes, I'm good, thank you.'

You looked up and down the corridor.

'You're not back already, are you?' you asked.

'No,' I said, smiling.

*When I chose not to say anything else, you seemed to realize what I
was driving at: I was here to see you. You finished what was in your
mouth, and said, 'Right.' A pause. 'Right, okay.' A brief smile. 'Well,
it was nice to see you, anyway.'*

'I've got something for you.'

'Oh?'

I handed it to you, wrapped in plain brown paper.

'Something to remember me by,' I joked.

*You didn't make eye contact this time and opened it in silence. I
assumed it was because you were embarrassed. I wanted to tell you that
you never have to be. I wanted to say, You never have to be embarrassed
with me, Derryn. I'll never make you feel small, ever. And I remember
things. I remember things that are important.*

Like this.

*I just watched you as you opened it, and I thought about all the days on
the ward with you. When we'd talked, it had been about books. Do you
recall? We discovered we had a shared love of Eva Gainridge. You said
your favourite book of hers was* No One Can See the Crows at Night,
*which has always been my least favourite. I think Gainridge was finding
her feet at the time. I don't think it's anywhere close to being her best work.
But I never told you that. I just nodded, and smiled, and – when you asked
me what I thought of the book – I said I admired it as a debut.*

'So which one of hers do you like best?' you'd asked me.

*'*The Man with the Wolf's Head.*'*

'Ah, the old favourite.'

*You'd said it with another smile, and I didn't think much about it at
the time, even in the immediate aftermath of leaving hospital, but – during*

our two weeks apart — it gradually started to come back to me; and, I'll admit, it began to slightly bother me too. Did you mean that my choice was worth less than yours because it had been Gainridge's most successful novel? Did you mean that, because The Man with the Wolf's Head *was studied and analysed the world over, and mentioned by academics in the same breath as* The Catcher in the Rye *and* Lord of the Flies *and* To Kill a Mockingbird, *it was somehow a less deserving choice? Would you have said the same thing to me if I'd chosen one of her less popular and less acclaimed novels?*

'Thank you.'

I realized you'd unwrapped the gift. I'd got you a copy of No One Can See the Crows at Night — *your favourite.*

'That's the 1998 edition,' I told you. 'It's very rare.'

You smiled again, but it looked harder for you to form.

'I didn't mean to embarrass you,' I said.

'It's very . . .' You frowned. 'Very kind, thank you.'

I pointed to it. 'There's a message inside.'

You tentatively opened the book and found the piece of paper I'd placed a couple of pages in. I watched you read it back, knowing exactly what I'd written.

Derryn: Thank you for our special time together x.

You smiled again. 'Uh, right. Well, thank you.'

'You're welcome.'

'I'd better be going.'

'Oh. Okay.'

'Thank you,' *you repeated, and held up the book.*

I nodded, watching you buzz yourself into the ward, watching you through the glass panel of the door as you headed towards the nurses' station, book in hand.

But something was wrong, I could tell.

You didn't react how I thought you would.

Now I needed to speak to you again and find out why.

Day Four

34

I woke in my bed again – on top of it, fully dressed – but this time there was no sun, no smell of cooking, no noise from anywhere else in the house. There was just a weak grey light escaping through the curtains and the soft sound of rain at the window.

Slowly, I hauled myself up.

My head had stopped thumping, but I felt sore and unsteady, even with my feet pressed into the carpet and both hands planted on the mattress. Next to me, on the bedside cabinet, the clock now read seven fifty-eight in the morning. I tried to make sense of it, of everything that had happened, but I couldn't. I couldn't hear her in the house now. I couldn't smell the meat or the potatoes or the vegetables. Her perfume wasn't threaded through the air and she wasn't calling me for lunch.

I looked around the room, checking to see if anything was out of place, and then got to my feet and opened the wardrobe. It was full of clothes – but only mine. There was nothing belonging to the woman inside. It was exactly the same in the drawers. In the bathroom cabinet, there was my deodorant and aftershave, my razor, shaving cream, moisturizer I'd bought, aspirin, throat lozenges.

On the floor next to the bed, I spotted my phone. It was face down, as if it had spilled out of my hands. Picking it up, I saw the battery icon was flashing red. It was out of power. I dug around for a charger and plugged it in, then moved out into the hallway. The doors to the office and spare room were now open.

Dusty light spilled in from either side, pooling in the hallway ahead of me, and when I looked inside the rooms, I found them exactly as they always were, the office a mess, the spare bedroom set up for guests I rarely had. When I reached the living room, it was light despite the rain and the curtains had been pulled open, revealing a wet garden, plants swaying in the wind. The room smelled of a scented plug-in, of wooden floors and furniture.

The table was empty, cleared of all the food that had been on it, of the plates and the knives and the forks. There was no present. No wrapping paper. No copy of *No One Can See the Crows at Night*. On the clock – the one with the triskelion for a face – it said it was Sunday 31 December.

It wasn't my birthday.

I'd gone to see McMillan at 9 p.m. on 29 December; now it was 8 a.m. on the 31st. I'd lost almost a day and a half, save for a tiny sliver of time in the middle when I'd woken up and found the woman in my house. Or had I? Had she really been here? Had any of it happened? For a short moment, I felt a sense of relief. If it was a dream, that meant I wasn't really sick – because she hadn't been here, there was no meal, there was no moment when I'd allowed my conviction to wane and held her against me. There were no tears; none of it was real. If it was a dream, I could explain it all.

Except it hadn't felt like a dream.

It had felt utterly real.

From the bedroom, I heard a series of beeps and remembered my phone was on charge. There was enough battery now for missed call and text message alerts to have begun appearing. I discovered five voicemail messages.

The first was from Erik McMillan.

He'd called at 7.02 a.m. on 30 December – ten hours after I'd met him at St Augustine's and right in the middle of my first blackout.

'David, it's Erik McMillan. I wanted to make sure you got home safely last night, and to implore you to accept my help. I don't know how much you remember about what happened, but you passed out here at the hospital. I looked after you until you came round and offered to pay for a taxi to take you to Queen Elizabeth Hospital, but you refused, and I'm sad to say you ended up leaving here in an angry, confused and dis-orientated state.' He sighed gently. 'You need to seek help, David. Blacking out like you are – that's not normal. It is, to be frank, entirely *ab*normal. If you won't accept my help, please at least go to see your GP. I'm concerned you're risking the safety of not just yourself, but others too.'

The message ended.

What the hell had happened to me?

Could there be any truth in his account of how I got home? Had I really refused to go to A&E? I'd blacked out, that much was true, and now I couldn't remember anything except when I'd woken up at home and found the woman in the house, cooking dinner, talking to me, crying for me. If it had all happened as I remembered it, where was the evidence the woman had ever been here? Where were her clothes and her toiletries? Where was she now?

The next message was from Annabel, an hour after McMillan's call. Listening to her voice gave me a momentary buzz, a shot of hope, some respite from the discord.

'I just wanted to see how you were,' she said. She was obviously driving, her voice a little distant and echoey inside the vehicle. 'I also wanted to say that I'm sorry. All the stuff I read about you and that woman on *FeedMe*, the way she looked, I realized I must have sounded like I didn't believe you when we spoke. But I do. I really, honestly do.'

The third and fourth messages were both from news-paper journalists asking for a comment on the *FeedMe* story. I deleted them immediately.

The fifth message had come through forty minutes before I woke up.

'It's DS Field. You're going to want to hear what I have to say.'

35

Field wasn't in the office, so I tried her mobile. As soon as she answered, I could hear traffic and the murmur of a police radio. She was in a car.

'I've been trying to get hold of you since yesterday afternoon,' she said. 'Where have you been?'

'Nowhere.'

'You've been at home the whole time?'

Her voice was hard, combative.

'Mostly,' I said, deliberately trying to keep it vague. But vague answers came with the same risk as the truth: I had no idea where any of it was taking me.

'Where else have you been?'

'Why?'

'Because it's not particularly helpful when I can't get hold of you. I asked you to remain contactable.'

'You only left me one message.'

'But we came to your house.'

That stopped me dead. *She and Kent came here.* My car had been on the driveway. Lights had been on in the house. The curtains had been pulled. They would have known that I was home – they just would have thought I'd been refusing to answer. Did that make me guiltier in their eyes?

'When did you come here?'

'Yesterday afternoon *and* yesterday evening.'

So she and Kent had driven to the house twice yesterday. That entire period – late afternoon, evening, the whole night until almost 8 a.m. – was a blank. I wondered if, rather than being unconscious, I just couldn't remember what had happened. Was that possible? But then why would I remember that single hour or two when I'd woken up and the woman had been in the house, and then absolutely nothing either side of it? If I wasn't willing to entertain the idea of it being a brain abnormality, a tumour, some syndrome that switched me off like a light, then I *had* to believe I'd passed out because McMillan had laced my coffee with something. But why? The only time it felt like I'd got close to making him remotely uncomfortable was when I'd started asking him about who had called him from the payphone in Plumstead, and that had happened before I'd even taken a sip. So had he drugged me for some other reason? Had he simply wanted me unconscious? What if something had happened to me in the black spaces either side of waking up? I felt dread start to pool.

'Mr Raker?'

'I was here the whole time,' I told her.

But maybe I wasn't.

'Then why didn't you answer the door?'

'I was feeling . . . I was . . .'

I stopped. *Ill.* That was what Field wanted to hear. That would make her life a whole lot easier because it would help answer a whole bunch of questions. Me being sick played into the entire narrative concocted by Erik McMillan and the woman.

'You were ill?' she pressed.

'No,' I replied, too quickly, and wondered whether my denial might actually have made things worse. Just as rapidly, I added, 'Just a little bit of a cold. I've managed to shake it off fairly quickly.'

'Right.'

I could tell she didn't believe me, so I shifted things on: 'What is it you wanted? You said you had something I needed to hear?'

She didn't respond and, from the front of the house, I heard a car pulling up. I went through to the kitchen. The Volvo had barely stopped before Field was getting out of the passenger side, followed by Kent on the driver's side. Out of one of the back doors came a third person: a guy in his late thirties, smart in a tie and jacket. He was carrying a black bag.

'So you're home now?' Field asked.

It was too late to deny it.

'Yes.'

'Good,' she said, and a second later our eyes met through the kitchen window as she ended the call and started to make her way towards the house. Behind her, Kent was shrugging on a grey raincoat.

Between them was the man in the tie and jacket.

The closer he got, the more I could see of him, and what he had wrapped around his neck and shoulders: a stethoscope.

After last night, I was starting to worry that everything was in my head.

Now I was about to find out for sure.

36

'How often do you get headaches, David?'

The doctor had introduced himself as Gregory Carson. He was good-looking, square-jawed and lightly tanned, with dark brown eyes I could see myself in. When he leaned in, I could smell deodorant on him, a faint scent like pine, and as I did, I pictured the deodorant I'd found in the bathroom that belonged to the woman, and the fact that it was no longer there; the fact that all evidence of her was missing.

Removed, when I was unconscious.

Or never there in the first place.

'Once in a while?' he said. 'Once a month? Every day?'

He had a southern Irish accent, which reminded me of Kennedy. As I thought of him, I thought of my parents' old cottage in which he was staying. For the first time in a long while I actually wanted to go there, to be next to the sea, to seek solace in the silence and isolation of the house. I wanted to be anywhere but here.

'David?'

'I don't know,' I said.

'But you get headaches regularly?'

'At times of stress, I suppose.'

'Are you stressed now?'

He'd already shone a penlight into my eyes, but now he did it again. When he was done, I blinked and looked over to where Field and Kent were standing on the other side of the room, just blobs of yellow light for a second.

'Well, I've got two police officers in my home,' I replied, 'and a woman pretending to be my dead wife – so, yes, it's fair to say that I'm not feeling at my most relaxed at the moment.'

Carson just nodded.

'Have you suffered any more blackouts?'

Yes. And this one lasted nearly thirty-five hours.

'David?' Carson prompted.

'No,' I lied.

'No more blackouts?'

'No.'

'Are you sure?'

'I think I'd remember.'

He began fishing around in his bag for a blood pressure kit. There was silence in the room as he attached it to my arm, and when I looked at Field, she simply looked back, a hint of pity in her eyes. Kent had his head down and was busy typing on his mobile.

'Have you ever suffered memory loss?'

'No.'

'Ever been diagnosed with depression?'

'No.'

'Post-traumatic stress?'

'Three years ago, a doctor said I might be suffering from mild PTSD. I didn't agree with him.'

He checked the blood pressure gauge and then began removing the strap from my arm again. As he did, he took a fractional glance towards Field and Kent and I could see the remains of something in his expression.

The first tremor of panic hit me.

Does he know I'm lying about the blackout?

'We've spoken to Dr McMillan,' Field said.

It was the first time she'd talked since entering the house. I turned to her. 'What?'

'We spoke to Dr McMillan on the phone yesterday morning. He said you went to see him on Friday evening at St

Augustine's.' She let me digest that, and then continued: 'He said you blacked out, and then – when you woke up – you were extremely confused. He said he tried to help you, tried to pay for a taxi –'

'McMillan's a liar.'

'Are you saying you *didn't* black out?'

'He drugged me.'

Kent finally looked up from his phone, a half-smile tracing the edge of his lips, as if he thought I might be joking. By contrast, Field was absolutely still: no reaction.

'He *drugged* you?' Kent smirked.

'He put something in my coffee.'

'So you *did* black out?' Field asked.

I looked at her. 'Yes.'

'Which means you lied to us just now.'

'I lied, because I knew I'd get this exact reaction.'

'And what reaction's that?'

'Don't play me. You know exactly what I'm talking about. Anything I say gets treated with immediate suspicion. Anything McMillan says – or this woman – is taken as cast-iron fact.'

'That's not true.'

'Isn't it? Are you even looking into McMillan?'

'Looking into him how?'

'He's lying about me.'

'He's an eminent psychiatrist, Mr Raker.'

I stared Field down, saw I wasn't going to get anywhere, and then turned my attention to Carson: 'When I blacked out three years ago, that was stress, exhaustion, whatever you want to call it. A friend of mine . . .' My words dropped away and I gave myself a moment, thinking of Kennedy, needing to pick my words carefully. It was the search for him that had almost broken me. 'Eventually, I found him,' I said, 'but he was dead.'

Another lie.

193

'I'm sorry to hear that,' Carson replied.

'This isn't the same. I didn't black out due to some biological defect; I blacked out because McMillan put something in my coffee.'

'Why the hell would he do that?' Kent asked. He was off his phone now, his arms in a downward V in front of him, his left hand gripping the RSI bandage on his right wrist.

'Maybe the same reason he's lying about my wife.'

'That's a very serious charge.'

'It's not a charge, it's the truth.'

'How can we trust someone who lies to us?'

'You seem to have trusted McMillan.'

'Okay,' Carson said, looking between us all, holding a hand up. 'Okay, maybe we should all calm down for a moment.'

'Take my blood,' I said to him.

'Why?'

'Because then you'll be able to see if I'm right.'

'About what?'

'About whether McMillan drugged me.'

Carson looked at Field and Kent, as if seeking permission, and when neither reacted, he said softly, 'David, do you ever find it difficult concentrating on things for long periods?'

'What?' The change of direction had thrown me. 'No.'

'Have there been any changes to your sleep patterns?'

'Well, I was roofied two nights ago . . .'

'What about before all of this?'

'No.'

'You don't have trouble sleeping normally?'

'No,' I said, but that was just another lie to add to the others: even now, even eight years on, I'd sometimes lay awake all night.

'How do you feel about leaving the house?'

I looked at him. 'How do I *feel* about it?'

'Does the thought seem unappealing?'

'No.'

'What about being around people? Do you like interacting socially?'

'It depends who with,' I said, and glanced at Field and Kent. Kent stared at me hard, but just for a second Field's mouth twitched, as if she'd seen the humour in it.

'Do you feel unusually anxious?'

'Yeah, you could say that.'

'What about outside of the current situation?'

I looked at him again: this was going somewhere and I wasn't sure where. 'No,' I said, 'I don't generally get anxious unless people are actively trying to ruin my life.'

'Do you ever feel like you're being watched?'

'Watched?'

'Watched, or maybe followed, or harassed by someone.'

An image filled my head: standing out in the alley beyond the garden, the path shrouded in darkness – and thinking that I'd seen someone there.

A face.

'No,' I said.

'Have you ever had hallucinations?'

I swallowed. The face that hadn't been there. The heart on the window that left no trace of itself afterwards. The woman in my house – all her clothes, her things – and waking up and finding nothing of her left. Could they have been hallucinations?

'David?' Carson prompted. 'Do you ever get anything like that?'

'No,' I said, deliberately trying to keep my voice composed this time – because I knew exactly where this was heading now. All his questions, all those symptoms, were pointing to one thing.

Schizophrenia.

Carson kept going, pushing me with variations on the same themes, but this time I was much less expressive, conscious of giving him too much or too little.

'Take my blood,' I demanded as soon as we were finished.

He didn't wait for permission. Instead, he reached into his bag and pulled out a pair of gloves and a syringe. While he was finding a vein, Field took a couple of steps forward and said, 'If, like you say, you were drugged, there may still be traces of it in your bloodstream. But I need you to be honest with me, Mr Raker. I need you to tell me, if you remember, exactly where you've been over the last twenty-four hours.'

I looked at her. Was telling her the truth better than lying? If I lied, I'd have to pluck something out of the air and precisely recall the lie every time we spoke from here on in, but it would, at least, lead me away from this diagnosis they were trying to make fit. If I told her the truth, I had to admit I didn't know. I couldn't say for sure where I'd been for the last twenty-four hours – for the past *thirty-five* – apart from the few short hours I'd spent with the woman. And telling Field that would only make things worse.

Because the woman was supposed to be missing.

That was the other thing. That was the anchor chained to my ankle. Two nights ago, when I'd been to see McMillan in his office, he'd asked me if I was responsible for her disappearance. The police couldn't find her and no one had seen her since the night she went to the flat.

No one except me.

'Mr Raker?'

'I've been at home,' I reiterated.

'You've been at home since yesterday?'

'Yes.'

Field and Kent looked at one another, something unspoken passing between them. Alarm bells started going off in my head.

'Have you found the woman yet?' I asked, unsure if I was heading off whatever was coming, or creating new problems for myself.

'No,' Field said.

'You didn't go to see Dr McMillan yesterday?' Kent asked, still in the same position, his fingers at his wrist. 'That would have been Saturday the 30th of December in case you're struggling to keep up.'

'No. I told you, I saw him the day before – Friday.'

His eyes stayed on me as if he were trying to read my thoughts, and then he readjusted himself and said, 'You're absolutely positive about that?'

'Yes.'

Or maybe I'm not.

Kent got out his leather notebook.

Beside him, Field came further forward: 'So, just to be clear, the last time you spoke to Dr McMillan was Friday night when you went to his office?'

'Yes.' I looked between them. 'Why?'

'Because we have a separate problem now.'

'What do you mean?'

'I mean,' Field said, 'that we can't locate Dr McMillan now either.'

37

McMillan was missing now too.

As Carson packed up his things, I felt a thick sludge move through my stomach. Was this another part of the game for McMillan? Was this his latest effort to keep the focus on me? I thought of everything that had already happened: the death certificate I couldn't find; the funeral paperwork I didn't have; the column that had run in *FeedMe*; having to admit to following the woman to the flat in Chalk Farm just before she disappeared; McMillan inviting me to see him at the hospital; the message he'd left on my voicemail about how he'd tried to get me to A&E, about how – disorientated, agitated – I'd refused, and about how my illness could eventually get someone hurt; and the way he'd subsequently told the same story to Field on the phone, in all likelihood emphasizing the risk that I posed.

Now, like the woman, he'd disappeared.

Then there was my blackout.

He'd been utterly relentless in pushing the idea that I was sick, and the blackout was the perfect way to illustrate it; all I'd been able to come up with in return was a vague, essentially baseless accusation – at least until the blood tests came back – about him spiking my coffee. I had no proof. It was simply a hunch. I could only remember a couple of hours, maybe less, in almost thirty-five. I didn't even remember how I'd got home from St Augustine's. And so – even when, in my strongest and most lucid moments, I was able to deny it – some small part of what he was saying still hung on: a contaminant, an infection I couldn't shift. And the more it hung on, the more the same old questions kept resurfacing.

What if I *had* been hallucinating? What if I really *was* ill? Why could I remember a red door? And what if I'd done something terrible during my blackout?

'Mr Raker?'

I looked up, found Field and Kent standing either side of me, like they were about to arrest me, and realized I'd totally zoned out. Carson had already gone out to the car. It was just the three of us, the room suddenly claustrophobic.

'Have you got any idea where Dr McMillan is?' Field asked.

I shook my head. 'No.'

'Now would be the time to tell us.'

'I don't know where he is.'

'I say "now would be the time to tell us" because you've already admitted to lying to us this morning, and any more lies . . .' She rocked her head from side to side as if weighing up what she was about to say. 'Any more lies would make it very hard for us to believe what you're telling us. So I implore you to be honest with us.'

I tried to think. 'He's got a daughter, right? She's studying up in Edinburgh. Maybe he decided to go and see her?'

Field shook her head. 'We've already spoken to her. She was with him over Christmas – he stayed with her in Scotland – and then he flew back to London on the 28th. He hasn't returned there.'

The day before he arrived home from Edinburgh, I'd still been at Annabel's, still been with my family, comfortable, happy – not alone and attacked.

'She hasn't spoken to her father since he vanished,' Field added. She flicked a look at Kent, who was making some notes, and said, 'I feel it fair for us to update you on a couple of things. You'll be pleased to hear that the blood we tested from the flat in Chalk Farm isn't a match to your DNA.'

I felt some of the weight shift.

'So who does it belong to?'

'I can't tell you that.'

'Is it hers?'

'Whose?'

'You know who I mean. The woman pretending to be my wife.'

She didn't respond, but her silence seemed to be pregnant with something and I wondered for a moment if she was telling me *yes* without having to voice it. Even if she was, why would she choose to do that? Why would she tell me anything, especially after everything that had happened since she'd arrived? Kent looked up from his notes, as if he sensed something was up, but Field simply kept her gaze on mine.

'There's something else,' she said.

It was only three words, but they sounded severe, uncompromising and sharp coming out of her mouth, and any relief I'd felt a moment ago vanished like smoke.

'You said you were at home yesterday.'

I looked between them. I'd told them I was, but now it was obvious where they were going. They had something; something they could use to contradict my claims.

'You were at home yesterday?' she repeated.

I had no choice now. I had to tell her.

'As far as I know,' I said.

Field stiffened, but Kent actually stepped away from me, as if I were infected and he might catch something. He crossed his arms in front of himself again, adopting the same position as before: arms in a V, left hand on his right wrist.

'As far as you know?' he said.

'I can't remember most of it.'

Kent looked at Field. She was on the opposite side of me, perched on the edge of the living-room table, her arms crossed.

'Why not?' Kent pressed.

'Whatever McMillan gave me, it knocked me out.'

'You mean, this drug he dropped in your coffee?'

I could hear the scepticism in his voice.

'Yes,' I said simply.

Field interjected: 'You believe you were at home yesterday?'

'I *know* I was at home for some of the time.'

'What time would that have been?'

I knew exactly: I'd woken up in bed and seen the time on the alarm clock – 11.57 a.m. *11.57 on 14 July.* I glanced out of the windows and saw the flash of Christmas lights in adjacent houses.

'Mr Raker?'

'Around midday,' I said, keeping it broad.

'Until when?'

'I didn't look. Maybe a couple of hours. Maybe less.'

'So you only remember being conscious for a few hours yesterday?'

'Yes.'

'And what did you do during that time?'

I watched her cook me a meal.

I let her hold me, and I held her back.

I cried.

'Nothing,' I said. 'I didn't feel well.'

She nodded and, finally, looked towards Kent.

'We pulled footage from the streets around 2 Sovereign House in Chalk Farm,' he said, 'the night the woman claiming to be your wife called to say you followed her there.' He stopped again, watching me. Inside, it felt like a storm was raging, but I tried not to show it. After a moment, he continued: 'We believe that we may have evidence she went to that flat and was subsequently taken against her will.'

It wasn't my blood on the door and I could account for my whereabouts during that entire evening. Unlike yesterday, I knew for sure what my movements had been. So, whoever took her, it wasn't me.

'She was kidnapped?' I said.

Neither of them responded.

Instead, Field said, 'I'd like to discuss Dr McMillan with you.' She reached into her inside jacket pocket, took out a folded piece of card and began unfurling it. Very quickly, I realized it wasn't card but glossy printer paper. 'What can you tell us about this?'

It was a printout of a photograph.

It had been taken from one of the CCTV cameras at the front of St Augustine's, close to the first security gate. It was dark, already evening, the street lamps nearby casting a pale glow across the entrance, and the road leading to it. Vaguely, in the background, I could make out dots of light from boats passing on the river, and the rest of the new hospital buildings across to the far right of the picture.

But there was really only one thing to focus on.

I was sitting on the ground outside the front gate, my back against it, my knees scooped up to my chest. The quality of the shot wasn't great, but it was good enough.

I was crying.

'What can you tell us about that?' Field repeated.

She was pointing to the timecode in the bottom left. It was marked with yesterday's date – and the time was listed as 18.49.

Twenty-two hours after I'd blacked out in McMillan's office, only hours after I'd woken up at home and found the woman in my house, I'd returned to the hospital.

And I didn't remember any of it.

38

'I, uh . . .' I paused, my eyes fixed on the picture. 'I don't know.'

'You can't tell us anything about this photograph?' Field said.

'I don't remember being at the hospital.'

'At all?'

'No.'

Field moved, pulling a chair out from the living-room table and sitting down opposite me. She bent her head slightly, ensuring she was in my eyeline, and then said very softly, 'We've known each other for a few days now, Mr Raker, so would you mind if we just switched to "David" instead?'

I studied her. What was she doing?

The room was so quiet that I could hear the scratch of Kent's pencil. He'd started writing again, head bent, at the very edges of my peripheral vision.

'David,' she said, her voice still at the same volume, 'let me tell you what I'm seeing from my side, okay? I've got a woman claiming to be your wife – who seems to know things about your marriage she shouldn't, and who looks enough like your wife to have turned even *your* head initially – and now she's missing. I've got a respected doctor supporting her claims, who you say drugged you two nights ago, who is now also missing. There are question marks in both their stories, I'm certainly willing to admit that, but the one constant in all of this is you. You were one of the last people to see the woman before she disappeared on Thursday night. You followed her to that flat in Chalk Farm. And now' – she placed a hand at the corner of the CCTV shot – 'it's clear that you were one of the last people to speak to Erik McMillan as well. We got in touch with the staff at the hospital and they checked McMillan's security card for us, and they confirmed that he came in on his day off yesterday. They said he left at 7 p.m., eleven minutes after this image was taken.'

'You think I was waiting there for him?'

'Evidently you were,' she said, pressing a finger to the photograph, to my face, the pale pink of her nail contrasting against the whiteness of my skin in the picture.

'How do you even know he's missing?'

Field's head tilted slightly; Kent stopped writing.

'It's New Year's Eve,' I continued. 'He's on holiday until Wednesday. And even if he changed his plans, it's not 9 a.m. yet so no one in his office is likely to have called this in. Plus, as far as I know, he lives alone, doesn't he? So there's no wife at home, his daughter's in Scotland – there's no one to notice that he didn't come back to the house last night. What makes you think that McMillan's disappeared?'

I thought I'd managed to corner them, but Field turned everything on its head: 'We asked him to come to the station last night.'

I jerked, as if I'd been hit.

Field didn't seem to notice, but Kent did: he was absolutely still, pen poised above his notebook, eyes drifting from one side of my face to the other, my shoulders, my chest, trying to read more into my physical reaction.

'He said he needed to pop into work to pick something up,' Field added, 'so we agreed a meeting time of 7.30 p.m.'

But he never made it.

'Maybe he forgot,' I said, clutching at straws.

'Maybe,' she replied, but it was obvious that she didn't believe that and she was about to tell me why. 'Thing is, he was supposed to get on a 5.30 a.m. flight today from London City

Airport as part of a two-night break in Florence. He never caught the flight. The airline confirmed he never even checked in. We can't find him at home and DC Kent has spoken to St Augustine's and they tell us that he definitely *hasn't* changed his plans and clocked in with work either. In fact, he hasn't been at work in an official capacity since before Christmas — apart from a brief visit on the night of the 29th to meet you, and then briefly again last night.' She pointed at the picture. 'According to all the information we have so far, you were the last person to come into contact with him yesterday.'

My guts were twisting. I felt sick.

'No,' I said.

'No what?'

'I haven't got anything to do with this.'

'How can you be sure?' Field asked. 'You can't remember anything about last night, isn't that what you said?'

I looked at the photo again, my face illuminated by a street light. The tear tracks were clear on the right cheek: two shiny, vertical ribbons, one running in a straight line towards the corner of my lip, one running in a curve towards my jaw.

'Do you know why you were crying?' she said, trying to sound soft, empathetic, but not quite carrying it off.

I just continued to stare at myself. It was like I was looking at a stranger. This moment in time, caught on a CCTV camera, meant nothing to me. I had no connection to it. It was a blank.

'David? You don't remember being there at all?'

I swallowed again, and then again.

'No,' I said.

'You said you only remember a little from yesterday?'

I nodded.

'Twelve o'clock through to 2 p.m., 3 p.m. at the very latest?'

I nodded again.

'What were you doing during that time?'

'I told you, I was at home.'

'Alone?'

No. Not alone. I was with the woman you think I might have harmed.

'Were you alone?'

No. Yes. I don't know.

'David?'

She was here. And for a second, I let myself believe it was Derryn.

'I was alone,' I said.

Field's eyes didn't leave mine. 'You told Dr Carson just now that you've never experienced such a long period of amnesia before.'

I looked at her. *Amnesia.* That was the first time I'd thought about it in those terms. Amnesia. Memory loss. Chunks of time that were gone and might never come back. I'd worked a case where a man had lost everything in his life – every memory he'd ever held dear. I'd seen its devastating effects. But, at the time, I'd tried to approach it just like any other case. I'd sympathized, but I hadn't truly understood.

Now it was *my* life.

'Were you being straight with us about that?' Field asked. 'About this being the first time you've suffered memory loss?'

'Yes.'

Kent started writing something new down.

'I wouldn't have hurt anyone.'

They were both silent.

'I wouldn't,' I said, but the words didn't sound convincing this time, even to me. Conscious, coherent, there was no way I would go out to injure someone; not deliberately, cold-bloodedly, with intent. But that was just the problem: yesterday, I hadn't been conscious *or* coherent. I wasn't sure what I'd been.

'Have you got the death certificate?' Kent asked. His eyes skirted the room and then drifted along the hallway. 'You told DS Field you had a copy of it in the loft. Have you had a chance to get that?'

Shit.

'David?' Field pressed.

'No,' I said. 'I haven't had time.'

'You haven't had time?' Kent repeated, contempt in his voice. It was even worse than when they'd come to the house two days ago, because then I could actually get away with the idea that I hadn't had time to go through the loft. Now it sounded exactly as hollow an excuse as it was. The truth was, I *hadn't* had much time – not between their first visit, seeing McMillan, and the blackout – but I'd had enough. One of the key pieces of evidence, one of the things that could instantly shift suspicion away from me, and I'd failed to even look for it. It seemed to change the dynamic in the room: Kent snapped his notebook closed and Field's face set hard, like concrete, her arms crossing in front of her.

'Would you let us search your loft for you?' she asked.

'I'll do it.'

'You said that the last time we were here.'

'I mean it this time.'

'And you didn't last time?'

'There's been so much going on . . .'

My words tailed off, flimsy, unconvincing, even though there was some truth in them.

'So you're not giving us permission?'

'No,' I said.

What other choice did I have? It was only a temporary fix: if they really wanted to find proof that I didn't have the death certificate any more, they'd just go out, get a court order and come back. My hope was that Field would wait, though: according to her, in twenty-four hours' time, the registrar at Ealing was due to return from holiday, and had promised to get her a copy of the certificate as soon as possible. I just had to stall things until then.

But it didn't help much in the here and now. Field was unemotional, stoic, but I knew enough about her, had seen enough of her, to know that she was pissed off. Kent was less adept at hiding his feelings: he looked like he wanted to get me by the throat and choke me out until he got to the truth. Again, I didn't blame him. I was either sick, or I was a pathological liar, or I was both.

But whatever I was, my story didn't add up.

Field said, 'You know how these things work by now, David,' and those grey eyes fixed on me, a hawk tracking its prey. 'Because of that, I'm going to spare you the official version. At this precise moment, we don't have enough evidence to arrest you, but it's a matter of time. Hours. You'd make your life a lot easier if you were honest with us. Are you responsible? Are these still just disappearances?'

The insinuation was transparent.

Or are they something worse now?

'I don't know where either of them is,' I said, and this time there was conviction in my voice. 'You think I don't *want* to know? If I knew where they were, I could stop this nightmare dead.'

Field responded like she hadn't even heard me: 'What we *do* know, and what we *can* say with a degree of certainty, is that you were one of the last people to see the woman, who claims to be your wife, alive – because you followed her to that flat – and, last night, you were waiting outside the gates of St Augustine's hospital in the minutes before Erik McMillan finished work.'

I turned to the picture again.

And then a thought occurred to me.

'So where's the image of him?' I asked.

'I'm sorry?'

'Have you actually got CCTV footage of McMillan leaving through the front gate? Have you got a picture of me

208

confronting him?' If they did, if they had footage of us together, why weren't they showing me that? That would have been even more problematic because it would confirm their suspicions about me. Instead they were using this photograph: me, on the floor outside the hospital, alone.

With no sign of McMillan.

'There isn't any footage, is there?'

Kent had reverted to the same stance, opening and closing his right hand. He glanced at Field and then at me, looking unsure whether to step in or not. But I ignored them both, my thoughts already skipping ahead: if McMillan had popped into work, as he'd told them he had, as the data on his security card had confirmed, then he must have exited via the main gate because that was the only way in and out of the hospital. And if I was there waiting for him before his 7 p.m. departure, why wasn't there footage of that? Whether he was in a car, or on foot heading to the train station, there should have been video of me confronting him. That should have been the evidence the police needed to really turn the screw on me. But Field had already told me they didn't have *enough* evidence for them to place me under arrest.

They couldn't put McMillan and me together.

It was a chink of light.

'His security card says he left St Augustine's at 7 p.m.?' I asked.

'I already told you that.'

'So you're relying on what the card says?'

Field's eyes narrowed. 'As opposed to what?'

'As opposed to what you can see with your own eyes.'

'I can see plenty with my own eyes, David.'

'Here's what I think,' I said, ignoring the jibe. 'I think McMillan has fiddled the system somehow. He's made it look like he left the hospital at 7 p.m. when he didn't –'

'David.'

'— leave at that time at all. Can't you see this is a set-up? It's all a set-up. There's only one way in and out of that place and if McMillan didn't take his car, he walked — and if he was walking, you should have him on film. You should have had us togeth—'

'David, *stop.*'

'Have you got footage of McMillan leaving the hospital?' I asked.

Silence.

'Have you or haven't you, just tell me that?'

And then I saw it again, that same look in Field's face as before, as if she was trying to tell me something: I wasn't sure how I was reading her, why she would even let me do it, but I could see it. It was in her eyes. She was telling me, *No, we don't have footage of you and McMillan together.* Or maybe this was some deliberate act. Maybe she wasn't tipping me off, but laying a trap.

'It's time we were going,' she said, standing.

I carried on watching her, looking for any further clues that I was right, that she had been communicating with me, but her face was a mask again, fixed and unreadable. I couldn't, for a second, imagine why she would help me, which made me even more dubious about her intentions.

She pushed the photograph across the living-room table and said, 'Keep this. See if it jogs your memory. I'll talk to Dr Carson about any steps we might need to take from here, based on your assessment, but it goes without saying that, if you *did* happen to recall anything about last night, it would be helpful. It would be helpful for us and it would certainly be helpful for you.' She let her silence press home the point. Then, more ambiguously, she said, 'Someone is lying to me, David.'

Two hours later, I found out who.

#0717

I've never told anyone this, Derryn, but, when I was young, I used to get into trouble a lot. I don't think I was naughty necessarily, although I'm sure there were times when I was, it was more that I was just different from the other kids. I didn't like the things they liked. At school, when they went off at lunchtimes to play football, I never went with them. At weekends, when they caught the bus into town, or went to each other's houses to talk about girls, I never joined them. It wasn't that I was antisocial, it was just I didn't feel the same way they did. The things they thought were important, I considered dull. The things they talked about, laughed about, worried about – they all seemed incredibly trivial to me.

I expect psychologists and doctors would look back at my childhood, at my lack of friends, at my decision not to join in, and say it was a consequence of something. I don't mean any offence, Derryn, but with doctors, with medical people, everything has to be rationalized and categorized. They'd probably look at me and put it down to the way my father spoke to my mother and me, the way he would sometimes grab her by the arm when they argued, his teeth gritted, and squeeze until she backed down. He would hit me sometimes, on the backside mostly – but a few times he hit me in the face. With my father, it tended not to be the things that he did, but the things that he said.

He could be cruel.

After what happened at the hospital with you, I thought of my father for the first time in years. I spent the next couple of days trying to figure out how I might have upset you by giving you the copy of No One Can See the Crows at Night, *but then I started to get frustrated instead. That was how it always started with my father. Frustration. Because, the thing is, you didn't seem as happy as you should have been when I gave you the gift. You didn't seem to appreciate it, or the note I'd written for you inside the book. You didn't seem to realize how rare that edition was or how difficult it was to get hold of.*

So, a week later, I decided to return to your ward, just so we could clear the air. I wanted the chance to go to dinner with you, to share an evening with you. I didn't want you to know me only as a patient, as someone sick who was admitted into your care, and then treated, and then discharged.

I wanted to be more than that.

I wanted to see you for another reason too: I didn't want my frustration to turn to enmity, or even worse to bitterness.

I didn't ever want to become my father.

39

An hour after Field and Kent left, a courier arrived with a package.

I signed for it, closed the door, and hurriedly tore along the top of the padded envelope. Inside were a slim USB stick, unmarked, and a piece of paper. Feeling a shot of adrenalin – my body starting to come alive, my thoughts instantly clear – I put the USB stick into my laptop. It contained four movie files.

It was the CCTV footage from Ewan Tasker.

I'd asked him to source two batches of surveillance tape for me. I'd wanted to try and ID the person who'd made the call from the payphone on the corner of Cavanagh Avenue in Plumstead, but I realized almost immediately that it wasn't going to be possible. The folded piece of paper inside the envelope had a message on it: *Re*: *Plumstead, no working camera close enough*. Maybe that was exactly why the person who'd called McMillan had chosen it. Identifying them was going to be hard now, but I still wanted to get a sense of the phone box, the location and why it might have been chosen, and – with or without the footage – the best way of doing that was by physically going there myself.

The other footage I'd asked for was from 2 Sovereign House in Chalk Farm on the night I'd followed the woman to the flat on the fifth floor. Field had said the blood on the door frame wasn't mine and had seemed to suggest it belonged to the woman. In turn, it seemed likely it had ended up there when she'd been taken – in Kent's words – against her will. If that really *was* true, I wanted to know who was responsible.

The footage was split into four-hour chunks covering the time period I'd asked for: 4 p.m. on Thursday 28 December through to 8 a.m. on Friday the 29th. The camera was situated opposite the stairwell for 2 Sovereign House. In the foreground, I could see cars parked up, a few empty spaces, and the play park with the roundabout; in the background, to the left of the block of flats, were indecipherable lights from the city. I could see some of the first-floor walkway and about ten doors, and the same on the second floor. Despite the camera being elevated, possibly attached to the side of an adjacent building, that was as much of a view of the flats as I had.

It would do: whatever happened, the woman had to come down the stairwell, and she had to exit in front of the camera. All I needed was one clear shot.

At 4 p.m., the place was quiet, populated mostly by young kids at the park, and teenagers walking home from school. I used the cursor to propel the footage on, going through it at 2x speed and then 4x. Even before the footage had really started, it was obvious that the sun had begun to set, but, over the course of the next hour, the light completely altered, the palette becoming black, white and grey.

The woman had arrived at the flat at around 7.25 p.m., so I kept fast-forwarding through the footage until I got to 6.30 p.m. Before that, there was little of any real interest: younger kids drifted back inside once it became fully dark, people started to arrive home from work, and then older kids began to emerge from hibernation, gathering in the folds and clefts of the building.

Just after 6.30, I noticed someone else.

He came in at the left-hand side of the frame, from the direction of the Tube, and was wearing a long raincoat, its colour hard to pin down in the gloom. To start with, I couldn't place him, even though he seemed familiar: thirties, black hair, his skin pale under the glare of the street lamps, five ten maybe, stocky. It looked like he had a suit on, and had come straight from work; certainly his shoes looked smart – black, highly polished or brand new. He appeared for only a matter of seconds, and then he was gone again, swallowed by the stairwell as it corkscrewed around on itself.

I replayed the footage. This time I slowed it all the way down, using the cursors to inch through frame by frame. When the man came into the shot, he was briefly side-on to me before his body turned ninety degrees and he headed in the direction of the stairwell. I played it once, still couldn't ID him, and then played it a second time. This time, it clicked.

Gavin.

The guy from the rental agency.

I grabbed my pad and went back through my notes. I'd spoken to him the morning after talking to Adam Reinsart, the owner of the flat. I'd been trying to figure out why someone would have been using the property, and how they'd gained access to it, when it was supposed to have been unoccupied until 6 January.

Gavin's second name was Roddat: he hadn't offered it, I'd got it from the Hammond's website. That was where I'd seen his picture too, and why it had taken a moment for his face to register with me. I'd never actually met him, only talked to him over the phone. I looked at the transcript I'd written up of our short phone conversation, where I'd pretended to be from the Met:

There's definitely no one living in the flat?
No, not until the 6th of January.
Because we've got witnesses that say there is.

At this point, I'd written: *Pause/didn't reply.*

Gavin?
There shouldn't be. Here at Hammond's, we pride ourselves on —
Would anyone else there know anything?
No. I handle that property.

Was it possible he was looking after another flat at Sovereign House? Maybe it was, but it seemed like a coincidence, and my eyes kept returning to that middle section of the transcript. *Pause/didn't reply.* Had he been silent because he was thrown by what I'd told him — or because he was trying to think on his feet?

I thought of what Field had said to me.

Someone is lying to me, David.

Did she mean Gavin Roddat?

Had he gone to unlock the flat? Had he gone there to wait for the woman? I couldn't see any keys on him, but even if he'd been holding some, it would have been hard to make them out, given the low-quality light and the high angle of the camera. As the footage continued to play, I looked down at the transcript again, thinking about how Field might be approaching this. It seemed hugely unlikely that she wouldn't have already watched this same piece of footage, and so she'd have seen Gavin Roddat enter the stairwell not long before the woman arrived. Whether that meant anything to her depended on whether she'd phoned Adam Reinsart, got hold of the name of his rental agency, and, like me, called Hammond's and found out that Roddat was looking after the flat.

I had to assume that she had. She was smart and organized. She wouldn't have missed something like this, wouldn't have overlooked a line of enquiry so obvious. So it was safe to assume that she knew what Roddat's connection to the property was. It was safe to assume she'd ID'd him on the video. So where had she gone from there? Had she been to see him? Had she brought him in for questioning?

Someone is lying to me, David.

I wondered, for a second, if this meant that Roddat was already in custody. Was he lying to her from the inside of an interview room?

The video rolled on, past 7 p.m., a few people coming and going but no one I recognized or who gave me pause. I kept trying to retrofit Gavin into what I'd found out in the case so far, making notes while watching the film, but I couldn't see the links. I couldn't connect him to McMillan – or to the little of what I knew of the woman.

For the next hour, the scene at the flat was quiet.

But then, at 7.26 p.m., the woman finally arrived.

40

She was holding the Post-it note between her thumb and finger, just as I remembered her doing, and as she came to a brief stop beside the play park, the roundabout turning gently in the breeze, she used a tissue to wipe her nose. She did it once, and then again, and then she looked at the Post-it note and did it a third time. As I watched her, I thought of her in my house, sitting on the edge of the mattress, the tears rolling down her cheeks.

She started moving again.

A few tentative steps, as if she wasn't sure what was coming – or maybe the total opposite. Maybe she *did* know. Maybe she'd met Roddat before. Maybe she was frightened of him. As if on cue, she looked up, out beyond the very top of the frame, following Sovereign House into the night sky as it rose five floors. She stayed like that for a moment, a hesitation in her movement, and then I saw her shoulders rise – as if she was taking a long, deep breath – and she headed in the direction of the stairwell.

About twenty seconds after she disappeared from view, I saw myself. There wasn't much of me – the back of my head and neck, part of my cheek, the top of my shoulders – but it was me. Field would have seen this too: the confirmation that I'd been there that night, but also that I hadn't followed the woman up to the flat, just as I'd stated. On the video, I stood on the other side of the play park and looked up.

I couldn't see what was happening on the fifth floor using the footage, but I remembered what I'd seen when I was there. She'd moved along the walkway towards the penultimate door – wiping her nose with the tissue again – and then she'd stopped, pausing there for a moment, looking down at the Post-it note. Then, finally, she'd placed a hand flat to the door, as if knowing already that it would be unlatched, and pushed. Once it had opened fully, she'd stepped inside, swallowed up by the darkness of the flat, and another small detail came back to me: the door hadn't closed again – not immediately.

It had stayed open.

That night, I hadn't lingered for long, and as I'd tailed her to the flat, I'd kept my distance the entire time. But, sometime later on in the evening, she'd called the police, given them the address of the flat in Chalk Farm, and told them I'd followed her there. I'd never been able to figure out how she'd spotted me. She hadn't said *why* she'd been at the flat, she'd never mentioned it in the interview with Field, and there was nothing connecting her to the property. But, when she'd made the call, she'd sounded distressed – so distressed that Kent had driven out to Sovereign House to check on her. By that time, she was gone, but it was enough to sow seeds of doubt about me in Field and Kent's investigation. They thought *I* was the reason she'd been so distressed. But what if it wasn't?

What if the woman hadn't seen me tailing her at all?

I'd shadowed a lot of people and had become good at it. I'd done it so many times, on so many cases, I felt certain I'd have known if I was compromised. That night, I didn't remember the woman looking back once in all the time I tailed her from Charing Cross – yet, somehow, she was able to tell police I was there.

Because it wasn't her that saw me that night.

It was Gavin Roddat.

I looked at myself in the bottom corner of the screen, lingering for a few seconds after the woman had entered the flat. I thought of how the door had remained open briefly afterwards, the dark of the flat showing out at me. What if Roddat had been just inside the door? What if he'd looked out and spotted me five floors below?

I let the video run, watching the timecode tick over. It was 7.29 now. Field said the woman had called them on a prepaid mobile an hour after leaving Charing Cross station: the walk from the police station to the Tube was about five minutes; the train journey on the Northern Line about fifteen; and the walk from Chalk Farm station to the flats no more than ten. Thirty minutes: that meant she'd made the call to Field – or rather Kent, as Field had already gone home by then – at around 8 p.m. So did she make the call from the flat? Did that mean the prepaid mobile belonged to Roddat? What did they do there for half an hour before she called Kent?

I sped up the footage, stopping at 8 p.m., thinking that she may have exited the flat immediately after the phone call. Nothing happened. More people came and went – a young couple; an old woman, slow, limping, being helped by what must have been her son – but no one I recognized; cars pulled into the parking spaces; teenagers began to drift out of shot. After that, the only thing that moved were the swings and the roundabout in the play park. I fast-forwarded it again at 2x speed, trying to catch sight of the two of them coming out of the stairwell. Still nothing. It was after 8.30 now, sixty minutes since she'd entered the flat, thirty since the phone call. By this time, Kent would have been well on his way – probably, depending on traffic, only a couple of minutes out.

Then, finally, she appeared again.

I hit Pause on the footage as she emerged from the stairwell into the glare of the street lights. She looked exactly the same as when she'd gone in, except she seemed to have recovered some of her composure. But then I started the video again, and – in motion – I began to realize it wasn't that at all. I thought I'd seen something positive and assured when I'd looked at her frozen image, but as the footage began to play again, as she started walking, I saw that her movements were slightly off, as if she was agitated or hurt. What I'd seen as poise was actually the opposite. Her face was empty, her eyes dead. She wasn't composed. She was stunned.

What was wrong with her?

She took another step forward and then I could see him. In the space directly behind her, almost hiding from view. Roddat had pulled the collar up on his raincoat so that it covered the sides of his face, some of the front too, and because of the shadows, there was only a minimal amount of face showing: an eye, a mouth, half a nose. I couldn't see his hair now either because he was wearing a black beanie.

Alarm blared inside me as I watched him guide her out into the evening. There was a mark on her cheek, one on her neck too. I thought they had been shadows to start with, but as she came further forward, she altered position and, even with the quality of the CCTV film, I could make them out under the glare of the street lamp. The one on her neck looked like a bruise, but the one on her cheek was a cut. It was fresh and it was spreading, black lines escaping from it.

It must have been how the blood had ended up on the door frame.

Shortly after that, they were gone.

I rewound the footage, starting it again at the point they appeared. This time I went through it frame by frame, taking screenshots of the moments when Roddat wasn't entirely hidden behind her. There weren't many. After I was done, I rolled the footage on and began going through the screenshots: three, maybe four usable shots, and even those weren't great. But they were enough. I could see it was Roddat; Field would have been able to see it too.

Now she had a suspect that wasn't me.

Onscreen, six minutes later, a car pulled in: Field and Kent's Volvo. Kent got out quickly, slammed the door shut, didn't even bother locking the car, and hurried to the stairwell. The call from the woman must have been bad – bad enough to have got this reaction from him. It made me wonder what she'd said, but mostly it made me wonder what Roddat had done to her; why she had blood on her face. Where would he have taken her from here?

He must have known that, over the days that followed, the police would be looking at the footage; and even if he'd gone to the trouble of – at least, partly – disguising himself on the way down with the beanie, he hadn't bothered on the way up, so he would have guessed the police would ID him pretty quickly. Maybe all he'd needed was time: by temporarily shifting the blame on to me, by getting the woman to speak to Field and Kent and tell them that I'd followed her from Charing Cross that night, Roddat would create enough breathing space to do whatever it was he needed to do. Get the woman somewhere. Hide her. Make sure she wasn't found.

As I processed that, I started to wonder if Roddat might also have been the person who'd made the call to McMillan from the payphone in Plumstead just before I'd walked into the police station at Charing Cross. What had he said? Had it been a call to warn McMillan what was happening? Was that when the two of them had come up with a plan to corner me, frame me, hurt me? I had no idea how I'd got home from St Augustine's, I didn't know how the woman had ended up at my house, or disappeared again, or how I'd ended up *back* at the hospital, but to Field and Kent, even to myself, by not being able to see those answers coherently, I looked like a man on the brink of collapse: the sort of man who might think he saw a heart drawn on to a window, or a face in an alley when there was nothing there; the sort of man who couldn't account for great swathes of time. And all of that played into the same story that the woman had started, that McMillan had continued, and now – it seemed – Roddat was set to carry on: that in telling the world Derryn was dead, I'd been lying.

But why target me at all?

And there was something else that didn't make sense: Roddat didn't live anywhere close to Plumstead. It took one thirty-second Internet search for me to get an address for him – and it was near Tottenham Marshes, over ten miles away.

I turned away from my laptop, trying to think, but all I could see now was the woman's face. It was there, impossible to delete: in the shadows at the foot of the stairwell, Roddat behind her and then beside her, directing her out, away from the flats, her expression absolutely set, her gaze fixed and empty.

As if she'd been hollowed out.

It was an image that hit like a hammer. It took me back to all the times I'd been sitting alongside Derryn, my hand in hers, as cancer doctors delivered devastating news like they were reading off a menu. It took me back to the weeks and months afterwards, when her hair was gone and her body was going, and I would glance at her and see that same hollowed-out look and realize there was nothing I could do for her. There was nothing I could say. All I'd had then were words, and they stopped working the second she got sick.

Again, I glanced at the screenshots I'd taken of the woman.

They were hard to look at now. The expression on her face had got to me, had dug into my skin like nails. I couldn't shake the image, even as I looked away: it was her eyes. They were absolutely empty. What the hell had he done to her in that flat?

She'd turned my life inside out, she'd lied about who she was, she'd made me a suspect in the eyes of the Met, and I still didn't know why she was doing it. But, in this moment,

I found it hard to generate any anger for her. Something had shifted, the axis of the case had tilted, and – despite all the lies she'd told – I saw distinctly who she was in this moment. Not an instigator, or a mastermind. Not someone in control. Someone vulnerable and fragile.

A pawn, just like me.

Everything snapped into focus: to end this, I needed to find her. It was all that mattered. I needed to know why she'd pretended to be Derryn, how she knew so much about us, and how she fitted into this nightmare.

I needed to find her for another reason too.

Her face on the video was a cry for help. It was the face of someone mixed up in something they no longer had any control over, and – if I wanted to help her, and in turn help myself – there was only one place to start.

I had to find out who Gavin Roddat really was.

41

Roddat lived in a plain two-up two-down terraced house in Tottenham, a mile south of the North Circular. There was a tiny square of paved-over front garden, empty except for a green wheelie bin and a white wooden bench.

I rang the doorbell and looked around. The street was busy: families were milling about, kids were kicking a ball against a wall further down, and a man was washing his car. Closer, a few doors away, an old couple were sitting on their garden wall, enjoying a coffee and the faint warmth of the winter sun. I had my picks with me, but it would have been insane to use them with so many eyes on me.

I looked through the window in a vague attempt to see whether he was hiding inside, but the TV and all the lights were off, including those on a modest, two-foot high Christmas tree. Getting out my phone, I tried the mobile number listed under his name on the Hammond's website. It went unanswered. Heading back down the path, I happened to look right, past the old couple, to a cul-de-sac halfway down. On the corner, only the front of it visible, was a grey Vectra.

Two men were sitting inside.

They were watching me.

I walked back in the same direction I'd come, as if I hadn't noticed them, but I knew who they were. Cops. If they were watching the house, it meant I was right: Field and Kent had seen the video of Roddat and the woman at the flat in Chalk Farm. They were on to him.

And now they knew that I was too.

It took me ten minutes to walk to the Overground station

at South Tottenham and, during that time, I knew that the call would have been made to Field and Kent at Charing Cross about my visit here. So what would Field do? Try to head me off? Try to prevent me from interfering in their hunt for Gavin Roddat? Or would she sit back and wait, and see if I led her somewhere new?

I got the train to Upper Holloway, and then walked from there to the bottom of Highgate Road. Hammond's was at the end, near the beginning of Kentish Town Road. I wasn't certain if I'd even find it open today, given it was New Year's Eve, but I caught a break: the lights were on and people were milling about inside. It was more like a coffee shop than a place to buy a house, a mix of red-brick walls, black-and-white photographs and highly polished floors. All the desks were in a line at the back behind four red sofas, a coffee machine and a fridge full of bottled water.

A woman in her twenties standing just inside the door, a clipboard in her hands, greeted me: 'Good morning,' she said, beaming. 'Welcome to Hammond's. I'm Louise.'

'Hi, Louise. I'm looking for Gavin Roddat.'

Her smile fell away.

'Oh,' she said. 'Oh, right.'

She looked worried now, immediately on edge: someone from the Met had clearly been here asking about Roddat already. I looked over her shoulder, towards the back of the room. All four desks were occupied. Gavin Roddat wasn't at any of them.

'Has someone already been in asking about Gavin?'

'Yes,' she said. 'Aren't you from the police then?'

'I'm working with the police,' I replied. 'I guess we got our wires crossed about who was coming here today.' I smiled at her, attempting to put her at ease, and before she could quiz me any further, said, 'So, to double-check: you told my colleague that Gavin isn't in?'

'That's right.'

'Is it his day off?'

'No. He called in sick.'

He'd called in sick, but he wasn't at home.

'He said he was ill?'

She frowned. 'Yes. Why?'

'It's just, I spoke to him on the phone yesterday.'

'Oh,' she said. 'Yes, he seemed fine then. Is Gavin in trouble?'

'He's fine,' I said, pretending to consult my notes. 'From our records, I see that Gavin lives in Tottenham. Do you know if he owns other properties in the city?'

'I don't think so.'

'Has he got a girlfriend?'

'No, he's divorced.'

'Do you know where his ex-wife lives?'

'Uh . . .' Louise paused. 'Somewhere up north, I think.'

Could he have gone there? He could have been hundreds of miles away already – and the woman could have been with him.

'Do you know where exactly up north his ex-wife lives?'

'No. I think her name's Carly, though.'

There was a hint of something else in her expression.

'Louise?'

'I say "I think" because he tends to just call her "the bitch",' she said quietly. 'I don't think they separated on good terms.' She turned, as if she could sense that she was being watched by her boss – which she was. A smartly dressed black guy was getting up from the desk, eyes fixed on us. 'He's always calling her a "bitch",' Louise went on, her voice dialled down, clearly relishing the opportunity to tell me what she knew about Roddat. For the first time, I noticed she was the only female employee here, which made me think this wasn't just her gossiping; it was a culmination of weeks, months, perhaps years of having to listen to Roddat and the rest of the men she worked with. 'He's really cruel about her – but, you know, you reap what you sow.'

'What do you mean?'

She looked again at her boss, saw he was coming towards us now and talked fast: 'Gavin's an arsehole when it comes to women. From what I hear, he's been screwing around for years. I don't blame his wife for calling it a day. In fact, I'm surprised the marriage even lasted five years.'

'Everything all right?'

'Fine, thank you,' I said to the branch manager, snapping my notebook shut.

'Are you from the police too?' he asked.

'I was following up on some things my colleagues asked this morning,' I said by way of an answer, and then thanked them both and quickly headed out.

On the way to the Tube, I tried to locate Roddat's ex-wife. If they were divorced, it was likely she wasn't using his surname any more. But, as it turned out, I got lucky: next to an address in Stalybridge, I found a C. Roddat in the telephone directory. A woman answered after a couple of rings: 'Hello?'

'Is that Carly?'

'Yes.'

'Carly, my name's David Raker. I'm an investigator from London. There's no need to worry about anything, but I need to get in touch with your ex-husband about a case involving a property that he looks after, and unfortunately I can't locate him.'

'I don't know why you think I can help.'

'You haven't seen him lately?'

'I still live in Manchester. He moved down to London after we separated. The last time I saw Gav was in July, and we both had our solicitors with us at the time.'

'So he hasn't been in touch?'

She gave a little grunt. 'No. And I wouldn't expect him to be, not after all the shit he pulled during our marriage. If you can even call it a bloody marriage. I wouldn't go within a thousand miles of that bastard if he was the last man on Earth.'

'Okay,' I said, trying to keep her on point. 'So, have you got any idea where I might find him?'

'No.'

'Has he got any family down here?'

'Daniel,' she said quickly.

'Who's Daniel?'

'He's, like, a third or fourth cousin or something, but they grew up next door to each other, so they've always been close. Sometimes Gav used to go down to London to housesit when Daniel was away with work; he's got some job where he's out in Asia a lot. Anyway, housesit is a pretty liberal interpretation of what I imagine Gav got up to when he went down there. Mostly I think he used it as a place to get his end away.'

I took down Daniel's name and address.

'Has anyone else been in touch about Gavin?' I asked.

'Like who?'

'Anyone else from the police?'

'No,' she said.

Hanging up, I tried calling Roddat on his mobile again, but I killed the call as soon as it went to voicemail. Next, I tried his cousin's landline. There was no response there either. That didn't discount the idea that Roddat was lying low there – in fact, it didn't mean he wasn't there at this precise moment – but if he was, I wondered what the best strategy would be. Should I watch? Scope him out?

Or should I just doorstep him and go on the attack?

If I was planning to do that, it was best not to do it in broad daylight, with neighbours and passers-by milling around, able to give a full account of what they were seeing and hearing, so I inverted my plans: at some stage after this, I'd intended to go to Plumstead and take a look at the phone box McMillan had been called from, and the area surrounding it. Instead, I'd go there first and then come back up to Camden Town – where the cousin's place was – as soon as it was dark. Cover of night wasn't the only reason for doing it this way round: it was New Year's Eve, so the longer I waited, the more partying there would be, and the easier it would be to go unnoticed.

Back on the Tube, I thought again about Gavin Roddat. I seriously doubted that he was sick, but alarm bells were definitely ringing, otherwise why go to ground? The weird thing was, though, as much as I knew I now had a lead that the police didn't – the location of his cousin's place – and, in turn, a potential way of locating him, something didn't feel right. I had zero sense of achievement, just a low-level dread humming in my blood.

And I knew why.

This was heading somewhere bad.

#0722

At the ward, I waited outside the security doors for you.

I had a takeaway coffee and a notebook with me that I used for work. It was full of names and addresses: people I had to visit as part of my job. On a fresh page, I wrote down the things I wanted to say to you. I know it seems stupid. I just wanted to get things right in my head before I said them out loud to you, because I knew I might only get one shot at this. I didn't think you were the type of woman who'd punish a man for being inelegant with words, but, at the same time, if I stood there in front of you and didn't articulate myself properly, if I seemed uncertain or garbled my words, that wasn't likely to help me very much.

This time, though, you never appeared.

Not in the morning, not in the afternoon either. I thought about going on to the ward, nipping in after someone had been buzzed in or out, but the nurses there were clever. They'd have worked out that I wasn't a patient any longer, and I didn't want to create a scene, or embarrass you at work.

So I came back the next day, and waited some more.

Eventually, on the third day of hanging around, I caught one of the nurses as he left and asked if you were on holiday. I recognized him from when I'd been on the ward, and I think he recognized me. His name was Alejandro and – the day after I'd been admitted with that skull fracture – I heard him telling the guy in the bed next to mine that he was from the south of Spain. I didn't really like Alejandro back then – he had this superior attitude, this way of looking down his nose at you, which really annoyed me – and I didn't much like the way he looked at me now. You remember how I said once before that some people don't smile from their eyes? He was one of those.

'Is Derryn on holiday?' I asked.

He frowned. 'Not exactly.'

'Where is she then?'

'I'm sorry,' he said, 'what was your name again?'

'Is she in work or not?'

'I can't give that information out.'

I could see him starting to get suspicious, looking at me like I'd committed some crime in asking about where you were, so I told him I was just a friend of yours – which wasn't a lie – and immediately left. By the time I got to my car, I felt annoyed. Why were you taking so much time off? How was I going to get hold of you? How was I going to tell you about how rare the book was?

How would we ever get to spend an evening together?

I slid in behind the wheel and tried to take some deep breaths. I thought of my father again, of how I never wanted to become like him, and then looked out of the windscreen at the building where you'd taken care of me for those few, wonderful days. And a couple of minutes later, feeling calmer and more rational, I made a decision.

It seemed so obvious.

I'd just find out where you lived instead.

42

It took over an hour to get to Plumstead, and another fifteen minutes to find my way to Cavanagh Avenue. By the time I arrived, the sun was starting to disappear behind rooftops to the west of the Common.

The payphone was on one side of the road, overshadowed by a huge oak tree in someone's garden, and on the other was the bank of shops and businesses I'd seen online when I'd been using Street View: the grocery store-cum-off licence, the Polish deli, the Bangladeshi takeaway and the newsagent.

I crossed the road to the payphone, briefly looked it over, and then checked up and down the street. Ewan Tasker was right: there were no cameras trained in the phone box's direction. There *were* cameras – I could see at least two, one mounted to the front of the grocery store, and the other on a pub about five hundred feet away – but they'd been adjusted so that their focus was on the building entrances, not on the Common Road itself – and certainly not on Cavanagh Avenue.

So what now?

I looked around me and saw a woman walking a dog in the park. She was studying her phone. She bore little resemblance to the woman who'd pretended to be Derryn, except perhaps in her hair colour, but the vague similarities in her height and weight, in her age, made me think of her. It made me wonder where she'd gone after that night at the flat in Chalk Farm. Where had Roddat taken her? Could they be up north? Or was he keeping her at his cousin's place? A part of me wondered whether it had been a mistake to come here and not go to Camden Town instead, but the idea that

Roddat would take her somewhere so obvious – or, at least, somewhere he could be tracked to without too much trouble – didn't feel right.

Grabbing my phone, I brought up a picture of Roddat and headed to the first of the businesses, the grocery store. It was run by a Pakistani guy in his fifties. I showed him the photo and asked if he recognized Roddat. He said he didn't. I then showed him the picture of the woman that had been used on *FeedMe*. He leaned in, taking the phone from me as if he needed to have a closer look, as if he wasn't sure – and, briefly, I allowed myself a moment of hope. But then he shook his head, gave me the phone back and any hope fizzled out.

I moved on to the deli, then the takeaway, then the newsagent, and then away from the Common and towards the pub. It was packed inside, New Year celebrations already kicking off. Music blared from a jukebox in the corner, people were laughing, some were in party dresses, clearly using the pub as a stopping-off point on the way to somewhere else. It gave me a lot more potential leads, but ultimately it came to nothing. No one recognized the woman from her photo, and no one had seen Gavin Roddat around either.

I headed back to the payphone.

If someone had used this phone, they hadn't just done it because there was no way to trace them, or no surveillance cameras close by to put them here at the time of the call. They'd done it because it was convenient. It surely had to be local to them, or local to where they worked, or close to the social circles they existed in, otherwise why use this particular phone? It made me wonder if Roddat had other family members in the city, not just his cousin in Camden Town – people he may have spent the Christmas break with, which would explain why he was down this way in the first place. Or was the truth simply that Roddat never called McMillan three days ago?

Was it someone else entirely?

I watched the lady in the park with her dog again, her phone still in her hands, moving away from me, between the skeletal trees that bordered the Common, and then I headed back in the direction of the station. There was nothing for me here. Whoever had made the call from the payphone had made it knowing they'd have complete anonymity.

No cameras.

No witnesses who might remember anything.

And then I stopped again. Fifteen feet ahead of me, where the Common jagged around a row of tired-looking terraced houses, most of them converted into flats, I spotted another business. This one was different from the others I'd just been into: its sign was above a doorway that was marked 13B, and it looked like it might once have been residential – a second-floor flat that was no longer being lived in.

It had been converted into a community library.

I moved towards it, a CLOSED sign under the number, its opening hours listed on a piece of laminated plastic to the left: 11 p.m. to 4 p.m. every day except Christmas Day. But that wasn't what had got my interest.

It was its name.

Immediately, I rewound back two days, to what I'd found when I'd been hunting around the loft for a copy of Derryn's death certificate: the edition of *No One Can See the Crows at Night* with a message inside.

Derryn: Thank you for our special time together x.

On the first page, there had been a stamp: *PCCL*.

I hadn't understood what the stamp had meant back then, hadn't even known if it was relevant. But it was. It stood for Plumstead Common Community Library.

This was where the book had come from.

I looked around me, back along the road towards the pay-phone. It was hard to think clearly, but harder still to believe this might just be some huge coincidence. I'd found the book, and the message tucked inside, after turning the loft inside out. I might never have found the message, ever, if the death certificate hadn't been missing, but the death certificate *was* missing, the message *was* inside the book – and Derryn had relegated it, and the person who'd given her the novel, to the attic.

Could it have been Roddat who had given it to her?

One thing was for sure: everything linked together too well now. There was no way the payphone that McMillan was called from just *happened* to be metres away from the library in which a book had been loaned, or bought, for Derryn. Not in a case like this.

Not when someone was pretending to *be* her.

I looked at my watch, at the sky – a charcoal smear – and thought about my next move. But there was really only one move to make: even if I'd wanted to go into the library, I couldn't. It was already shut.

So that just left Gavin Roddat.

If I found him, I found the woman.

43

Roddat's cousin lived in the middle of a three-storey terrace, about a minute's walk from Regent's Canal. The houses on both sides were smart and the street was lined with expensive cars. It was obvious why Roddat might offer to housesit and why he'd prefer to bring women here rather than to the less auspicious surroundings of his house in Tottenham.

I walked up and down the street, partly to get a sense of the road, but mostly because I was on the lookout for more police. I'd spent an hour in Plumstead, and over two hours going there and getting here, so there was every chance they'd used the time to connect Roddat to his cousin and his cousin to here.

But if they were watching, they were well hidden.

There were no vehicles in the road that I would have immediately identified as unmarked cars; certainly no cars with people sitting inside them. I walked to one end of the street and into a connecting road, double-checking there too, then came back and did the same on the opposite side. I checked the windows of the houses as well, even though I was pretty certain the Met wouldn't be camped out in someone's home yet. Sometimes it came to that, but this case wasn't quite at that stage. Even so, as I returned to the house, I still felt on edge.

There were no lights on inside, though it was dark now, and the only things I could see through the semi-opaque ground-floor window were an extravagant wreath hanging from the living-room door close by, and a tall, decorated fir tree – almost as high as the ceiling – next to a fireplace off to the left. All its lights were off. The cousin must have been at home before Christmas at some point, but it didn't necessarily mean he was around at the moment. In fact, if it turned out Roddat *had* actually come here, if he was using this place to lie low in, it was probably likely he was doing it because his cousin wasn't home, and wasn't due back for a while.

I rang the doorbell.

As I waited, I checked the road again. It was almost six o'clock and – just like in Plumstead – the New Year's Eve celebrations had begun. Nine doors along, I overheard a man talking on a mobile about a dinner party; in the other direction, I could hear music, the dull thud of a bassline; across from me, a group of four women were in a doorway, smoking and laughing.

I tried the doorbell again.

As I waited, I checked the houses either side of me: on the right, in an identical garden to this one, a wicker reindeer had fallen over; to the left, I could see through the window to where an old couple – their backs to me – had just finished setting a table for dinner. There were two places, one for each of them. They had a gas fire going, its flames casting a warm glow, and the man had now taken his wife by the hand and was beginning to waltz her towards the kitchen.

They erupted into laughter.

I thought of my own parents then, who'd still laughed with one another, even after years together, and felt a flutter of sadness as I remembered how long it had been since they'd died. I felt it again as I thought of Derryn, except it hurt even more. In moments like this, in the fractional glimpses of a life we could have had, it always hit me how much I missed her. And it hit me even harder now as I dealt with the fallout from four days of lies, as the grief I'd buried, and made some sort of peace with, was exhumed.

Further down the street, there was another eruption of

laughter from the women gathered outside having a smoke, a shrill noise that brought me crashing back to the present. I looked from them to the door I was standing in front of, and – ignoring the doorbell completely – knocked hard.

This time, I heard something.

A click.

It took me a second to work out what had happened, the lack of light from the inside of the house not helping. I stepped closer, checking the shadows around the door – and then I understood.

The front door had shifted.

It was already open.

44

With the sleeve of my jacket, I pushed at the door and watched it swing back into the shadows of the house. There was some peripheral light ahead of me, but not much.

The hallway ran front to back, with a living room on one side and a kitchen on the other. From the living room, there was a leak of residual light through the front window, but not enough to show me more than the edge of a sofa and a square TV cabinet. At the end of the hallway, a glass door led out to a small garden. Solar-powered lights had been added to a couple of flower pots immediately outside the door, and now they were emitting a ghostly hue.

'Gavin?'

Nothing from inside the house.

'Gavin, it's David Raker.'

I double-checked the street, studying windows, looking into cars that were parked along the side of the road. I still couldn't see any eyes on me, not in the houses or in the vehicles, but neither of those things steadied my nerves. As I turned to the door again, it began inching back towards me, moaning on its hinges, and I noticed something else: the faint, very distant whine of a breeze carrying through the house.

'Gavin?'

For a third time, all I was met with was silence.

I wiped my feet and pulled my sleeve down, covering my hands, conscious of leaving a trace of myself here. As soon as I stepped inside, I heard the wind again, felt it streaming past me like the fast flow of a river, drawn to the front door from somewhere else in the house: another open door at the back of the property, or a window in one of the other rooms. The moment I was inside, the carpet thick beneath my feet, I checked the front door to see why it had been open. A bunch of keys was hanging from the rear. Because the keys had been turned in the lock, the latch was off. I pulled the keys out, placed them on the side and closed the door properly. The sound of the breeze ceased.

'Gavin?'

Removing my phone, I opted against using the torch function – it was too bright and too conspicuous if anyone was looking in from the outside – and opted for the duller glow of the home screen. It was enough. As I inched into the living room, everything came alive in sepia: two sofas, a table, the TV cabinet, some DVD box sets piled inside. It was small, but it had been done nicely: the furniture looked expensive, the television too, the wallpaper shone new. Left on one of the sofas was a Dell laptop in a slipcase.

I picked it up with the sleeves of my coat, unzipped the case and removed the laptop. As I left it to boot up, I went back out into the hallway and across to the kitchen, which looked out to the back garden. There was no shed, no storage of any kind; nowhere to hold someone. I checked the kitchen for anywhere that looked large enough to store a person the woman's size, but again there was nothing.

Back in the living room, the laptop had brought up a password screen and a corporate logo. It was a work computer; his cousin evidently worked for a shipping company. I closed it and headed upstairs.

The moment I hit the landing, I could feel the air chill, breath forming in front of my face in a fine mist. There were three doors, forming an L-shape: a bathroom, a main bedroom and a spare room. I checked the bathroom over, found nothing, checked the main bedroom, then made my way to the last room.

The door had swung most of the way closed. Even before I reached it, I could feel the temperature alter again, the ice in the air. This room was at the back of the house, looking out over the garden. I knew, behind the door somewhere, I would find a window open, and it had nothing to do with the cold: I could hear traffic from Kentish Town Road; I could pick up the voices of the women I'd seen outside earlier; and I could hear the same music – its pulsing bassline – but even clearer, coming from this side of the terrace.

I shoved at the door.

It swung open, and a sudden rush of wind met me. My exposed skin prickled, my eyes watered: the room was like an ice box, the window wide open, pushed as far as it would go on its fixings.

He was in the space beside the desk.

His feet dangled a foot and a half off the floor as he hung next to the legs of the chair he'd used, his body somehow appearing smaller than it should have, as if it had collapsed in on itself, an inflatable that had lost its air. He seemed to have compressed and shrivelled, his hands half-formed fists, his trousers slipping away from his waist and legs. Every part of him had receded in death – every part, except one.

His head.

That was still upright, facing forward, his eyes wide and filled with blood, his neck rigidly held steady by the noose. The rope ran from his neck to a ceiling fixture, then looped down to the open window in an inverted V shape, where it was attached to one of the window fittings. There, it had been tied in a series of knots so it wouldn't come loose after the chair had been kicked away beneath him.

I tore my eyes away from Gavin Roddat and took in the rest of the room. There was a desk with an iPad on it. A pot with some pencils and pens. A few sheets of paper – bills, correspondence – and another laptop. This one was already open, the power on, a video of some kind paused onscreen. A split second later, I realized what: the snow, the Alpine houses, a woman in the centre of the shot, looking back.

Nausea gripped me.

It was the home movie of Derryn in Austria.

I'd watched it three nights ago. I'd watched this whole section, from start to finish: Derryn walking through the snowdrifts in the town, towards the restaurant, talking over her shoulder at me, joking that she was going to have glüh-wein for every meal.

On the desk, beside the laptop, was a suicide note.

It only had two words on it.

I'm sorry

#0733

You lived in Ealing. I couldn't find out much about you online, even though you had an unusual name. But you were in the phonebook, listed as D. Raker, so – after work one day – I took a drive out to where you lived, hoping that you might be at home.

You weren't.

I wasn't exactly sure what I was expecting, but I've got to admit that I found your home quite plain and unremarkable. It was a bungalow, which was unusual for London, but everything else was so staid. I thought, given that smile of yours, that little bit of mystery you had in your eyes, that I'd get to the house and find something unusual, out of the ordinary. But it was just another house, in another street, with the same finishes and flourishes, the same flowers at the front.

It was the middle of the day, and I didn't want a neighbour to think I was snooping around, so I wandered on to the driveway and went straight to the front door. You didn't have a doorbell. Instead, you had a timber door with a brass knocker. I tapped it twice and waited.

There was no answer.

From the front porch, I could see part of the way into the kitchen. You must have left in a hurry that morning, because there were bowls in the sink and a half-finished cup of coffee on the worktop. I leaned a little closer and my new angle gave me a view all the way across to a door on the right, into the hallway. Next to that was a fridge, things stuck to it: paper, magnets, a notepad.

Photographs.

The photographs were too far away to be certain of who was in them, but I thought I could make you out in one. I thought I could see that smile, even from where I was. In another, I wondered if you might have been with your parents because there were three people, and two of them looked like they had grey hair. It made me wonder about your family. Were your parents still alive? Did you get on with them? Did you have a brother or a sister?

I returned to your house twice over the following week.

The first time, I waited outside in my car, almost opposite the gates of the house, but – after four hours – you never came back. The second time, I woke in darkness and tried to get across London before you left for your shift at the hospital, but the house was already locked up by the time I arrived, and I started to wonder if you'd changed shifts in the time between my visits. Maybe you weren't on the day rota any more; maybe you were working the night shift now.

I've lost count of the visits now, because there have been so many, but some I remember more than others. One time, at night, I scaled your side gate. I stood there, protected by the blackness, and looked out at your simple little garden, and then peered in through the rear windows, into the living room and the main bedroom. Again, I'd expected the decor to be more unconventional, but the bedroom was all cream and grey and mauve, like a bland show house. Was this the limit of your imagination, Derryn? Was this really as far as it stretched? Almost immediately, I had to remind myself that successful relationships aren't always built on similarities but on differences, and on being able to embrace those differences, and, in the grand scheme of things, knew that these were small niggles – but, even so, that day, for the first time since I'd started coming to your house, I felt that same sense of frustration building. I felt the echo of my father coming through again. I didn't want to be sneaking around. I just wanted to talk. But you're never at home, Derryn.

Why are you never at home?

The more I've thought about it, the more I've got it into my head that you're playing games with me. So is that what this is? A game? All I want, all I've wanted, is to sit down and talk to you, like we did when I was in hospital and you were looking after me. Back then, it felt so natural. It felt like we understood each other. But it's clear something has changed. I've started to wonder if you're deliberately avoiding me. I've started to wonder if that Spanish nurse said something to you: the one who'd dismissed me as I'd waited outside the ward; the one who'd eyed me with such suspicion, as if I were committing some crime in standing there. Maybe he'd gone back inside the ward afterwards, or he'd called you on his way home and told you I wanted to talk to you. He probably called me strange or weird or creepy. In fact, he probably had a good laugh at my expense. Did you join in with him, Derryn? Did you laugh at me too? I hope not.

I never would have pegged you for that type of person, but then I never would have pegged you for the type of person who might dismiss the choice of gift I gave you – that rare copy of No One Can See the Crows at Night – in such a callous fashion. I mean, I get that a relationship is about compromise – I just told you I understand that – so I have to accept your character flaws if we're ever going to be together, but I can't pretend you didn't insult me a little the day I gave you that gift. There are only about a hundred copies left in the entire world, and now you have one of them. Did you know that? So, when you reacted like you did, barely even remarking on my gift, I'll be totally honest: you hurt me, Derryn.

You hurt me greatly.

And, in turn, for the first time, I really wanted to hurt you.

Day Five

45

My watch beeped gently.

It was 5 a.m.

Beyond the walls of the interview room, I could hear traffic out on the main road, the intermittent drone of engines as lorries rolled by, and the occasional rogue firework as the New Year celebrations bled into the first morning of January.

In front of me were three plastic coffee cups, all of which I'd emptied, and an untouched cheese and ham sandwich one of the officers had bought from a petrol station down the road. He said it was the best he could do because the canteen was closed and nowhere was open this early on New Year's Day.

It didn't matter. I wasn't hungry.

I looked down at what I was wearing now: a pair of grey tracksuit trousers and a hooded top that didn't belong to me. My clothes, the ones I'd worn yesterday, the ones I'd been wearing when I found Gavin Roddat's body, were in evidence bags. As soon as I'd arrived at Kentish Town station, I'd agreed to be fingerprinted, to let the police take nail scrapings; I'd answered an hour's worth of questions about what I had been doing at the house, why, and what I'd discovered. I'd even had to justify my decision to call Field directly, as if my choice to phone her and tell her about Roddat, and not to call 999 instead, had in some way been questionable. I assumed that would get straightened out once she arrived at the station, because there was no way she and Kent weren't coming. Roddat was the prime suspect in their potential kidnapping.

At five thirty, the door finally opened and three officers filed in: Field, Kent, and a Scottish DI in his fifties called Carmichael, who'd spoken to me already. He had thinning blond hair, a goatee, and was built like a truck. His bulk seemed to be made up from fat more than muscle, his shirt struggling to house his belly, but I still wouldn't have fancied my chances in a straight fight. In the brief conversation I'd had with him on arriving, he'd been the one cop who appeared willing to take me at my word.

As Carmichael sat down, Field pulled out an adjacent chair and Kent went to the corner of the room where a third seat was propped against the wall.

'Hello again, Mr Raker,' Field said. I greeted her and then glanced at Kent. He had his notebook out, his legs crossed, his eyes fixed on me. It was clear he thought that this was some elaborate attempt by me to play them, or to alter the focus of the case. Or maybe he just didn't like the turn that everything had taken.

I didn't disagree with him.

Gavin Roddat had come completely out of left field. He worked for the estate agency that looked after the flat at Chalk Farm, but until he appeared on CCTV the night the woman was kidnapped, he'd been so far off my radar he'd barely registered as a blip. Now he was on a mortuary slab, a suicide whose last moments were spent watching an old, stolen home movie of Derryn and me. Nothing about that made sense.

Carmichael started the tape, introduced everyone, made it clear that I wasn't under arrest – although I could feel a *yet* hanging there, unspoken – and, because of that, I'd waived the right to a solicitor for the time being. After we were done, he asked me to go over my account of finding Roddat again – how I ended up at his cousin's place and why, and a step-by-step version of how I entered the property. I repeated the same things I'd said earlier, not just because they were easy to remember and were the truth, but because it was basically a test: they were seeing if my story had holes in it.

After I was done, there was a long silence.

This was another test, one I'd seen repeated many times; one I'd used myself on occasions. Long silences tended to make people uncomfortable, and when they were uncomfortable, they felt the need to fill gaps, to talk, to answer questions that hadn't been asked, and that was when they made mistakes. It was basically a fishing exercise on Carmichael's part, an attempt to pounce on any contradictions or errors.

So I just stared across the table at him.

Eventually, I saw a flicker of a smile on Field's face, her eyes on what she'd written: she could see I'd figured out Carmichael's tactics, and then so too did Carmichael himself. He came forward at the table and said, 'DS Field and DC Kent were telling me about the woman claiming to be your wife.' He was softly spoken, his voice just a notch above a whisper. I wasn't sure if it was actually the way he talked, or another, subtle ploy. 'Have you found out her identity yet?'

'No.'

'Nothing?'

'Nothing.' I glanced at Field. 'Why, have you?'

She shook her head. I couldn't see any obvious signs that she was lying, nothing in her eyes or her face, although the truth was, I didn't know her, so it was hard to be sure. I returned my attention to Carmichael, then to Kent. Carmichael was staring at me, unmoved; Kent was busy writing.

'Any idea where we might find her?' Carmichael said.

'You don't think I'd tell you if I knew?'

No one responded.

'No,' I sighed. 'I don't know where she is.'

'What do you think "I'm sorry" means?'

He was referring to Roddat's suicide note.

251

'I hope it means he was repentant.'

'Repentant?'

'Before he killed himself.'

'What should he be repentant for?'

'I'm sure you can guess.'

I'd already admitted to him that I'd seen the footage of Roddat and the woman at the flat in Chalk Farm, although I'd stopped short of revealing how exactly I'd got hold of the footage. Carmichael had tried to press me for details, but if I told him, I sold Ewan Tasker down the river – and there was no way I would ever do that.

'Mr Raker?' Carmichael prompted.

'Like I said, you've seen the CCTV footage of him and the woman.'

'You think he's sorry about that?'

'I *hope* it's that.'

'As opposed to what?'

'As opposed to him being sorry for killing her.'

A hush settled across the room.

I'm sorry could easily have meant that she was dead; they knew that already, they just wanted me to say it. And maybe she *was* dead. I really, desperately hoped not, but I had no real idea what Roddat was capable of or how far he was prepared to go. But what I knew, and what the cops didn't, was that she was alive for a time *after* being taken from the flat – because she'd been in my house. I didn't understand, and couldn't see, the link between a psychiatrist and an estate agent – McMillan was a respected doctor, a father, a pillar of the community; Roddat was an estate agent who liked to shag around – but it was clear that they were working together.

Whatever their arrangement was, they must have brought her to me, presumably because they knew I wouldn't be able to admit as much to the police without looking complicit in her disappearance; and in doing so – in refusing to tell the police about those hours in my home – my account of what I'd been doing during the time I'd blacked out looked even flakier than ever. It was a set-up and, in large part, it had worked: it helped play into the idea that I was either sick or a liar. So, if their plan had worked, why did Roddat kill himself and where the hell was McMillan? And there was another thought creeping into my head too, growing like a weed: was I putting the woman at risk by not telling the police what I knew?

'So you think this woman's dead?' Carmichael asked.

'I don't know anything about Gavin Roddat,' I said. 'I'd never heard of him until a couple of days ago, had never even met him in the flesh, and then all of a sudden he's there on film with the woman, he's trying to set me up, he's breaking into my house and stealing videos of my wife and me. Is it possible he's killed her? I don't know – because I don't have the first idea who he is or what he was up to.'

'And you think he's working with Erik McMillan?'

'That would be my best guess.'

'But McMillan has mysteriously disappeared too.'

I could read between the lines: despite everything, they weren't ready to abandon their suspicions about me. I still had over thirty hours I couldn't account for and McMillan had vanished within that time frame. Somewhere in the blackness was the truth about him, I felt sure of that; about Roddat too, what connected them, and about who the woman was and what happened to her after she'd left my house – but as long as I couldn't extract it, I had to accept the police's mistrust. I'd never admit it to them, not on tape, but there was a part of me that still doubted my own judgement. I'd lost a day and a half and the only thing left among the wreckage was my time alone with the woman. A woman that no one could find now.

I couldn't have hurt her. Could I?

'Okay, Mr Raker, thank you.' I tuned back in as Carmichael reached across Field, switched off the tape and started to gather up his things. 'I appreciate your honesty.'

Thrown, I looked between them.

'That's it?'

'Yes, you're free to go.'

'I've been waiting here half the night, and you wrap things up in ten minutes?' I looked between them again, trying to read their faces. Field wasn't looking at me; Kent had a half-smile on his face, as if enjoying my confusion; and Carmichael barely seemed to be registering anything I was saying. That was when I realized I'd been wrong about him: I'd expected a fair crack of the whip, had maybe even held out some hope that he'd be open to an exchange of information – some of what I knew for some of what he and his team had gathered from the suicide. Instead, he was shutting me down. I looked to Field, her head still low, then back to Carmichael: 'Seriously? That's all?'

'For now, yes.'

'You made me wait around all night for that?'

'You were free to go at any time.'

I smiled, but there was no humour in it. Technically, he was right: they'd never placed me under arrest and had never read me my rights. But this had been more than just a voluntary attendance. I'd found the body. I'd called it in. Roddat had, for whatever reason, tried to ruin my life. Those were the reasons I'd spent nine hours here, with only my phone and machine coffee for company, and all four of us knew it.

'What aren't you telling me?' I said to Carmichael.

'What are you talking about?'

'I want to know what you're keeping back.'

'Don't be paranoid, Mr Raker,' Carmichael said, buzzing the door open, and looking back at me. Field and Kent got to their feet, neither of them making eye contact, and moved past him, into the corridor. 'This is an active police investigation,' Carmichael continued, 'not some question and answer session at the town hall, so whatever it is you think we're keeping back, and whatever you want answers to, it's going to have to wait. If you want my advice, Mr Raker, I'd go home. We'll call you if we need you – but I think it's highly unlikely.'

I went to reply, but he was already gone.

46

I left the station exactly the same way I'd arrived: in the dark. The city was quiet, there was rain in the air, and I was no closer to understanding why Gavin Roddat had killed himself, why he'd broken into my home, or why he'd stolen the home movies from me. Had he taken Derryn's death certificate? Was he the one who gave her the book? Was he the face I thought I saw out on the path behind my house and the one who drew a heart on my bedroom window? And where was the woman in all of this?

Could she really be dead?

It didn't help that I was angry now too. I'd sat there for nine hours waiting for answers, and I'd come away with nothing. What I couldn't decide was if Carmichael was laying down the prelude to some carefully constructed strategy, or if this had simply been a joke at my expense, a stunt, a way to belittle and frustrate me, and keep me away from – and uninformed about – about the investigation.

It started to rain properly as I approached the Tube, a sudden eruption from the black sky, but I was so deep in thought, I barely registered it. I barely registered the vibration of my phone in my pocket either, the chirp of a text message pinging through, not until I was down on the platform and it chirped a second time. I got out my mobile and checked the screen.

I know what the police aren't telling you.
Salmon Bridge railway arches. 15 minutes.

The number was listed as PRIVATE.

I looked around me, automatically, instinctively, as if the message had been a whisper from somewhere close by. There was a group of teenagers further down the platform, some of them clearly still drunk from the night before, but no one else.

I reread the message. *I know what the police aren't telling you.* A warning went off at the back of my skull as I thought of finding Gavin Roddat's body at the house; of the woman being manoeuvred away from the flat; of Erik McMillan. All the questions I had, all the frustrations of the last nine hours — and, suddenly, a text lands out of the blue.

It was a trap. It had to be.

I headed back up to street level, going to the maps on my phone. I had no idea where Salmon Bridge was, but it didn't take me long to find it: it crossed the line out of Kentish Town train station about half a mile away. The arches were built under it on a road that ran adjacent to the tracks.

I had ten minutes to get there — *if* I was going. Taking in the street, I watched as the rain got heavier, crackling against the pavements, the clouds so dark it was like the middle of the night. I tried to think straight, tried to imagine where this might end up, who I was meeting and why they'd try to get me alone. The risks didn't require imagination. There were countless reasons not to go because there were always countless reasons not to walk into a meeting totally blind. But what would happen if I *didn't* go?

Maybe nothing.

Maybe everything.

I took off, heading east, as light finally began to break in the distance. Soon, the railway lines emerged to my left and then I arrived at the bridge itself. It rose slightly as it straddled the line, and on the other side some steps led down to the road that the arches were on. From my position at the top, I couldn't see much more than the first few, fenced off and filled with shadows. The rain was coming down so hard now, it made it difficult to see even that much.

I took the stairs down.

There were ten arches in total: a couple had been turned into businesses; the rest had been fenced off to prevent them being used as shelters and drug dens. The fences had been breached or broken in two of them: one was closest to me; the other was much further along. I used the torch on my phone to illuminate the interior of the one opposite: it had been used as a dump, the ground awash in old machinery, tyres, bottles, cans and food. The whole thing smelt of urine.

No one was waiting for me there.

I looked along the other arches, formed like a row of open mouths, all of them full of nothing but the darkness of early morning. But then, inside the seventh one, I saw something. It took me a moment to realize what: cigarette smoke. It drifted from the shadows before being instantly doused by the rain.

My heart started beating a little faster.

Slower this time, I headed in the direction of the archway, angling my head in an effort to see who was waiting. There wasn't enough natural light down here, though, no street lamps nearby, and the rain was falling too thickly.

But then I started to see more clearly.

Twenty feet short of the archway, I spotted a hand in the dark – a cigarette pinched between two fingers – and the edges of a figure. The figure took another long drag on the cigarette and then flicked it out into the street.

'You're late,' a voice said from the darkness.

#0734

No. No, wait. No, I'm sorry. I'm sorry. I didn't mean those things.

I don't want to hurt you, Derryn.

I should never have said that.

If you were ever at home, we could have straightened this out a long time ago, I wouldn't have become so frustrated and there wouldn't have been any grey areas. I mean, I would have been honest with you. I would have said to you, 'It's been eating me up, Derryn, the way you didn't seem to appreciate the gift I gave you; the way you reacted when I told you I loved The Man with the Wolf's Head, that it was my favourite Eva Gainridge book, not No One Can See the Crows at Night.' It felt like you believed my choice was conventional and predictable – less worthy than yours – and that hurt me.

That's why I ended up saying those stupid things.

If I could just see you again, I'm sure I would put your mind at rest very quickly. I really believe that. I've been over it again and again in my head. I'd tell you, 'It's okay, I'm not angry with you any more, I just want you to apologize for the way you treated me.' And, after that, you'd realize what a bitch you've been and you'd say sorry to me. 'I'm sorry,' you'd say, 'I'm sorry,' and I'd tell you, 'It's fine, it's all forgotten. You're forgiven, Derryn.'

And then you'd invite me in, and we'd maybe have coffee together, and I'd make you smile and laugh, and then – over time – we would start to grow closer; you'd confide in me, and me in you, and we'd go to dinner – just like I've always wanted – and talk about books and art and the places in the world we'd always wanted to see. And then, eventually, at a time when we felt completely comfortable with one another, we'd make love, and it would be wonderful, and it would really mean something,

259

and afterwards we'd lie beside one another, beneath crisp white sheets, and you'd feel so at ease with me, so close to me, that you'd tell me a secret, something you've never told anyone else, ever – and I'd tell you one in return. And it would be the one about why I love The Man with the Wolf's Head so much more than any of Eva Gainridge's other novels. More than any book I've ever read. I would tell you what I've never admitted to anyone else in my entire life, Derryn, and it's this: I honestly, genuinely believe that book was written for me.

I know how that comes across. I know you probably think I sound crazy at this point, but it's true.

See, the main character, Oliver, he's like me: he looks like me, he's about the same age as I am, he thinks like I do and says the same sort of things; he had his heart broken by the callous actions of a woman, a slut, a whore, and he meekly accepted what Maisie did to him, just like I did with Nora. I let the woman I loved and the man that she was screwing get away with it, and so did Oliver. And afterwards, it played on my mind constantly, just the same as it did with Oliver in the book, and neither of us could let it go. We were the same. It ate away at us, him and I; it burned us, it made us so angry, all the time, with everything. And although, subsequently, we both met other people – he met Roberta, you'll remember; and I met you – that anger, it never really goes away, it just gets buried under a thin covering of earth. And, because of that, sometimes it resurfaces, and I become like my father. And sometimes it comes back even worse than that. Sometimes it just hits me so suddenly and violently that I can't control the frustration and the anger, which is exactly what happened to Oliver in the book.

I mean, you know how the next bit goes.

You might not know my story yet – not fully – but you know Oliver's. You've read the novel. After she cheated on him, you know what he did to Maisie.

He punished her, and he silenced her.

Because, in the end, that's all a liar deserves.

47

Field looked out at me from the darkness of the railway arch.

'*You* sent me the message?' I was completely thrown. 'What the hell's going on?'

She didn't respond. Instead, she turned and headed into the black of the tunnel. I followed her, reluctantly at first, drizzle trailing us as we moved through the shadows. Beneath my feet I listened to the crunch of broken glass, I brushed the edges of mattresses with the toes of my boots, and smelt old water and older sweat. There was no one else here, I could tell that much, but there had been recently. They'd been sleeping rough, their clothes still strewn everywhere, empty wine bottles on the ground.

We stopped.

Field turned to face me. It was harder to see her than it had been at the edge of the arch, but there was enough light for us not to be in total blackness. She was wearing a dark, knee-length raincoat and she'd put her hair back, but that was the only change I could see from the interview room.

'Did you speak to anyone about meeting me here?' she said.

'How could I do that when I didn't even know it was you that I was meeting?' I looked both ways and then back at Field: 'Why did you send me that text?'

'I've got thirty minutes before I have to be back,' she said, 'so do me a favour and don't interrupt unless you have to. Can I trust you to keep this between us?'

'I don't even know what "this" is.'

'Yes or no? Can I trust you?'

'Yes,' I said, and watched her, wondering if I could do the same with her.

'If you sell me down the river, I'll burn your life to the ground.' She stared hard at me, her eyes dark, slightly narrowed, perhaps looking for the hint of a man who might betray her. But then she must have seen enough, because she said, 'I'm going to tell you some things. And part of the agreement you automatically make with me when I do that is that you never, ever call or contact me about anything. Never. When I call you next, for whatever reason this investigation determines we need to talk, you're going to pretend we never spoke. Because – as far as the Met knows – we never did. Do you understand me, Raker?'

'Yes.'

'Because I promise you I will –'

'I get it, Field,' I said.

She was quiet for a moment, her eyes still fixed on mine, and then, her voice soft, so slight it was like an echo from the rainstorm, she said, 'Carmichael's a DI, so he's a ranking officer, and everything big in this case has happened on his patch, not ours. The flat that woman was taken from is half a mile down the road from here; Roddat's body turned up in a house in Camden . . .' She faded out, then fumbled around in her pocket and removed her cigarettes. 'Carmichael has a dead body and what looks like a kidnapping – or, who knows, maybe even a murder now; we can't find the woman anywhere – and Kent and I have her disappearance, McMillan's vanishing act, and you. So, for the time being, it's Carmichael's show. He's the tip of the spear now and he can play it exactly how he likes. And how he likes it played is you out of the loop, because he's heard all about you from his drinking partners at the Met, he doesn't trust you, and he thinks you're lying through your teeth.'

'About what?'

'About everything.'

'And you don't?'

She thumbed a cigarette out of its carton, pinched it between her front teeth and used a Zippo to light it. Her eyes didn't leave mine as she inhaled, blowing the smoke off to her left, where it vanished instantly. 'I'm not sure about you, Raker,' she said. 'That's the truth. I've read about you too. Some of the shit you've pulled, it doesn't sit well with me. But there are things in this case that are sitting even less well with me.'

'Like what?'

She watched me. 'You said this Roddat guy never appeared on your radar before last night?'

'No.'

'Never?'

'I chatted to him once on the phone a few days ago about the flat, but the call lasted less than a minute.'

'That's it?'

'That's it,' I insisted.

She nodded. 'So, this guy barely registers as a blip, but it appears that he's obsessed with you and your wife. I mean, in a search of his house last night, Carmichael's team found fourteen home videos he must have stolen from you and digitally transferred, all saved on a hard drive – that's about twenty-one hours of film. They found editing software on a second laptop that he used to capture very precise screenshots of you both: he had literally *hundreds* of printouts of you and your wife in a locked container under his bed, and *thousands* of shots saved to his laptop. Every angle you can possibly imagine. It was like he sat in front of those videos screenshotting the bloody things frame by frame.'

I couldn't imagine why Field was telling me all of this, but I had even less idea why Roddat would go to those lengths. Why would he steal those movies from me? Why would he sit in front of them and capture them all? Why was he so infatuated with Derryn and me? Immediately, an idea started to form. *Was this the fallout from an old case? Had I crossed paths with Roddat before?* While it wasn't impossible, it seemed unlikely: I'd barely started working with missing people by the time Derryn died. I'd closed five, maybe six, cases by then, and none of them had been like this. They hadn't been like the major ones mentioned in the *FeedMe* article either.

This wasn't to do with an old missing persons case.

The alternative was that it had something to do with my time as a journalist – a story I'd written, a piece that had exposed people, the unravelling of corruption, greed, crime. But, again, I just couldn't see the connection, couldn't imagine which of those stories might have had this type of ripple effect.

'They found the death certificate.'

I looked at her. 'What?'

'Derryn's death certificate,' Field repeated.

'Roddat had it?'

'It was in his house.'

I let out a breath, as if I'd been holding it in for days, and the relief flooded through me. *I'm not going mad.* I turned away from Field, the emotion forming a lump in my throat, my vision smearing. *The death certificate hadn't just existed in my head. I'm not going mad. He stole it from me.* That was why it hadn't been in the loft. Did that mean the face in the alley had been real? The heart on the window? Those hours alone with the woman in my house? If one was real, all of them had to be real. And if that was true, I wasn't losing it. I wasn't sick.

I was being played.

When I returned my gaze to her, Field was staring at me. It could just have been the way the shadows lay across her, but it looked as if there was an apologetic slant to her face now. She understood why I'd tried to fudge the question of the death certificate: because I'd gone up into the loft and it hadn't been there. It had been taken.

'So is this why you've had a change of heart?' I asked her. 'You realize now I'm not some fantasist?'

'They found pictures of the woman,' she said, by way of reply.

With her spare hand, she reached into her jacket pocket, unlocked her phone and went to her photographs. In the lack of light, I could see everything on the screen: she'd taken shots of some of the evidence recovered at the scene of Roddat's suicide, all of it bagged and marked. When she got to the picture she wanted, she turned it around and held it up for me to see. Another evidence bag, this time with an actual, physical photograph inside it. It was a close-up of the woman's face.

'He had hundreds of these,' she said.

'Just photos of her face?'

Field shook her head. 'Her face, her body – every inch of her, basically. They're all taken against a blank wall, but they're all of the woman. Different clothes, front on, profile, chin up, chin down, hair up, hair down. But she's fully clothed in every single one of them. These aren't sexual. It's like some kind of academic study.'

I thought of the article on *FeedMe*.

'He was the source,' I said.

'What?'

I looked at her. 'Now we know who "Crime and Punishment" must have got the woman's photograph from. Roddat was the source for their story. He must have scanned in one of these pictures and emailed it anonymously. Have you tried tracing the origins of the email that *FeedMe* received? That way, we can confirm it's him.'

Field didn't say anything.

'Field? Are you listening to me?'

'No.'

'No? No what?'

'We haven't tried tracing the origins of the email.'

I frowned. 'Why not?'

'Because Roddat wasn't their source,' she said quietly. 'I was.'

48

'You *what*?'

'Before you blow your top,' she said, her voice hard, unrepentant, 'hear me out. I couldn't find any trace of this woman anyw—'

'*You* took that picture of her they published?'

'Just give me a chance to explain.'

'Explain *what*? That you sold me down the river?'

She held up a hand, waited. 'Are you going to give me a chance to speak?' When I didn't respond, she said, 'I needed to try and ID this woman. I couldn't find any trace of her anywhere — I *still* can't find any trace of her anywhere. And now it's even *worse* than that because we can't actually find her. On that first day, the only thing I cared about was trying to work out if this woman was actually your wife.'

'I told you she wasn't.'

'I'd never even met you before. Did you really expect me to sit there and take your word for it?'

'So you let it play out in the *media*?' I stepped back, could hardly even look at her. Deep down, I knew I was a hypocrite: in the past, I'd done things I shouldn't have in order to progress cases. But, right now, I didn't feel like playing fair — not when it was about my wife, the woman I'd loved, and the way her death had scythed me in two; not when it was about her memory being perverted, bent out of shape, played with like some toy. 'Have you got any idea what you've done?' I said to Field, my voice throbbing with anger. 'Thanks to you, half the country thinks I'm a liar.'

'I thought it would help.'

'Help who? *Me?* I've got tabloid journalists crawling all over me now. They're digging into everything. Even my own *daughter* thinks I'm lying.'

'I wanted to ID her as quickly as possible,' Field said, 'not wait around for all the boxes to be ticked at Charing Cross. The minute Kent phoned me at home and told me about the call she made, the way she sounded so distressed, the fact that she wasn't even *at* the flat when he finally got there – I knew we had to move fast. That same night. If I got a story posted to *FeedMe* the next morning, maybe her family would see her picture and call us, or a neighbour would recognize her. But no one came forward. No one seems to know who she is. That bothers me as much as anything else. Does it mean her family haven't seen the article, or does it mean she doesn't *have* any family?'

'You asking my opinion now?'

'You would have done the same,' she said, her tone barely changing at all. She really didn't think it was a mistake.

I just looked at her.

'Do you want me to say sorry?' she said, but if she did it would only be a word, empty of any meaning. 'Is that what you want, Raker?'

'That piece was a hatchet job.'

'I didn't have any control over what they wrote.'

'You knew what they would say about me.'

She nodded, which was about as close to an apology as I would get.

I took a breath, looking out at the rain. I was angry at her, at everything her actions had set in motion – but, ultimately, what did it matter now? There were bigger things to worry about, starting with where the woman was.

'Why would he call you and Kent?' I said.

She leaned in. 'What?'

'I think it was Roddat who forced the woman to phone

into Charing Cross the night she went to the flat. He saw me tailing her. But why? Why would he get her to tell you that I followed her?'

'To shift the spotlight away from himself?' She shrugged. 'Maybe he needed to create some breathing room for himself. Maybe he just needed us to spend some time looking at you while *he* took the woman to wherever they went next.'

'So he did it in order to buy himself some time?'

I wasn't convinced, and I got the feeling she wasn't either.

'Whatever his reasons,' she said, 'the evidence is there. The woman went to the flat in Chalk Farm where Roddat was waiting for her. We've got that on film. He leaves with her. We've got that on film too. She called the station. That's on record.'

'So why would he kill himself? Why would he go to all that trouble, successfully buy himself some time, and then kill himself? He'd shifted the attention on to me. He'd put you and Kent on alert. It had got to the point where you were in my house taking my DNA; I looked guilty as hell when you asked to see the death certificate, we both knew that, and that story on *FeedMe* was busy colouring everyone's opinion of me.' I paused, looked at her, and then thought of McMillan. 'I've got a whole chunk of time I can't account for, and a respected doctor telling the world I'm sick, either because he was working with Roddat, or because Roddat had something over McMillan and was manipulating him. Whatever the reason, Roddat was winning. The trap had gone off. So why would he kill himself?'

'Maybe he knew we would find out the truth eventually.'

'Maybe. But something isn't right.'

From her face, she seemed to agree.

In the brief lull, I thought of the video of Roddat taking the woman from Chalk Farm. 'Have you got any witnesses?'

'To what?'

'To anything. Did anyone see anything?'

'The suicide, no. We spoke to the neighbours at his cousin's place and no one saw or heard anything. There's no CCTV in the street either. As for the night the woman was kidnapped: we've managed to identify most of the people who appeared on film before and after Roddat entered the stairwell, and again when he came back down with her, and we've spoken to all of them but one so far. They're all dead ends.' She put her cigarette between her lips and drew in the smoke. 'It would help if we could find McMillan.'

As she said that, I realized something.

'I forgot to follow up on McMillan's relationship history,' I admitted. 'If he's got a daughter, he must have been married, or engaged, or at least attached.'

'Married. His wife died ten years ago.'

'Of what?'

'She cut her wrists in the bath.'

'Another suicide?'

'Don't get too excited,' she said. 'The coroner said it was open and shut. She'd suffered from depression for most of her adult life.'

'What was her name?'

'Kelly.'

I got out a pen and wrote it on the back of my hand. I didn't even bother to hide what I was doing now.

'So what tipped Kelly over the edge?'

'Unclear,' Field said. 'Maybe we can ask McMillan when we find him.'

'He's definitely not with his daughter?'

'He's not in Scotland, Raker, I told you that yesterday.'

I looked at her. Was there something else she wasn't telling me?

'Do you think the woman's dead?' she asked.

I studied her, trying to work out if that was what had gone

unspoken a moment ago. 'I think "I'm sorry" could mean any number of things,' I said.

'You mean it's possible Roddat killed her?'

'Or McMillan did. Or Roddat killed him too.'

Was McMillan a cold-blooded killer, though? Was Roddat?

'Something feels wrong,' I said again. I looked at her for a moment and thought about the death certificate, about Roddat taking it. Should I tell her what else I'd found in the loft?

'I can see your brain going,' she said, a half-smile on her face.

I nodded, hesitated for a moment more, and then could see more reasons to tell her than not: 'When I went up into the loft to try and find the death certificate, I also found a book. I think there's a chance that Roddat might have given it to Derryn before she died.'

I watched Field's expression change.

'Are you serious?' she asked.

'I'm serious about the book; whether Roddat gave it to her or not, I'm not so sure about. It was *No One Can See the Crows at Night* by Eva Gainridge. Have you read that?'

'Gainridge? She wrote that *Wolf's Head* book.'

'Yeah, that's her most famous one, but *Crows* came before that. It's her debut. It's about a woman whose husband returns home from the Second World War, and she starts to think that it's not her husband at all, but an impostor.'

She instantly understood the connection.

'Derryn loved Gainridge,' I said. 'She was her favourite writer.'

'So what makes you think Roddat gave her the book? Or that he knew her before she died?'

'I don't know. But someone gave it to her.'

Thank you for our special time together.

'You've been through McMillan's phone records, right?'

'Yes,' she said.

'You saw the call he got from a payphone in Plumstead?'

'Yes. You clearly have as well.'

'The book came from a community library about a minute's walk away.'

'What?'

'That's not a coincidence. It can't be.'

'I didn't know Roddat had a connection to that area.'

'That's just the thing,' I said. 'He doesn't, not as far as I can tell. He doesn't have any connection at all to south-east London. He lived in north London, same as his cousin, and his family's in Manchester.'

'That doesn't mean he couldn't have been there.'

'Why would he go to a library ten miles from his house?'

'Maybe he knows someone there. Maybe he has friends down that way. Maybe he just likes their selection of books. Why do any of us do anything? We've got half his house in evidence bags now, so we'll probably know the answer before long.'

'What if Roddat never made that call to McMillan?'

'So someone else is involved now?'

'You think it's so unlikely?'

She didn't reply for a moment, looking out of the archway, towards the street. She checked her watch. 'What if it isn't even relevant?' she asked.

'The phone call? It's got to be.'

'Because the phone box is so close to the library?'

'Yes, but not just that: who calls from payphones these days?'

'A lot of people do.'

'All right,' I said, 'a better question is, *why* do people call from payphones? I can only think of two reasons: one, they don't have a mobile and they desperately need to use a phone; two, and more relevantly, the call can't be traced back to them.'

Again, she didn't reply.

'Can I have a look at the photos of the woman?'

Field checked her surroundings again and then handed me her phone, letting me scroll back and forth through the pictures. Roddat had positioned her in various ways – facing him; in profile; some of the photos taken from above and others from below – and many were only fractionally different from the previous one, so it was almost impossible to tell them apart. It was like he was trying to document every angle, every curve, every natural line, every tiny flaw. The more I looked at her, the more I saw what Kennedy had been talking about when we'd been discussing the department at St Thomas's that studied so-called 'twin strangers'. He'd said the doctors there had computers that in seconds could separate physical characteristics that looked identical – or pretty close – to the human eye, and prove they weren't identical at all. From the front, the woman did have a striking similarity to Derryn. Not anywhere close to exact, but close enough to fool someone who didn't know Derryn like I did. When she was side on, though, the differences were much clearer. Her mouth protruded further than I remembered Derryn's doing, and her chin was less pronounced. She wasn't a natural blonde either, I realized now. From a top-down shot that Roddat had taken, I could see the faintest hint of roots emerging along her parting. So why would she go to such lengths to pretend she was my wife?

'You've definitely never met Roddat before now?' she asked.

I shook my head as I handed her back her phone. 'No. Never.'

'You're certain?'

'I think I'd remember if I had.'

'But you reckon Derryn might have known him?'

'Like I said, someone gave her the book.'

I pictured him: not the version of him I'd found at the end, with a noose coiled around his neck, or even the man I saw on the CCTV video at Chalk Farm, but the person in the photograph on the Hammond's site. *Could* he have known Derryn?

'How would he have met her?' Field asked, echoing my own thoughts.

I tried to think, tried to seek any sort of answer, but then I turned to Field and saw something in her face that stopped me dead. A second question lay unspoken on her lips and I knew exactly what it was. Slowly, a terrible idea began to re-form in the blackness of my thoughts, one I'd already faced down – and dismissed – after finding the book.

'No,' I said to Field.

'I have to ask it.'

'The answer's no.'

Thank you for our special time together.

'Raker, did Derryn ever cheat on you?'

49

'Derryn never cheated on me.'

'Do you know that for sure?'

'Are you listening to me? I said it never happened.'

'Would you know if she had?'

'I said *no*.'

My words were hard and laced with anger. I didn't blame her for asking the question, but even thinking it made me feel sick. I swallowed it down, took a breath, and calmly, more in control, said, 'She and Roddat could have met, yes. I mean, that's possible. I don't know where or when or how, but it's possible. There's no way in hell she ever had an affair, though. It never happened. I'll never believe that.'

Field nodded, but her expression still held the idea.

'I mean it.'

'Okay,' she said.

'You don't understand,' I replied, and could feel rain drift into us, blown our way by the wind. 'You don't understand what we had. No one does. What we had, it was . . .' I stopped, the words disintegrating, the emotion like a tremor in my throat. I didn't need to defend fourteen years of marriage to Field. I didn't need to defend the woman I loved, mourned and missed.

All I had to do was know.

And I *knew*.

Field watched me for a moment longer, taking another drag on her cigarette, then said, 'So we don't know why Roddat became so obsessed with your wife, we don't know why this woman is pretending to *be* Derryn and how she knows so much about you both, and we don't even know where she is – or where McMillan is either.'

I looked at her. 'Are you accusing me of something?'

'I'm just laying out our predicament.'

'"*Our* predicament"?' I studied her in the dark of the tunnel, half-formed in the shadows. I'd let most of my anger go, but not all of it, and as I continued, it clung to the edge of my voice: 'What is this, Field? Are we working together – is that it?'

'No,' she said. 'We're not working together.'

'So why are you doing this?'

'I told you, some things don't sit right with me.'

'Some things don't sit right with you? Come on. You decide to put your entire career on the line to tell me about Roddat because something *bugs* you?'

'I can walk away, if you'd prefer.'

'I just want to know why you're here.'

'What does it matter?'

'You know why it matters.'

'Are you scared that this is some sort of trap?'

'You think that's so unreasonable?'

She took a last drag on her cigarette and then dropped it to the ground. It flashed orange briefly, hot ash scattering, but then everything died and the gloom returned.

'You can work the angles I can't,' she said eventually.

I smirked. 'So you want me to do your job?'

'You've been doing that from the minute that woman turned up at the station, Raker, so don't take the moral high ground with me, okay? Carmichael's barking up the wrong tree with this. I don't like the way he works, I don't like the way he runs his teams or his investigations, and I don't like the way he sees this case as a vessel to do his mates in the Met a favour – the ones you've managed to piss off at various points in the last six or seven years. We're wasting time trying to connect you to this, trying to slap some crime on you based on how much of a pain in the arse you are, when we *should* be try-ing to figure out where the bloody hell Roddat magicked himself from and how this woman has vanished into thin air.'

I calmed myself and tried to think.

'It's definitely a suicide?' I asked.

'As opposed to what? A *murder*?' She shook her head. 'No, you can forget that. Roddat had no defensive wounds, there was nothing to indicate a struggle. His injuries and bruising were consistent with suicide by hanging. In all my years work-ing murders, I've never seen someone fake a hanging. It's too easy to balls it up: you've got to take into consideration body weight, the knot, the strength of the rope, the suspension of it. You've got to think about how much the body is going to jerk after the platform is gone. Whatever else, he definitely hanged himself.'

Her attention shifted to the road, then to me: 'There's something else you should know. After McMillan didn't turn up for his flight yesterday, we got a warrant and went to the hospital to look around his office.'

I eyed her. 'Did you find something?'

'His file on you is a page long.'

I didn't know what to say to that; all I could feel was relief.

'The notes he made on a guy he treated for a year and a half, supposedly the victim of a quite rare and extremely ser-ious condition, extend to a single page. So that doesn't make sense. And then, this morning, we got the results back from the blood test Dr Carson did on you at your house.' She paused. 'They found benzodiazepines.'

Tranquillizers.

I felt another weight lift. 'So McMillan really *did* drug me?'

'It looks that way.'

Again, there was no apology – not in words – but her head tilted slightly and I saw enough. This was as contrite as Cath-erine Field ever got.

'McMillan drugged me. Maybe he made Roddat look like a suicide too.'

'It was a suicide, Raker, okay? It's not a set-up. The only person who set it up was Gavin Roddat when he climbed on to that chair and put the noose around his neck.' She stopped for a couple of seconds and then said, 'Look, for what it's worth, I had to ask the question about Derryn and Roddat because it was an obvious place to go. If they didn't meet that way, then they must have met somewhere else, some*how* else. He has her picture all over the place, and he marches a woman who *looks* like Derryn out of a flat, having previously taken hundreds – who knows, maybe thousands – of photos of her as well. You don't do either of those things on a whim. The question of who this woman is and why she would pretend to be Derryn, why I can't ID her, why I can't find her anywhere, and where the hell she's been hiding for the last eight years, *if* she's been hiding at all – clearly, the answers lay in the life of the *real* Derryn Raker.'

She looked at her watch again and, as she did, I felt my guts twist: I didn't want to have to go back, as much as I knew Field was right. I wasn't scared that I might find out something corrupting about Derryn, about our marriage, about who she was, because I believed – in every single part of me – that that thing didn't exist. When I told Field that Derryn had never cheated on me, it wasn't just my ego talking. It was the truth.

The reason I didn't want to go back was much simpler: it hurt. Every time I got on to my knees and scooped away more of the earth that covered her, every time I questioned everything that I knew to be true, I ruined a part of her memory. I would have given anything for it to have been her, on that first day, in the interview room at Charing Cross – but now I wanted the opposite. I just wanted to find the woman and ask her why she was doing this. How did she know so much about me? Why was she ruining my life? I just wanted Derryn – *my* Derryn – to be laid to rest.

'I've got to go,' Field said. 'Is there anything else?'

I was about to say *no*, but – as I thought again about the ways in which Derryn and Gavin Roddat may have crossed paths – an idea came to me: 'How long has Roddat lived in London?'

'About two years. He moved down in November 2015.'

I tried to align my thoughts.

'What's on your mind, Raker?'

'I was going to suggest checking his medical history.'

'For what purpose?'

'I was thinking he might have met Derryn when she was a nurse.'

Field nodded. 'He could have been a patient of hers – but the timings aren't right.' She meant Roddat hadn't moved down from Manchester until 2015; Derryn had already been dead for six years by then.

Except something was niggling at me.

'Raker?'

And now it wouldn't stop.

'Raker, are you all right?'

A patient of Derryn's.

Field said my name again, and then again, and then came closer, but this time I barely registered any of it. All I could see was a series of disconnected images, a memory, shuddering to the surface.

'*Raker.* What the hell is the matter with you?'

'Wait a second,' I said, 'wait a second.'

'What?'

I closed my eyes.

'Raker?'

I didn't answer, trying to form the memory properly.

'*Raker*, are you going to talk to me or not?'

'Give me a second. There was this one time, I . . . her and I . . .'

I trailed off. The memory was still opaque.

It had come out of nowhere, but as I held up a hand to Field, as I asked her to wait, as I tried to connect the images, everything became a little more distinct. Not lucid, but lucid enough.

'There was this guy – way back.'

'A guy? What guy?'

'This was years and years ago.'

'Who was the guy, Raker?'

'He was someone she treated.'

She paused, suddenly understanding why I'd stopped responding to her, why I'd become so distant. 'Someone Derryn treated? A patient of hers?'

'Yes.'

'You remember someone?'

'Yes. Not clearly – I only met him briefly – but . . .'

'But what?' Field pressed, taking another step closer.

'I haven't thought about him at all since it happened,' I said, looking out towards the street, trying to form his face against the grey blur of the rain. 'All I remember is, this guy, this patient of hers, there was something weird about him.'

#0762

I started waiting outside the ward for you again. You didn't come out. I watched the other nurses leave, bleary-eyed from the night shift – but not you. I looked through the glass panel on the security door, and could see staff milling around, doctors sitting slouched over reports and paperwork, and then a few patients shuffling about in the background, pale-skinned and sick, but you were nowhere to be seen. You weren't at home, you weren't at work, so where were you?

I got my answer two days later.

I'd spent whatever time I could in the hospital foyer, sitting on the benches in the corner next to the pharmacy, hoping to catch you, because you'd have to come out this way, from the ward, to get to the staff car park or to head to the Tube. But the longer I went without seeing you, the more I started to wonder: were you on a different ward in another department, leaving from an exit I didn't know about? Had you got a new job at another hospital, or somewhere else in the city?

In the end, it turned out to be none of those things.

I finally got to see the real reason you'd become so hard to find. I came to understand why that Spanish nurse had seemed so reticent to talk about you outside the ward, and why your hours were so irregular.

You were no longer just an employee at the hospital.

You were a patient.

One of the porters wheeled you into the foyer, talking to you as he did. You were smiling. Even as sick as you looked – your skin as grey as ash and as thin as tracing paper, your body small in your clothes, shrunken, rolled in on itself – you still managed a smile. As I watched you, I could barely move, my entire body glued to the seat. It was like looking at a reflection of you, a distortion, an image in a fairground mirror. Where was Derryn? Where was the woman I'd come to know? Why had you never told me you were sick? That's what happens when you have a connection with someone. You tell them important things. You share. You help each other through.

I got up, my legs unsteady, and watched as the porter carried on pushing the wheelchair across the foyer. You said something to him, which he didn't hear, and then he slowed down and leaned in to you and you said it to him again, and he erupted into laughter. A few people glanced in his direction, seeing where the noise had come from, and then their eyes came to rest on you instead, and they stared as if you were some circus freak. Out of nowhere, I felt a tremor of anger. How dare they do that. How dare they stare at you like that. One of them, a woman in her late fifties with an awful sagging face and small eyes like a pig, made a comment to a man seated beside her, and that was when I started moving. I headed towards her, my fists clenched, teeth clamped so hard together I could hear ringing in my ears.

When I got to the woman, I knelt down beside her and said, 'Excuse me,' my voice just a whisper. She turned in her seat, surprised, uncertain if I was addressing her, and then I said, 'If you ever pass comment on that woman again, I'll rip out your fucking heart.'

She sucked in a breath, shocked, appalled.

I stood, looking down at her, my eyes boring into hers, and I saw her wither and shrivel under my gaze, and then I began moving again: you'd briefly gone out of sight, as the porter wheeled you to the main entrance, but I soon found you.

Slowing down, I settled on a viewpoint about eight feet back. You'd come to a halt, side on to me, the porter adjusting the blanket that had been placed over your legs.

'You need to keep warm,' I heard him say.

'I'm fine, Clive,' you replied, your voice faint, a little crackly, a needle trying to find the grooves of an old record. 'Honestly,' you said as the porter continued to adjust the blanket. You said it so gently, so kindly, and squeezed the porter's arm. 'I don't even really need this wheelchair.'

'I know, I know,' he replied, and stopped moving the blanket, dropping to his haunches beside the wheelchair instead. He smiled at you, said

something I couldn't hear, and then looked out of the front entrance. From the way he was around you, the way you were so comfortable in each other's company, it was obvious that he knew you: not just because he'd wheeled you out here, but because you'd talked before, lots of times, during the period you'd worked here as a nurse. You and this Clive person knew each other, liked each other, had some sort of bond, even if only small.

As I recognized that, I felt a stab of jealousy.

'I can walk from here,' you said to the porter eventually, and when he replied that he would tell you off if you did – his voice half-disguised by the noise of a bus pulling in outside – you said, 'Okay, Clive, I'll stay here. But I'll be all right on my own. I'll see you again the next time I'm in, okay? You can update me on Amy.'

'I'll tell her you said hello.'

'Do,' you said. 'I hope her exams go well.'

Clive stood, gave your arm a gentle squeeze, and you smiled at him again. Despite how you looked, how you sounded, despite everything you were now, nothing could dilute that smile. It lit up the entire atrium. It was like breath to me.

The porter left, looking back at you as he passed me. I watched him go, disappearing along the corridor until it took a left turn, and then I approached you.

'Derryn?'

You turned in your wheelchair.

Up close, you looked terrible. It was hard to even reconcile the woman who'd looked after me on the ward only months ago with the woman in front of me now.

'How are you?' I asked.

A flicker of recollection this time, and then you said, 'Oh, hello.' Your voice sounded worse up close – torn, and frayed, and broken – and I could see that your hair had started to fall out. It looked like a forest after a fire had passed through, sparse, fitful lumps of hair still rooted in place, clinging on even after everything else had been destroyed.

'You're ill,' I said.

You broke into a smile. 'Yes. It seems that I am.'

It was a stupid thing to say, and I instantly regretted it, but you didn't make me feel small. Instead, you turned the wheelchair slightly, rotating it around, and then reached under the blanket that was covering your legs, looking for something.

I watched you.

Finally, you brought out a book from your lap, your hands white and very thin, the bones showing through, your fingertips covering some of the front cover.

But I knew what it was.

It was a copy of The Man with the Wolf's Head.

In that moment, I think I fell in love with you even more than before, because it was obvious that you were reading it for me. You were reading my book, for me.

'Thank you,' I said.

You frowned. 'For what?'

But I barely heard your response. I'd spent months being so angry at you for the way you seemed to suggest The Man with the Wolf's Head *was worth less than Eva Gainridge's other novels, for the grati- tude you seemed to lack when I gave you that rare copy of* No One Can See the Crows at Night, *but suddenly the embers of how you'd made me feel before – the frustration I'd had, the anger, the confusion – were gone. I felt renewed. This was a fresh start.*

I took a step closer and said, 'I thought your favourite Gainridge was No One Can See the Crows at Night?'

'Oh, it is,' you said, looking down at your copy of the book. It was the 2008 anniversary edition with the blue and silver cover. 'It's just, I haven't read this one for a while – so I thought, as I had the time, I may as well refresh my memory.'

You smiled again.

How were you still managing to smile when you looked so bad? How could I tell you how much you'd consumed me and hurt me in the time since we'd last met?

'Have you been away?' I asked.

You frowned again.

'I just haven't seen you around, is all.'

'Why, have you been back in hospital?'

'Yes,' I lied.

'More complications with the skull fracture?'

'Yes.'

'Oh, I'm sorry to hear that.'

I hated lying to you.

The frown remained, a look on your face that I couldn't quite interpret, and then it dissolved and you said, 'Yes, I've been away, down to the coast. I was trying to do something other than think about this worthless body of mine.'

'It's not worthless.'

'That's sweet. The truth is, I don't really need this wheelchair to get around, but I figure I may as well get used to it.' You forced another smile and then showed me the book again. 'Anyway, this is a way to distract me.'

When I looked into your eyes, something shimmered in them, the hint of tears, and I realized, in that moment, I truly did love you. I just wanted to wrap my arms around you and keep you safe. I wasn't like that porter. You wouldn't persuade me to leave you here, waiting for a taxi. I'd refuse to go. I was going to take you home, and undress you, and bath you, and run my fingers over your skin, even though your bones were starting to come through. It didn't matter that you'd upset me, that your home was so staid, that you'd dismissed me on that last day I'd been in hospital like I was just any other patient. I'd watched you walk away from my bed and you hadn't even looked back, hadn't even been there to say goodbye when I was discharged. I had to seek you out, had to wait for you outside the ward, in order to continue what we had. But none of that mattered any more. I'd forgiven you your mistakes. I was here for you. Me, no one else.

'Do you know why you first caught my eye?' I said.

You frowned. 'I'm sorry?'

'When you were looking after me, when I started having problems with my fracture, have you got any idea why you first caught my eye? I mean, it wasn't just because you were my nurse. You were everybody's nurse in there.' I dropped down to your level, on to my haunches, and you

284

leaned away slightly, suspicion now evident in your face. It annoyed me, but I let it go. 'Your eyes were so full of light.'

You just stared at me.

'Your smile lit up the entire room, Derryn.'

'I, uh . . .'

'It's okay. I realize this is a lot for you to take in, especially when you're like this. My timing's not great, I know that. But I so desperately want to tell you something. I want to tell you that I lov–'

'Sorry, sweetheart.'

I looked up. We both did. A man was standing in front of us, tall, handsome I suppose, dark hair, a week's beard growth. He looked tired, drained. The whites of his eyes were forked with tiny blood vessels and I couldn't decide if it was a result of exhaustion or tears. He looked at me, his expression hardening, as if he'd glimpsed an animal – a threat that might concern him.

'I thought I could pull up out front here,' he said, his eyes on me, although obviously addressing you, 'but they only let buses and taxis into this bit, so I've had to park a little further around. It's only a couple of minutes. Not too far, I promise.'

He finally glanced at you.

'Is everything okay?' he said softly.

'We were just having a conversation,' I replied, sharp, pointed.

He looked at me again, then at you, and I could see something pass between the two of you, something wordless that I couldn't understand or grasp, because he immediately came around to the back of the wheelchair and grabbed the handles.

'We're having a conversation,' I said again.

'Well, now the conversation's over.'

'You can't do that,' I replied, automatically trying to stop him, trying to grab the handles of the wheelchair, trying to push him aside. But he caught me by surprise. He planted a hand on my chest and shoved me, pushing me away so hard, I almost lost my footing. I looked around: a few people were staring at us. And then I looked at you: I expected you to defend me, to say something – but I could see the reality in your face.

You were on his side.

'Derryn?' I said.

'What's your name, pal?' the man asked.

'None of your fucking business is my name. You can't do this. You can't come in here and do this. Derryn and I are friends. I was just having a conversation wi—'

'I want to go home, David,' you said to the man.

I stared at you. 'Derryn?'

'What's your name?' he asked me again.

'What the fuck's that got to do with you?'

'It's got everything to do with me. I'm her husband.'

Husband.

A single word more powerful than any hand he could lay on me. I looked at you, then back to him. 'Husband?' The word tasted sour in my mouth. 'Husband?'

You were married.

You'd lied to me.

He began wheeling you away — almost inviting me to follow, just so he could assault me again — and, when I didn't, you looked back, over your shoulder, and I saw an expression on your face that I recognized immediately. It was a mix of hostility and fear.

Once upon a time, Nora had looked at me exactly the same way.

You remember Nora, right? I told you about her. I told you about how she broke my heart. I opened up to you that day on the ward and I told you that Nora had hurt me, had cheated on me. I told you that she was the one, before you, that I loved. Well, she would look at me in exactly the same way as you did when you left the hospital that day.

She would do it all the time.

So I've seen that look before, Derryn, the one you had. I've been betrayed like this before. I've seen that look of hostility in the faces of both women I've loved now.

But it's easy enough to get rid of hostility.

And, once you do, all you have left is fear.

Because that's all anyone has left before you kill them.

50

'Could it have been Roddat?'

I looked at Field.

'It could have been,' I said, still unable to quite picture the man, his face, his profile. 'It was a long time ago: the third time Derryn was diagnosed with cancer – so after April 2009. It could even have been May or June. She'd had a round of chemo, I remember that much, and I remember she made the decision to stop shortly after.' Once more, I tried to visualize him, but it had been nearly nine years. All I could see were fragments from the scene: how he'd been kneeling down beside her when I'd turned up; how he'd gestured at me when I started to wheel her out; some of the things he'd said; how I'd asked Derryn who he was as we made our way to the car, and how she'd told me he'd been a patient of hers once. And what else? *Think.* What else had she told me?

Field checked her watch, looked out at the road, and then, in her pocket, her phone pinged. She removed the handset and eyed the screen.

'Shit,' she said through her teeth. 'Carmichael. I really have to go.'

I nodded, but my mind was still on the grey outline of the man in the hospital, irritated at my inability to recall him clearly. I had a good memory for faces, a decent ability to store and retain information like that, but eight years was way too long. In the December previous to that, we'd moved back from the US, and as an experiment, as I followed Field out towards the street, I tried to recall the faces of the people who'd worked in the same office as me while I'd been in

LA – but I struggled to remember more than two or three of them, and they were people I'd had daily contact with. The others, the ones I interacted with less often, were just blurs, or in some cases total blanks. How, then, could I ever remember the face of a man I'd seen for two minutes in a hospital foyer getting on for a decade ago?

And yet, I remembered how I'd *felt* when I met him. I'd told Field that there was something weird about him, and I vaguely recalled having to step in front of him, or around him, and I recalled Derryn being in a wheelchair as well, even though she didn't want to be. If I'd sniffed any immediate danger, if I'd felt Derryn was under threat in any way, I would have headed it off. But I hadn't felt the need to do that. I tried to rebuild the moments that followed that incident in my head, tried to think of how Derryn had described the man, but all I could remember was her telling me it didn't matter, that he'd just become attached to her, that sometimes that happened on the wards. If I'd got the impression she was lying, that she was avoiding the truth or trying to deliberately downplay it, there's no way I would have let it go like I did. But she'd been happy to forget him.

Could it have been Roddat? Was that brief moment in the hospital that day why he was doing this to me? Why the woman was? Why the hell would they want me to believe that Derryn was alive? Or was my inability to remember or recognize Gavin Roddat because he wasn't that man at all?

'Raker?'

We'd walked almost to the end of the arch, cars passing on the street a few feet from where we were standing, and I'd barely even noticed. Field was looking up and down the road, jittery now, skittish, worried about being seen here, with me.

'I can't be certain if it was Roddat or not,' I said to her.

'So this guy in the hospital could be no one important?'

'Maybe,' I said, but now the memory had resurfaced,

something about it stayed with me, some instinctive sense that it was relevant. Derryn, for her part, had been happy to forget it. But had the man felt the same way? Did that one tiny moment have the same insignificance to him?

Or was it where all of this had begun?

'Have you located the pharmacy in Woolwich?' I asked Field.

I was trying to work out if the woman had actually gone there, and, if she had, whether the police had footage of the guy who took her. A car out on the street. The registration plate.

She shook her head, checking her watch, her phone, the road: 'There's seventeen in the area. Twelve of them have got cameras close by, five haven't. It looks like he chose the one he took her to carefully, because we haven't located the car she arrived in – make, model, who was driving. Nothing. And because she never actually went in, the people working in the pharmacy wouldn't have seen her. We chased down the council in an effort to find out the identity of the traffic warden who got into an argument with the driver, and – when we found him – he gave us a description. He says the car was light blue or grey, and either a Mondeo or a Lexus. He says the guy was medium height, medium build, dark hair, possibly a moustache or a goatee.'

'So this traffic warden didn't actually get around to issuing a ticket?'

'No.'

'But he got the car reg?'

'The last two letters. MX. The rest of the plate was covered in grime. Unfortunately, those last two letters have got us precisely nowhere.'

We looked at each other and, again, I saw the same thing in Field's face that I'd spotted earlier when we'd been talking about McMillan's daughter.

'Is there something else?'

'At this point,' she said, 'I'm sure I don't need to remind you of what I said earlier. None of this came from me. We didn't have this meeting.'

'I get it. But is there something else?'

She checked the street again.

'You asked about McMillan's daughter,' she said, her eyes still on the road, on the people passing us, on the cars. 'She really doesn't know what's happened to her father, I truly believe that. I've phoned her, I've talked to her on Skype twice, and a guy from the missing persons unit up there – a guy I used to work with for a while down here – went around to interview her for me. He says she's either the most flawless liar he's ever met, or my hunch is correct: she's not holding out.' Finally, she looked at me again, her expression almost pained. 'I've got to be honest, it was hard talking to her about McMillan, because she basically idolizes him. Her mum's dead, he's everything to her. She's up in Edinburgh doing a degree in medicine because she says she wants to follow her old man into psychiatric work. But as much as she worships him, there's no way she's hiding him; and I don't believe, for his part, that McMillan would jeopardize her safety in that way.'

'Okay,' I said, because there obviously *was* something else.

'That call that was made to McMillan on the payphone in Plumstead on the 28th of December – I don't want to know how you got hold of his phone records, or from who, but were his the only phone records you got?'

'As opposed to what?'

'Do you know what other calls were made from that payphone the same day – specifically, immediately *after* the call to McMillan?'

'No,' I said, watching her. 'Do you?'

She nodded. 'There was only one other call made from

that payphone on that day, and it was twenty seconds after the call to McMillan.'

'So it was made by the same person?'

'That would be the assumption.'

'Who was the call to?'

'Caitlin McMillan. Erik's daughter. She mentioned the call on both occasions I talked to her, and to my colleague up in Scotland too. She said someone – a male – phoned her on her mobile and said – and I quote – "Ask your father about Dartford."'

'That's it?'

'That was all he said.'

'Dartford in Kent?'

'That seems most likely.'

I tried to think if the town of Dartford had ever come up in anything I'd discovered so far, but felt certain it hadn't.

'So did Caitlin speak to her father about it?'

'Yes. She said she couldn't get hold of him on the 28th, so phoned him at home first thing on the 29th and he told her he didn't have the first idea what the call was about. He seemed concerned that she was getting strange messages.'

'Has anyone from your team been down to Dartford?'

'I sent someone down there yesterday to take a look, speak to the police there, ask around. No one's seen McMillan.'

'Anything at his place in Kew?'

She reached into her pocket, took out her notebook and began flipping through its pages. When she finally stopped, she'd got to a page with nothing on it but a five-digit number.

'We did a basic sweep,' she said. 'We didn't find anything at his house.'

I eyed her. 'But?'

She tore out the number and held up the piece of paper.

'But maybe you can.'

I looked at the number. 'What's this?'

'It's the code for his house alarm.'

For a second, I thought I'd misheard. I looked from the piece of paper to her, and said, 'What are you doing?'

'What does it look like?'

'You want me to break into McMillan's home?'

'What, you're going to pretend you've never picked a lock before?'

I smiled, but there was no humour in it. If I took the piece of paper from her, what then? Was this some kind of elaborate set-up? Would I get to Kew, get the door open and suddenly be overrun by officers lying in wait? I tried to imagine if this might be some plan dreamed up in an office, Carmichael pulling the strings. Field had already admitted that he wanted me stopped, punished for perceived slights against the Met, and the law.

'You still don't trust me?' she said, her expression somewhere between disbelief and amusement.

'How can I trust you when I don't even know you?'

'I don't know you either, Raker – except by reputation – but I've just spent the last thirty minutes destroying the integrity of an entire investigation, so, if you sell me down the river, I'm in just as deep as you are.' She looked at the piece of paper in her hands, at the digits written in pencil. 'We've been to his house and taken a number of items already – including his electronics – but so far we haven't found anything. That's why I think it's worth a second look.' She checked her watch and then her phone. 'But take it, don't take it, I don't give a shit. The woman, McMillan, Roddat – they're destroying your life, not mine.'

Studying her, I tried to see the lie in this, the deception that was going to send me to jail, but she looked right at me, unblinking.

I took the piece of paper.

'Now I *definitely* need to go,' she said.

I followed her out on to the street. It was still raining,

292

water running off the curve of the brickwork. She had a hood on her coat, its edges finished in faux fur, which she flipped up before turning to me for the final time.

Our eyes stayed on one another for a second.

'What?' she said, the rain against her shoulders.

'I still don't understand why you're doing this.'

'I already explained to you why.'

I shook my head. 'I don't believe you.'

'You don't believe I want this case solved?'

'No, I believe that,' I said. 'I believe that you think Carmichael's running this investigation the wrong way. I believe everything you've told me about what evidence was recovered from the scene.'

'Then what else is there?'

You're a cop, I thought. *And cops hate me.*

She rolled her eyes at the lack of a response and looked out at the rain. 'Just go and do what you do best,' she said.

And then she headed out into the storm.

51

I went straight home.

I needed a shower; ideally, I needed to sleep. I'd been awake for over twenty-four hours and I was starting to feel it, the exhaustion a needle picking away at the seams. But even if I tried, I knew I wouldn't drop off.

I was too charged, too focused on what was ahead.

I wanted to go back to Plumstead, to speak to someone at the library about the book I'd found in my loft, but, despite the fact that it felt like the middle of the afternoon, it was still only 8.15 a.m. The library didn't open until eleven.

There was McMillan's house as well.

I'd memorized the numbers for the alarm and dumped the piece of paper that Field had given me into the nearest bin. I'd kidded myself that it was to protect both of us, that the fewer trails leading back to our meeting in the arches, the better – but, in fact, I was primarily protecting myself. Despite everything, despite seeing all the sense in what she'd told me – how she was jeopardizing her career by contacting me, how the meeting could sink the legality of the entire investigation – I still wasn't prepared to trust her completely. My doubts lay in those moments at the end, in her response to me – or lack of it – when I'd asked what she was keeping back.

Because she was keeping *something* back.

I could feel it.

As soon as I got through the front door, I went to the sideboard in the living room and pulled out the home movies. The one of Derryn and me in Austria that I'd watched two nights ago was still there. So was the other one I'd selected, from the Christmas the year before she'd died. I couldn't remember exactly what else was on the rest of the tapes but as I went through them one by one, there didn't seem to be any glaring omissions. All the holidays I remembered were here. The trips. The birthdays. The Christmases. Whatever tapes Roddat had stolen, whenever it was that he'd broken into my house, he must have put everything except the death certificate back.

I showered, changed and then went through to the kitchen. I stood there and sank a glass of water, exhaustion ghosting through me again. My bones ached. My body was tired. Outside, in the street, the parties were all over, the skies were like granite, the rain was still hammering against the roof, and except for the sound of it, my house was absolutely silent. I wandered back through to the living room, taking in the home I'd once shared with my wife, and then stopped again: it had been like this for eight years, the walls and the floors, the air itself, heavy with the scent of loneliness — but most of the time I'd been able to ignore it. Now, though, it was impossible. I knew I wasn't losing my mind any more, but I still felt haunted. I was haunted by the silence of my house, of my life, and by the same questions, repeating themselves over and over.

Where the hell was the woman?

Where was McMillan?

Why were they doing this to me?

I thought of Gavin Roddat again, swinging from a rope while a video of Derryn and I played beside him, and realized the questions didn't end there. I had no idea why he'd become so obsessed with us. I had no idea why he would kill himself.

From the bedroom, my phone started ringing.

I snapped it out of the charger and saw it was the landline for my father's old cottage down in Devon.

Kennedy.

I wedged the phone between my shoulder and my ear, and, as we spoke, started to pack a bag full of things I'd need over the next few hours. A copy of the woman's photograph that Field had emailed to *FeedMe*. The edition of *No One Can See the Crows at Night*. Printouts of Gavin Roddat's face. My prepaid mobile.

My lock picks.

'Can I call you later?' I said to Kennedy, trying to head off a lengthy social call. 'I'm in the middle of something.'

'I think you'll want to hear this.'

He sounded sombre, severe. I stopped packing.

'What's up?' I said.

'We might have a problem.'

'What sort of problem?'

'After I got off the trawler yesterday, I arrived home and found this guy waiting outside the cottage. He said he was from the *Tribune*.'

Shit. The UK's biggest daily.

'He left his card. Connor McCaskell.'

I recognized the name instantly: he'd tried calling me three days ago, a few hours after the *FeedMe* article had been posted, and I'd hung up.

'Raker?'

'Yeah, I'm here.'

I rubbed at my forehead. I didn't need this now.

'Why's some arsehole hack turning up on my doorstep?'

'Because someone at the Met screwed up,' I said.

Field had no idea of the harm she'd done when she'd leaked the story to *FeedMe*. Maybe she really *had* done it for the right reasons, but that didn't make it any easier to deal with. Not only had she invited the entire media into my life, exposed me to them, put my work and my choices under completely avoidable scrutiny, she'd sent ripples even further out. Kennedy was the biggest and most damaging secret of all. If anyone found out about him, he was going to prison, and I was going with him.

'What did he say to you?' I asked.

'He knew you owned the cottage, but didn't realize it was being rented. He asked what my name was.'

'Did you tell him?'

'I told him I didn't speak to journalists.'

It was hard to say if that was better or worse than him just giving McCaskell a name. We were always going to be vulnerable, whatever direction Kennedy went in.

'You need to leave,' I said, trying to think fast.

'And go where?'

'Anywhere. Just grab your things, go to Totnes, get on a train and head north. I've got a credit card I only use in emergencies. I'll give you the details. Get a hotel and lie low.'

'He said he was writing a story about you.'

My stomach dropped again.

'He wanted to know if I knew anything about the woman who says she's your wife.' Kennedy sighed. 'What the fuck have you got yourself into, Raker?'

'I'll explain everything later.'

He was silent.

'Just get out of there, okay?'

Again, he didn't respond.

'Are you listening to me?'

'I'm listening.'

'Take your passport as well. Just in case.'

'Am I going abroad too?'

'You're going wherever no one can find you.'

'Why is this woman pretending to be your wife?'

'I don't know,' I said, heading off any other conversation he might be about to start. I told him to get going and call me when he was safe, and then zipped up the bag and carried it through to the living room.

The home movies were still scattered across the floor.

I thought of Derryn, of the places I'd captured her in, of how she would have looked at the time – and then my mind changed direction entirely and I thought of another video I'd watched, much more recently: the CCTV footage from Chalk Farm.

That was the only direct connection I had to the woman now.

The four movie files from that night that I had on my laptop, that I'd watched over and over again already, remained the single, most powerful snapshot of her – and of Gavin Roddat – that I had in my possession.

I had to make them count.

52

I was back in Plumstead forty-five minutes before the library opened, so found a café and loaded up on some much-needed coffee. The sun had come out, it was cool but bright, frost sprinkled across the Common, and in a window seat overlooking it, I got out my MacBook, plugged in my headphones and opened the Chalk Farm CCTV footage.

Fast-forwarding it to the point when Roddat first emerged from the dark, I hit Pause, inching it through frame by frame from there. I wanted to try and see if I could spot something else – *anything* – that might provide me with a glimpse of an answer, a connection between him and Derryn, the woman and Derryn, between any of this. Instead, it played out exactly the same as it had every other time: he came into view at 6.31 p.m., and vanished into the stairwell.

I moved it on almost an hour, to the point at which the woman appeared in frame for the very first time, at 7.26 p.m. I let her come into shot, stop there, look up to the fifth floor, and then I hit the space bar, freezing it on the best angle I had of her.

Who are you?

I watched her for a moment more, frozen within the confines of the laptop's screen, and then started up the film again as she vanished into the stairwell.

Look again.

I rewound it, back to the moments before and after the woman turned up at the flat. I watched people come and go in the minutes either side, and watched her come into frame, pause there with the Post-it note in hand, and glance towards the flat.

Were you nervous about meeting him?

I thought of her expression as she'd exited the flat afterwards. Something had happened up there, beyond Roddat hurting her physically. The bruise she now carried, the fresh cut, the specks of blood she'd left on the door frame – it wasn't any of that. It was something else.

What did Roddat say to you?

I went through all of it again, all the way up until she and Roddat left, then did the same on repeat. After yet another run-through, I stopped, leaning back in my chair. My body felt tight, rigid and uncomfortable from leaning over the laptop for so long. I stretched, finished my latest cup of coffee, and looked at the frozen image of the woman emerging from the stairwell. What was I doing?

This was madness.

I ordered another coffee, felt it make no impact, and bumped on the footage a couple of frames until both the woman and Roddat were visible.

It's not madness. There's something here.

There was no denying what the police had found in Roddat's possession – the photos, the videos, the death certificate – and I couldn't argue against the idea of him killing himself, because Field was right: it was so hard to dress a murder up as a suicide – or, at least, it was easy enough to dress it up at the scene, but almost impossible to sustain it once forensics and a pathologist became involved. Roddat *had* killed himself, that much was certain, and he *had* hurt the woman during the hour they'd spent inside the flat. But there was something else.

Something I wasn't seeing yet.

I went all the way back again and tapped at the cursor keys to edge the footage on. I watched the same faces come and go – a young couple; an old woman, slow, limping, being helped by what must have been her son – and saw the same cars pulling into the same parking spaces. Teenagers drifted out of the shadows beneath the flats once more and out beyond the side of the frame, and then all was quiet again. The clock ticked on, and then – when the readout got to 8.33 p.m. – the woman finally emerged, Roddat behind her.

I hit Pause.

Wait a second . . .

Rewinding the footage all the way back, I started it again at the point the young couple came into shot. As soon as they did, I paused it, studying their faces, remembering what Field had said to me at the arches: *We've managed to identify most of the people who appeared on film before and after Roddat entered the stairwell, and again when he came back down with her, and we've spoken to all of them but one.*

I looked at the screen again.

All of them but one.

I moved the video past the couple and on to the old woman and her son. This time I stopped it at the best angle I had of them. It was easy to see her: she was in her late eighties, slightly crooked, her limp pronounced. Her face was caught under the full glare of a street lamp. Next to her, though, I could see hardly anything of her son. A line of shadows bisected the two of them, she as bright as he was dark. His face was mostly covered.

After they disappeared from view, I replayed the section over again, slowing it down once the two of them came out of the stairwell.

And then it hit me like a punch to the throat.

As soon as they appeared in shot, the son said something to his mother, and she came to a halt and looked back at him. She responded, although I couldn't see her lips, just the movement of her jaw. There was a momentary lull before she broke out into a smile. After that, he took her gently by the elbow, saying something else to her, and the two of them went right.

I rewound it and stopped it just as they first appeared in the stairwell.

She doesn't know he's there.

That was what I was missing on the video, the speck of grime on an otherwise featureless canvas. *Him.* The son was what was wrong with it. When he appeared in the stairwell behind her, when she stopped and looked back at him, she didn't know he was there.

Because he isn't her son.

He wasn't even someone she knew.

He was a total stranger.

Field had said there was one potential eyewitness at the flats that night whom the police hadn't been able to speak to yet.

This was the one they couldn't find.

I rewound the section and played it again.

At the bottom of the stairwell, when he first spoke to the old woman – when he presumably asked if he could help her, take her arm, walk her out – she stopped and looked back because she was surprised, and she was suspicious.

Until then, she hadn't seen or heard him at all.

After that, he must have worked fast, made her feel at ease; told her he would help her, accompany her to wherever she was going. Maybe, if she was still suspicious of his intentions, he'd made up a story on the spot: he lived close to her, or he knew her family or a friend of hers; or maybe he'd played on her age, the way memories became cloudier over time, and pretended they'd talked before. It was impossible to tell on the video, and impossible to know for sure, but however he'd accomplished it – however he had got her onside – it had worked, because the next moment, she'd let him take her by the elbow and the two of them walked out of shot. He'd hidden behind the fiction he'd created – the mother and son – and let the shadows do the rest. Because no one was going to look twice at a son helping an elderly parent.

Field must have seen this too, and she – or one of her team – would have talked to the old woman about it; in turn, the woman would surely have confirmed the guy wasn't her son. If the police couldn't find this person, they couldn't interview him, which was why they had one outstanding witness.

That wasn't what bothered me, though.

What bothered me was the fact that Field hadn't said anything about the son when we'd been at the arches, about suspicions she might have had, just that there was a potential witness they hadn't located yet. So why would she keep that information back? The more I thought about it, the more I could only think of two possible reasons.

Either Field genuinely didn't think it was important.

Or she'd chosen to lie.

53

The door to the library was propped open by a couple of bricks. Beyond, there was a short hallway leading directly to a staircase. I entered and headed up.

It was a former flat, so at the top I found a landing with a toilet in the middle and two doors either side: one into what used to be a kitchen-diner, one into the former bedroom. All the furniture had been removed, replaced by wall-to-ceiling bookcases.

In the kitchen, at the counter, there was a man in his fifties, lean and sinewy, with the beginnings of a grey beard. He sat on a stool, leaning on the worktop, his head in a biography of the film star Glen Cramer.

He looked up and said, 'Hello there.'

'Hi. My name's David Raker.' I handed my card to him. 'I'm trying to find someone who might have come in here.'

He looked at the card. '"Missing persons investigator". Wow. Well, that's a bit more exciting than this.' He snapped his book shut. 'I'm Roy.'

We shook hands.

'Welcome to the Plumstead Common Community Library,' he said, his accent local. 'Have you ever been here before?'

'No, never.'

'We've been open fifteen years in February,' he said proudly, gesturing to the room. I followed his eyes across the bookshelves, paperbacks and encyclopedias, annuals and graphic novels crammed into every available space. 'We've been very fortunate,' he went on. 'We got a grant the first year, which got us up and running, then the former landlord decided to waive the second year's rates and offered us the tenancy rent-free. This was his first flat – plus, he's a big campaigner for children's literacy.'

I placed my notebook down on the kitchen counter and got out a pen. 'The owner of this place,' I said, 'would it be possible to get a name?'

'Carl Goshen.'

It rang a bell.

'He does something with the Internet,' Roy went on, waving a hand airily around his head, and as soon as he told me that, it clicked: Goshen had founded a video-based social media platform in the late 2000s, had sold it for billions, and now worked in California at a second company he'd set up. It seemed unlikely he would be a route to anything, least of all answers in this case.

I looked around the shelves briefly, eyes on the spines, trying to see if I could spot any of Eva Gainridge's novels. But there were so many books, stacked vertically and horizontally, I couldn't tell for sure.

Slipping my bag off my shoulders, I unzipped it and grabbed the printouts I'd made of the woman and Gavin Roddat.

'Do you recognize this man?'

He took the printout from me. I'd decided to show him Roddat first because the picture was clearer, more defined, and might get me further, faster.

As I waited, I looked around the room again. Above one of the shelves, taped to the wall, was a handwritten sign: *The books in this room are all for sale – most are £3 or less! If you only wish to borrow, head across the landing.*

'No.'

I looked at Roy. 'You don't recognize him? He hasn't ever come in here?'

He held up the photo of Roddat again. 'I don't think so,' he said, studying it. 'He certainly doesn't seem familiar.'

'Is it just you who works here?'

'It is, yeah.'

So there was no chance anyone else might come up with a different response. I swapped pictures. 'What about her?'

Roy took the printout of the woman from me. It was much fuzzier than the one of Roddat, especially blown up. The original picture that had been sent to *FeedMe* had been small and low resolution – I imagined because, at that stage, as she sent the woman's image out into the wild, Field was still trying to contain the spread of the story, even as she attempted to use the media as a tool to advance it. That decision may have seemed minor to her, but its reverberations were huge. If she'd taken a decent image of the woman, a clearer one, I might not have spent four days petrified that I was ill; I might not have had journalists picking apart my life, my own daughter uncertain about whether I was telling the truth.

'I'm not sure,' Roy said finally.

It was better than the blanket no he'd given me for Roddat.

'Have you got a better image of her?' he asked.

'No, that's it,' I said, frustrated. Field had had images of the woman on her phone, taken through the wrinkled plastic of evidence bags at Gavin Roddat's house. Why hadn't I asked her for one of those?

But then I thought of something.

I went to my mobile, punched in the code and then paused again. *Roddat had the death certificate in his house. You're not sick. You know that now. She's not Derryn.*

They're not the same person.

I repeated it all to myself again, and then again, a third time, a fourth, and then I went to my photographs and scrolled to the top where I had some pictures I'd moved across from previous handsets. I tapped on one of them.

'She looks a bit like this,' I said.

It was a photo of Derryn the February before she'd died.

It was a Sunday. I remembered it clearly, could almost see the image moving in front of my eyes. It had snowed, and we'd been out on Ealing Common, carving trails with our feet, watching kids building snowmen, and then we'd ended up at a café. She'd tried an eggnog latte and had almost gagged drinking it, and after that it had become a running joke between us every time we went for a coffee.

Roy took my phone from me.

The woman isn't Derryn.

The woman isn't –

'Oh, that's Derryn,' he said.

I swallowed. 'What?'

'That's Derryn. She used to come in here all the time.'

54

It felt like my throat had closed.

I looked at the phone, at the picture of my wife – stopped in time on a snowy day almost nine years ago – and then back to Roy.

'Are you okay?' he asked.

'How do you know her name's Derryn?'

I sounded exactly what I was: rattled, shaken, unnerved.

He shrugged. 'Because she told me.'

I took a moment, gathering myself.

Which Derryn did Roy mean?

Mine? Or the impostor?

He handed the phone back, sensing something was off with me, but I avoided his stare and looked out to the books. *Breathe. Concentrate.* On one of the shelves closest to me was a sci-fi novel with an illustration of a skyscraper on it, a maze of trees in semicircles at its apex, three people – just dots compared to the trees – lost at the centre. As I studied the image, it reminded me of the design on the clock I had hanging in the living room, the spirals of the triskelion, and the way the clock had shown a different date during the hours when I'd been alone with the woman in my house. The thought of her – of those moments when I'd given in, closed my eyes and pretended it was Derryn – made something inside me cramp.

What if it *had* been Derryn?

I rejected the question the moment it formed. Roddat had Derryn's death certificate in his house. McMillan had lied about treating me and now he'd gone to ground. The man on the CCTV footage was still out there, and he was a part of this just the same as the other two. And then there was the woman herself.

For whatever reason, they were *all* lying.

'She told you her name was Derryn?' I asked.

He frowned. 'Why, are you saying that wasn't her name?'

I sidestepped the question. 'You said she *used* to come in here?' My voice was still unsteady. I breathed in again, cleared my throat, repeated myself.

'Are you all right, son? Do you want a seat?'

'I'm fine. You said she used to come in here?'

'Yes,' he said, still watching me, his brow furrowed beneath the silver of his hairline. 'She hasn't been in for a while. A couple of months maybe, maybe more.'

'You two must have talked a lot if she told you her name?'

'I guess. But I talk to most people who come in here; I know a lot of names. She just happens to be very nice, very easy to talk to.' He looked away, reeling in a memory. 'She has lovely eyes. They're this really bright blue. A lovely smile too.'

'What did you talk about with her?'

'Books, mostly.' He shrugged, glanced at my mobile, which I still had in my hand, and then at the business card on the counter between us. Something occurred to him: 'Is Derryn missing then?'

'No.'

I said it automatically, instinctively. But the truth was, his version of Derryn – the one who came in here – hadn't been seen in four days.

'Uh, well . . .' I tried to sound composed. 'That's what I'm trying to establish.'

His expression changed: a flash of concern.

'Did she say where she lived?'

He shook his head. 'No.'

'You don't have library cards here?'

'No,' he replied, 'it's not that sort of library.'

'But do you know if she was local?'

'I don't know that either. Sorry.'

I looked around the room again.

'Any CCTV?'

'No. No, we don't have anything like that.'

And there was none immediately outside. It might be possible to trace her to this general area – Plumstead, the surrounding districts – on one of the days she'd come here. It might be possible to source footage from cameras within the radius of the library and try to pick up her trail that way, but it would be hundreds of man hours of work. Roy couldn't remember the exact date she last came in, and with no idea in which direction she'd approached or exited, I'd basically be asking for weeks, *months*, of tape with no real idea of where to start.

'She loves the work of Eva Gainridge, I know that.'

I looked at Roy. 'What?'

'She's a big fan of Eva Gainridge.'

'She told you that?'

'Yes. She said that was why her husband told her to come here.'

I felt a prickle beneath my scalp.

'Have you ever seen her . . .' I could barely say it. ' . . . husband?'

'He used to come in here a lot on his own when we first opened this place, but he hasn't been in for a while. The last time I saw him, they came in together.'

I took a step closer.

'He came in here with her?'

'Yes,' he said, trying to figure out if he'd hit on something useful.

'When was this?'

'Oooh, four years back. Five, maybe.'

'How many times did they come in together?'

'Once. Twice at most.'

'What did her husband look like?'

'I'd say he was probably in his thirties. Your sort of build and height.' Roy stopped, looking me up and down. 'Same colour hair as you too.'

I dropped my head and looked at the counter, at my business card, not because I was reading from it, but because I needed something to focus on. I didn't want Roy to spot the doubt on my face. I'd been past this, I'd broken through to the other side. It wasn't Derryn. I wasn't sick.

The woman's husband wasn't me.

I gathered myself and zeroed in on something I knew for sure: there was a man vaguely matching the description Roy had given – medium build, my sort of height – on the Chalk Farm CCTV footage.

'You sure you're all right, son? Do you want something to drink?'

I looked up at him again, back in control. 'I'm fine,' I said, smiling, trying to tell him everything was normal. 'Anything else you remember about the husband? Any identifying features? Did he wear glasses? Did he have facial hair?'

'A couple of days' beard growth, maybe.'

'Was he smart? Scruffy?'

'I don't know. Just kind of . . .' He paused. 'Average.'

'Short hair? Long hair?'

'Normal, really. Just a normal length.'

Medium height and build, normal length hair, average in terms of the way he dressed, maybe a bit of stubble, maybe not – it wasn't going to take me anywhere. If he had worn glasses, if he was smartly dressed, there had existed the faint possibility this 'husband' might have been Erik McMillan. But, deep down, I knew it wasn't.

It was the guy in the video.

'Wait,' Roy said, his tone suddenly different, more frantic. 'Wait a second. He could have had a tattoo.'

I looked at him. 'A tattoo?'

'I can't remember where exactly.' He glanced at himself. 'Or maybe I'm mixing him up with someone else.' He frowned, rubbing the side of his hand against his brow. 'I don't know. It's been a long time since he's been in.'

'Any idea what the tattoo was of?'

He shook his head. 'No. Sorry. I wish I could remember.'

I scanned the room again.

'You said Derryn liked Eva Gainridge?'

'Yes. But she told me she's a big reader generally. She reads all sorts. When she comes in here, she buys rather than borrows, which is another reason we got talking. We obviously appreciate her custom – I mean, borrowing books is fine, but buying is better, right? We still have to pay rates, after all.' He smiled, but then the smile fell away when he saw my expression. I was struggling to suppress my anxiety. It was all over my face. *My Derryn had been a big reader. She'd loved bookshops. She'd loved libraries.* Roy said, 'She usually spends about twenty quid whenever she comes in here.'

I gave myself a second to think.

'You said her husband told her to come in here because she liked Gainridge.' I looked around me. 'Does that mean you're well stocked?'

'With Gainridge? Oh yes, definitely.'

'Are you a fan too?'

'A big fan,' he said. 'She's a genius. I love all her books, but my favourite one is definitely *Exit Music from Cemetery City* because of the –'

'So you're always on the lookout for her books?' I said, cutting him off.

He looked a little hurt.

'Always,' he said, quietly at first. 'Some editions of her novels are extremely rare and worth a lot of money. People give us all sorts of old novels – paperbacks they've found in boxes they've dug out of the loft, or in the garage or wherever – and they genuinely have no idea of the worth of what they've let gather dust.'

'So some of the old editions sell for a lot of money?'

'They can. Some I'll keep back, for my own collection . . .' He faded out, more sheepish now: siphoning off the best stuff wasn't exactly in the spirit of a community library. 'Anyway, we have people – like Derryn – who obviously know what they're looking for.'

'What about her husband – was he a Gainridge fan as well? You said it was him that suggested she should come here in the first place?'

'He probably told her I knew what I was talking about. I mean, back when he used to come in on his own, he'd always ask if we had any new Gainridge stock in. He especially loved *The Man with the Wolf's Head*. He'd always look out for that.'

'You mean, he keeps on buying the same book over and over again?'

'*Reissues* of the same book,' Roy said, correcting me. 'I assumed he was some sort of collector, because *The Man with the Wolf's Head* has been reissued in fifteen different editions over the years, with fifteen different covers, and some of those are extremely hard to get hold of. The 1982 reissue – to coincide with the release of Gainridge's third novel, *Garden Apex* – is just one example of that. They'll go for two hundred quid each. There are other examples.'

I thought of the book I'd found in the loft.

'What about *No One Can See the Crows at Night*?'

'Exactly the same.' Roy dug around in a drawer next to him and brought out his own mobile phone. He started to hunt on it for something. 'There was a 1998 print run of *Crows*,' he said, 'that had a typographical flaw in it, and a mistake in the artwork. It was basically one big balls-up, so they ended up pulping most of them. There are only about a hundred copies left.'

He handed me his phone. On it was an edition of *No One Can See the Crows at Night*: a close-up of a crow on a branch, blood on its beak, a Normandy cemetery reflected in its eye. It was exactly the same edition as the one I'd found in the loft.

Derryn: Thank you for our special time together x.

'Did you ever get one of these in?' I asked.

'I've only ever had one.'

'Do you remember who you sold it to?'

He nodded. 'I sold it to Derryn's husband.'

#0799

I've decided to forgive you, Derryn.

I realize now that your husband acted the way he did at the hospital because he thought he was protecting you. He was under the mistaken belief that you and I didn't know each other, that we didn't have countless things in common, that we didn't share a connection. When he saw us together in the hospital, he had no idea.

He was jealous too, I think.

He seemed simple and oafish, and I'm afraid that type of person will always exist in a very black-and-white world; they can't see the complexities of life, the texture. A man like that could never hope to understand the way our relationship works, its layers and subtleties, and I suspect he saw the way we were together and the only way he could counteract it was through a physical show of force. When he pushed me away from you, he was basically demonstrating the extent of who he is.

And I get it, I really do: you're sick, and — psychologically — you need someone at your side who you feel will physically protect you, in some way, from the cancer. But he can't, Derryn. Your husband has no power to stop what is happening to you. So what, in the end, is his purpose? What does he bring to your life? When you get better, what then? Is he going to sit down with you and talk about art, or literature, or music, or politics? Will he be able to look you in the face and see what is on your mind without you even having to utter a word? Will he forgive you your mistakes like I have? I mean, I can't pretend that I'm not hurt that you would lie to me about being married, but all of us, at one time or another, have lied about things. For the last four years, I've lied about what happened to Nora. When I run into her friends and they ask me if I've seen her around, I tell them she cheated on me – which she did – and she left me without saying goodbye.

That bit's only partially true.

She left me, but she didn't do it voluntarily. I took her to a patch of land close to where I live, this remote spot where no one would see us, and I said I needed to tell her something. And when we got there, when she started to twig that something was up, she started screaming and shouting and making a noise, and I basically had no choice. I grabbed the first thing I could find. I hit her.

I buried her among the rubble.

See? We all lie, Derryn. I'm not proud of what I've done and I don't enjoy keeping things back from you, but we do whatever we think is best, don't we? You married your husband thinking it was for the best, and maybe it was at the time, but it's not any more. Now he's simply in the way; a blockage, detritus between us.

So I've started following him.

As we're being honest, I feel I need to tell you that. I've been following him since the events at the hospital. Last night I followed him into the supermarket. I saw him walking the aisles with the trolley, getting things for you both. He bumped into someone he knew, a woman, and they talked for a while, and the way he was around her – smiling, pretending to put a brave face on things – it was disgusting. He's already moved on from you in his head, Derryn – do you realize that?

He's mourned you already.

He's given up on you.

I stood in the shadows and watched him loading the shopping into the back of your car and I thought to myself, 'I could end this now.' I realized how easy it would be: it would be as easy as walking across the car park and severing his carotid artery. There was no one else around. There was no one to stop me.

He'd be dead inside a minute.

And he'd never see me coming.

55

Ninety minutes later, I arrived in Kew.

I spent half an hour doing circuits of McMillan's house, trying to get a sense of who was at home in adjacent properties, who might have an uninterrupted view of his home, and whether this was a trap. I saw no cars parked up and watching, as I had done the night I'd gone to Gavin Roddat's home in Tottenham, and I had no sense that the police were here. On the back of my hand, I still had *Kelly* written in biro – the name of McMillan's wife – and, in my head, the five numbers for the alarm, but as much as I wanted to get inside, I refused to be rushed.

I needed to be completely sure Field hadn't sold me out.

I retreated to the shadows and watched the house, thinking again about what Roy had told me at the community library. He'd said he'd sold the copy of *No One Can See the Crows at Night* to Derryn's husband. Except that man hadn't been me, and the woman who went there looking for books wasn't Derryn. It was all a trick, a blurred line between what was true and what wasn't, what was fiction and fact. The two of them – the husband and the wife – were frauds.

But, among their lies, I could see one grain of truth.

If my Derryn – the *real* Derryn – had been given a copy of the book, if its first page had been marked with a PCCL stamp, if the only copy Roy had ever had pass through his doors was that one, then it meant the edition the so-called husband had bought there had been the one I'd found in the loft. If that was the case, it meant he'd definitely known my Derryn before she died, he'd written the message that I'd discovered inside the pages of the book to *her* – not to the woman pretending to be her – and he'd given it to my Derryn as a gift. And then she'd dumped it in the loft.

I was certain that man was the same one I'd met at the hospital. I was certain he was the figure in the shadows at Chalk Farm.

Now I just had to prove it.

I checked my watch and saw that I'd been waiting forty-five minutes. That was enough time. I headed for the front door of McMillan's house. It was under a porch, a hanging basket swinging gently to one side of it, a solid wall on the other, and there was enough shadow – because of where the sun was at this time of day, the cloud cover, the pallid tint of winter – for me to hide from view.

All the same, as I got out my picks, as I slipped on gloves and a pair of shoe covers, I checked around me again. Everything was quiet.

The lock on McMillan's door was more complicated than the one I'd popped at Chalk Farm, so it took me longer to get in. A few times I had to pause, hands steady, tension wrench in place, and check over my shoulder as a car passed. Once, I heard voices and laughter in a house close by. Mostly, though, it was quiet.

Finally, when I heard the familiar click, I dropped the picks into my pocket, and – still in a crouch, checking the street again – pushed the door open an inch.

Immediately, the alarm began to beep.

I found the panel on the inside of the door, a series of lights flashing on it. As I put in the code Field had given me, I looked over my shoulder, still unsure why she would do this for me, why she would jeopardize her career and the integrity of the investigation, but when the house fell silent, I realized it really wasn't a trick. The code worked and no one was coming for me.

I closed the door and took in the downstairs hallway.

Despite the fact that it was the middle of the day, the house was still gloomy, but on one of the walls closest to me, I could see a nest of family photographs. I used the torch app on my phone and approached it. A lot of them were the same: his daughter, Caitlin, at various stages of her childhood, sometimes alone, sometimes with McMillan, often with what must have been his wife, Kelly.

Right at the edge of the wall of pictures was one of Kelly and McMillan back when they must have first started dating. He was in his early twenties and couldn't have looked more different from now, his hair an untidy shock of black, the sharp angles of his beard replaced by a thin moustache. His glasses were different too: simple and conventional, with thick rims that hid the tops of his cheekbones and the entirety of his eyebrows. Kelly was mixed race and about the same age. She was wearing dark lipliner and pink blusher, acid-wash jeans and a neon T-shirt, but none of her questionable fashion choices could dim her beauty. Dark-haired, dark-eyed and petite, she had a genuine smile and a face that carried the glow of it. Field had said she'd cut her wrists in the bath ten years ago and it made me wonder how she'd reached that stage. Had she been suffering from depression even back then? Or was it something that had crept in later, becoming a part of her in more recent times?

Caitlin was a good mix of her mother and father: she had Kelly's beauty, the smoothness of her skin, the radiance of her smile, but her father's eyes, hints of the same expression I'd seen in the hour before my blackout at St Augustine's. As I looked at her, I wondered if it was possible that she had misled the police. She'd said she didn't know where McMillan was, that she hadn't heard from him since she'd phoned him about the mysterious 'Dartford' caller on the 29th, but was this just another story to add to the ones her father had told me?

319

Somehow it seemed unlikely. To believe that, I had to be willing to believe she'd fooled Field twice on Skype, and a detective from Edinburgh face-to-face, and while people capable of lying that effectively *did* exist – I'd met them myself – they were rare.

As I found more photos of the three of them at the other end of the hallway, of extended family too – his mother and father, Kelly's parents, cousins – I thought about Derryn again. *My Derryn.* If this was all about her, if it had started with her, where were the links to her in McMillan's life? Where were the links to the woman pretending to be her? How the hell was I ever going to find her if I couldn't find McMillan?

I moved further in.

To the left was the living-room door and a staircase; to the right, a dining room, what appeared to be a study, and a kitchen at the rear. The back garden was fenced in, and had a patio, a shed, and a row of fir trees at the bottom. Beside me, I could hear a soft gurgle from the nearest radiator and moans in the walls as pipes pumped hot water around.

I entered the living room and found expensive furniture, shelves in coves next to a chimney breast with a woodburner in it, a piano near the TV, surround-sound speakers, and modern art on the walls. More photos too, mostly of Kelly and Caitlin. I checked them over, looking for things that didn't seem right. A few had been removed from their frames, presumably by the police for use in any future appeal for information.

Upstairs, at the top of the landing, I looked both ways. To my left were two doorways and some windows at the end, part of the converted chimney stack I'd seen from outside the first time I'd been here. Built around the windows were shelves, filled with books, more photos and trinkets.

I looked over the rooms, going through drawers, opening

cupboards, using the light from the torch to illuminate murky interiors, and – when I came up short again – headed upstairs to the third floor. It was a loft conversion, a master bedroom with a wet room built at the end, behind a three-quarter wall. Skylights were on either side, above a row of built-in wardrobes, and there was the continuation of the chimney stack too, more of its windows flooding the floor with grey light.

I started with the wardrobes, going through his clothes, boxes he'd stacked at the bottom, pulling them out and digging around inside. When I was done with those, I moved on to his bedside cabinets: one was basically empty, except for a few charging cables; the other was full, clearly the one he used every night.

Inside, I found more photographs, these ones loose. They must have been twelve years old, as Caitlin looked about eight or nine. In one, the three of them were at Disneyworld. In another, presumably on the same holiday, they were at Kennedy Space Center. There was one of Caitlin and Kelly on a British beach somewhere. Another at a waterfront in Spain. One in a meadow. One of them eating fish and chips in St Ives. There were also photographs of McMillan with his parents, and McMillan and Kelly together, all pretty innocent.

I put them back, feeling a strange sense of guilt as I did – not at being here, illegally, inside McMillan's home, but at invading the sanctity of his family through their pictures, through the only medium in which the three of them existed now.

And then I stopped again, realizing I'd made an error.

I'd missed something.

Behind the shot of the three of them at Disneyworld was another photograph, its corner poking out. The two of them had become stuck together over time, one disguised behind the other.

I prised them apart.

The one I'd almost missed was taken at an office party,

balloons tacked to a wall above two desks. There was a cork-board full of notices off to one side. In the middle of the shot were four men and three women. Neither Kelly nor Caitlin was in this one, just McMillan.

This was somewhere at St Augustine's.

Faintly, stencilled next to the corkboard, I could see its name spelled out above some sort of coat of arms, and one of the men was still wearing a lab coat, pens in his breast pocket. I turned the photograph over, but there was nothing written on the back – no description or date – so I flipped it again and drew it closer to me.

My gaze returned to the doctor in the lab coat. He was the same sort of age as McMillan, but not as handsome or well turned out – his hair was thinning, he was a little overweight – but he had vivid green eyes and his arm was around the woman next to him and they were laughing about something.

I looked at him, trying to figure out what it was that had caught my attention. Did I recognize him from somewhere? Where would I have seen him? Could he be the man in the CCTV footage from Chalk Farm? Could he be the man I'd found talking to Derryn that day at the hospital? Derryn had said that man was a patient – or, at least, that's what I recalled her saying, but all of that had happened almost nine years ago. Could I have misheard her, or just misremembered?

Could he have been a doctor?

Even if all I had was a vague memory of the person at the hospital, the doctor in the photograph was definitely too chunky to be the man in the CCTV video, probably too tall as well, and the man in the footage – from what I'd been able to see of him in the shadows – was shorter, more toned, and had a fuller head of hair.

So what had given me pause?

I looked at McMillan and then back to the man in the lab coat, his face, the people he was with, and then my eyes drifted to his breast pocket again, to a name badge clipped to it. I had to look hard, because the writing on it was small, but – at the top, in precise, bold type – I could just about make out his name.

Instantly, I felt a charge of electricity.

Ask your father about Dartford.

That had been what someone had said to Caitlin in the second phone call from the payphone in Plumstead on 28 December. Field had told me they'd sent someone down to Kent to look into it – but what if whoever had made that call wasn't talking about the town in Kent? What if they'd been talking about a person?

I looked at the doctor's badge again.

It said, *Dr B. Dartford*.

56

I pocketed the picture, knowing I'd got lucky: because it had got stuck to the back of another photograph, because the police hadn't done a detailed forensic search of the house yet, they'd either not seen the photograph or they'd missed it completely. Now I had to make the most of it.

I found the number for St Augustine's and hit Call. After a couple of rings, I got through to the main switchboard.

'Hi,' I said. 'Can you put me through to Dr Dartford, please?'

'Dr . . . ?'

'Dartford.'

'Um, that doctor's not on my list. Can I put you on hold for a moment?'

I told the operator that was fine and, as I listened to a rendition of Beethoven's Sixth, I headed downstairs. At the windows in the living room, I peeled back the curtains and made sure no one was approaching the house.

The street was quiet.

The woman came back on the line: 'My colleague tells me that Dr Dartford hasn't worked here for seven years. She says he died in 2010.'

'He's dead?'

'That's what I'm told. It was before I started here, I'm afraid.'

'Does your colleague know what he died of?'

I heard her place a hand over the phone and ask the question. When she came back on, she said, 'He was killed in a car accident, apparently.'

I thanked her and hung up, going to Google. It took me less than ten seconds to confirm what she'd said: Bruce

Dartford had been killed in a pile-up on the M1, coming back from a medical conference in Sheffield. He'd hit a jack-knifed lorry.

Ask your father about Dartford.

Was I wrong then?

What if the call to Caitlin *was* about Dartford, the town?

I looked around the house, wondering if there might be anything else here, hidden away somewhere, that might help answer the question. For now, though, I dug around for a number Field had given me for Caitlin McMillan and fished out the prepaid phone I'd packed earlier. It rang for so long I thought I was going to have to leave a message – but just as I was about to terminate the call, she picked up.

'Hello?'

'Is that Caitlin?'

'Yes. Who's this?'

'Caitlin, my name's Detective Smith. I'm part of the team looking into your father's disappearance.' The words felt sour in my mouth: I hated the idea of lying to her – it felt almost like lying to Annabel – but it was the quickest way to get her onside. 'Have you got a few minutes to answer some questions for me?'

'Yes,' she said. 'Yes, of course.'

Her voice sounded small, troubled.

'How are you feeling?' I asked.

She didn't answer for a second. 'I don't know. Sick, I guess. I feel a long way away too. I just don't know why Dad would do this. Why would he disappear?'

Carmichael, Field and their teams had clearly avoided giving Caitlin too much information, partly because they needed to contain the search for McMillan, but also – I suspected – because they needed Caitlin to be as lucid as possible in moments like this. If she knew the extent of McMillan's problems, based on what Field had said about her idolizing her father, it would completely destroy her. His flawless outline would crumble in front of her. Yet, despite the damage that McMillan had done to me, I didn't want to be the one to send the wrecking ball to his daughter.

'As soon as we know anything, Caitlin,' I said, 'I promise you we'll tell you, but in the meantime, could I ask you those questions?'

'Okay.'

'You last heard from your father on Thursday – is that right?'

'Yes. I got this weird call and I wanted to ask him about it.'

'"Ask your father about Dartford."'

'That's right,' she said. She sounded perplexed, misled.

'He told you he didn't know what that meant?'

'Neither of us had the first idea, no.'

'And you didn't recognize the caller's voice?'

'No.'

I wandered through to the back of the house, checking the garden. As I did, I said, 'Did the caller have a regional accent?'

'Not that I noticed.'

'And he hasn't called since?'

'No.'

I was still holding the photograph of Dr B. Dartford in my hands. 'Did your father ever mention anyone called Dartford? Maybe someone he worked with?'

'Not that I can remember.'

'Ever remember him mentioning a colleague called Bruce?'

'Bruce?' She thought about it. 'No, that doesn't ring any bells either. Sorry. Dad used to talk about his work with me all the time, because I wanted to be a psychiatrist, just the same as him, especially after my mum got ill. I guess . . .' She stopped. 'I don't know,' she said, her voice breaking up a little, 'it sounds really naive and simplistic saying it aloud, but maybe I thought I could make her better.'

326

Except no one could make her better.

Not Caitlin, not McMillan himself.

I gave her a moment.

'Did he talk much about his colleagues?'

'Not a great deal. When we talked about Dad's work, it was always about the *work* side of things – you know, the actual blueprint of psychiatry, what it took to get to where Dad is, his view on things, how he became so well respected. He said one day maybe we'd end up working in the same facility.'

'At St Augustine's?'

'Maybe.'

That was another wish that would never materialize now. McMillan's lies, the paucity of his file on me, the total lack of evidence that I was ever in his care – those things would cast long shadows. They would end his career.

'Can you think of anywhere your dad might have gone?'

She took a long breath. 'Nowhere,' she said, and then I felt a flicker of a change in her tone, as if she was getting suspicious. I didn't blame her. She'd already answered these questions.

'I know we've been over this,' I said, trying to reassure her. 'I'm sorry for dragging it out.'

She sighed a little, seemed to relax again. 'I can't think of anywhere I haven't said already,' she went on. 'I mean, I gave you guys all the places we used to go to on holiday. I basically gave you everything I could think of. If he's not in those places . . .' She faded out, sniffed. 'I just don't . . .'

She was choking up.

I wondered which places she'd suggested to the police, and how I could get her to run through them again without raising suspicion. But then I wondered if it even really mattered. If he'd gone anywhere obvious, it was almost certain the Met would have picked up his trail and located him already – which meant it was much more likely he'd gone somewhere no one knew about, including his daughter.

Once I'd thanked Caitlin for her time and tried to give her some small measure of encouragement – even if, ultimately, it was just another lie – I hung up and turned off the mobile. As I was putting it back into my bag, I noticed something: behind the living-room door was a rack, its pegs loaded with keys.

There was a car fob hanging from one of them.

I peeled back the curtains again, peering out at the street, and then grabbed the fob from the rack. Pointing it out of the window, I pressed the Unlock button. Over on my left, eight or nine cars down, a series of flashing lights went off.

Wherever McMillan had gone, he hadn't taken his vehicle with him. And there was something else too: the morning the woman said she'd been dropped off at the pharmacy, her driver – the man who had taken her there – had got into an argument with a traffic warden. Field said the traffic warden had described the driver as having dark hair and possibly a goatee. McMillan had black hair and a beard. And the same traffic warden said the driver was behind the wheel of a Mondeo or a Lexus.

I looked along the road at McMillan's car.

It was a Lexus RC.

57

I checked my surroundings as I approached the car and then opened the driver's door and slid in at the wheel.

It smelled new, the leather seats smooth and unblemished, but the car wasn't entirely unmarked: I could see fingerprint dust on the steering wheel and along the passenger's door — on the area above the glove compartment too. The police must have spotted the car and made the same connection I had, then dusted the passenger side in the hope of confirming that the woman had been in here. It made me wonder why Field hadn't told me that McMillan owned a Lexus. Was this something else she'd deliberately kept back from me — or was it simply because she'd already dismissed it as a coincidence? The car definitely wasn't the right colour: the traffic warden had said the vehicle he'd seen was light blue or grey, while McMillan's Lexus was a bottle green. And the registration plate didn't match either: the one at the pharmacy ended in M X; McMillan's was personalized.

Even if she *had* written it off as a coincidence, Field had still had the car dusted, maybe because a fluke like this never sat entirely comfortably with a detective. But even as I accepted that as the most likely sequence of events, I couldn't let my suspicions go entirely: what if the reason Field hadn't mentioned McMillan owning a Lexus was because she really *was* keeping me in the dark? When I'd left her at the arches, I hadn't been able to kick the idea that she was hiding something, and since then I'd found out about the man on the CCTV video *and* McMillan's car. So if she didn't want me digging, if she didn't want me knowing these things, why tell me about the case and give me the alarm code for McMillan's house?

Uncertain of the answers, I refocused and leaned over, checking the glove compartment, but only found manuals, handbooks, a packet of mints and some hand sanitizer inside. Snapping it shut again, I checked the rear seats. They were pretty much spotless.

Getting back out, I went around to the boot and popped it open. There was a gym bag, a picnic blanket rolled up at the very back, and a collection of 'bags for life' scrunched into the corner. A bottle of de-icer, an ice scraper, some towing cables. It was certain the police had been in here too.

I pulled the gym bag towards me and unzipped it. It smelled fresh, washed. I yanked everything out, checking the interior of the bag. There were two zip pockets but all I found was a membership card for a gym in Thamesmead and a fixture list for a five-a-side league. Zipping it up again, I pushed the gym bag all the way to the back and lifted up the hatch for the tyre well.

Just a breakdown kit and a spare.

Leaving everything as I'd found it, I slammed the boot shut and used the fob to lock the car.

Then I stopped, a fresh idea forming.

Unlocking the door again, I got back in at the wheel and started the engine. On the dashboard, the seven-inch screen sprang into life.

I tapped a finger to *Nav.*

This sort of thing was always easy to overlook.

Some options appeared in a horizontal strip. I tapped *Destination* and then *Previous Destinations.* A list of the places that McMillan had been to – and had used the satnav for – were in a list on the right. He'd utilized the function a lot in the short time he'd had the car, especially on his daily journey to St Augustine's, not because he didn't know his way across

330

the city, but because the satellite updated the system in real time with information about traffic accidents and roadworks, helping him to avoid hold-ups.

I moved down the list.

Using my phone, I started cross-checking postcodes that I didn't recognize in Google. A lot turned out to be conference centres, universities and hospitals, places he'd gone to deliver talks or to lead workshops or to train people. There was a postcode in Edinburgh, close to the university, which must have been where Caitlin was living, and a cemetery in Richmond that he'd been to three times in two months. That was obviously where Kelly was buried.

There was one place, though, that didn't quite fit.

It was a London postcode, with a street address on Earls Court Road. I stuck it into Google and it came back with the URL of a storage company called Eaz-E-Stow. I clicked on the link to their website. They had four facilities in south-west London, nine in the city as a whole. One of the facilities was 64,000 square feet and built on three floors, but the one on Earls Court Road was much smaller, more like a post office, with mailboxes, and design, print and copy services.

Somehow, I doubted McMillan was driving five miles across London to get some photocopying done – and if he wasn't using the print and copy services, I could only see one other reason for using Eaz-E-Stow.

He was storing something there.

58

From the outside, Eaz-E-Stow was just a cramped single-door unit wedged between a chemist's and a money exchange, but its size was deceptive. The moment I entered, I saw that it extended back a long way. At the front was a bank of computers, printers and photocopiers, and a woman behind a desk, her head down, reading something; at the back, through another door, I could see brass mailboxes – hundreds of them – in towers six feet high.

The woman looked up and said hello.

I smiled. 'Hi, how are you?'

Over the desk counter, just behind her, I could see a computer. I needed to try and figure out which mailbox was McMillan's.

'I had a phone call about my mailbox,' I said.

She frowned. 'A phone call?'

'Yes, someone left a message saying there was a problem with it.'

Understandably, she had no idea what I was talking about. 'What is your name, sir?' she asked.

'Erik McMillan. That's Erik with a *k*.'

'Okay. Just give me a second.'

I told her that was fine and pretended to look away, at the photocopiers. As soon as she swivelled on her chair to face the computer, I glanced at her screen. She put in an access code, which I struggled to follow, and clicked a couple of options on the next page.

McMillan's account came up.

I saw his name at the top, and his address below that. I

scanned the lines and numbers underneath those, trying to see what might be a box number, and right at the bottom, beneath confirmation that he was paying £30 per month, I saw it: D–2888. When I looked towards the mailboxes, I could see signs hanging from the ceiling, arrows pointing off either left or right into A, B, C and D sections.

'I can't see anything here, sir,' the woman said.

'Oh.' I made a show of looking at the screen briefly, as if it were the first time, and then in the direction of the mail-boxes. 'Oh, that's strange.'

'Do you know who called you?'

'Maybe it was one of those scam calls.'

She leaned back in her chair, nodding. 'It could be. We *have* had some issues with that sort of thing. You did the right thing to come in here and check, though.'

We talked politely about scammers for a moment.

'It says here you're paying by cash every month,' the woman said. 'Would you prefer to switch to direct debit? It's a lot more convenient.'

'I think I'm fine for now,' I replied, and told her that as I was here now, I may as well check my box. But all I could really think about was McMillan's decision to pay in cash every month.

He didn't want anyone to find the mailbox.

I headed down to D section. It was as far back as you could get, but I still had to be careful. Because the banks of mailboxes ran in straight lines all the way down, the woman could still see me from where she was. When I got to 2888, I checked she wasn't looking my way, got out my picks and started trying to spring the door. It was fitted with a simplis-tic tumbler, probably because most people were using these things as mail drops, not to store valuable items. And maybe that was what McMillan was using it for as well.

But somehow I doubted it.

I heard the woman coughing, stopped what I was doing and checked she still wasn't looking, careful not to move my hands, and then gave the lock a final twist.

The door bumped out towards me.

There was only one thing inside.

An unmarked brown envelope.

59

I took the last seat in the end carriage on the Tube back to Ealing, well away from anyone else, and opened up the envelope. Inside was a series of A5 lined pages, their tops frayed, and stapled in the corner to keep them together. I wasn't sure what I'd been expecting but it wasn't this: fourteen pages of written notes in a hand that was near-illegible. At an initial glance, the most I could do was make out some dates: 21 October 2011; 3 May 2012; 19 August 2014.

I went back to the first page, wondering if the notes might be a combination of bad handwriting and shorthand, but if this was shorthand it was a system I didn't understand. As a journalist, I'd learned to read and write Pitman, and had learned to read Gregg during my time in the States, but it was neither of those. It could have been another system entirely, or it could have been something that McMillan himself had developed, one that only he could read properly. The more times I went through the notes, the more likely that seemed: he'd kept them locked away in a mailbox five miles from his house because he didn't want anyone to see them; and if anyone did come across them, like now, he didn't want them to be interpreted easily. He wanted to be the one to *do* the interpreting. Which made these notes what? A way for him to protect himself? An insurance policy of some kind? Was this the rabbit he'd pull out of the hat at the end when he had nowhere else to go?

I grabbed a pen and started at the beginning, circling any words that I could read or felt that I definitely understood. His system seemed to use a combination of different techniques: regular words, properly spelled; abbreviated versions of things – *reocc* instead of *reoccur*, or *i/n* instead of *illness*; similar curves to the ones used for consonants in the Pitman shorthand as well as the straight lines of its vowels, but not necessarily applied to either consonants or vowels here; and then some of the punctuation techniques used in Gregg.

It was a total mess.

I got to the end, grabbed a separate pad from my bag and wrote down every word I thought I could read properly. By the time I was done, the train was pulling into Ealing Common.

At the surface, I took a detour to a Chinese on Uxbridge Road, grabbed some crispy chilli beef and noodles and hurried across the Common. The smell trailed me as I walked, and I realized I hadn't eaten properly all day. I was famished.

Once I was home, I fired up the central heating, pulled a floor lamp in close to the living-room table and laid everything out in front of me.

As I wolfed down my meal, I went through the list of words that I'd understood – or thought I had – in McMillan's notes. It was like reading the answers to a spelling test, or orderless extracts from a dictionary. There was no coherence to any of it. They were just random words; unrelated.

Or were they?

I'd lifted twenty-seven different words from the notes, which wasn't much from a total of fourteen pages, but there was a lot of repetition – such as his use of *i/n* for *illness* – so I'd only included duplicated words once. *Illness. Presenting. Treatment. Milligrams.* These were all terms he'd repeated a lot and that he might also use in his capacity as a doctor – so did that make these medical notes? Why would he use such scruffy paper, and why lock them away in the mailbox? I paused, trying to think, and remembered what Roy had told me at the community library about the woman pretending to be my wife, and the man claiming to be her husband.

Could these notes be related to them?

Could they be *about* them?

I looked through the pages again, trying to get my head straight. If McMillan had treated them, why were these notes here and not in a steel cabinet somewhere in St Augustine's with the rest of the patient records? Where were their actual files? Why would their medical histories be handwritten on sheets of paper that looked like they'd been ripped from a spiral notepad?

I spun back to what I'd been thinking about on the train home: I'd wondered if these might have been some sort of insurance policy, perhaps leverage of some kind, a way for McMillan to protect himself.

Or maybe they were a way for him to fight back.

He'd pretended to be my doctor, had told the police he'd treated me, had been willing to sacrifice his entire career to sustain that lie, for however long it held firm – but what if he hadn't done it out of choice? What if his hand had been forced?

What if he'd been blackmailed?

I thought about the doctor I'd seen in the photograph at McMillan's house. *Bruce Dartford.* The man who'd made the call to Caitlin from the payphone in Plumstead had told her to ask her father about Dartford. It seemed to be a suggestion to dig into McMillan's past; a suggestion that there might be something waiting there, interred and forgotten. Could that be why McMillan had lied about me? Was it because someone was threatening to tell the world his secret – whatever this Dartford thing was – and he didn't want it to come out?

As that slotted into place, a flash of a memory resurfaced: in the seconds before I'd blacked out in his office, McMillan had dropped to his haunches at my side.

I'm sorry, David.

I thought of the woman pretending to be Derryn, and then of the man in the CCTV footage. The wife and her husband.

They had to be the ones blackmailing him.

Blackmail explained why the notes were so difficult to interpret. It explained why he kept them locked up. If this was how
he hoped to fight back, he had to make them impenetrable, just
in case they fell into the wrong hands. What it *didn't* explain was
why, if these notes were his reprisal, the way he went on the
attack, he hadn't utilized them as a weapon. Why wasn't he
threatening to release the information contained here?

Was it because he'd never had the chance to come back for
the notes?

Was it because he was already dead?

I tried not to let the thought derail me and went back to the
pages, reading from beginning to end, making sure I'd written down every intelligible word I could pick out. By the time
I was done, I still had the same twenty-seven words. I went
through them again individually, counting how many times
they appeared in the notes, cross-checking everything. The
house faded to black around me, the only source of light the
floor lamp angled in above my head, like someone leaning
over me. Out of the twenty-seven, one word bothered me.

Malady.

McMillan had used that word seven times, including twice
on one page under the date 3 May 2012. It wasn't that the
word didn't belong here; if a synonym for illness belonged
anywhere, it was in a set of medical notes, however unconventional. It was more that the word was hard to read. I
wasn't sure it was even *malady.*

I went over the notes yet again, trying to gain some sort of
context, anything that might give me a steer on what the word
might be if it wasn't *malady*, and then I noticed that the first *a*
was different from the second *a*. He hadn't written them the
same way. Each was a different style, the first *a* much less obvious than the second.

Because the first a *isn't an* a.

'It's an *e*,' I muttered.

As I realized that, I could suddenly see it so clearly. There were no *a*'s at all here – because the word wasn't *malady*.

It was *Melody*.

It was a woman's name.

#0806

I went to see Erik this morning and he showed me your medical records.
  Oh, Derryn.

I didn't realize this was the third time you've had cancer. Back in January, when I was on the ward with my skull fracture, it had only been five months since you were given the all-clear the second time around. I never would have guessed. That smile of yours, it hid no hint of anxiety or unease. And now here we are again, in July, and it's back, and in your medical records it says you're not going to have chemotherapy again. It says you don't want it, that you've had enough. I suppose I understand now why your house looks so boring. It's because you've been sick or in treatment, on and off, for the last two and a half years. When would you have had the time to decorate, to think about that sort of thing? Maybe, if your husband had any vision, any competence beyond the use of his fists, he could take the lead, change things, improve them, but he hasn't. If that was me, Derryn, I'd turn that house on its head. I'd bring you home, and I'd show you inside, and you'd have tears in your eyes when you saw how wonderful everything looked. You'd say, 'Thank you so much,' and – despite being weak – you'd throw your arms around me and you'd touch your lips to mine.

  'I love you,' you'd say.

I've actually been in your house a lot. When you and your husband are out, I get inside and wander around. I just like running my fingers over things. I look in your drawers and your wardrobe. I lean in and smell the perfume that lingers in your clothes. Sometimes, I pick up photos of you and your husband and I drop them on to the ground, so the glass in the frame shatters. I twist and break the frames so there's no way they can be used again. I leave them on the floor, making it look

340

like they fell off a sideboard, or a dresser, or the wall. I do it well and I don't do it a lot, otherwise you might realize someone has been snooping around, but I do it just enough so that, when I return, there are fewer photos of you and your husband together. I like coming back and seeing empty spaces where he should be. It's just better like that.

It's better when it's just you and me.

I've studied your movements over the past couple of months, and today you went to a cemetery in north London to choose a plot for yourself. It was hard for me to see that. I didn't follow you in, although I very much wanted to. I felt that, if your husband spotted me, it would become a distraction, so I left the cemetery and went to work and tried to concentrate on what I was doing. I got a little done, but not much. We had a few people in, a few homes to go to, and I sorted some paperwork out. It wasn't busy, but even if it had been, I doubt I would have been able to focus.

Later, I went and saw Erik again, and as I walked through St Augustine's, I started to realize something: all the doctors working in here, all the people – like McMillan – who get paid all this money to help others, to be the very best in their field, and not a single one of them is any use to you whatsoever. They're the wrong doctors. They specialized in the wrong thing. They're as worthless as the fly that buzzes behind the curtain in summer, bashing against a locked window, over and over again, trying to reach the sky. If I ground all of these doctors into paste, if I chopped every one of them into pieces, and dumped their remains in the same place I once left Nora, if I let the crows and the buzzards and the gulls peck at them and feed on their bodies, what difference would it make?

It wouldn't make any to you.

They can't help you.

So, by the time I got to Erik, I was angry, I couldn't stop myself. I got hold of him, punched him, kicked him. When he started begging me to stop, I just carried on. It's not his fault, really, I know that. But I hate him for his inadequacy.

I hate everyone.

When I feel like that, I go back to your house and watch all the old home videos of you. I like watching them. They can be corny and sentimental at times, but I like watching you in motion. You really can be so beautiful. Just the way you move, the way you speak, the way you hold yourself. A few weeks ago, I took one of the tapes home with me and made a copy of it, and then returned it the next day. When I realized neither of you had noticed it was gone, I took more. Tonight, I've just finished copying the very last one. I've got them all now, and I watch them constantly. I'm starting to know what's coming – what you'll say, how you say it, what your reaction is going to be. I like seeing you well, healthy, because it's hard seeing you as you are now. When you leave the house now, you're grey and fragile. You look like a baby bird, featherless and blind.

I don't want you to die, Derryn.

I want everything to be normal again, not to have to pretend that it is. Even though I know you've decided against the treatment, that there's only one way we're going from here, I've had to make out that I'm fine, and I hate it. Inside, I'm a wreck, I'm ruined, but outside I just look the same as ever. I maintain this horrible façade. Because no one knows about you, Derryn. No one knows what we have.

Well, no one except Erik.

He became my doctor after Nora fucked with my head. He did help me back then, I admit that much. He helped get me out of a deep spiral. After he worked with me, I could see clearly again. In fact, Erik helped me realize that, in order to move on, I needed to redact Nora from the pages of my past.

So, after I got rid of her, I told him what I'd done, what I'd done with her body, and he was horrified. He said he never meant for this to happen and that he would have to call the police. I told him he wasn't to do that. I told him, instead, that he was to continue treating me, but he would have to stop writing things down. See, I never make a point of walking in blind. I always make sure I know people's secrets. When you know people's secrets, you can get them to do anything; and I can get Erik to do anything for me.

But, sometimes, even secrets can't help us.

I don't want you to die, Derryn.

Please don't die.

60

It didn't take me long to find her.

In a search for *Melody* on the website Missing People, I discovered three females registered by their families with the charity. One was under eighteen, a kid who'd run away from home and had never been seen again; another was a woman in her late sixties, suffering from dementia, who'd been gone two days. The third was a woman in her forties who'd been missing since February 2010.

Her name was Melody Campbell.

I clicked on the link. Next to her entry was a photograph. At a quick glance, it was hard to identify her as the same woman who'd turned up at Charing Cross four days ago, except in the eyes. But, even then, you had to look hard. Physically, she was like a different person. The accompanying text said she'd been missing almost eight years, and that tallied, just about, with what the woman had told Field that first day at the police station. I turned to my notes, went right the way back to the start and tried to remind myself of exactly how that conversation had gone. Field had told me that the woman had mentioned once – and only once – that she'd been gone for eight years, but then, in the interview I'd watched on the monitors, the woman had put it down to a misunderstanding. I'd managed to note down a rough transcript of it.

FIELD: You told us earlier that you were missing.
WOMAN: Did I?
FIELD: For almost eight years.
WOMAN: I don't think I said that.

343

FIELD: You did.

WOMAN: I'm sure I didn't.

FIELD: You did. But you say you're living with David. So how is that missing?

WOMAN: It's not. I said we got separated, not that I was missing.

FIELD: You and David got separated?

WOMAN: Yes. Perhaps that's where the confusion comes from.

FIELD: Where did you get separated?

WOMAN: At the pharmacy.

Had she been playing a game with Field? Or was she genuinely confused? A lot of the things she'd said in that interview – her lack of knowledge about London and about using the Tube; her easily disproved claims that she worked as a nurse; her sudden need to come to Charing Cross – hadn't added up, and I'd never been able to work out if it was duplicity or sickness. If she was sick, and McMillan was treating her, why wasn't he helping her through the usual channels? Why were his notes confined to fourteen scruffy pages hidden in a mailbox? Field had said that they'd been through McMillan's office – it was where they'd found his meagre file on me – so it was likely, after securing a court order, they'd been able to cross-check the description of the woman with photographs of other patients he'd looked after during his time at St Augustine's. If they hadn't found Melody Campbell, then she had either never been a patient at the hospital, or everything that had been collated on her had been dumped before McMillan went to ground.

I looked at her photograph again.

Within the confines of a picture an inch and a half high, it was difficult to spot her similarities to Derryn, because eight years ago they were so small – really, just her eyes – so it

344

would have been even harder for the police: they'd have been looking at hundreds of photographs, countless faces in huge missing persons lists, and with no idea what her name was – no hint, like me, that it was Melody – there was nothing to grab their attention. Without a name, there was no starting point for a search other than the physical description of the woman the day she'd turned up at the station – and, here, she looked nothing like that.

I enlarged the image. The more I looked, the more I started to see it wasn't just the eyes: the brow and the nose were the same as the woman's too – and close enough to Derryn's – they were just disguised behind starker, more dominant differences. Eight years ago, Melody Campbell's hair was a chestnut brown, not blonde, and she was wearing it much shorter, almost boyishly. The Melody Campbell who'd turned up at the police station on Thursday was slim, but the Campbell in this photograph wasn't. Here, she was probably two or three stone overweight, thin spirals of fat gathered on top of each other beneath her shirt, the material exposing their outline. Her neck was puffy, and her arms carried the excess that came with weight gain. It had subtly changed the topography of her face, obscuring many of the main lines and contours that – years later – would make her a near-facsimile of my wife.

Melody Campbell was pretty, well dressed, her smile full and rich, but she wasn't Derryn; and she certainly wasn't her back then. If I hadn't had such a connection to the woman she was trying to ape – if I'd been in Field's shoes, or Carmichael's, or someone who didn't know Derryn at all – I'd most likely have passed right by her.

There was a link to a proper missing poster on her page. I clicked on it. The same photograph was on the left-hand side, but there was some additional information on the right. Her birth date confirmed her age as forty-three, which made her a year older than Derryn would have been, and she'd vanished on 27 February 2010.

Beneath that was a very brief outline of her last sighting:

Melody Campbell was last seen at the Hilton Birmingham Metropole.

What had she been doing in Birmingham?

I googled her disappearance. It had made a minor splash, but only in local newspapers. I'd expected those local newspapers to be based in the Midlands, but they weren't.

They were in Northern Ireland.

I followed a link to a story in the *Belfast Telegraph*. It didn't amount to much, just an appeal for information, but halfway in, I got the background I was after: she and her parents were from Berkshire, but they'd moved to Belfast after her father got a job at Bombardier, the aerospace company, in 1989, when Melody was fifteen. After leaving school, she'd ended up working at Bombardier too, in the HR department, and had been in Birmingham attending a recruitment conference at the NEC when she'd vanished.

I hunted around for more details, but while her parents had never stopped in their efforts to find out what had happened to her, they'd died within a year of each other in 2012 and 2013, and Melody had no siblings to continue the work.

She was never found.

Until now.

I looked at her face, trying to imagine what had happened at that conference. In the newspaper article, it said she'd gone outside for a cigarette at the end of the night, after enjoying drinks with some colleagues at the hotel bar, but didn't come down for breakfast the next morning. One of the men she worked with went up to check on her, couldn't get a response, and raised the alarm. When the manager opened up her room,

Melody's clothes were all gone, her toiletries too, her hand-bag but not her phone. That was the only thing she'd left behind.

So where did she go? Why was she back now? And why, on her return, was she pretending to be Derryn?

I looked again at the location of her last sighting: a hotel outside the country's largest exhibition centre. Was there any link between the location of her disappearance and the fact that Erik McMillan frequently attended conferences? Could they have been in Birmingham at the same time?

As I turned everything over, a separate idea formed.

I put in a fresh search, this time using the terms *Derryn*, *Melody* and *Raker*. The first result was for the 'Crime and Punishment' blog on *FeedMe*. Under that were links to other newspaper stories, some years old, written off the back of cases I'd worked, and long since put to bed, that had bled into the public eye, none of which was relevant to this. I scrolled back up.

Beneath the search bar and the number of results was:

Did you mean: **Kerrin Melody Raker?**

I clicked it to see where it would take me, and found an altered set of results. At the top was a link to a tweet from an account called @merrigoldsdeli.

Merrigolds Deli on Twitter: "The weirdest thing just happened . . .

http://www.twitter.com/MerrigoldsDeli/status/96464497474.html

There had been no keyword match for Raker, and in the preview Google had provided there was only a description of who the account belonged to:

Merrigold's Deli is an award-winning restaurant and delicatessen in the beautiful Sussex village of Killiger. Tweets by Pat Merrigold.

I followed the link, uncertain about why it had been rated as the most relevant hit in Google – but then I read it and something began to congeal inside me.

Merrigolds Deli @MerrigoldsDeli 12 Sept 2013

The weirdest thing just happened. A woman came in asking for directions to, erm, Belfast (???) She seemed confused & didn't have an Irish accent. Uh?

A second and third tweet had been threaded to the first.

Merrigolds Deli @MerrigoldsDeli 12 Sept 2013

Maybe even weirder, I asked her what her name was and she said it was Kerrin (? I think). But then before she left she said it was Melody. Uh x 2?

Merrigolds Deli @MerrigoldsDeli 12 Sept 2013

She didn't even know it was Killiger. Not sure if it was a joke or if I should be concerned. Very short blonde hair & slim. Anyone seen her around the village? #twilightzonemusic

No one had responded to say they'd seen the same woman, but it simply had to be her. It had to be Melody.

It didn't matter to me that the owner of the deli seemed to think she referred to herself initially as *Kerrin*. I was almost positive she hadn't; instead, I believed the woman at the deli had misheard *Derryn*, perhaps because both names – *Kerrin* and *Derryn* – were unusual, perhaps because the woman's request was so odd. The connection to Belfast tallied with what I'd found out about Melody already.

The question was why.

Why had she gone in there to ask directions to Belfast? Why didn't she seem to know where she was, where Belfast was, even the area the deli was in?

What had she been doing in Sussex in the first place?

I went to a new tab and started reading about Killiger. It was a tiny village, right on the English Channel, between Seaford and Eastbourne, barely more than a single street with a pub, a newsagent, a grocery and a butcher's. From London, it was an easy two-hour drive.

I looked at the date of the incident in Killiger: September 2013. That was two and a half years after Melody Campbell disappeared, and over four years before she walked into the police station at Charing Cross. So was there anything to be read into the timings? I couldn't see an obvious pattern.

I couldn't see anything about this that made any sort of sense.

I switched to Google Maps, zooming in for a close-up of the village, and kept swapping between Map and Satellite views, trying to see if anything leapt out at me.

There was nothing.

But then, right at the edge of the laptop's screen, on the eastern boundaries of Killiger, something caught my eye and I realized I was wrong.

It was a cove, a beach, cut into the sweeping chalk cliffs that ran along this part of the coast. A road led down to a small car park, and next to the car park was a café and a children's play area.

Above the play area hovered its name.

The Dartford Memorial Park.

61

There was nothing about the memorial park on Google other than a small description on the East Sussex County Council website, which described exactly what was there – some swings, a roundabout, a climbing frame. There was no direct link to Bruce Dartford.

I put in another search for him and found the same stories I'd already read: he'd been travelling back to London from a medical conference in Sheffield, a lorry had jackknifed in front of him on the M1, and he'd ploughed into it. Two cars had smashed into the back of his Mercedes and he died later in hospital from severe brain injuries. From what I could tell, he'd been in London for years; certainly there was no obvious information online that connected him to a village on the East Sussex coast.

So was it just a huge coincidence that a park there carried his surname?

It was after seven o'clock at night, so even if I'd wanted to cold-call the deli, the butcher's or the grocery store in Killiger, I couldn't. So that really only left me two options: either I had to try and cold-call every single house in the village – from what I could tell, that amounted to about fifteen homes – or I gave the pub a shot first, hoping something would land.

I dialled the pub on my prepaid.

A gruff male voice answered: 'The Crown.'

'Evening, sir. I'm calling from the Metropolitan Police in London.' I paused for a moment, letting him take that in. I could have called on my own phone and told him who I was, but I needed him to focus, and pretending to be from the police was always the quickest way to get someone's attention. 'We're looking into a case that involved someone we *think* came from Killiger, and I'm afraid I haven't had a lot of success so far in getting the information I need. Have you got a minute?'

'Yeah,' he said, his voice softening.

'Have you heard of a Bruce Dartford?'

'Yeah, of course. His mum lived here.'

I felt a shot of adrenalin. 'His mum?'

'Margaret. Mags.'

'Is she still around?'

'No,' the man said. 'Mags died, ooooh, ten, eleven years back. Nice lady, that one. Lovely sense of humour.' He was starting to warm up now. 'Anyway, Bruce used to come down here to visit her a lot. He had some fancy job up in London somewhere – a doctor of some kind. Psychologist or psychiatrist or whatever you call it. Never know the difference. Uh, you know he's dead as well, right?'

'Yes, I read that.'

'He died in a car accident on the M1, up near Luton.'

I looked at my laptop again, at the satellite map of the village.

'So was the play park named after him?'

'Yeah.'

'How come?'

'Cos he died,' the man responded, 'obviously.'

'Yeah, but people die every day, don't they? So why was Bruce different? What made the village commemorate him in that way?'

'People liked him round here. He did a lot for this place. Back in the mid 2000s, some big shot from Brighton wanted to build an industrial estate half a mile inland. It would have been a disaster. Traffic, pollution, half the green belt destroyed. I mean, the guy was a total arsehole. I hated him, refused to serve him in here. I told him one night, "You can't –"'

I cut him short, before we got wildly off topic.

'Bruce didn't agree with the industrial estate being built either?'

'No way,' he said, clearly disappointed that I didn't want to hear about how he'd refused to serve the developer a drink. 'No, he ran a campaign against it. Did it almost single-handedly. When it went to court, he even paid all the legal fees himself.'

Bruce Dartford was generous, altruistic – how was that relevant? Where was all of this going? Dragging the map back and forth with the cursor, I kept zooming in and out, trying to see something new at the play park, but instead my gaze snagged on something else: a line I'd just added to my notebook.

Mother lived in Killiger.

'You said his mum lived there?' I asked.

'Mags? Yeah, all her life.'

'Where was her house?'

'Just out of the village,' he said, 'between here and the beach.'

I looked at the map again, trying to find it on the satellite image.

'He turned it into two holiday cottages,' the man said.

'Who did?'

'Bruce. After she died, he turned her house into two holiday cottages. Did it really nicely, actually. Quiet, minimal fuss. Respectful of his surroundings, the scenery, that sort of thing. It's all – what do you call it? – green. Renewable energy and all that. He named it after his mum – Margaret Cottages.'

Finally, I found it on the map.

It was alone, among fields, half a mile from the beach.

'He was pretty generous with that too,' the man said.

'What do you mean?'

'After he died, he left it to the hospital he worked for in London.'

That stopped me.

'Are you talking about St Augustine's?'

'I don't know what it's called,' the man said, 'but it was their charity arm. The hospital doesn't run it, the fundraising bit does. Same thing, I suppose.'

Except it wasn't the same thing at all.

If the police had even thought to look for property that St Augustine's might have owned, which was doubtful, the cottages in Killiger weren't in the hospital's name, they were in the name of their charity, Asclepius. I'd read all about it on the hospital website. That made it harder to find, not just because it was named after a Greek god and wasn't easily affiliated to the hospital, but because the charity arm would most likely be registered, structured and organized in a completely different way. Its contracts, paperwork, accounts and legal documents were probably at another address entirely.

'Do you know if the cottages are occupied at the moment?'

'First week of January?' the man said. 'I doubt it. The tourist trade tends to be dead until Easter and then it all kicks off.'

'But you don't know for sure?'

'Trust me, no one ever stays here at this time of the year.'

And that was the whole point.

That was what made the cottages such a good hiding place.

#0858

It was your wedding anniversary yesterday.

I know that from going through some of the papers in your loft. I watched your house most of the afternoon and evening, to see if I could catch a glimpse of you. I thought your husband may have done something for you, the kind of perfunctory celebration that only he would think was deserving of you. A cake, perhaps. A meal. Some tacky little gift.

Did he do that, Derryn?

I don't know, because until today I hadn't seen you for a week. That's the longest we've ever been. I didn't catch a glimpse of you in any of the windows; I hardly saw your husband either. I spent seven days watching the house, trying to understand what was going on, and the only time anything changed was on day five when a man in a silver van turned up. He went inside, spent forty minutes with you, and when he left again, I could see that your husband had been crying.

I only realized later that the man was from the hospice.

So are you really sick now, Derryn?

If you are, your husband's weakness isn't going to help. You can't fight if you have a man like that at your side. He may be physically big, but I realize now that he's vulnerable. He thinks all of this is about him. Those tears are about him, about what he's losing, not about you. He's not good enough for you, and I imagine this is the point at which you're starting to realize it. When the man from the hospice left, your husband looked a mess, an absolute fucking mess. I can only imagine what effect that must be having on you. You're there, fighting for every breath in your lungs, and all he can do is sit and cry. He's pathetic, isn't he? You're too kind, too graceful, to admit that he is, but I know you must be thinking that. You must look at him with utter contempt.

In fact, while I was watching the house yesterday, I started thinking about something: what if I really did get rid of him? I've thought about it a lot since the night I followed him to the supermarket. I've thought constantly about how much better it would be if he wasn't here. I could make the world forget him, just like they forgot Nora. I'm good at planning things like that. I have the patience for it. After I split up from Nora, as Erik was helping me clear my head in our sessions, I watched her for months and she never even realized I was there. I wanted to know what she did, her routines; that way, I knew how to lure her in, to get her where I needed her to be. I would do the same for your husband if you wanted me to.

He would never see me coming, I promise.

Knowing the type of person you are, I'm sure you would want it to be over quickly for him, despite the way he's let you down, and I'd do that for you, Derryn. I would. If I severed an artery, just like I imagined that night at the supermarket, he'd be unconscious in ten seconds. He wouldn't suffer, even though he deserves to.

And then it would just be the two of us.

I think you'd like that, especially if you really are in a bad way now. You'd remember what a connection we had and I think it would give you a lift. We could talk about whatever you wanted. I could read you passages from No One Can See the Crows at Night. *Even though it's not my favourite Gainridge book, I would read the entire thing to you if it helped.*

I would do anything for you.

But then I saw you again today and everything else — all the plans I was making — faded into the background. It happened after your husband finally left the house. He was crying again. I watched him come out and get into his car, and as he drove past mine, wiping his eyes, it dawned on me: I would still kill him, if that was the most effective way to bring us closer, but I didn't have to wait until then to be alone with you. It seemed so simple, so clear, I wasn't sure why I'd never thought of it before.

I'd been inside your house many times.

I'd just never thought to go inside when you were there.

I gave it a couple of minutes, just to be sure he definitely wasn't going to come back and disturb us, and then accessed the back garden in the same way I'd done before, when you'd both been out. I scaled the fence at the side and then picked the door at the rear. Inside half a minute, I was standing in your living room.

The house had changed since I'd last been in. It smelled of sickness. In the kitchen, there were unwashed plates. It felt dirty and unclean. I stood there for a moment and listened, tried to hear if you were moving around. But all that came back was silence. As I went through to the hallway, I felt anger throb like a pulse in my throat. He hadn't left the house in seven days, so why had he let it get like this? Why was he failing you so badly, Derryn?

I walked to the bedroom door.

Even before I got there, I could hear you, the air rattling in your chest. Your breathing sounded like an old motor struggling to turn over. When I looked in at you, you were under the sheets, asleep, your eyelids fluttering, your skin waxy and pale. You looked like a mannequin. I'm not sure what I was expecting, but it wasn't this. I gripped the door frame and edged further inside, but you didn't even move.

'Derryn?' I said.

I went to the foot of the bed.

You were so gaunt. Your skin had settled on your bones like wet paper, falling around your cheeks, your chin. You were a skeleton covered in a sheet of silk; a husk, a meagre reflection of the woman I'd first seen walk on to that hospital ward, confident and smiling and beautiful. As I came further around the bed, your breath staggered in your throat, struggling to make it to your mouth, and I watched your windpipe shift like a piston – up and down, up and down – as your body went into panic. I reached forward and gripped your hand, and the touch of your skin on mine – even as thin and as brittle as it was – sent a charge of electricity through me. I hesitated for a moment, watching you, and as you settled, I leaned in and kissed you gently on the forehead.

When you didn't stir, I did it again.

'I love you,' I whispered.

Your eyelids fluttered, but you didn't wake, and then I noticed that there was saliva at the corner of your mouth, bubbling. It looked undignified, unattractive, so I looked around the room for something to wipe it with. There was nothing to hand, so I tried the drawers of your bedside cabinet, searching for tissues.

But, in the second drawer, I found something else.

A copy of No One Can See the Crows at Night.

It was a hardback edition. I reached in and took it out, and as I did, the book slid away, as if its covers didn't fit properly, and the novel tumbled to the floor.

Except it wasn't a novel inside the covers.

It was something else.

62

A light came on in the house just before 11 p.m.

I'd been waiting for an hour in the car park at Killiger, my Audi covered in shadows, looking up the slope towards the holiday cottages. Beside me, circled by knee-high fencing, was the children's play park, the swings moving back and forth as the wind rolled in off the sea. To my left was Killiger itself, or what amounted to it, little more than a few squares of light and wisps of chimney smoke. Behind me was the cove that everything was set around: a crescent of beach hemmed in on both sides by huge chalk cliffs, sloping upwards like giants hauling themselves from the shingle.

From what I could see with binoculars, there were two main doors on the house, at either end of the property, one for access to each holiday cottage. The building had been divided in two, and because of that, there were matching slate patios at both ends. Until now, I'd seen no activity in either part of the house – no hint of anyone.

I focused the binoculars on the window. It wasn't very big and its glass was frosted, so it seemed likely that it was a toilet, or maybe some sort of utility room. I watched for signs of movement inside and adjusted the focus a fraction more. As everything sharpened, I picked up something: a distorted hint of a shape. Was it the woman? McMillan?

The room went dark.

I'd kept the engine running, the heaters going and the headlights off, but now I silenced the car, got out and went to the boot. The light in the house had only been there for

358

thirty seconds, maybe less, but someone was inside and that was all the confirmation I needed.

Grabbing my bag, I slipped it over my shoulders, locked the car and headed away from the car park, back up the narrow, single-track road I'd driven down. At the top was a lane running west to east. I headed east, rain in the air. The weather had slowly started to change on the drive down from London, cloud knotting together in the clear winter skies. The closer I'd got to the coast, the fiercer the wind had become, and as I tried to pick up the pace now, it pressed against me even harder, almost as if it were trying to drag me back, some premonitory force telling me to turn around.

Ahead of me, a gap in the hedgerows emerged, a wooden gate set into it separating the road I was on from an uneven, loose-stone track that led down to the house. I stopped at the gate and looked over it. From where I was, it seemed as if the cottages were clinging to the edges of the headland, about to plunge on to the beach itself.

I waited for a moment.

There was very little natural light here, just whatever was leaking across the fields from Killiger, and what had made it this far from the lighthouse at Beachy Head, three miles further along the coast. There were no street lamps. No other houses nearby. If it had been a clear night, it would have helped me; instead, the rain had started to get heavier, crackling against my jacket, the clouds letting nothing through from above.

I scaled the gate and dropped down, on to the other side. As the track was full of loose stones, I switched to the grass either side, using it to disguise the sound of my approach. At one point, I looked back over my shoulder and realized that hardly anyone would see this place from the main road if they were driving past. It would have been visible from out to sea, from the beach and the car park, but not really from Killiger itself. And because the beach and the car park weren't used as regularly in winter, especially in weather like this, the house would exist in relative isolation at this time of year.

That was why it was such a perfect hiding place.

As I arrived at the entrance to the near-side cottage, I checked for signs of movement around me. It was hard in the rain, the wind shifting the grass, the sea crushing the sound of everything else, but when nothing registered, I returned my attention to the house and moved around to the other half of the building.

That was where the light had come from.

The first window was a bedroom, the bed made, some ornaments on a set of drawers in the shadows. Next to that was the kitchen. It was hard to see into, but there was enough residual light from the digital readouts on the cooker and the microwave for me to see plates and mugs piled up in the sink, packets of food on the worktops, and one of the chairs pulled out from the table, an anorak hanging from the back of it. Through the bi-fold doors, I saw an untidy living room, cushions bunched up where they'd been used as head pillows, a remote control on the floor and some scattered DVD boxes. Close to me, only a few inches from the doors, I saw something else: the phone socket. The Internet had been disconnected.

I headed past the utility room and the bathroom and then stopped short of the window into the second bedroom. Swinging my bag off my shoulders and leaving it on the grass, I leaned against the wall and peered inside. A man was lying on the bed, asleep, facing me.

McMillan.

I'd found him.

But any flurry of excitement was brief.

Inside, he moved, moaned. I looked in at him as he rolled on to his back, a hand coming up towards his chest – and that was when I saw blood all over the mattress, his shirt, his hands.

He wasn't sleeping.

He was dying.

63

I rushed to the front door and tried the handle. It didn't move. Dropping to my knees, I reached for my picks and started trying to spring the lock. It took me longer than it should have done, the pressure getting to me, my hands trembling, the image of McMillan in my head.

But then I heard a click.

I pushed at the door. Ahead of me, muddy footprints glistened on the oak flooring.

Someone else is here.

I glanced around in vain for a weapon and then out to the blackness of the fields surrounding the house. Everything was movement: rain and grass and wind. I switched my attention back to the interior of the house, unzipped my bag and pulled out a torch. Flicking it on, I shone it deeper into the cottage.

Its beam reflected off the walls, the wooden floors.

It came back at me from a nearby mirror.

And then so did my reflection: I was bloodless and frightened. I could hardly remember the last time I'd slept, could feel the exhaustion weighing on me like chains. Before I'd driven down from London, I'd managed an hour on the sofa, but it had been fitful, agitated, and eventually I'd given in: I hadn't wanted to sleep, I'd wanted to get to Killiger and find out who was using the cottage as a hideaway.

Now I wanted to be anywhere else but here.

I made a quick half-turn, out towards the fields again, the beam of my torch cutting through the rain like a knife, and – when I couldn't see anyone – grabbed my bag off the floor and slipped it over my front. It was the best I could do, the only way I could shield my torso from any blade.

I didn't want to end up like McMillan.

The house was warm, the heating on. I listened to a radiator ticking in the hallway, and then passed the door to the downstairs bathroom, my eyes trained on the kitchen. That was where the muddy footprints led. There was no exit in there, so if that was where McMillan's attacker was, they'd have to come back this way.

I paused at the bathroom.

It was the one that had been used less than ten minutes ago. The door was open an inch, enough for me to see – with the torch – that there was no one inside. On the floor were the same muddy footprints – and there was blood in the sink, partially washed away. Bandages on the top of the toilet. Tape. Antiseptic.

McMillan hadn't used the bathroom.

Someone else had.

So had they been trying to *help* McMillan? Had they found him like this? Or had something got out of hand?

Even with the wind howling outside and the rain against the roof, I could hear his moans, and the closer I got to the doorway, the louder they got. He was saying something too, his words indistinct.

Keeping my gaze on the kitchen, I stepped up to the door, then took a quick look in at him. He was on his side, facing me, blood-soaked sheets beneath him.

He'd seen me.

'Look,' he wheezed, eyes on me.

I frowned, checked the kitchen for any sign of his attacker, and then mouthed: *What?*

'Look,' he repeated. 'Look . . .'

Look at what?

He shook his head.

I turned towards the kitchen again, trying to angle my head in order to see more of it, and then McMillan started coughing.

I glanced at him again.

'Look . . .' He coughed. 'Up.'

And then it felt like I got hit by a sledgehammer.

I was on the floor before I even really understood what had happened. Somewhere beyond the rain and the wind and the crash of the sea, I heard the squeak of wet shoes on wooden floors, someone breathing, and then frantic, rhythmic footsteps, dulling as soon as they hit the fields. Everything pinged back into focus only a couple of seconds later, but I was still on my back, staring up at the vaulted ceiling, at the timber beams criss-crossing above my head.

I turned, trying to prop myself up on to an elbow, and pain streaked across my chest: whoever had landed on me had crunched my collarbone, the edges of my throat and neck. I took a deep breath and looked out into the night.

Vaguely, I spotted a shape sprinting away.

They were making a break for the beach.

64

I hauled myself up on to all fours, took another even deeper breath and then tried standing. I felt unsteady, dazed, but I started running all the same. Ahead of me, maybe two hundred feet away, a silhouette was tearing across the fields, following a faint chalk path in the direction of the cove.

For the first time, I saw something else too, faint against the night, but unmistakable: a boat.

It had been pulled up on to the shingle.

I tried to pick up the pace, but the faster I went, the more nauseous I started to feel. I was blowing hard, struggling to find my footing in the wet grass, the chalk slick and the wind fierce. The next time I looked, the figure was at the stern of the boat, shoving the vessel towards the water.

Grey light from the village and a lingering, pulsating glow from the lighthouse showed the figure's outline, and then my torch beam confirmed it: stocky and well built, dressed in black waterproof trousers and a dark anorak, the hood up. Instantly, I thought of the shadow man in the CCTV video: he'd moved the same way.

Because it's him.

He's here.

Again, I tried to move faster, to raise the torch so that more of the man might come into view, but he was only appearing in flashes now, blinking in and out of existence as the torch beam jerked around. I was still woozy from where he'd landed on me, and my throat was burning as I breathed.

His feet started kicking up water.

'Stop!' I shouted instinctively, but the wind carried it away, a worthless word that was never going to be heeded. I'd caught him up by a few yards, but it wasn't enough: he was in a foot of water now, the boat beginning to glide. Once it did, he gave it another, much harder shove and then leapt into it.

The boat rocked on the waves, left and then right, but he adjusted his balance, staying at the stern, by the motor. He began fiddling with something close to the throttle, then the choke.

It spluttered.

As he tried it again, I closed the gap, feeling a charge of electricity – *I can get to him, I can still get to him* – but the motor erupted into life, the boat jolted forward, began to move smoothly away on the water, and he grabbed the tiller.

An ashen glow washed in from the lighthouse again. He was out in the water now, more exposed to its beam, his identity no longer protected by the darkness and the slopes either side of the cove.

But he knew the light was coming.

A second earlier, he'd been side on to me, looking at the engine, reaching for the tiller, the profile of his face inching out beyond his hood. But then he made a fractional movement away, out towards the horizon, and all I could see as the boat took off, as the lighthouse blinked, was the back of him, his coat, his hood.

The beach became dark again.

The boat began dissolving into the night.

And then there was nothing left of him.

Except that wasn't quite true: as I moved to the shoreline, I realized he'd left something behind. When I'd been running after him, I'd missed it because it was so faint, but now, as I looked at it more closely, I saw how it trailed from the edge of the sea right back to the grass in infrequent, sporadic dots. It was on the shingle and in the field. It was all the way back at the house.

Blood.

I thought of the mess that had been left in the bathroom at the cottage – blood in the sink, a bottle of antiseptic, bandages, tape.

McMillan hadn't made the mess, the man had.

He was injured.

65

Once I was back at the house, I headed for the bedroom. There was blood everywhere. McMillan had moved, dragging himself off the bed and on to the floor. I leaned down, grabbed him under the arms and hauled him into a chair.

He wheezed, looked at me, his eyelids fluttering.

I grabbed my phone, trying to second-guess the fallout for me from dialling 999. But I didn't really have a choice. McMillan was dying. He needed an ambulance. If I tried to save my own skin, I was condemning someone else.

As I was speaking to an operator, I looked around the room. On the bed, half-covered by sheets, was a knife. It was small, but it was sharp and serrated, probably taken from the kitchen. McMillan must have been sleeping with it under his pillow.

I put the rest together: his attacker had come to the house with his own knife – judging by McMillan's wounds, a proper hunting knife – and stabbed McMillan just under the ribcage. It was bad. As he started coughing, blood escaping on to his lips, I started to realize how bad. The injury was making a sucking sound. Every time he breathed in, air was escaping into his chest cavity. If his attacker had been able to run for a boat, his injury was nowhere near as bad as McMillan's, but it was bad enough: bad enough that he would try to patch it up in the bathroom. And, as he was doing that, he must have seen me from one of the windows, approaching.

He'd climbed up, on to one of the cross-beams.

And he'd waited.

I finished calling for an ambulance, pocketed my phone

and looked at McMillan's wound again. He stared back at me wordlessly. He was a doctor: he knew better than I did.

He didn't have long.

Hurrying through to the kitchen, I searched around for some cling film, grabbed the tape his attacker had been using in the bathroom, and returned to McMillan. Lifting up his shirt, exposing the wound, I tried to create a makeshift dressing, laying a folded sheet of cling film over the injury and taping it to his skin on all four sides.

When I was done, he looked at me, blinked as if he couldn't focus, and softly said, 'Thank you,' but we both knew it was only a temporary fix. If the ambulance didn't get here in the next ten minutes, he wasn't leaving this cottage alive.

'Erik, I need you to focus, okay?'

He tried to shift himself, and grimaced.

'Where's Melody?'

I wasn't sure if he'd even heard me.

'*Erik.*' I took a step closer to him, his blood tacky against the underside of my shoes. His eyes started to close. I knelt down beside the chair, laid a hand on his arm and said, 'Erik, listen to me. Where's Melody Campbell?'

'She's . . .'

'She's where?' I squeezed his arm. 'Where is she, Erik?'

'She's gone.'

Panic hit my bloodstream.

'She's *dead*?'

He didn't respond. My memory fired up: the woman sitting in an interview room at Charing Cross; approaching the flat at Chalk Farm; in the living room at my house; in my arms for those few short minutes.

'Melody's dead?'

'He got rid of her,' he murmured, staring off into space.

'He? You mean the man who was here?'

He nodded slowly.

I took a breath, collecting myself. 'Who is he? What's his name?'

'John.'

'John who?'

'I don't . . .' He faded out. 'I don't know.'

He winced, jamming a hand to the dressing I'd made.

'I don't know anything about him,' he breathed, *about him* barely making it past his lips.

I looked around the room, as if the answers might be hidden in its corners, but then – when I turned back to McMillan – it hit me properly: Melody was dead. I was never going to find out why she'd pretended to be Derryn.

They were both gone.

'Do you know where Melody's body is?'

He looked at me, his eyes filling with tears. One broke free and he tried to wipe it away, his hand juddering towards his face. All he did was smear fresh blood across his cheek.

'My letter,' he said, almost incoherent now.

'What?'

He began weeping again.

'Where can I find Melody's body, Erik?'

He shook his head.

'You treated her, right? I found your notes in the mailbox in Earls Court. You treated her. You must know *something* about her.'

He glanced down at himself, at the wound, at the blood slowly spreading like an oil slick beneath the cling film. 'I'm dying,' he said quietly, his words slurred, gluey. 'This is . . .' He sucked in another breath. 'This is the ending I deserve.'

'What about Melody, Erik? I need to find her.'

He returned his gaze to me, his focus drifting in and out, like a camera struggling to adjust. 'I'm sorry for what I did.'

'What did you do?'

'I lied . . . about you.'

We stared at each other.

'You were . . .' He swallowed. 'Never my patient.'

'So why did you say that I was?'

He answered but I didn't hear him, his throat wet, the words doughy and indistinct. I leaned in closer to him and asked him the same question again.

'Scared,' he mumbled.

'That's why you said you treated me?'

He nodded.

'Who were you scared of?'

His eyelids began to droop.

'Were you scared of this John guy?'

Another nod of the head.

'He said . . . he'd tell . . . everyone.'

I frowned. 'Tell everyone about what?'

He started coughing again.

'Tell everyone about what, Erik?'

He was starting to drift again.

'*Erik.*'

He looked up at me, disorientated, and then – as he glanced at the wound, like a mouth beneath his ribcage – he started whimpering.

'*Erik.* Where's Melody Campbell?'

'My letter,' he said again.

'What letter? What are you talking about?'

He shifted his head slightly and looked across the room, towards the bed. I followed his eyeline. All I could see were bloodstained sheets. The knife. Some books on the bedside cabinet. A pen.

A spiral notepad.

I grabbed it but it was empty. He'd used pages in it – I could see the thin slivers of paper caught in the spirals at the top – but there was nothing written inside. All its pages were blank. I looked back at him, confused, and saw that his eyes were on the top drawer of the bedside cabinet.

I opened it up.

There were two solitary sheets of paper, torn from the notepad, sitting on top of some underwear. He'd written on both of them, front and back, and not in the deliberately illegible hand he'd used when he'd been writing about Melody. He wanted the recipient to be able to read this.

Because the recipient was his daughter.

He was asking Caitlin to forgive him.

66

I finished reading the letter and looked across the room at McMillan. He stared back, tears in his eyes. He'd managed to gather himself slightly but the pain was still humming close to the surface. His mouth was permanently turned up at the edges, as if he couldn't breathe properly.

'You really want your daughter to see this?' I said to him, floored by what I'd read. He nodded. 'This will destroy her, Erik.'

He nodded again.

'She idolizes you.'

There was a flicker of something in his face this time, and then a spark of uncertainty flared. It was clear that he'd been going back and forward on this, and not just over the last few days – over months, years. He'd wanted to tell his daughter the truth for a long time, about the things he'd done, about his wife, Kelly. It had been eating him up. But he loved Caitlin more than anything in the world, and he'd realized the truth would devastate her. It would ravage their relationship.

There would be no going back.

I looked at the letter again. These words, this truth, was how it was possible to manipulate him. This was why he'd gone along with the lies of Melody Campbell, of the killer I'd chased to the boat. This was how McMillan had been blackmailed.

Dear Caitlin . . .

He started by saying how much he loved her, that she was the centre and circumference of his life. He said nothing could, or ever would, change that, but he needed to tell her something. She needed to know the truth about her mother, about why Kelly ran a bath ten years ago, and cut her wrists.

I looked up at him.

He was crying, grieving. He was bleeding from the wound in his chest, and he was dying. But the decay had started a long time before tonight.

Your mum had been depressed for years . . .

It had been pretty much since the start of their marriage. But they'd managed it – with pills, with therapy, Kelly had managed to survive, to maintain an equilibrium, and Caitlin had been a big part of that. Their daughter had been their light, the tether that bound them all together, the perpetual life jacket that had kept Kelly afloat. Except, a rot had been festering the whole time: Erik McMillan had a secret.

I wanted to tell your mum from early on, even before you were born, but I'm not sure I was certain then. Or maybe I was just frightened about how people would react to me, what they might say about me. I felt like I couldn't give into it.

But then he met Bruce Dartford.

And that was when he stopped denying who he was.

Kelly had found emails between the two of them on McMillan's computer. An accident – she hadn't been prying. But, low at the time, in a funk, it sent her even lower. Three weeks passed and she didn't get out of bed. Caitlin asked her dad what was wrong with Mum and he told her it was just another period of decline, a trough that her mum would crawl out of, just the same as before. Erik assured her that he had no idea why it had suddenly hit her so hard like this.

A day later, Kelly was dead.

I looked across the room at him.

If I could help it, I rarely opted for lies, especially among family. But, even though I didn't know Caitlin, except through a single ten-minute call, I could see how huge this would be. Everything would fall, because she'd built everything on following the example of her father: how he'd tried to help her mother; how he helped patients at the hospital; how people respected him and looked up to him; how he loved them both, mother and daughter, and supported them – Caitlin especially, but even Kelly, however platonic his real feelings for her had been.

If the truth was just that he was gay, Caitlin might be shocked, but she would probably accept that over time. But the issue wasn't McMillan's sexuality, it wasn't even necessarily the way he'd kept it secret, it was the way his wife had found out, the things she had read in the emails between him and Bruce Dartford, and the aftermath. She cut her wrists because he had an affair, because that affair was with a man, because he didn't love her as a husband was supposed to love a wife, and because he'd lied to her about who he was for the entirety of their marriage.

'You really want Caitlin to read this?' I said again.

He was definitely unsure now. Eventually, things were going to come out, his deception about me would be exposed, but there were degrees of severity. How he'd deceived the police, the way he'd played along with Melody and whoever the hell John was – that could potentially be explained away, fudged somehow, even if he'd suffer the consequences of it over the years to come. Because lying to the police would be much lower down the list in Caitlin's eyes than the actual reason an eleven-year-old girl went through the trauma of watching her mother kill herself.

He started coughing again.

I knelt down beside him and said, 'Where can I find Melody, Erik? If she's dead, I need to know where she is. I need to find John.'

'A . . .' He stopped. ' . . . gus . . .'

'Angus?'

He shook his head.

' . . . gus . . .'

'Angus? Who's Angus?'

He swallowed, took a breath; winced.

'Who's Angus, Erik?'

But this time he shook his head.

'*Augustine*,' he breathed, and then started coughing again.

I stopped, looking at him.

'*St* Augustine's?'

He nodded.

'What about it?'

'He's . . . there . . .'

'John works at St Augustine's? He works at the hospital?'

His eyes started to glaze over. I grabbed him by the arm, pressing hard, trying to force some function back into his body.

He didn't react, his eyes still closed.

Somewhere in the distance, I could hear sirens now. The ambulance was close; the police would be too. I didn't have long.

'*Erik.*'

He jolted again.

'Will I find John at the hospital?'

It was weak, barely discernible, but he nodded, once.

I looked around me, trying to make sense of it. *John works at the hospital.* I thought back to the night I'd gone there to see McMillan and the moments before I blacked out. I'd heard someone else enter the admin block. I'd left McMillan's office to look for them – but no one was out there. It had felt like I was losing it at the time. But I wasn't. Someone *had* been there.

John.

'Melody . . .'

I snapped back to McMillan.

'Melody? What about her?'

'Not dead . . .' He drew in a breath. 'Just gone.'

I frowned. 'What are you talking about?'

His head began to drop.

'*Erik*.'

His head stayed where it was, but his eyes opened. I crouched down further so we were on the same level, and – in a voice barely above a whisper – he repeated something he'd said to me earlier: 'He . . . got rid of her.'

'"Got rid of her"? What does that mean? Is she dead or isn't she?'

'Not dead. Someone new.'

And that was when I finally understood what he was trying to tell me: the name Melody Campbell was gone, the identity – the person that had existed before her disappearance in February 2010. That was what had been got rid of. But the woman herself was still alive.

She was just someone else now.

'Ease war.'

'*What?*' I leaned in towards him again. 'What did you say?'

'Ease war.'

'"Ease war"? What does that mean?'

'He erased Melody . . . at . . . ease war . . .'

He stopped again.

'Erased Melody . . . at . . . ease war . . . made Derryn.'

His eyes fluttered shut, like the wings of a dying bird, and in my head a picture formed, and it was one that I should have seen coming a long time ago. But as clearly as I saw it now, as much as I wanted to ask McMillan if I was right, I couldn't. I could barely bring myself to form the idea in my head, let alone say the words out loud.

Not this.

Not what had been done to Melody Campbell.

#0899

I need to tell you something, Derryn.

As I stand here at your grave, it's been four months since you died. I've had to go back to Erik again, get him to help me. I can see he's not trying as hard as he could be — not after what happened last time, with Nora — but he knows that he has no choice but to listen; not unless he wants his daughter to hear all about the dirty little secret that cost her mother her life.

And I think, really, that's all I need him to do.

I just need someone to sit there and listen to me. I need to unpack everything in front of him so I can look at it more lucidly. I need to articulate to him how much I miss you. We never got the chance to be together, not properly. In your final few weeks, whenever your husband left, I got inside your house. But it wasn't the same as being together, as actually existing together, living, cooking dinner, making love. You were barely conscious most of the time. It wasn't like when we were in hospital together, when you'd sit on the edge of my bed and we'd talk about books. It wasn't like that.

But something has happened.

This is what I need to tell you about.

Five weeks ago, I got told I had to go to this tedious recruitment conference in Birmingham with one of the idiots from Psychology. And as much as I wanted to scream in the faces of the people I worked with and tell them I didn't give a shit about any of it, I told them it was fine and I went. And, Derryn, I think it might have been fate that I was there. If I believed in that sort of thing, I might have seen it as destiny, some thread of a connection between wherever you are now, and me. Because I saw you.

I saw you in someone else and it floored me.

She was staying at the same hotel as me. When I went to the conference the next day, I spent my lunchtime searching the show floor for her, and I found her on the Bombardier stand.

Derryn, it's you.

It's you.

You and Melody, you aren't identical. Actually, in quite a number of ways, the two of you are very different. She's overweight, a brunette, her nose isn't quite right and her skin much less pristine. She doesn't have your smile – it's nearly there, but it's not quite the same – and her movements are less refined, less lithe, because she's fat. She doesn't quite have your confidence either, that little, deliberate hint of mystery. But as soon as I saw her, I saw an echo that was impossible to ignore. As soon as she walked into that hotel, I saw you.

I saw you in her face, her traits, her characteristics.

When you died in November, when I watched them take your body out of the house, its scant shape barely existing beneath the sheet, I never thought about how this would end. I know I talked about killing your husband, but there doesn't seem to be a point now. What would it achieve? It would just make my life more complicated. I hate him for his inadequacy – for the way he failed you when you were sick – but if I killed him and buried him next to Nora, it would just bring questions. It would bring suspicion.

And I can't afford for that to happen now.

See, I've got her tied up in the basement. I'm still having a hard time getting over you, and I don't want to do anything before I've cleared this fog away. I need to be absolutely lucid again, like I was when I dealt with Nora.

I don't want to make any mistakes.

But I've started trying to talk to her about you; she's a sounding board, a way for me to get my head straight at home, at night, when I'm not in my sessions with Erik. I've admitted to her that I've had a breakdown. I tell her all about it. I tell her that McMillan is treating me, and I pretend I have this thing called Capgras delusion, which is where you get all fucked up in the head about the people close to you. I don't have that at all, but she seems to believe me. Admittedly, in these early days, she doesn't always play ball, which is why I sometimes have to keep the gag on, or tie her up. Sometimes I have to hurt her, even though I don't want to.

But, over time, I know that will change.

I have a system I'm going to use.

You know how we used to love to read, don't you? Well, you wouldn't believe how much reading I've done over the past five weeks. I've studied these techniques over and over again, every day since I brought her here. I've watched documentaries on the Korean War, on Patty Hearst, on Manson, on Koresh. I've now read so many books and written so many notes, I've watched so many DVDs, you could fill an entire room.

Soon, we will get to the first stage.

I've isolated her.

Next, I will start the assault on her identity.

You know, Derryn, I think — even when I stood at your bedside in those last few days, holding your hand, seeing how sick you were, how you could hardly even breathe — I still didn't accept you were dying. I didn't believe anything would get in the way of us — not even your illness.

Now I realize something.

It doesn't have to.

Because I have Melody. All the things that are different about her I can change. Her weight, her hair — those things are easy. I can get contact lenses made for her eyes so they're exactly the same as yours. Her movements, her confidence — I can alter those too. They can be taught, like an actress playing a role. They can be refined. I can teach her to talk like you and eat like you, remember all the things that you did in your life. We can watch the home videos of you that I stole. I'll edit out anything with your husband in it, so it's just about you. Only you. She'll learn about you, and she'll behave the same way you do, and eventually she'll believe it's her. She'll look at the screen and talk about herself. She won't get sick like you. She won't go to work like you. She won't have friends.

She'll just be mine.

So, yes, I miss you so much, Derryn, and I'm sorry that your hus-band got between us. I was going to kill him, and I lied to you – I was going to do it slowly. I'm sorry I have to admit that now, as I stand at your graveside.

But none of that matters any more.

Because now I have Melody.

And I'm going to make her into you.

67

I stood, using the nearest piece of furniture for support, and my eyes started to blur. The confession fell from my hands.

McMillan just looked at me, tears in his eyes, bleeding out.

John turned Melody into Derryn.

All the pieces began to click into place. I remembered the tweet I'd read about how Melody had walked into the deli here, acting strangely, asking for directions back to Belfast. Whoever John was, he'd brought her here. He must have called it a holiday, acted like they were a real couple, that their relationship wasn't built on a kidnapping, on lies, on keeping Melody a prisoner until she became what he wanted. The woman at the deli said that Melody had referred to herself as Kerrin – *Derryn* – but, later on, changed her mind and told them her actual name. Was it because she was scared? Panicked? Disorientated? Had she managed to get away from John for those few short minutes?

Had it been an escape?

If she'd got away from him somehow, beyond his control for a time, it had been a failed attempt. He must have found her again quickly, because I hadn't discovered a single mention of her anywhere else on the web after that. But then another detail stuck with me: the description of her having very short blonde hair.

I blinked, another terrible idea starting to form.

No. No, not this.

Had he wanted her to be so much like Derryn, he'd shaved her head? Had he wanted her to be like Derryn at the end, when she was sick? Nausea spread like vines through my throat. The obsession had started with Derryn in the time before she died, and in one tiny moment, forgotten entirely by me for eight years, that obsession had spilled out into both of our lives when I found him bothering her at the hospital. She never talked about that man again, which must have meant he didn't try to speak to her before she passed on – but he would have been there. A man like that, wired how he was, couldn't turn it off like a light; all I'd done in confronting him that day, in pushing him away, was to force him into the shade. So had he followed us after that? Had he watched those final months of her life play out from a distance?

Or had he got closer than that?

The idea almost cut me down. Could he have got inside my house years before I ever found his book in the loft? Could he have tried to get close to Derryn again? And then, off the back of that, something else landed so hard it really did wipe me off my feet and I dropped to my knees: it would have been safer and easier for him to wait for me to go out and *then* get close to her.

He'd been there alone with Derryn.

He'd been at her bedside in her final weeks.

The sirens were just outside now, but it took a second for it to hit home. I was barely functioning, consumed by the idea that this man had been inside my home when my wife was dying. I tried to dismiss it, to tell myself it was only a theory, nothing more, but it was an image I couldn't unsee, one that blinked like a strobe behind my eyelids.

Wiping at my eyes, I attempted to gather my composure, to ready myself for the police, but my whole body felt like it was withering. I tried to imagine when he might have invaded my home, why he would ever do what he did to Melody afterwards, alter her like that, and one thing kept returning to me: he wanted to nurse her back to health. He wanted to succeed where no one else had.

The doctors. The hospitals.

Me.

He wanted to be the one who saved Derryn.

Day Six

68

Erik McMillan died in the back of the ambulance.

I stood at the entrance to the cottage, the wind still blowing, the rain chattering against the roof, and listened to the paramedics desperately try to revive him. By the time McMillan was dead, the police had arrived in force.

Officers began cordoning everything off, laying down metal plates for detectives and forensic staff to walk on, and eventually a mobile incident unit parked up on the grass at the front of the house, and I was shuffled inside before I could contaminate any more of the crime scene. From its windows, I watched officers and forensics moving between the bedroom of the cottage, the living room, kitchen and bathroom, photographing and collecting evidence, the brief anonymity of McMillan's existence here destroyed for ever.

Three hours later, after my clothes had been bagged and I'd been given replacements, and after a detective from a Sussex Major Crime team had conducted an initial interview with me, I watched another vehicle emerge off the main road and head down the stone path towards the house. It pulled up behind the truck, but I could see enough of it to know who was inside: Carmichael clambered out, his big frame encased in a black raincoat. There was no Field, no Kent, just him and someone else from his team. He walked up to the cottage, showing a uniformed officer his warrant card, and then he talked to another detective for a while. Finally, he turned and looked at me.

We stared at each other through the half-misted windows of the vehicle, and I thought of what Field had said yesterday beneath the railway arches. Carmichael was the tip of the spear. He was driving the entire investigation now, which was why he was here and not her. And, worse than that, he didn't like me, didn't like what I did for a living, how I went about it, or any success I might have had.

I was tired, bruised, as drained as I could ever remember being.

But I'd have to forget all of that for now.

Because he was coming for me.

Carmichael set up the interview in the truck.

The detective from the Sussex Major Crime team sat beside him: she was in her early forties, and had introduced herself as DI Mulligan during the initial interview with me. On a stool behind them was a DC called Yedborough, pale and serious, who had travelled down with Carmichael from London. He sat in silence, taking notes.

Carmichael first made me go over my visit to Killiger.

I gave him exactly the same account as I'd given Mulligan. It was four in the morning and I was starting to flag, but it wasn't hard to maintain my story because, for the most part, it was true. The only things I altered were details that might incriminate me, or give Carmichael a foot-up: when he asked about the fourteen pages of notes that McMillan had written, I told him I'd seen them on McMillan's desk at St Augustine's the night he invited me there, and that was how I found out about the mailbox and, in turn, discovered the name Melody. It was hard to say whether any of them believed me, but it was harder for them to disprove it. I'd placed the notes I'd got from the mailbox inside the top drawer of the bedside cabinet at the cottage, so it looked like McMillan had brought them to Sussex with him. In the moments before the paramedics entered, I'd also asked McMillan what he wanted to do with the letter he'd written to Caitlin. He could barely talk by then, but he said enough with his eyes. I ripped it to pieces and flushed it down the toilet.

The more frustrated Carmichael became, the more he fixated on my decision-making, on the reasons why I might not contact them as soon as I found out the woman was called Melody Campbell. 'You knew her name and you chose to remain silent,' he said, almost spitting the words through his teeth. 'It's unacceptable.' I suspected most of his irritation came, not from me failing to give him the name, but from the fact that I'd got there before him. After that, he tried to paint all of my decisions as some grand conspiracy of silence and, because the same questions got asked by him so often and with such force, he eventually got what he wanted.

I lost my cool.

'You want to know why I didn't pick up the phone to you?' I said, coming forward at the table. My words were quiet but my voice was taut. 'Because everyone at the Met thought I was involved in her disappearance and, when you and I spoke last time, it was clear you wanted me kept entirely out of the loop. So, when I found out her real name, I'll be completely honest with you: I couldn't think of anyone I would *less* want to call than you.'

Mulligan's mouth twitched. I got the sense that she didn't particularly care for Carmichael and I wondered if it was just coincidence that she was the second female detective I'd met that had felt that way. Was he chauvinistic? Did he have a problem with women? It was hard to tell for sure, but if he did, it was something I could use to lever them apart.

'We need to find Melody,' Carmichael said, undeterred by my last comment.

'I agree.'

'We need to find her *now*.'

He phrased it like an accusation.

'I said I agree with you.'

'You really don't know where she is?'

I frowned. 'If I knew where she was, don't you think I'd tell you? Whatever you might think of me, there's no way you can seriously believe I would put her life at risk — *further* at risk — by pretending I didn't. Why the hell would I do that?'

He eyed me with mistrust. 'You tell me.'

'You think I want my moment in the media spotlight, is that it?'

'Maybe,' he said. 'You used to be a journalist, after all.'

'So?'

'So, it's not such a stretch from one to the other, is it?'

'As much of a prick as you are, even *you* don't believe that.'

His cheeks coloured. Yedborough looked up from his notepad briefly; Mulligan kept her head down. Carmichael stared at me, unblinking, until the colour washed out of his cheeks, and — calmly and deliberately — he said, 'You told us you saw Melody's name in those fourteen pages of notes that McMillan had written?'

'Yes.'

'And those notes are what exactly?'

'I think maybe they're an account of his meetings with Melody, and with this John guy — this man who calls himself her husband. There are a lot of dates in there, and many of them seem to relate to Melody. Maybe they're dates on which he helped them.'

'Helped them?'

'Treated them.'

'McMillan was giving them *therapy* sessions?'

'No. From what I could tell from the notes, it was more like simple medical help. I mean, there was no way that this guy could ever take Melody to an actual doctor if she was ill, otherwise too many questions would get asked. But McMillan was in Edinburgh with his daughter over Christmas and he didn't get back until late on the 28th, so that's why I think this "husband" took Melody to a pharmacy earlier that day. He probably delayed and delayed the decision, but the cut on her arm was too badly infected.'

'So you think McMillan was using those notes as an insurance policy?'

'I think that the original idea – maybe the *ultimate* idea – was for McMillan to tell the police, or the media, or someone at the hospital about the things he'd seen and been forced to do; about Melody, about John. But the problem with McMillan was that he was frightened.' I stayed on that last thought for a moment. *Frightened of losing his daughter.* 'And that fear was why those notes – all those details about Melody and the man who kidnapped her – never got handed over to you, or the newspapers, or to someone – *anyone* – who could do something about it.'

'And that was why he made them so hard to translate?'

'Right. Because he didn't want anyone else to be able to read them, especially the man who took Melody. In McMillan's mind, I think he saw them as a last resort; a way out if he was ever cornered – if his life was truly under threat, or he was arrested.'

'You said he mentioned something else before he died?'

'"Ease war."'

'Any idea what that means?'

I shook my head. 'He said the guy who took Melody "erased her" at ease war – as in, turned her into Derryn – so maybe it's a place. But it doesn't relate to anything in his notes, or anything I've found out.'

Carmichael finished writing, making me wait for him, and when he looked up, I could see in his eyes that he was preparing to go on the attack again. The friendlier, calmer tone of the conversation was about to be jettisoned. He was trying to unsettle me by shifting back and forth.

'So you've really got no idea who this man is?' he said, leaning back, his seat creaking under his weight. 'The one who took Melody?'

'No.'

'You don't know what his surname is?'

'No.'

'Or where he lives?'

'No. But he works at St Augustine's.'

'McMillan confirmed that?'

I nodded. 'Yes.'

Carmichael glanced at Yedborough, and the younger man began to furiously write something down. For a long time, the scratch of his pencil was the only sound.

'We think his surname might be Bennik,' Mulligan said.

It was the first time she'd spoken since the interview had started. Carmichael glanced at her, a twist of frustration on his face. He preferred it when I knew nothing, floundering in the black of confusion.

'Does that ring any bells with you, Mr Raker?'

'Bennik?' I said to her. 'No. Who is he?'

She shrugged. 'We don't know much about him. He's got no criminal record and we can't find any pictures of him. We're still digging around, though.'

'So how have you made the connection?'

She held up a hand, reassuring me that the answer was coming. 'We think he was reported missing by some people he worked with.'

'Missing? When?'

'He rented a flat in east London between November 2007 and February 2009,' Mulligan said. 'Neighbours said he was sharing with a woman, possibly a girlfriend, who introduced herself as Nora. We think that could be Nora Fray. She disappeared too, in January 2009. Her name wasn't on the tenancy agreement so it's hard to say for certain, but no one has seen Nora since the beginning of '09.' She studied her notes for a moment. 'Anyway, in the middle of January 2009, he was admitted to hospital with a skull fracture.'

'How did he get that?'

'He told hospital staff that he came off a bicycle.'

But the inference was clear: as far as they were concerned, he hadn't got it coming off any bike; he'd got it from Nora Fray. *She'd fought back.*

It wasn't a disappearance.

It was a murder.

I felt a flutter of panic take hold: was it already too late for Melody? Had he done the same thing to her that he'd done to Nora Fray?

'Weird thing is,' Mulligan went on, 'there's no medical records for John Bennik prior to his admission.'

'So that's not his real name?'

'No. In fact, the only John Bennik we've been able to find, anywhere, is a 57-year-old man from Bournemouth who died of a heart attack in 2002.'

I understood immediately: 'He stole someone's identity.'

'Correct.'

The panic I'd felt for Melody became something else now: conflict, guilt. Was I any better than this man I was trying to find? Because I'd done the same as him. I'd stolen an identity when we'd created Bryan Kennedy. We'd taken a man's life, the pieces of his biography that serviced our need, and transplanted it on to someone else entirely. I hadn't thought about it then, because the need had been so desperate, but it hit me hard now. In this moment, it was difficult to feel anything but shame.

'Mr Raker?'

Mulligan looked at me, Carmichael stared harder: they could see I'd tuned out, and Carmichael especially wanted to know why.

'You said his work reported him missing?' I asked Mulligan.

'Yes. The fake John Bennik was studying at the University of East London,' she said, 'but he was also working part-time in student services there. He was a mature student: an undergrad between 2004 and 2007 – aged twenty-one to twenty-four – and then he completed an eighteen-month Masters in Applied Psychology a couple of months after your wife died.'

'And he just disappeared after that?'

'According to what we've been able to find out, just after he finished his Masters he accompanied one of the psychology lecturers to a recruitment conference at the NEC, on behalf of the university. This would have been the end of February 2010.'

'The same conference Melody was at.'

'Yes. We called UEL and they said they used to use the conference as a way to recruit talented lecturers and that Bennik – as part of his role working in student services – would have been there to do a lot of donkey work for the other staff. Two days in, he vanished. The last time anyone saw him, he was talking to a woman matching Melody Campbell's description outside the hotel.'

We fell into silence for a while, processing everything.

And then, quietly, Mulligan said, 'Before that, in January 2009, when he was admitted with the skull fracture, he was treated at the Royal London Hospital.'

She looked at me and got her answer, even before the question had formed in her mouth. Derryn had started work at the Royal London Hospital just before Christmas. She'd been really excited about it, even though it was a fifty-minute commute. She loved nursing, loved being on the ward, loved helping people. Her career had always been a calling. And that particular job had felt like such a break, such a huge stroke of good fortune, because she'd walked straight into it a fortnight after we got back from our year in LA.

But nothing about it seemed fortunate now.

Because, inside a matter of weeks, she'd met the man who called himself John Bennik – and that had been the spark that, nine years later, would become a fire that had almost consumed me.

69

Derryn had treated a killer.

She'd talked to him, dressed his wounds, reassured him. Knowing her, she would have smiled at him, laughed politely, listened when he tried to be serious. The very idea of her doing those things for him, basic though they were, cleaved me apart. As I pictured her, unaware of who he was and what he'd done – of what he would become after that – I felt nausea bubble at the base of my throat.

'As DI Mulligan told you,' Carmichael said, returning me to the moment, a subtle emphasis on *told you*, as if Mulligan had betrayed the entire investigation, 'we don't have a clear idea of what John Bennik looks like. We have a description from the lecturer he attended the conference with, but after eight years, it's vague. Medium build, medium height, dark hair. We're not going to get very far with that, are we?'

I looked at him, saw his mouth moving, but it was like my hearing was defective, ringing from the aftermath of an explosion. All I could hear was Derryn; all I could see was her talking to a man – faceless, impossible to identify – from the edge of a hospital bed.

'He never applied for a driving licence,' Carmichael continued, 'or a passport in the Bennik name before he – quote, unquote – "disappeared", and we've managed to speak to a few people at UEL, but after all this time they barely remember him. We're waiting to hear back from some former students he attended classes with, but in the meantime, can you think of anyone else who might be able to give us a description of what this John Bennik looks like?' He meant

McMillan was dead, so was Gavin Roddat, and Melody was still missing. 'Something more useful than just medium build, medium height,' he added, forcing the point home.

I ignored the jibe and tried to gather myself, to push the image of Derryn and the shadow man from my head. 'He may have a tattoo,' I said.

Carmichael leaned in slightly. 'A tattoo?'

'Maybe.'

'How do you know that?'

'I don't, not for sure. If he does, I don't know where on his body it is, or what the tattoo is of, but if he's an employee at the hospital and he *does* have a tattoo, that should make him easier to find. The fact that he wasn't working last night and he's going to be returning to London with some sort of injury from the stab wound that McMillan gave him will help too. And if all of that fails, there must be CCTV cameras around the hospital.'

'Check the hospital's CCTV cameras.'

I looked at Carmichael.

'Never thought of that,' he said caustically. 'Good job you're here.' I felt a pulse of anger, but said nothing. Carmichael carried on: 'What about Gavin Roddat?'

'What about him?'

'Well, we know it was a set-up,' he said. I was guessing they'd known for a while. The files on his laptop, the hard drive under his bed, every piece of digital evidence would have shown the same thing: movement of data on or around the date of Roddat's death – because all those things had been planted after his suicide. 'So you think, whoever Bennik really is, he had something over Roddat, just like he did with McMillan?'

I shrugged. 'That would be my best guess.'

'But what exactly? Roddat's got no record.'

'That's totally irrelevant. McMillan didn't have one either, and he spent the last five days lying to you. What McMillan and Roddat had, were secrets. My guess is something was weighing on both their consciences.'

'McMillan never mentioned anything to you?'

Yes.

I shook my head. 'No.'

'And what would Roddat's secret be?'

'Again, I don't know.'

'And Bennik was threatening to tell the world about whatever it was these men had done, *if* they didn't do his bidding?' Carmichael paused, letting the question hang there: he made it sound improbable, but it was what had happened. I felt certain of it. It was patently Bennik's speciality: he zeroed in on a weakness – a mistake, an emotional vulnerability, a fear – and he used it like a weapon. That was exactly what he'd tried to do to me as well.

'So, whatever Roddat did,' Carmichael said, trying to maintain the pressure on me, 'it was serious enough that he'd let himself be manipulated like that?'

'A lot of us have done things in our past that we regret – or that we never want made public,' I said.

'Are you talking about yourself here?'

'I'm making a general point.'

'I'm sure you are,' he said dismissively. 'So Roddat walks Melody out of that flat in Chalk Farm, in full view of a camera, knowing it will totally fuck up his life?'

'I doubt, even for a second, he thought about being caught on camera. Roddat was just a patsy. He was petrified. Whatever happened to Melody at the flat in Chalk Farm that night, whatever the reason for her having blood on her face and a bruise on her neck, it wasn't Roddat who did those things, it was Bennik. The guy in the footage you can't get in touch with, the guy who walks the old woman out of the stairwell, that's him. That's Bennik. He was already waiting outside the flat when the other two arrived. He must have gone there early to scope out the area.'

I watched Carmichael: he was trying to remember if he'd ever told me about the guy in the footage, about the fact that they hadn't been able to ID him, which he hadn't. Field had.

'That night,' I went on, 'Roddat arrived and opened up the flat for Bennik, because that's all Roddat was to him: a guy with access to empty properties and a secret that Bennik could make use of – at least, until Roddat had enough of being blackmailed and took his own life. Bennik put the bruises and the blood on Melody. He was the reason she looked scared shitless as she left. He was angry with her for wandering off at the pharmacy, so he said something to her, must have hit her, and after it was over, he told them to meet him somewhere. That was what he also needed Roddat for: to be the one caught on camera, leading Melody back out again.'

'You tailed her that night at Chalk Farm,' Carmichael said, his tone heavy with the accusation.

'I've already admitted that.'

'Why would Melody call Field and Kent to tell them you did that?'

'Panic,' I said.

'Panic?'

'Bennik was panicking. He was in the flat, saw me arrive after her, the alarm bells went off, and so he got her to make the call. He's smart and devious, but a lot of what he's done over the past week isn't thought through. It's a reaction. Trying to shift the attention to me with that call to Field and Kent; using Roddat in the way he did. He must have been watching me, and when I figured out where McMillan was hiding, he must have done the same. I mean, he'd been to these cottages with Melody before – did you know that? So he knew where they were. He knew they were affiliated with St Augustine's and that, this time of year, they'd be empty. But Bennik's lack of preparation is all over the bedroom in there: he came here to kill McMillan because he realized everything was getting out of hand, and he succeeded eventually – but not before McMillan managed to stick him with the knife he kept under his pillow.'

'If he's such a panicker, why is he only just coming up for air now?'

'Because he's never made a mistake as big as the one he made at the pharmacy. He's become extremely good at keeping Melody hidden, at isolating her enough, at controlling her when they're out in the open and disconnecting her from the world when they're not. In fact, in some ways, in how he's managed to break her down, in the way he's built this model of a husband and wife – one that she seems to believe, that she's totally compliant in now – he might be one of the most frightening people I've ever known.' I looked between them. 'When he brought her down here in 2013 for a holiday, he must have found out about the cottages from McMillan. He probably got McMillan to book it, to organize it, and then he came here with Melody as a couple. That wasn't a role he was playing, that was what he genuinely believed they were. A couple. Holidays are what couples do. I imagine it was the first time he'd ever chanced anything like that – and, after what happened at the deli here, probably the last.'

'You mean, her wandering off?' Mulligan asked. I'd told them already about the tweets I'd found, how they'd allowed me to zero in on Killiger as a location.

'Yes. Maybe she didn't do it deliberately, but she wandered off from wherever they were. She'd been with Bennik for two and a half years by then. Two and a half years is a long time to be under someone else's control, but maybe not enough time to turn you completely. That was why she acted so strangely with that woman in the deli, why she still felt a connection to Belfast, to the name Melody.' I shrugged. I didn't know any of this for sure – none of us did, not yet – but it fit too perfectly to simply be a hunch. 'Like I said, while he let her out in public again, to go to places like the library in Plumstead, I suspect he was always with her, even if it didn't appear like that. He'd be close by the whole time. He was never going to let her out of his sight again like he did down here – or, at least, that had been the plan until last Thursday, at the pharmacy.'

Mulligan said, 'I want to ask you about the pharmacy in a second, but why did she go to the flat in Chalk Farm? I mean, how did she even know about it?'

I'd thought about that a lot. Why go to Chalk Farm?

'She was carrying a Post-it note,' I replied, 'I assume with the address of the flat on it. I think she'd probably written it down. Or maybe it was another location, like Charing Cross, that she "felt" she should go to. That was what she said that first day: she "felt" she had to come to Charing Cross police station. She told DS Field that "something sparked" – a recollection, a memory. Maybe something sparked about that flat. Maybe in the same way something sparked for her in 2013 when she remembered Belfast.'

'So is she suffering from amnesia?' Mulligan asked. It was clear she was having a tough time filling in the blanks with a lot of this. I didn't blame her: it was so hard to drop into something this dense. '"Something sparked" – it sounds like she's suffering from some sort of memory loss if she's struggling to recall things.'

'I don't think it's that.'

'So what do you think it is?'

'It's like I said, I think Bennik completely broke her down.'

'Broke her down?'

'In order to rebuild her as someone else.'

Mulligan became more animated. 'Are you talking about thought reform?'

'Thought reform, coercive persuasion, whatever you want to call it – but yes, that's exactly what I'm talking about. The way he's isolated her, the way that she's become entirely dependent on him, the fear she has of him, and the way she seems to dread the idea of stepping out of line – they're the kinds of techniques that cults use all the time. They're what Manson and Jim Jones did. Destroying a person's sense of self, that's the kind of thing the Koreans were doing to American POWs back in the fifties. Remember, Melody has probably been under his control for the entire time she's been missing. That's almost eight *years*.'

'So you think she's lost her sense of self?'

'Exactly.'

'Do you know anything about her upbringing?'

I saw what Mulligan was driving at, had already noted her use of the term *thought reform*, and wondered if she, like Bennik, had a background in psychology.

'No,' I said. 'Only what I've been able to find out on the web. Her parents are dead, she has no siblings. I don't know much more about her, really.'

'So if Bennik is her "husband", is he pretending to be you?'

I shrugged again. 'I'm not sure. I don't have any proof, just a working theory. But, yes, I absolutely believe he's told her his name is David Raker.'

He's pretending to be me. My name. My history.

Even thinking about it made me sick, the way he'd created a different version of me, a copy, and had used it to control and imprison someone.

As I thought of that, I thought of that time alone with Melody in the house. That was the first and only occasion we met face-to-face. At the police station, I'd been in another room, watching her on a CCTV feed. So when she'd been asking Field if she could see David Raker, she didn't mean me – she meant Bennik's version of me – and because Melody and I never met that day, she thought the person watching on CCTV was Bennik.

Which meant what?

It means, at the house, she must have been playing a role at Bennik's behest. It was all just an act. He told her to pretend, for those few short hours, that *I* was her husband, and she agreed, because that was how their relationship worked. That almost certainly explained why she was in tears by the end, bewildered about who I was, uncertain about why her husband was making her cook dinner for a stranger, hug him, pretend he was the person she loved. I started to turn it all over in my head, trying to see everything clearly, and then I remembered something that Melody had said to me right before I'd blacked out for the second and final time.

I don't even recognize you.

I thought she'd meant she didn't recognize the man I'd become – the illness I was supposed to have, the way I treated her – but she didn't mean that at all.

She meant she literally had no idea who I was.

'You really think he's calling himself David Raker?' Mulligan asked.

'Privately, when he's alone with her,' I said. 'Not publicly. Publicly, he'll be someone else entirely. If he has a degree in Applied Psychology, if he works at the hospital, you're looking at someone smart, adaptable, probably extremely well liked and sociable. He won't be odd and insular; he won't appear aggressive and hostile. That would just bring questions he doesn't want.' I shrugged again. 'I don't know any of this for certain, but if he *is* me, he believes he's a *better* version of me. He kept her alive when I failed –'

'You're talking about *brainwashing*,' Carmichael scoffed, and for the first time I saw an overt flash of irritation on Mulligan's face. She tried to disguise it by looking down at her notes, but it was clear that she saw some sense in what I was trying to argue; its echoes in the evidence.

To Carmichael, it was just another lie for me to hide behind.

'From what I can tell,' I said, looking pointedly at Mulligan, not him, 'Bennik developed a fascination with my wife in the months before she died in 2009. I'm not sure he realized she was sick until quite late on – so whatever plans he had for her, and for me, got cut short. One of the reasons he became so interested in Melody was because he saw the similarities between her and Derryn – he saw beyond the fact that Melody was overweight, that she had different-coloured hair, all of that, and he zeroed in on the physical characteristics they *did* share. But it was more than that. I saw it that first day at Charing Cross too. It's not just a physical likeness: it's behavioural, emotional.'

'So you *are* talking about brainwashing?' Carmichael asked.

'Yes,' I said. 'At this point, I doubt she even remembers Melody Campbell – just flashes. I believe she went to Charing Cross because she was confused, unsure of why Bennik had left her at the pharmacy, and because she had some memory of the station. He drove off because he got into an argument with a traffic warden about where he'd parked, and then became concerned that the traffic warden would note down the registration of the car and, worse, issue a ticket, find out who he was and put his details into the system. And if his details were in the system somewhere, he was suddenly on the radar. It was another moment of panic. I think I'm right in saying there are no CCTV cameras near the pharmacy, which would have been the point – he'd definitely have known that – so I can only take a guess at this, but I'd be willing to bet that Bennik was gone very little time at all. I bet he went away, turned around and came back for Melody, knowing that the traffic warden would have moved on – but Melody was already gone.'

Silence.

The fact that Carmichael wasn't arguing with me about any of it suggested he and his team – perhaps Field and Kent too – had all assumed the same thing, or something close to it.

As I waited, I thought of that first day, of Field telling me that Melody had £22 on her, of me following her to Chalk Farm that night and seeing her glance at a digital watch she'd been keeping in her pocket. Bennik must have given her enough money to buy whatever the pharmacist recommended for the cut on her arm, and set a timescale to do it in: the watch was to make sure she didn't take longer than he ordered. Again, that fed into the way he'd changed her – controlled her, governed her.

'So she wasn't escaping him?' Mulligan asked. 'After he left her at the pharmacy, she wasn't fleeing him, she was simply confused?'

'Yes,' I said, nodding. 'She is, basically, deeply confused. At Charing Cross, she claimed to Field that she'd been missing eight years, and then denied ever saying it. Maybe she gets these flashes – these moments of clarity, of truth – like instinctively knowing the police station at Charing Cross, or the flat at Chalk Farm, or the fact she's been missing – but then it all goes again. The rest of the time, she's Derryn.'

Carmichael kept going with the questions, but it became obvious that he was no longer trying to fill in the gaps; instead, he was attempting to catch me out. I batted back his attempts to corner me, Mulligan watching silently, until he finally called time on the interview.

By then, the sky had lightened outside the windows of the truck.

I sat on a bank of grass, overlooking the cove I'd chased John Bennik across the previous night, and watched the sun bloom in the sky. I thought about Melody, the person she believed that she was now, where she might be and how the police would ever find her. I thought about the terrible things Bennik must have done to her over the last eight years to make her think she was Derryn. And then, finally, I thought about the last weeks of Derryn's life. Without the adrenalin charging through me, without the tightrope walk of trying to keep Erik McMillan alive and breathing, it fully started to hit me: Bennik had been there. He'd been there at the end of Derryn's life.

He could have stood next to her bed.

He could have touched her.

He could have done all of that, and worse, and I never even realized. I felt the anger course through me, trapped in every muscle – every fibre and vein and artery – and, once that began to subside, I started to feel light-headed and sick. I retched, and then again, and again, until eventually I took myself away, out of sight, and vomited.

And after that, away from the police and forensic teams, away from the locals gathered on the road looking on, I bowed my head, and I closed my eyes, and I cried.

70

I pulled into my driveway, switched off the engine and just sat there, looking out through the windscreen at my house. It was dark, its windows opaque, silent as a crypt except for the rain running out of the gutters and into the drains. I didn't want to go inside. I didn't want to be in there, in the hallways and rooms whose purity had been destroyed, whose entire history had been rewritten in the last few weeks of Derryn's life without me ever knowing. Once, it had been a unique part of our identity, a place in which we were going to start a family; eventually, I managed to make it some sort of a sanctuary in the months and years after she died.

Now it was nothing to me, just bricks and mortar.

Just a place John Bennik had poisoned.

I let myself in, grabbed a change of clothes and then left again, driving south to Kew, where there was a motel I'd used before for people I needed to keep hidden. It was big and ugly on the outside and basic on the inside, but it was quiet and clean, and – because of the time of year, the decorations gone, the festivities doused – I didn't have any trouble finding a room. I paid for two nights, but told the woman on reception it was likely I'd need more, and then hauled my luggage up to the fourth floor. Once I was inside, I collapsed on to the bed.

I went into a dead sleep and didn't wake until 9 p.m. Briefly disorientated, I got up and sat at the edge of the bed, trying to clear my head in the dark. I felt nauseous, there was a dull pounding behind my eyes, my muscles were compressed and painful, and – somewhere deeper and more difficult to locate – I felt absolutely broken.

I got up and went to the window, watching the lights of the city blink, and then showered and changed and headed downstairs to the empty restaurant. There wasn't much of a choice on the menu, so I ordered a sandwich, a bowl of chips and a pint of beer and sat in the corner with my phone and my laptop, trying to find out how much my home was worth. I looked at houses in Ealing, in Brentford, Chiswick, Kew, and then realized, if I really *was* going to move, it made no difference if I stayed in this part of London any more; maybe it didn't make a difference if I stayed in London at all. I was on my own; alone. I could live anywhere I wanted. The house was supposed to have been the beginning, not the beginning of the end, and the only thing that had ever kept me in Ealing was the emotional connection I had to it.

A moment later, my phone went.

It was Annabel.

I picked up. 'Hey, sweetheart.'

'Hey. How are you?'

'I'm okay.'

She didn't respond straight away, halted by the fracture in my voice. I mostly tried to protect her from moments like this, from concerns about me, but it was hard to rise above it now.

'You sound sad,' she said, obviously thrown. 'Are you okay?'

'I'm fine. I'll tell you about it some other time.'

'Is it this case? This thing with . . .'

She was going to say *Derryn*, but stopped.

'Yes,' I said. 'It's been hard.'

'I'm glad I called, then,' she said, and I admired her, and loved her, for how reassuring she was trying to be. 'I wanted to say that I'm sorry again. All the stuff I read about you and that woman on *FeedMe*, the way she looked, I realized I must have sounded like I didn't believe you when we talked. But I do. I really do.'

'I appreciate that.'

Neither of us spoke for a moment.

'I was thinking,' she said, 'after this is over, maybe you could come down again and stay with Liv and me for a while. We loved having you here over Christmas, and there's at least three more board games in the loft that we haven't played yet.'

That made me smile.

'I'd love that. Thank you.'

'I'm so sorry again for doubting you,' she said, but I told her not to worry, and meant every word of it. She didn't need to apologize. I'd quickly come to understand her suspicions on the morning she'd found the *FeedMe* article.

I'd been questioning my own sanity.

Maybe, quietly, I still was.

Day Seven

71

The next morning, I was having breakfast in the restaurant, alone except for a group of tourists and two men talking about a work colleague, when the call came through.

It was a private number.

I put down my knife and fork and picked up.

'It's me,' Field said, as soon as I answered.

'Have you found her?'

I could hear the desperation in my voice.

'No,' she said.

I pushed my half-eaten plate to one side and slumped back in the booth, a knot forming in my stomach. It had been over a day since I'd left Killiger, and the police still hadn't located Melody Campbell.

There was, however, some good news.

Field had already called me early this morning – the first time we'd spoken since our meeting under the arches – and told me that, in their search for John Bennik's real identity, they'd zeroed in on a man called Evan Willis. Willis ticked all the boxes. He'd been a counsellor at St Augustine's since 2012 and hadn't been seen since the night of the events at Killiger. He'd called in sick that day, presumably so he could watch me and track my movements down to Sussex, and then hadn't phoned his manager since, not responding to text messages or repeated phone calls. When the police went to his flat in Forest Hill, they found it empty. Clothes were missing from the wardrobe, his wallet, phone and passport were all gone, and at four thirty yesterday morning – about the same time as I was sitting with Carmichael and Mulligan answering their questions – Willis had withdrawn £250 from an ATM on the South Circular. A few hours later, he'd used a credit card at Gatwick Airport to pay for a flight to Madrid. A couple of hours after that, he landed at Barajas Airport. Willis – who also matched the physical description of Bennik: stocky, dark hair, a beard – was in Spain before the police had even finished scouring employee records at St Augustine's.

'Has he used his card again?' I asked.

'That's what I'm calling about. He used it an hour ago.'

'Is he still in Madrid?'

'Looks like it. He withdrew two hundred and sixty euros from a cash machine in the lobby of a hotel on the Gran Vía. The Palacio Verde. He's staying in Room 439. We're speaking to police in Madrid now. All being well, we should have the bastard in cuffs in an hour.'

I felt a slight sense of relief, although it was only brief. Even with Bennik – *Evan Willis* – in custody, it didn't help Melody Campbell. It had been six days since she disappeared in Chalk Farm, almost four since she was in my house, and she still might not have had treatment for the cut on her arm. If Bennik had put her somewhere, there was no way he could move her now that he was hundreds of miles away. That meant her injury could be worse than ever. It could be critical.

I just hoped she was still alive.

'Have you found any CCTV footage at St Augustine's of Bennik and McMillan together?'

'Willis,' Field corrected.

'Willis, Bennik – it doesn't really matter much any more, does it?'

'No,' she said, 'we haven't. Well, not in the same room together, anyway. The administration block, where McMillan's office is, has two entrances, but only one of them has a camera. The west entrance, opposite the lift, we've got; the south entrance, accessed via the stairs – which is the route that you were brought in on – doesn't have any CCTV. We've managed to get some film of Willis going into the administration block a couple of months ago, although we can't confirm whether he went to see McMillan or not. My guess is that he did, because that backs up the idea that he would visit McMillan when he needed something.'

'But there's nothing more recent?'

'No, nothing. Listen, are you free this morning?'

'Why?'

I heard the line drift, the echo of footsteps and a door close. She was moving somewhere more private. 'You're still on Carmichael's shitlist,' she said, 'but he can't find anything to corner you with. So, in the spirit of cooperation, I need you to help me with something. It'll aid your cause here, with Carmichael and all his friends, and it'll make it look like you don't have anything to hide . . .'

She trailed off, letting her words hang there: the two of us had found a middle ground, a place where we were willing to work together, to trade information, but it didn't mean she found me entirely trustworthy. The feeling went both ways: I still wasn't one hundred per cent clear on why she'd offered to help me. I'd asked her what her real motivation was then, because it had felt like she was holding something back from me, but she'd palmed me off. And then I'd asked her this morning why she'd never told me about the man on the CCTV video or the fact that McMillan owned a Lexus, and she put both down to an oversight, to the pressure of having to tell me so much, so quickly, at the arches. It didn't feel like the truth.

So what was her game?

'Anyway,' she said, 'Carmichael wants you to physically walk us through that night at the hospital. The night you went to see McMillan.' A pause. 'The night you . . .' *Blacked out*. 'We're trying to piece together the timeline.'

'In order to do what?'

'In order to figure out what the truth is. You went there on the 29th of December, your blood test seemed to suggest he drugged you, you woke up at home, say you spent the whole *day* at home on the 30th of December, but we've got security camera footage of you wandering into shot – on the evening of the 30th – and plonking yourself down outside the front gates of St Augustine's.'

'I told you, I don't remember –'

'Before you get all antsy with me, we're not suggesting you deliberately lied to us. McMillan roofied you. You were clearly confused. But we need to figure out what happened on the night of the 30th of December, including how you ended up getting back to the hospital and *why* you came back, because that was *also* the night that McMillan – according to his security card – clocked out at 7 p.m., and almost certainly made a break for Killiger. If Willis gets picked up in Madrid this morning, there's just no way we can go into a potential prosecution with big blank spaces like this. I mean, you could sail the *Titanic* through this case, which means the defence will have a field day. So, with McMillan dead and Willis in Spain pretending he's Ronnie Biggs, you'll have to do.'

She said it as a joke, but it wasn't. If the Met could have avoided using me to help their case, they would have.

'Okay,' I said.

'Carmichael's got half the hospital cordoned off, so you won't be able to park on site. There's a housing estate next door, so you'll have to use the street there. That might be for the best, anyway: the press have caught wind of this.'

'Great.'

'They're sticking to the front gates like flies on shit.'

'I bet they are.'

I'd been part of that feeding frenzy once, so I understood their motivation perfectly. A kidnapped woman kept prisoner

414

for almost eight years, the killer of a respected doctor still on the run, the missing persons investigator who couldn't stay out of trouble: it had all the ingredients they, and the television networks, would need. I'd spent much of my morning screening my calls and not listening to any of my voicemail messages. I'd gone out for a run to try and escape them and had returned to find a journalist waiting in the motel reception for me.

As I thought of that, I thought of Kennedy, of the journalist who'd turned up at the cottage down in Devon, asking questions. Kennedy had called me just before breakfast to say that he was in a motel in Newcastle for now, but it didn't make me any less anxious about the reporter from the *Daily Tribune*, or how much digging he might be prepared to do. I'd lied to everyone about Kennedy's death, including Annabel. I'd perjured myself in front of the Met for his benefit, in an effort to give him some version of a life. But if the press found him, the police would too, and none of that would matter.

If they found him, I was going to prison.

'Is there any way for us to avoid the press altogether?' I asked Field. 'Or is there genuinely only one way in and out of that place?'

'That's what they tell the public,' Field said.

'So there *is* another entrance?'

'One other, but it's only accessible on foot and you have to go through the nature reserve. The hospital don't use it any more and keep it locked up, but they told Carmichael about it and he made them open it for us. So we can come and go through there without having to speak to the media. That's part of the reason why I said to use the housing estate.'

'Is it easy to find?'

'Yeah. The gate's on Mountford Road, just next to the hospital.'

I didn't say anything, my head filling with images of the

last time I'd been inside St Augustine's – listening to McMil-lan's lies, glimpsing Bennik's shadow in the half-light of the office.

Blacking out.

'Raker?' Field said. 'I'll see you in an hour, okay?'

I didn't want to go back there.

I just wanted this to be over.

'*Okay?*'

I told her it was fine, but something didn't feel right. It curdled in my stomach. I just couldn't decide if it was the idea of going back to the hospital, the thought of being cornered by the press – or the fear that I'd missed something big.

72

Field arrived late.

It had been sleeting all morning and there was no shelter anywhere, so I just had to stand there, freezing cold and pissed off, and let the wind cut through me for twenty minutes.

Mountford Road was a long cul-de-sac lined with 1930s terraced houses that ran along the eastern boundaries of what was now the nature reserve, but had once been the other half of St Augustine's Hospital. The gate was halfway along the street, at the end of a path between houses, and was part of an eight-foot perimeter fence. There were signs all across it – NO ENTRY! TRESPASSERS WILL BE PROS-ECUTED! DANGER! – and the gate had been padlocked top and bottom. Beyond the fence, it was wild and overgrown, a sweep of rampant, unchecked greenery pockmarked by crumbling, long-abandoned buildings.

By the time Kent pulled into a parking spot further down Mountford Road, I was soaked to the skin, chilled to the bone and ready to head back to the motel. Field got out straight away, already in a raincoat, and came towards me. She'd seen the weather; she saw my expression.

'Sorry we're so late.'

'You said ten thirty.'

She held up a hand. 'I know.'

Kent joined us, sleet dotting the shoulders of his jacket, his face, his hair, and smiled apologetically. 'There was an accident in the Blackwall Tunnel,' he said. It was the first time he'd ever been anything approaching sympathetic to me, but I couldn't decide if it was because he genuinely believed I had no involvement in this – in the disappearance of Melody Camp-bell, in her imprisonment, in the crimes of John Bennik – or because he needed my cooperation for the time being.

'Well, we've got some good news,' Field said. 'Evan Willis is in custody.'

I let out a breath, the relief like a flood.

'Has he said anything?'

'He says he's not talking without a lawyer.'

That was a good sign. It spoke of someone who knew it was the end of the road.

I fell into line behind Field and Kent and we headed between the houses and down towards the gate. As we got closer, I realized Field must have called ahead, because one of the security guards was coming towards us on the other side of the fence, weaving his way through the remnants of the old sanatorium.

He greeted us, unlocked the gate and let us in.

As he locked up again, I looked around. The ground under my feet was a mix of mangled concrete and rampant weeds and, around me, everything seemed to sprawl, the layout of the nature reserve hard to gauge: the path the security guard had walked on ran vaguely through the middle, towards a huge, ruined building; off to the right there was a knot of much smaller structures, identical in size but different in terms of damage. Paths zigzagged between corroded walls, past trees and thorns and vines, routes snaking off at angles, like minor capillaries, into alleys created intentionally when this site was still being used, and accidentally in the years since its closure, as foundations and roofs imploded, and bricks toppled.

'Follow me,' the guard said.

Our footsteps soon became drowned out by birdsong, the squawk of geese, the chirp of starlings. The wind came, mut-ing everything for a second, and then it all faded in again. A bird broke from a tree to my left. Another took flight much further along, where the path became darker, the overgrowth denser, trees leaning in at one another, their canopies merging. Sleet continued dotting my face.

Eventually, we got to another fence, an almost exact replica of the one we'd passed through on the other side of the reserve, and then we walked up a grass bank into the hospital itself.

Inside, we took the lift up.

Built in a half-circle around the lift shaft was the rest of St Augustine's, contemporary and striking, constructed in the grey and white tiers I'd seen the first time; off to the far left was an even clearer view of the nature reserve, a labyrinth of half-broken buildings, consumed in a sea of green. There were birds everywhere, nesting on the damp, overgrown banks of the river, in what remained of roofs, in the ragged teeth of smashed windows. Despite it all, there was something weirdly beautiful about the decay, especially in the subdued light, the natural, primitive sweep of the reserve so at odds with the hospital's sharp, modern angles.

The lift opened, and we were immediately opposite the doors to the admin block. This was the west entrance – the one Field had mentioned to me this morning.

A man in his late thirties was waiting inside, as if expecting us. He introduced himself as Jerry Wragg. He spoke quietly as we headed to the corner office, trying to prevent himself from being heard by the rest of the floor, and said they'd been so shocked to read about the death of Erik McMillan in the newspapers. Field responded blandly and then we filed into McMillan's office, Wragg disappeared again, and she asked me to start running through my recollection of the night I came to see McMillan here.

They made the occasional note, but mostly the two of them just watched and listened. I told them what I could remember of the conversation that had taken place, talked about him making me a coffee – the machine, I saw, had already been dusted for prints at some point over the past day, the powder still evident on it – and then looked out of McMillan's office, to where the rest of the staff were.

'I thought I saw someone out there,' I said.

I'd already told Field this over the phone, but she nodded as if it were the first time she'd heard it.

'Had you drunk the coffee by then?' Kent asked.

'Yes.'

'So do you think anyone was *actually* there?'

'I don't think I was hallucinating.'

'So someone was there?'

'Yes,' I said to him. 'I think it was Bennik.'

'But you didn't see him?' Field asked.

'No. I heard a door open and close – the one at the south entrance – and I swear I saw movement out there.'

'So he came in through the south?'

'Yes.'

'To deliberately avoid any cameras?'

'That seems likely.'

'And what happened then?'

I shrugged. 'I went out and checked, and I couldn't find anyone.'

'And then what?'

'And then I passed out.'

Both of them stared at me. It was difficult to say what they were thinking. Field said, 'And then, when you woke up, you were at home?'

'Yes.'

'You don't remember how you got back?'

'No.'

Field frowned. 'I don't understand why he would go to the trouble of drugging you and then put you in the back of his car and take you home. That makes no sense.'

She was wrong. It actually made a lot of sense, it's just neither of them had the full context because I hadn't ever told anyone about Melody being in my house when I woke up. At the time, when I was still under a cloud of suspicion, I chose to remain silent because I knew I was the last person to see her alive, and if I admitted we were together, even if I didn't understand how or why, it looked bad for me. Now, it was hard simply because I'd left it so long. But those couple of hours definitely made sense: they'd been an attempt to box me in. Bennik knew how it would play with the police if I told them about Melody, and how it would eventually play if the truth came out and I'd chosen not to. He also knew how it would look if I admitted that I had no idea why I was waiting outside the gates of the hospital, how I'd got there, or why I seemed so upset. I was upset because of those disconcerting moments alone with Melody earlier that day, and I was confused because McMillan's drugs were still in my system.

Mostly, though, that time with Melody was his attempt to unbalance me, to have me questioning my own state of mind, and make me believe I really *was* sick. It had almost worked. I was willing to bet he'd been the one who'd drawn the heart on the window two nights before that, and the one who'd taken Derryn's sign from the fence and put it in the garage. And then there was the face in the darkness at the back of my house. It hadn't been a trick of the light, or a delusion. It was him. He'd been toying with me: haunting me, stalking me.

He'd been using my emotional vulnerability against me.

Field walked over to one of the walls where there was a framed map of the facility. I'd noticed it the first time I'd been here. She started looking it over, perhaps trying to understand John Bennik's movements, and how he and McMillan had got me out – and why they would bring me back here.

'When did you wake up at home?' Kent asked.

'Around midday.'

'And what happened then?'

I looked at them both, but didn't hold their gaze.

'It's, uh . . .' I stopped. 'It's hard to remember.'

'We need you to try,' Field said, turning to face me again.

'I've been trying for days,' I replied, too quickly, and while there was some truth to it, and a lot of that thirty-five hours was still a blank, I remembered enough – I remembered Melody – and Field seemed to pick up on it; a minor give-away, a flash of something in my face. I knew, then, that if I sustained the lie much longer, if I kept her in the dark, what-ever goodwill I'd built up would immediately go south.

'Anything?' Kent said.

I looked at him. 'Can I have some water?'

Both of them immediately looked cautious. He glanced from me to Field, who nodded at him, and then Kent headed to the door and went out to a water cooler. The people on the floor looked up and watched, as if Kent were about to deliver some news. I got up quickly, went to the windows and stared out at the view, so my back was to the door. Field was two feet away. She looked at me, eyes narrowing as if she sensed something was up.

'What's going on?'

'There's something I need to tell you.'

She glanced towards Kent.

I followed her gaze, to make sure he was still out of earshot, and then said: 'When I woke up at home . . .' I stopped again, swallowed. My mouth felt completely dry. 'She was there.'

'Who?'

'Melody.'

'Melody was in your *house*?'

I nodded.

'What the hell are you talking about?'

'She was in my house, cooking me dinner. I don't know what . . .' I stopped, knowing how it must have sounded to

Field. 'I don't even know how to explain it. She was there, and then she wasn't. I woke up and she had set the table. She'd bought me a present, a copy of *No One Can See the Crows at Night*. But it was Bennik. He was behind it, trying to make me feel sick – *seem* sick – unreliable, unstable. He knew I was having doubts about myself, and I . . .'

My words fell away.

'You what?' Field asked.

I looked off towards the other side of the hospital, to the withered remains in the nature reserve, to the echoes of the old sanatorium – its wards, its untold stories.

'David,' Field said, 'you *what*?'

'I was starting to think I might really *be* sick.'

'Do you still think that?'

Just then, Kent returned with a cup of water.

'David, do you still think that?'

I shook my head, rubbed at my brow and looked at the map on the wall, trying to understand that night, the practicalities of taking me out while I was drugged, transporting me, and doing it without raising any alarms. Had they pretended that I was a patient? Did anyone bother questioning the motives of the Clinical Director as he walked an apparently unconscious man out? The facility was quiet, anyway, because of Christmas, but the trust that people had in McMillan, the respect he'd built up over so many years, would have gone a long way.

'David?'

This time, Field's voice came through, but only at the very edge of what I was hearing. Something had caught my eye on the map. It was actually two maps, I realized now, one laid on top of the other – the hospital as it was now, and the hospital when it opened in 1901.

'David?'

I stepped in closer to it, concentrating my attention on the older version. This was before the nature reserve, when the

423

buildings were all still in use on both sides. Each building had a name, and pathways had been drawn where now there was only undergrowth and broken concrete.

'David?'

'Look,' I said, pointing at the map.

'Look at what?'

'This.'

They both came in closer and I pointed to the right-hand side. Back in 1901, there had been no fencing around the hospital site; instead, there had been walls, their measurements marked out – two and a half feet thick, eight feet high.

'What am I looking at?' Field asked.

'This wall here.'

I tapped a finger to the one on the right. It was where we'd come from today, what had existed there before it was knocked down and replaced by modern security fencing. Back at the turn of the century, there had been no Mountford Road and no housing estate. There were no houses at all.

There was just the wall.

'Raker?'

'Ease war,' I said.

'What?'

'That's what McMillan said to me before he died.'

'So?'

I drew a finger around each of the four walls that had surrounded the hospital site. The walls were no longer up, but the map still marked their positions.

North wall. South wall. West wall.

East wall.

'He was giving us a direction,' I said.

73

As we exited through the gate, the same way we'd come in, a wind suddenly ripped in off the river. Birds took flight behind us, sleet spattered against our jackets, and then we left the skein of old brickwork and trees, the grass and wild flowers, and broke back into suburbia. Once I got to Mountford Road, I stopped.

'What now?' Field said, drawing level with me.

I looked both ways, the street quiet, and then at Field and Kent. In their faces, the doubts had already started to gather like storm clouds.

'What now, Raker?' she said again.

I headed to my left, in a northerly direction, towards the end of the cul-de-sac, studying the houses as I passed them. They were all identical. Bay windows on the bottom floor, two windows at the top.

'You said Evan Willis lives in Forest Hill?'

'Yes,' Field said, walking beside me. 'He's got a flat there.'

'Does he own or rent anywhere else?'

'No.'

'What about his parents? Brothers? Sisters?'

'One sister, in North Wales.'

'No parents?'

'Look,' she said, glancing at one of the houses closest to her, 'I know where you're going with this, but Willis doesn't own a house here.'

That didn't meant he *wasn't* here. He'd already used and abandoned one ID – who was to say he hadn't used another in order to buy or rent here? This could have been where

McMillan had come to treat Melody whenever she was ill. This could be where Melody was at this very moment, hidden behind the walls of one of these homes.

'Raker,' Field said, struggling to keep up now. 'Raker, *stop*.'

But I didn't. I kept going, looking in at the bay windows, at what I could see of the interiors. I saw shapes moving around inside some of them, nothing in others. I didn't know what the hell I was even looking for – Melody at one of the windows? My face became frozen, my hands rigid with cold, my skin like ice. The sleet was starting to turn to snow, getting thicker and thicker, swirling in front of me like gauze, and the effect was disorientating: I felt like I was losing balance.

Suddenly, I felt Field grab my arm.

'*Raker.*'

I stopped.

'What are you doing?' she said.

'She might be in one of these houses. We need to find her.'

We were almost at the top of the road. At the end was a row of trees; in front of them was another fence, this one much lower. On the other side of the trees was the Thames Path, but there was no access to it from here.

'We could knock on some doors,' Kent suggested.

Field shook her head, keeping her eyes on me.

'No,' she said. 'We're not knocking on any doors.'

I hated how she was looking at me now – like she pitied me, like I was collapsing in on myself. I looked up and down the street again.

Come on, Melody, where are you?

'Why don't we go back to the hospital?' she said.

'I'm not going back there.'

'You'd rather stay out in this shitty weather?'

'I want to find Melody.'

'I know,' she said, taking a step closer to me, looking like she might be about to squeeze my arm in an effort to comfort me, or talk me down. 'So do we.'

'Then we should do what Kent said and knock on some doors.'

Field glanced at Kent, and he seemed to shrivel under her glare. She was telling him to keep his mouth shut next time.

'David.' She said my name like she was trying to shake me out of a trance. 'Listen to me: you need to get your head straight.'

I turned to her. 'Don't talk to me like I'm a fucking child, Field. I know I'm right about this. I *know* it.' I tried to sound confident, even though I wasn't. Where did I begin looking? Which house? Was it even this road? 'This is what McMillan meant,' I said. 'East wall.'

'He could have meant anything. He was dying.'

'This is what he meant,' I repeated, my voice harder. 'It's pretty much where the wall *used* to be. It's the name McMillan saw every day on that map beside his desk. I'm telling you: this is where he came to visit Melody whenever she needed a doctor. Bennik, Willis – whatever he's calling himself here – lives in one of these houses.'

I stared her down, my expression unmoved, but all I could think was, what if my hunch was wrong? How would I look then? What would happen to Melody?

I began walking again, and this time neither Field nor Kent followed me. I looked back over my shoulder at them, and they watched me go like a fractious child they couldn't control. I saw Field dig into her pocket for her phone and then bark instructions at Kent that I couldn't hear above the wind, and he started trudging back towards the Volvo, parked further down the street.

The closer I got to the end of the road, the more the dread started to build in me. *Where the hell is Melody? How was I ever going to find her?* In the next round of police interviews, in the

427

court case I'd eventually have to attend, I'd get ripped apart. Field and Kent would have to recount these moments, the moments when I marched off into a snowstorm trying to find a woman who wasn't here, and then it would all come full circle again, an echo of those hours in the station at Charing Cross: my state of mind, my choices, whether anything I said could be trusted.

I stopped, my feet sliding in the slush.

Ahead of me, a hundred feet down on the left, was a turning at the end of the street, beyond the last house. I hadn't seen it until now – until I was almost on top of it. It was big enough for a car – but only just – and as I realized that, I realized something else: it wasn't a turning, it was the start of a driveway. There were no other driveways on the street: every other resident had to leave their vehicle parked on the road. So why did only the last house have a driveway?

I started moving, more of the driveway coming into view, and as it did, I could see that it went past the last house, around towards the back of it, in the direction of the nature reserve. On the wall, at the entrance to the driveway, was a sign.

THE OLD CHECKPOINT

I thought of the map in McMillan's office and remembered that, at the east wall, there had once been a second entrance – not just a footpath like there was now, but a place for vehicles, horses and carriages to enter – as well as a second security checkpoint.

This must have been it.

I checked on Field and Kent, who were distorted by the snow. I could only vaguely see Kent on his phone. But Field was watching me from the same place, her head tilted, as if she was curious about what I might have found.

Now I was level with the driveway.

428

Offset from the other houses was another home. It was detached, fashioned from yellow London stock brick just like the structures that were crumbling to dust in the nature reserve, and was much bigger than the terraced houses that lined Mountford Road. Judging by its name, it must once have been the building that had accommodated the guards at the second security checkpoint; maybe, given its size, it had doubled up as something else back then too – a series of admin offices, even part of a ward. In the century since, though, it had been converted into another home.

I took a few steps forward.

At all the windows, top and bottom, the curtains had been pulled. As I left the road and headed along the driveway, I spotted a car as well, parked out front.

It was a light blue Mondeo.

Its registration plates had been removed.

I thought of the traffic warden the day that Melody was left at the pharmacy, of how he'd described the man who'd dropped her off as driving a Mondeo or a Lexus, in light blue or grey, with a plate ending in MX. But the realization about the car, of noting that every single curtain was pulled in the middle of the day, came fractionally after something else.

Before either of those, I'd seen the front door.

I recalled those two hours alone with Melody in my home, and then a sliver of a memory coming back to me, one that I could never fully understand and had pretty much forgotten entirely in everything that had happened since.

The vague, fractured image of a red door.

I'd started to believe it didn't matter, that it had been a glitch, a mistake, some trivial piece of information that I'd attached to that time with Melody. But it wasn't a glitch and it wasn't a mistake.

It was real.

The same red door was the entrance to this house.

74

I banged on the door.

'Melody? Melody, are you in there?'

When I got no response, I knelt down, peeled up the letter box and looked into the house. A hallway extended out in front of me, modern and tidy. Wooden floors, pale walls. A side table with a plant on it.

'Melody?'

I waited. Nothing.

'Melody?'

And then something occurred to me: *she doesn't know who Melody is.* She'd spent most of the last eight years thinking her name was Derryn.

'Derryn?'

Her name almost caught in my throat.

I swallowed. 'Derryn?'

I glanced behind me, not wanting Field to follow me down here and see me like this, crouched at a letter box, shouting my dead wife's name into the void.

But I was still alone.

I turned my attention back to the house. Ahead of me were the stairs. Beyond that was a kitchen, or what I could make out of one: its door was pulled most of the way shut. To the left was another door, maybe into a living room.

I bent down a little further, seeing if I could get a better vantage point for the top of the staircase, but instead, my eyes locked on to something else.

A bookcase.

On one of the shelves, all twelve of Eva Gainridge's

novels were lined up, their titles showing on the spines, each of them identical in colour and design.

I got up and hurried around to the side of the house, but there was a locked gate, with barbed wire on top. When I leaned in closer to the slats, I could see another door in the spaces between them.

Returning to the front door, I dug around in my pocket, my wallet, the zip inside: I got out my picks and switched my focus to the lock. My fingers fumbled. I was frozen by the cold, nervous, angry, frightened. They slipped again, and then again. Finally, the door popped open.

There was no alarm.

I headed inside. The house was smart and contemporary, but felt unlived in, soulless, as if it had been deserted. In a small living room, I found a television and a DVD player, but no other technology. When I returned to the hallway, I searched for the phone socket. Nothing was plugged into it. There was no Internet, maybe not even a working landline.

Off to the left was a poky office with a desk and a chair. No PC, no laptop, nothing on the desk, no filing cabinets or storage. Beyond that was a toilet. I went upstairs and found two bedrooms and a main bathroom. One of the bedrooms was actually being *used* as a bedroom, the bed made up, non-descript men's clothes in the cupboards and drawers, but the other was totally empty. There was no furniture in it, only a carpet on the floor and empty built-in wardrobes.

Worse, Melody wasn't in either of them.

She wasn't in the house at all.

When I got back down to the kitchen, I could see it had been cleaned and there was the faint smell of food in the air, as if something had been cooked in here recently. Out of the back windows, there was a small garden, well maintained and looked after, lined by thick oak trees on one side and at the back. It meant the neighbours couldn't see into it and, from here, there were only flickers of the nature reserve – of the fence too – in the moments when the wind picked up and the branches moved.

I turned and looked back down the hallway, towards the front door. I couldn't put any of this together.

Where the hell was Melody?

Panic took flight in me. I'd forced my way into someone's home and found absolutely nothing – and now what? Now I was just breaking and entering.

But this has to be it.

The car on the driveway. The Gainridge books.

The red door.

This *had* to be the place.

I kept telling myself that as I wandered through the house for a second time, going into all the rooms again, and by the time I was back downstairs in the kitchen, something had started to dawn on me: why was this place so small on the inside? The living room was undersized, the office was tiny, there were only two bedrooms upstairs, and only half of the house looked like it was being lived in.

Yet, from the outside, the property had appeared large.

I hurried back into the kitchen, a memory starting to flicker, something I'd seen but not properly taken in the first time, and then I stopped and looked across to the left-hand wall, at the end of the kitchen unit.

There was a door.

I'd overlooked it because it was in the same style as the rest of the cabinets. I'd assumed it was a pantry or a cupboard.

But it wasn't.

When I pulled it open, where there should have been shelving full of condiments, food packets, cereal boxes and plastic storage tubs, there was, instead – a couple of feet further inside – another door.

It had slide bolts on it.

I popped both bolts across, grabbed the handle and yanked it open, and then I finally realized what was going on, why the house felt so small.

It wasn't one home.

It was two.

75

I went through to the other side and found myself in a narrow corridor with two doors on the left and one on the right, much further down.

Looking around me, I searched for a weapon, something I could use, and saw a steel pipe among some building debris. It looked like it had been ripped out of a wall, perhaps was once part of the plumbing system. It was old and rusted, but it would do.

I reached back and pulled the door closed again, trying to recreate the same noise levels as before I'd entered, in case someone was listening. As soon as the door clicked shut, the faint noises of the main house faded to nothing.

Gripping the pipe, I moved towards the first room on the left. Both this one and the next were open, but evidently they were usually kept shut and secured: there were no handles, just metal plates with padlocks hanging loose.

I looked into the first room.

It was tiny. There was a workbench against one wall, hand-built, the surface gouged and blemished. At the end of the bench were medical supplies – plasters and bandages; antiseptic, a sewing kit, thread – and then a medical encyclopedia. It was open to a page halfway in and I could read the title.

'Treating Infected Wounds'.

That was exactly what Melody had.

Next to that were a laptop and a nest of leads, charging cables, plugs, and a pile of USB sticks. There was an old-style video camera that took DV tapes as well, and then a digital SLR with a long lens, and a photo printer. A set of speakers. A microphone. Beside the microphone was a very large desktop storage unit with a flip-up lid. I opened it.

Dictaphone tapes were piled up inside it, one on top of the other.

Some were facing up, spines out, each tape case marked with a hashtag and a number. #0012. #0184. #0430. #0635. #0734. There were hundreds and hundreds of them. I pulled one out at random – #0858 – and dug around for the Dictaphone. It was under a pile of leads. Sliding the tape in, I turned the volume down and pressed Play: *'It was your wedding anniversary yesterday. I know that from going through some of the papers in your loft. I watched your house most of the afternoon and evening, to see if I could catch a glimpse of you. I thought your husband may have done something for you, the kind of perfunctory celebration that only he would think was deserving of you. A cake, perhaps. A meal. Some tacky little gift –'*

I stopped it, fast-forwarded for a couple of seconds, and then pressed Play again. My hands were shaking so badly they almost slid off the button.

'I walked to the bedroom door,' the same voice said. *'Even before I got there, I could hear you, the air rattling in your chest. Your breathing sounded like an old motor struggling to turn over. When I looked in at you, you were under the sheets, asleep, your eyelids fluttering, your skin waxy and pale. You looked like a mannequin –'*

I switched it off.

But it was too late. Even as I threw it against the wall, watching the Dictaphone shatter, it was too late. He'd been there at the end. It was true.

The fucking bastard had been alone with Derryn in my house.

I backed up, into the corridor, clutching my hand to my mouth. I dry-retched, did it again, and then again, and then I swivelled in the direction of the second room.

Did I even want to look inside?

Slowly, I approached the door. It was difficult to make

anything out at first. My eyes were drawn to a desk in the corner and a solitary lamp on top, slim-line – like a metal tube – its neck facing down so that the bulb was barely inches from the desk's surface, creating a perfect disc of yellow on the wood. Not much of its glow escaped out elsewhere. Even as I used my phone to illuminate the rest of the room, it took me a second to understand what was in here; a second to grasp properly what I was looking at. And then I did, and it felt like my throat was closing up.

There were photos everywhere.

Every wall, every surface, even the ceiling.

I shuffled further in, barely able to carry myself. The photos had been divided into vertical strips, each strip separated by subject. I saw images of me, of the places I'd been during the past week – my routines documented by shots with infinitesimal differences – and then, higher up, pictures from way before that, long before Melody Campbell entered my life. Some were a decade old, taken by me, by Derryn, stolen, without me ever realizing, from the boxes I'd had in the loft. They were of the two of us: holidays we'd had, moments we'd shared, our marriage, our history. In many of them, my face had been scratched out with the point of a blade.

I barely processed the next strip of photos – tens, maybe hundreds, of close-ups of Melody Campbell's face – or the ones after that of Erik McMillan going about his life, his work at the hospital. And then there was Gavin Roddat in a blown-up 10 x 8, his arm around a woman in a nightclub. There was something off about the photograph, something that didn't sit right about it, and then I looked at the woman again, her face, and it dawned on me.

She was a girl.

They might have been in a nightclub, she might have fooled the people on the door, but the picture – the white of the flash, the shape of her face and eyes – exposed the lie: she wasn't eighteen. She was beautiful, mature enough to muddy the waters, but she was a child. A wave of dread crashed through me. This must have been how Bennik had controlled Gavin Roddat: his knowledge of the girl, of what Roddat had done with her, and what the consequences would be if anyone found out. And then I looked at her face for a second time, started to see more of her adolescence, and nausea began burning in my stomach again. What if it was worse than that? What if she hadn't even been sixteen?

Bile seared behind my ribcage as I realized what was in the next strip: hundreds of pictures of my house. They went back years, to old furniture I'd got rid of, to walls I'd long since painted a different colour. In the middle, filling the margins of another 10 x 8, was a shot that instantly chilled my blood: it was taken in the doorway of the bedroom, a wide-angled shot of the layout, the dresser, the wardrobes. Derryn was on the bed, her eyes shut.

'No,' I said quietly, unable to stop myself. '*No.*'

It had been taken in the last weeks of her life.

Tears blurred my vision as I looked at her, her face grey, her bones pushing out through her skin. I swung the light around and it got even worse. Her entire last year was plastered across the walls: her leaving the house for work; the months after she got sick; her going in to see the doctors; me wheeling her around in a chair; a shot over the back fence of her sitting in a seat on the rear deck. There were photographs of her inside the house, taken when Bennik was inside *with* her, and she didn't even realize it. He'd been behind doors, at the edges of frames.

And, in those moments when I wasn't home, he'd got his close-ups. When she slept, he'd photographed her from every position, like a scientific study. The angles of her. The way she held herself.

This time, I threw up.

Stumbling out of the room, into the corridor, I covered my mouth, trying to prevent myself from being sick for a second time, and leaned over, hands on my knees, gasping for air, breathing as deeply as I could. I wiped tears away, again and again, but they kept coming and, when I finally gave in and let them fall, I suddenly remembered something: there was a third door.

I blinked, trying to clear my eyes, and looked sideways. Just like the one leading from the kitchen, it had been slide-bolted shut from the outside.

I gripped the metal pipe harder, my head full of static, and looked over my shoulder, back the way I'd come in, wondering how far behind me Field and Kent were now, or whether they were coming at all. I thought of the tapes, Bennik's voice burning into my skull, and then the photographs of Derryn, of his camera in her face as she faded from this life. How could it be worse than this beyond the door?

And then my eyes returned to the slide locks.

He's keeping something inside.

Or someone.

As quickly and quietly as possible, I slid both locks across, their mechanisms giving a gentle squeal, and – as soon as they released – the door bumped back towards me.

Light spilled out.

My heart was thumping with such ferocity I could feel its tremor in my bones, the noise like a fist on a wall, pounding, ceaseless.

I eased the door all the way open.

The smell of furniture polish and air freshener wafted out towards me. Directly in front of me was a short hallway. At the end was a living room, but not the one I'd already been into. On the left was a kitchen, but not the same kitchen I'd just left.

This was a different part of the house.

It was a different *house*.

'What the fuck . . . ?'

I stepped into the hallway. *My hallway*. The carpet was identical, the furniture an exact match. The kitchen was laid out the same way, the units and the lino almost indistinguishable from mine. The dimensions of the hallway and the kitchen – of the living room, of all of it – was smaller, the rooms narrower, the ceilings lower, more cramped, some of the finishing and details were ever so slightly off, but it hardly seemed to matter. Even attempting to build something like this was enough, let alone almost getting it right. It was brilliant, and devastating, and absolutely deranged.

It was a work of art and a work of insanity.

He'd built a recreation of my house.

76

I stood there, stunned, my lungs like stone in my chest. I couldn't breathe, I couldn't move, I just looked at it, the intricacy of the design, the incredible attention to detail. How long had this place taken to build? How many times had he been inside my house in order to make this possible? How many photographs, measurements, drawings?

I could barely process it all.

I took a couple of steps forward, realizing now why I'd always felt so anxious about that night alone with Melody in the house, why my internal alarm had sounded: not just because she was there, and she was pretending to be Derryn, but because the house had never felt quite right. I hadn't ever put it together fully – not even for a second – but now I got it: the night McMillan had drugged me at the hospital, and most of the thirty-five hours that followed, weren't spent at home.

They were spent here.

The house had smelled of furniture polish that night; it had been spotlessly clean, just like now, because that was the way this version of the house was kept. I'd heard birds out in the garden – but it wasn't the garden, it was the birds in the nature reserve. All the curtains had been drawn that day, only thin shafts of daylight getting in, and now I understood why: because the windows didn't look out to my garden, or my driveway, or my garage. There was no decking on the other side of the living-room doors like I had at home, there was a lawn enclosed by oak trees and the fence of the nature reserve. If I'd got up and looked through the windows the day I woke up here, I'd have seen it and known straight away. So he'd closed the curtains, and he'd made Melody tell me it was because of my headaches.

And then there was the spare room and the office: I hadn't been able to get either of those doors open that night. They'd seemed jammed. But they weren't.

He'd just never built them.

I looked around the living room. The furniture, the sofas, the table – nothing was an exact match; the clock, designed with the maze-like triskelion, was home-made, not shop-bought. The ceiling was lower and the walls were closer in; the whole dimensions of the house were smaller. The differences were so obvious now, I could see them easily. But, stumbling about when I'd just come round from a blackout – confused, emotional, McMillan's drug still weighing heavy in my blood – none of it had clicked.

It had seemed like the real thing.

I closed my eyes, trying to make sense of it all. Bennik must have brought me across the nature reserve from St Augustine's, set everything up with Melody, and then returned me to the front gate. There, he'd deliberately avoided being caught on CCTV but ensured that I was in full view of the cameras in the minutes before a security card said McMillan exited the hospital site. The timings made it look like I'd returned to the hospital to confront McMillan by myself, to hurt him, and that was all Bennik needed: I had no memory of the incident, so I couldn't explain it away, and I was on film so there was hard evidence I'd returned here from my house on the other side of the city. What Bennik couldn't have known was that, in the hours after helping him set this up, McMillan would make a break for the coast. That had helped play into the idea that I'd hurt McMillan, because no one could find him after that – but suddenly Bennik didn't have control over the man he was manipulating.

Opening my eyes, I took in the house again, picking up one of the photos closest to me. It was of Melody, dressed in clothes that looked like Derryn's. Next to it was another, and then another.

All of them were of Melody.

I glanced down the hallway to the bedroom. More memories came flooding back. This counterfeit house, this copy, was why Derryn's clothes had been here, and why only old clothes of mine – clothes I'd thought were still in the loft – were hanging up in the wardrobe. He'd stolen them from me – slowly, item by item, over a long period of time, so that I didn't notice their absence.

He'd become me.

I thought of Melody that first day I'd met her, of being sandbagged by the way she'd looked – and then slowly, over time, the differences between her and Derryn starting to wash out like a dye. This was the same. I turned and began to head down the hallway, in the direction of the bedroom, and I saw the flaws: the plastering on the walls looked different; the door frames weren't made from the same wood. I got to the spare room and tried the door; when it didn't open, I tried the office – neither door was the same design I had at home, even if they'd been painted the same colour. In one of the frames, I saw fingernail gouges, the evidence of when I was here, when I'd stood there, listening to her call me to dinner and it had felt like my heart was coming out of my chest.

At the bedroom, I stopped.

Everything hit me at once. It wasn't laid out in the same way as my house was now; it was laid out like it had been in the weeks and months before Derryn died. The furniture had been returned to its original position; the striped duvet cover was the same design as the one she'd lain under – and died under – eight years ago. There was a lookalike bookcase next to the bed, the real version of which I'd chucked when one of the shelves snapped.

It was filled with Eva Gainridge novels.

There were paintings on the walls that Derryn had always loved, but which had begun to sting too sharply in the time after her death. I came to hate looking at them, at the heartache and memories clinging to every brushstroke and so I took them down and put them in the loft as well.

Now they were back up.

The photo frames weren't quite right and the pictures were all of Melody, but they'd been positioned in the same places as the ones Derryn and I used to have. It was so distressing seeing it like this – this portrait of a life, this time machine – that I had to reach out and grab the door for support.

I was back in the worst moments of my life.

The days before she died.

And then I noticed something else. Stepping further in, the carpet thinner than the one at home, I saw that the duvet was ruffled, untidy, as if it had been slept in. At first, I thought it was simply unmade, but then I realized that wasn't the case.

There was someone under the covers.

77

I rushed to the other side of the bed.

It was Melody Campbell.

She was lying under the duvet in a foetal position, dressed in one of Derryn's nighties. Bennik had abandoned her. As Evan Willis, as the man he was to almost everyone but the woman he kidnapped, he'd grabbed everything he could and he'd fled.

Her body looked so small, so fragile. The bones at her collar were like ridges on a hillside, the hollows of her cheeks sunken and dark. Her skin was almost yellow and she'd been sweating so much there were damp patches in crescents at her arms, her hair slick and coiled. She had a bandaged arm, but there was blood on the dressing and a thick residue had begun leaking out, a tendril of infection.

'Melody?' I said gently.

She stirred but didn't wake.

I dropped to my haunches, so our eyes were on the same level, and said her name again. This time, her eyelids fluttered, a bird trying to take flight. I caught a brief glimpse of an iris, a flash of blue-green, and then it was like the power had been cut as it snapped shut again.

Getting to my feet, I gently rolled her on to her back, the duvet twisted around her, and checked her pulse. It was slow. I swapped arms and began to peel back the bandaging. I'd only just pared it away from the skin when the smell hit me. The stench of infection was so strong, I had to pause for a moment.

I peeled back the rest of the bandage.

The wound had begun opening up, like a smile on her

arm. It had definitely been inflicted by a knife. *Bennik's knife.* I felt a burst of anger, a hatred for him that made my fingers close on her wrist. I released them again, conscious of hurting her, and saw that the wound was mottled with pus. She needed a hospital.

She needed one right now.

'Melody?' I said again more urgently.

This time, her eyes opened part of the way, struggling to focus. I gave her a few seconds and then said her name again, but now something was different. She looked like she was awake, like she was hearing me, but a frown was slowly forming.

'You,' she said, her voice hoarse.

She doesn't know who I am.

I was just a man her husband told her to trick.

She shifted on the bed, closer to me, turning her head so that it was no longer in profile. Her eyes flittered open and closed. She'd never looked like Derryn in profile, only like this, only front on; and as I looked at her, as I saw her up close again, as the past six days finally caught up with me, she looked enough like my wife to take my breath away.

I love you, D.

Suddenly, it was November 2009 again.

I'll always love you.

I was holding Derryn's hand.

I'll love you even after I'm gone.

'Where's David?'

I snapped out of the moment, wiping my eyes.

'What?' I said.

'Where's David?' she croaked.

She swallowed, her head rolling to the left, as if it were too heavy. And then her eyes began to close, her mouth pressed against the pillow and her breathing dulled.

I needed to get her out of here.

Throwing back the duvet, I saw the full extent of her, how

small her body had become. I looked around for something she could wear, couldn't see anything and then went to the wardrobes. There, I found all of Derryn's old clothes – as well as a mix of mine and Bennik's.

'David?'

I turned to the bed again, ready to respond.

Except it wasn't Melody's voice.

Spinning on my heel, I looked out into the hallway. The voice had come from out there. I left Melody for a second, heading to the front of the house.

Field was standing at the door. Something had happened to her. Her eyes were full of tears, glistening in the light from the house, and there was a bruise forming on her left cheek-bone. She sniffed, took a step forward.

'Field?' I said. 'What the hell happened?'

Kent stepped into view behind her.

I looked at him, even more uncertain than ever. And then, for the first time, I noticed something. He matched the physical description. Stocky, medium build and height, dark hair, a beard. Roy at the library had talked about the husband having a tattoo: I glanced from Kent's face to the blue RSI bandage that he'd been wearing since the first time we'd met – except he had no injury, I realized that now.

He was hiding whatever was inked on his wrist.

Suddenly, I understood what McMillan was trying to tell me the night he died: not that John Bennik worked at St Augustine's, but that he *lived* next to it. I suddenly understood the links to Charing Cross, why Melody had ended up there, how she knew to go to the flat in Chalk Farm that night, straight from the police station. I understood all of it as I looked at Kent and it froze my blood. Because John Bennik wasn't in Madrid. He'd never been called Evan Willis either.

He was here, and he was a police officer.

And he had a knife to Field's throat.

78

I backed up as he pushed Field into the hallway, and then, in the living room, he pushed her again and she hit a wall. I felt it bend against the impact. A puff of dust fell from the ceiling, a crack appearing in the plaster. The moment she recovered, straightening, he grabbed the collar of her coat, dragging her in front of him, the point of the knife at her neck.

'Put down the metal pipe and sit,' he ordered, indicating one of the chairs at the table.

My eyes moved to Field: she looked in shock, and I could see another injury at the top of her hairline. This one was starting to bleed.

I pulled out the chair and sat.

He hustled Field towards the table, yanked a second chair away from it and then shoved her down, hard. This time, he winced. *The knife injury.* For the first time, I noticed a stiffness in his left hip. He shuffled a little to his right, so that he could bear the brunt of his weight, and without taking his eyes off me, without moving the knife at Field's neck an inch, he reached behind himself to the sideboard, sliding out the middle drawer. He ripped the RSI bandage away with his teeth, dumped it in there, and I saw the tattoo.

It was four sentences in black ink, one on top of the other: *The body can wither. Memories can fade. But love never dies. RIP 26/11/09.*

It was the opening lines from *No One Can See the Crows at Night* and the date of Derryn's death. Anger pulsed in my throat.

Out of the drawer, he lifted a pair of handcuffs.

'Put these on,' he said, wincing again.

Field couldn't see what was going on, but as Kent tossed me the handcuffs, he pressed the point of the knife in harder against her jugular – a threat; a promise that he would cut her throat if I didn't follow his instructions. I watched her suck in a breath. It was a terrible, terrified sound, and a tear broke from her right eye. The whole time she looked at me, trying not to move, trying to remain silent, inert, as I snapped the handcuffs on.

I looked at Kent.

'You were right,' he said, smiling. 'I panicked.'

He was referring to the interview I'd done with Carmichael down in Sussex. He must have read the transcript. I'd said the reason Bennik tried to shift the focus on to me by getting Melody to tell the police I'd followed her, why he used Roddat at the flat, was panic. The rationale for driving off and leaving Melody at the pharmacy was the same – if he got a ticket, if his registration was taken and he existed on the system somewhere, he became visible in a way he hadn't been before. His real identity would be exposed. Later on down the line, he might get asked questions about why he was there, and who he was with. So he drove away before the traffic warden could give a detailed description of him, his car or his plate. He tried to stop a spiral – but the spiral had already started. It started when Melody wandered off, unsure about where he'd gone or where she should go.

I'd never been certain why Melody had gone to the flat at Chalk Farm that night, but now I knew: when Field was busy interviewing me, Kent had gone into the suite to see her. I tried to imagine what Melody's reaction might have been. Was she happy to see him? Scared that he might be angry she had wandered off? Whichever it was, he handed her the address, and directions, on a Post-it note and told her to go there afterwards. By then, he must have already organized it

448

with Roddat. I knew as well why Melody recalled Charing Cross – of all the police stations in London – so distinctly; why she would go there after being abandoned at the pharmacy. It was because, at some point during the eight years he'd kept her a prisoner, Kent must have mentioned its name, perhaps only accidentally, perhaps without even realizing it, and – in her confusion, in the gradual deterioration and loss of self over such a long time – she remembered it, and she mistook it for a place she might find refuge.

And then, finally, there was the CCTV footage from Chalk Farm. Kent had said that he was the person who'd picked up the telephone call from Melody; the one in which she'd sounded distressed and said she was being followed. Except the call, in reality, was never made – or, if it was, the paperwork was fudged by Kent – because he wasn't at the station at the time, he was in the flat with her. As I'd told Carmichael down in Sussex, Kent must have been waiting outside the flat for a while, but once Roddat opened up, once Melody arrived, he'd told them what the plan was, and then he'd walked out again, keeping to the shadows as he helped the old woman in the stairwell. A few minutes later, after Roddat and Melody were both gone, he pulled up in the Volvo. He was back to being Gary Kent, a detective constable with the Met – trusted, tenacious, honourable. His role there explained something else as well: how he'd manipulated Roddat. Kent would either have threatened to charge him, branding him a sex offender, or – if he'd kept his real identity as a police officer hidden – told Roddat he would tip off the authorities. Whichever it was, I was absolutely certain now that Roddat had slept with an underage girl. In the dark of a nightclub, she'd probably looked much older. He could have ended up in bed with her without realizing how young she was. Not that either of those things made a blind bit of difference. He'd had sex with a child.

Or was it even worse than that?

I thought of Roddat taking his own life, of the suicide note that simply read, *I'm sorry.* If he'd done it before, if he had a history of it, if he had sex with underage girls all the time, that was something Kent could *really* use. Suddenly, it wasn't one mistake in a nightclub, it was the actions of a prolific paedophile. Roddat's tastes would have been abhorrent, ruinous, and – just like he'd done with Erik McMillan – Kent would turn the screw on him until he got what he wanted.

'It just all went wrong at once,' he said, the sound of him breaking my train of thought. He was quiet, almost regretful, and something had altered in his voice: he didn't speak like the Gary Kent I'd met before. That version of him had a soft London accent, his voice expressive and dogged. Now, he spoke like the man on the Dictaphone tapes: almost no accent at all, more reserved, his tone more stilled, but with an anger behind it – a threat – that was truly frightening. 'The cut on her arm,' he went on, 'became infected while McMillan was up in Scotland; then there was the pharmacy, the traffic warden; and *then* she ends up walking into Charing Cross because of one tiny mistake I made over two *years* ago.' He sucked in a deep breath. 'I wrote down something about the police station and forgot to get rid of the note. I got complacent, I suppose. I forgot myself for a fraction of a second and that was all it took. I don't know how or why she remembered it, but she did.'

He meant that he was supposed to be David Raker. His story was supposed to be my story. But he'd let slip one small detail about his other life and it was enough.

'The morning I took her to the pharmacy, it was my day off. I'm driving around London, trying to find out where the hell she is, and she's already at my fucking place of work. I thought I got lucky after that: one of the guys in the office called me because he wanted to check something about another case, and we got talking and he said they'd had this woman turn up who was supposed to be dead. I was still south of the river then, driving around Woolwich, so I went down the road to Plumstead. I knew that place, knew that area, knew there were no cameras there, and I phoned McMillan and prepped him for everything that was coming. I told him the police were going to call and – when they asked – he had to pretend he'd treated you. But McMillan kept fucking me around, kept arguing. He said he didn't care any more if I told the world about Bruce Dartford. And I thought, "You don't care? *Really?*" So I put the phone down and called his daughter, and he caught a glimpse of what it would be like if his girl ever knew the truth, and, after that, he realized he cared quite a lot. Once I was done, I went into work, pretended I needed to check on something, and the moment she was alone, I switched off the CCTV, went into the interview suite and gave her the address for the flat.'

'But the cat was already out of the bag,' I said.

'It was like dominoes,' he muttered, his eyes briefly skirting the living room. 'You can understand why I panicked. This place took a lot of work. We loved it here. If Derryn hadn't made me so angry that day, none of this . . .' He faded out.

Derryn.

He wasn't talking about Derryn, he was talking about Melody – the woman he'd erased. He was talking about the reason she had the injury on her arm.

'But Derryn can be like that, can't she?'

It felt like nails were ripping at my skin. I wanted to grab him. I wanted to hurt him. I hated the sound of her name on his lips.

'She kept asking these questions. These fucking *questions.*' He said it through his teeth, flecks of saliva mixing with whorls of dust in the air. 'No matter how hard I worked, what I tried, the changes to her appearance, the techniques, how isolated I made her or didn't, I never *quite* turned her completely. Ninety-nine per cent of her is Derryn. But there was always that one per cent that wasn't, and when that one per cent was on, that was when the questions would start. Sometimes I'd just flip. I'd have enough of it.' Kent shrugged. 'That day, it just happened to be within reach.'

It. The knife he'd cut her with.

A hush settled around us.

'Who does she think you are?' I asked him.

A flash of anger. 'What sort of fucking question is that? I'm her *husband*. We have a life here. We talk about books and art; we watch movies together. We go out to the park and the library. We have a lovely relationship. It's full of kindness, and fun, and laughter. She trusts me.'

'You kidnapped her.'

He shook his head.

'You kept her prisoner here. You took her from her family.'

'No.'

'Her parents died without knowing what happened to their only daught–'

'*No*. Shut up. *Shut up*. She loves me.'

'You cut her with a knife.'

'*No.*'

'That night at Chalk Farm, she came out with bruises on her. You hurt her so badly she bled. Her blood was on the door frame. If you loved her, you wouldn't *ever* lay a hand on –'

'*Shut up.*' He closed his eyes for a second. 'Shut up,' he repeated, his chest expanding and contracting, his hand balled into a fist. He shook his head again, as if he were try-ing to exorcize my voice from his head. 'I was angry when she turned up there, I know that.' And then he was suddenly calm again, a switch so instantaneous, it was terrifying. 'I mean, of *course* I was angry with her. We'd just had that inci-dent with the knife and then, barely a few days after that, she upped and left me at the pharmacy. Of *course* I was angry.'

'So you hit her.'

He swallowed. 'Do you know why we spent almost an hour in that flat? Because I was hugging her, cuddling her, telling her I loved her and that she was safe.'

'Was that before or after you hit her?'

His eyes narrowed.

But then his expression neutralized and it was clear he'd thought of something: a way to get at me. 'You know,' he said, turning the knife at Field's throat, eliciting a gasp from her, 'when she and I talk, when we share these special moments, it's rather like old times.' He paused, waiting for me to catch up. He meant the times he'd spent talking to Derryn – the actual Derryn, *my* Derryn – when he'd been on the ward. 'I can just be myself again.'

Field and I glanced at one another. She swallowed, her eyes wet, her throat shifting up and down behind the blade. Every muscle in my body was on fire. I was shaking from the anger.

But then, with only two words, he cut me in half.

'Hey, sweetheart,' he said, his voice like an axe in the chest. I looked at him, at his body, into the blue of his eyes. He was aping my voice. Impersonating me. But not only that: somehow he'd changed himself physically too.

He'd brought his shoulders up, broadened himself in order to match my build. He held his head at a slight angle, tilted fractionally to the right, something I knew that I did – that I saw reflected back in the mirror sometimes – but was rarely conscious of. He brushed a finger against his eyebrow, another habit of mine when I was deep in thought. He smiled like me, and then he laughed like me, and then, finally, he said, 'Why don't you get undressed, sweetheart?' mimicking my voice again. It wasn't exactly right, but it was close. All I could do was watch, transfixed. 'Why don't you lie on the bed, sweetheart? Why don't you open your legs, sweetheart?' He stopped, and the whole façade dropped. 'You get the idea,' he said, and as his body relaxed, his voice changed back and he jerked a little, a reminder of the wound he carried.

I felt light-headed, woozy.

It was why Melody, on that first day at the station, had suggested that I'd threatened her, hurt her. Because, in the shadows of this house, this museum trapped in time, David Raker had. He was the one who loved her, and comforted her, and slept with her, but he was also the one who isolated her, and destroyed her; broke her, hurt her. To an outsider, even to me, it was impossible to believe that this prison had become normal to her, that she'd come to accept it. But then I remembered that she'd lived like this, every minute of every day, for eight years. He'd cut her to pieces and then stitched her back together, brainwashed her, converted and conditioned her. This was her version of normal.

'I know, sometimes, I let her down,' he said quietly.

He moved the blade at Field's throat, nicking her skin with the edge of it. She flinched and began to bleed from a faint line above her collarbone.

Kent didn't seem to notice.

'She'll ask to go outside and a lot of the time it's easier just to say no. It's too risky.' He shrugged. 'But I want her to enjoy herself and be happy. That's why the garden's nice here. It's enclosed; no one can see her, but she can be outside, in the air. And when we *do* go out – I mean, *out* out – I plan it all properly. We avoid the neighbours, go where people won't recognize us, and we only do it for short periods. She knows she can't be away from the house too long, because of the disease she has.' He eyed me. There was no disease. It was yet more fiction. But Melody believed it – perhaps because Kent used McMillan to reinforce the idea – and I remembered that at the station she'd suggested she couldn't be out for long periods of time. 'I told her she wouldn't ever be able to go outside for longer than a few hours,' he said, as if he could read my thoughts, 'otherwise she could become very ill. If she was out for too long, I told her, she'd become bewildered and detached from reality.'

He repeated it back like it was fact, like everything he was saying was logical.

'In the end,' he said, 'if you do things properly, most of what doesn't make sense gets forgotten, or accepted.'

He was talking about thought reform.

Brainwashing.

'I mean, Patty Hearst was running around robbing banks for the SLA after two months. Imagine what you can do to a person's mind after eight years.'

He was so matter-of-fact it was horrifying.

'Did you know that, last week, when she talked about you having a breakdown, she was really talking about me? After November 2009, I was very low.'

November 2009: the month of Derryn's death. I glanced at his tattoo again, the storm starting to return inside of me.

'I struggled for months and months to get past what happened to her, what she had to endure.' He adjusted his stance, grimacing slightly. He was talking about Derryn, not Melody, but maybe they were the same person to him now. As that occurred to me, something else hit home too: he couldn't acknowledge that Derryn was dead; he couldn't say it out loud. 'When I saw her up in Birmingham, my head cleared instantly. I could suddenly see a way through it. I'd work on her physical appearance, her weight loss, her memories of things; I'd shave her hair so that I could nurse her back to health, succeed where you failed.' He paused, the lines between Derryn and Melody becoming more blurred the longer he talked. 'Sometimes, at night, I take her out to the nature reserve, let her listen to the birds, the river, the sounds of the city. She always says how much she loves it.'

He looked at me, and a wordless question formed in his

455

face: *Why didn't you ever do that sort of thing for her?* And then it changed into something else.

I'm everything you weren't.

I'm everything you should have been.

'We kiss when we're there,' he said, 'and I tell her I love her, and she always forgives me my moments of weakness. Do you ever wish for that?'

It seemed like he was about to say *David*, but then he stopped himself, shifting from one foot to another, pushing the serrated blade harder against Field's throat.

'Do you ever wish for that?' he repeated.

He couldn't say my name. Saying it would be admitting he was a fake.

'Do you ever wish for that?' he said again.

'Do I ever wish for *what*?'

'Do you ever wish you could kiss Derryn like me?'

'You don't kiss her.'

He frowned.

'The woman in there isn't Derryn.'

He gave me a puzzled look, as if he genuinely had no idea what I was talking about – but then he broke into a smile.

'Derryn has had many different stages.'

And then it felt like the roof was caving in.

'No.' I shook my head. '*No.*'

'Yes,' he said. 'She's had many different stages, she's been sick and she's been healthy – and I've lain with her, and I've kissed her, in all of them.'

79

It took everything I had not to leap out of my chair and grab him by the throat – even if my hands were cuffed together. I wanted to choke him. I wanted him to feel my fingers crushing his larynx. I wanted his last moments to be raw and painful.

I wanted him to suffer like I had.

It coursed through me like a poison, a rush of blood so immense it made spots flash in front of my eyes. I closed them, sucked in breaths, felt the familiar pounding start up, a thump at the back of my skull. But then I looked at him again and I tried to show him he hadn't won. I tried to suppress every last ounce of revulsion and rage, because I knew I wasn't in control, and any move I made now put Field's life at risk.

'I kissed her,' he said again.

I stayed still, not taking my eyes off him.

'I kissed her on the lips, on the mouth, as she lay there.' His fingers wriggled at the knife, adjusting the position of his grip. I was almost retching again. 'One of us had to be there, because you were so worthless. So *weak*. I used to watch you come out of the house in those last months, and you were a fucking mess. Tears all down your face. Blubbing like a scolded child. She was in there, fighting for every breath in her lungs, and when she looked at you, what did she see? She saw a man who'd already committed her to the grave. She looked at you and saw no hope – nothing to aim for – so she thought, what's the point? She may as well give in.'

'She had terminal cancer,' I said, barely able to speak.

'Nothing is *terminal*, you fucking coward.' He spat the

words at me. 'Nothing gives you the excuse to fail her like you did. I spent time alone with her in hospital. I know what sort of woman she was. She and I, we were on the same wavelength. We understood each other. All the shit I'd been through before I met her, the way Nora *destroyed* me, all the crap Derryn had to deal with the first two times she got sick, we understood that sense of loneliness. She and I, we understood being abandoned and having to face down what scares you, alone. If I'd been there for her properly during her last few months, there's no way she would have suffered like she did. I would have made it –'

'You don't know anything about her.'

His eyes narrowed.

'You're the *same* as her – you believe that?'

'I don't believe it,' he replied, 'I know it.'

'You really think you're remotely like she was?'

'Yes. We were the same.'

'Of course you weren't the fucking *same*,' I shouted at him. 'You're *deranged*. I spent sixteen years with her, I saw every moment, and she was *nothing* like you. You have *zero* in common with her.' I paused, watching him colour. I knew I had to retreat, to step back for Field's sake, but I couldn't stop myself: the rage was spilling out of me. 'That day you and I first met, that day in the hospital nine years ago – do you remember that?' It wasn't a question I needed an answer to, because I knew that he did. 'I forgot your face. I forgot everything about us meeting until a few days ago, but – when I thought about it, when tiny fragments of it began to return – one thing came through the clearest. I saw Derryn's expression.'

He shook his head, knowing what was coming.

'She never even *liked* you.'

'That's not true.'

'You frightened her.'

'*No.*' He lifted the knife away from Field and pointed it at me. 'You're a *liar*.' He stopped himself, readjusted his stance. 'You've no idea what we were together.'

'You weren't together.'

'I was there at the end. I saw her every day during that time. I lay next to her in the bed and I held her in my arms. We kissed. She would say my name to me.'

'She didn't know *what* she was saying.'

'She did.'

'No.' My jaw clenched. 'She was barely conscious.'

'I would talk to her,' he went on, 'and she would listen – and where were you? All the times you left the house to do whatever it was that was so important, I was –'

'I hardly left the house.'

He shrugged. 'You left it enough.'

Enough for me to get inside.

Enough for me to lie with her.

It felt like I was rupturing open.

'You know,' he said, 'I did think about killing you once. I gave serious thought to it. Before I knew she was really sick, I even began planning it out. With you out of the way, things would have been a lot simpler for us. But, ultimately, killing is so messy, and complicated, and frightening. Any pleasure you derive from it is gone before you've even had a chance to appreciate it, because there's so much else to worry about. In *The Man with the Wolf's Head*, Eva Gainridge calls murder "an ephemeral act". I never really knew what she meant until I met Nora, but then it made sense to me. It really *is* like that: it's there, and then it's gone.'

He seemed to lose himself for a second, and I briefly wondered why he would talk so openly about Nora Fray. Then I remembered that Mulligan, the cop from Sussex, had identified her during our interview in Killiger. The police suspected that John Bennik had killed her.

Kent must have listened to that interview too.

He'd listened to everything, because it was the perfect way to keep ahead of the investigation.

'Much more interesting to me,' he said, 'is suffering. The things I found out about Erik McMillan, the way he lied to his wife about who he was, the way his actions made her kill herself; and then the things I found out about Gavin Roddat, the way I twisted and used his repellent taste for underage girls against him – both of those were true deaths. They happened slowly, over a long period of time. They weren't ephemeral.' But then he stopped, his face dropping; a flicker of sadness. 'The trouble was, I didn't expect Gavin to kill himself. That ended up being another moment of panic. I tried to head it off, to buy myself some time just to think straight, but you saw right through it, didn't you?'

He meant the evidence that the police had found in Roddat's possession: the home movies, the photographs, the obsession with Derryn and me.

'She's never said as much,' Kent said, 'but I rather suspect that DS Field saw through it too.' He brought the knife further around her throat. 'Am I right, *boss*?'

She nodded, her eyes on me, and in them I saw something else: the reason we'd met beneath the arches; the reason, when they'd been interviewing me in my home, that Field had appeared to be silently communicating with me, giving me responses to questions she wasn't supposed to. She hadn't gone behind Carmichael's back because she didn't like the way he was running the case – or, at least, that wasn't the primary driver. It was because she knew something was off much closer to home.

This was what she was keeping back from me.

'You started to suspect Kent,' I said.

'That's right, isn't it?' Kent asked her.

A single nod of the head. 'Yes.'

It was the first time she'd spoken since she'd arrived at the house. Her voice was small, ragged.

'Did you know he used to be John Bennik?' I asked.

'No,' she said. 'Never.'

'You just felt something wasn't right about him?'

'He was acting differently,' she said softly. 'Quieter, more on edge. He kept poring over case files – but not in a normal way. It was almost obsessive. He had to see everything. He was there before me every morning and after me every night. I just never realized it was *this* case he was looking at – all the evidence, all the interviews.'

'I thought I was being careful,' Kent interjected, 'but you saw right through it, didn't you, boss? And there were other things. Like, why would I come into the office on my day off like that when I never had before? Or, when she ordered me to call McMillan on the phone and ask some initial questions, why did I make an excuse and tell her I couldn't? Why was I *always* making excuses about not being able to call McMillan, or speak to him face-to-face?' He angled the knife slightly, taunting her with a sawing motion. 'McMillan didn't know I was a cop. He didn't know my name was Gary Kent. I'd told him my name was John. But he would have recognized my voice if I'd ever spoken to him on the phone in my role as a cop, and especially my face if I'd gone to his office. That was why I couldn't have anything to do with him, and that was why her curiosity was aroused.' He looked down at Field. 'Am I right, boss?'

'You wanted me to smoke Kent out?' I said to Field.

'I had no idea it was this,' she replied, 'I swear to you. I thought he might have been on the take, maybe protecting someone else. Not this – not *ever*.'

As she said that, something else slotted into place: this was the real reason that she leaked the story to *FeedMe*. Not because she wanted to know who the woman was, and what I might be hiding, or not *only* that; rather, it was because she knew the story would spread quickly, and the quicker it spread, the quicker it would reveal potential anomalies — anomalies like a liar embedded in her own team.

'So is Gary Kent your real name?' I asked him.

'Yes.'

He looked around the place he'd built.

'But I have lots of names for lots of things. One advantage that being a cop *does* give you is easy access to people's information. You choose the name of someone who's been missing a long time, or who's dead, and you bring them back in from the cold.'

Multiple identities. Nothing to tie one person to the next, one act to another. But his real identity tied him to this place. He must have realized that, if Field did decide to follow my advice and start checking properties in Mountford Road, she'd find him. That must have been why he'd grabbed her and brought her here.

Somewhere, a crow squawked, and then another, and then we could hear them on the roof of this part of the house, the *clack, clack, clack* of their feet, passing from one end to the other.

'Why don't you feel guilty?' he said.

I looked at him. 'What?'

'I don't sense one *iota* of guilt in you. Where's your guilt over Derryn?'

I didn't respond this time.

'Admit that you failed her,' he said.

I shook my head.

'Admit it. *Admit* it.' He brought the knife away from Field's throat again, using it as a pointer, an extension of his hand, jabbing it into the space above her right shoulder. 'Admit that you failed her,' he repeated, his voice more contained, 'and we move on.'

'Move on to what?'

'Derryn's ill again, and she needs help,' he said.

'And?'

'And I'm going to save her.'

'How the hell are you going to do that?'

'I'm not. You're going to do it for me.'

I frowned. 'What are you talking about?'

'You're going to go and get her dressed,' he said, 'and unless you want me to cut DS Field's throat, and then travel down to Devon and cut the throat of your daughter, you're somehow going to get Derryn into A&E, and get that injury of hers looked at.'

I thought of Annabel, of Olivia too, pictured him inside their house, the two of them trying to hide from him, and my stomach dropped like a stone.

'I'll do it,' he said, knowing where my head was at. 'And I'll make it slow.'

'Even if I *do* take her to A&E, how do I explain who she is?'

'That's the good bit. You'll tell them she's your wife.'

I looked from him to Field.

'You're going to give the world what they want to hear,' he said, 'what the Met have suspected for a long time, what the journalists have been itching to write about for ever: David Raker, the sham. The impostor. The fraudulent husband. The fake, the charlatan. The man who told the world his wife was dead.'

'She *is* dead.'

'And who will believe you?'

'None of this will stand up.'

'It'll stand up long enough to ruin you.'

I glanced at Field again, and then looked at him.

'And you?'

'Once you bring Derryn back to me,' he said, 'we're going to disappear for a while. We'll make a life for ourselves somewhere else. I'll feel sad about leaving the police force, it's been my existence for nearly eight years, it's where I've learned so much about investigation, science, psychology, guilt. I'll be even sadder to leave this place because I've put so much work into it. I mean, it's art, isn't it? It's a painting every bit as beautiful as the ones on the walls in Derryn's bedroom. Even you have to admit that. You have to admit this place is profound.' He waited for me to comment, and when I didn't, he said, 'Life moves forward. It always moves forward. So you'll get her seen to, and when she's better, we all walk away safely.'

Except that was a lie.

It was all a lie.

He might have had plans for himself and Melody, but Field and I weren't walking away from this safely. We weren't walking away at all. Because, for all his talk about killing being frightening and messy, our murders were the only way he could create enough breathing room for him to escape successfully. With the two of us out of the way, he had time to reimagine himself, relegating Gary Kent to history alongside John Bennik.

'How did you know so much?'

He studied me. 'What?'

'How did you teach Melody so much about me? About Derryn and me? How did you know the private conversations we had? Were you in the house when we talked?'

'I was never in the house when you were there.'

'Then how do you know?'

He broke into a smile.

'Trade secret,' he said.

'Just tell me how you know.'

'I said it was a secret.'

'*Please.*'

I heard the pleading tone of my voice, the desperation threaded through every word, and hated myself for it. I hated myself for ever having left her, for the moments when I'd gone out for an hour, trying to clear my head, to gather myself. He was right. I'd cried all the time in those last weeks, and it was because I'd known it was over, I'd known the fight was finally at an end, and I couldn't face it. I couldn't accept it. All the other times she'd fought, we'd glimpsed the light, some hint of hope like the first strands of a sunrise. The third time there had been no light.

It had just been a perpetual darkness.

'I will cut her open,' he said, bringing me back into the moment, the flat of the blade now pressed against Field's windpipe. 'I will slice Field's throat from ear to ear and then I will cut your daughter's heart out. If you don't do this for me, I will cut –'

'David?'

Everything stopped.

It was Melody.

80

She was standing in the hallway, looking in at us, her night-dress clinging to the meagre shape of her body. She was struggling to focus, unbalanced, a finger of blood creeping out from beneath her dressing. She looked brittle and dazed.

'Sweetheart,' he said softly, lovingly, dropping the knife away a little, bringing it around to the side of Field's neck so that Melody wasn't able to see it. 'Sweetheart, go back to bed. I just need to deal with something, okay?'

She blinked, looking in at us, struggling to focus.

'What's going on, D?'

She was looking at him, not me, addressing him, not me, speaking like Derryn, looking like her. When the tears started to well in my eyes, when my vision smeared and she became less defined, it was like I was back in that last month: a moment of déjà vu. Derryn had come down the hallway just like this.

D? Are you okay?

I'm fine, sweetheart.

What's the matter?

Nothing. Nothing, I promise. Can I get you something?

I'm thirsty.

Okay, you go back to bed. Let me get you a drink.

Are you sure you're all right, D?

And then she could see: I'd been crying. I'd left our bedroom, pulled out a chair at the living-room table, and sat there and cried. I hadn't wanted her to see me like that, unable to maintain control, unable to keep being the person she needed me to be.

'Go back to bed, sweetheart.'

His voice brought me round.

I wiped my eyes and, for the first time, Melody actually seemed to register me. She turned slightly, frowned, looked to Kent, then to Field, then back to me.

'It's him,' she said weakly.

I turned back to Kent, watched the knife drop another inch, the serrated edge coming away from Field's neck completely, angling down towards the back of her shoulder blade.

'Go back to bed,' Kent said, more sharply this time.

Field was staring at me.

Do something, Raker.

'Go back to *bed*.'

Do something now.

'Derryn, get back to your fucking *bed*.'

I sprang to my feet.

Field lurched to her side, dropping off her chair completely, as I smashed into Kent. The two of us crashed into the sideboard. Photograph frames spilled off, glass shattered. Melody screamed. I saw Field scramble across the floor, right at the periphery of my vision, and then Kent and I fell, him landing on top of me, his knees in my stomach.

My breath hissed out of me.

Lights. Noise.

When everything snapped back into focus, I saw he had straddled me and was looking around for the knife. I leaned forward, bringing my torso up even as my pelvis remained pinned beneath him, and swung my handcuffed wrists at his face. I hit him hard. He rolled left, stunned, and then Field appeared behind him, holding the metal pipe I'd brought in with me. A second later, he saw her, started to turn, an arm reaching up to try and grab the pipe.

I jabbed him hard in the ribs.

He collapsed again, his arm dropping – and then Field

moved in for the kill. She took a step closer, gripped the pipe and crunched it against the side of his head.

Kent became limp.

He swayed, leaned.

And then, finally, he fell sideways and hit the floor.

After

81

Once the police interviews were all over, I went to stay with Annabel in Devon. We'd talk at night over dinner, and we'd curl up with Olivia on the sofa and watch old movies, and then, when they went to bed, I'd sit at the window, looking out at the lake beyond their house. I'd watch birds come and go, darting out of the darkness, marks against the moonlit water, and would think of the crows on the roof of the house that Kent had built, and then the crow on the cover of the book I'd found in the loft. Some nights, I would manage to sleep. Most nights, I didn't. I'd stay awake until the sun started to bleach the sky, and when Annabel asked the next morning how I'd slept, I'd lie and tell her I'd slept well.

When she was at work and Olivia was at school, I would go over the things I'd said in the interviews. Carmichael had made it clear he didn't like me, and tried to hammer me on perceived inconsistencies, but – over time – Field's accounts helped to dilute much of his work. There were things he could have hurt me with – like breaking into Kent's house – but, ultimately, they were worthless time-sinks in comparison to the scope of what had existed inside. And, in the end, even Carmichael could see the bigger picture: going after me while a Met detective had imprisoned and abused a woman for eight years would play disastrously internally, and even worse in the public arena.

I never saw or heard from Kent again – except in the media when his picture, an official Met police photograph, would be used – but in the weeks that followed, Field and I spoke on the phone and she filled me in on things he'd admitted to and that investigators had uncovered.

He was an orphan, brought up as a teenager in the care system in Oxfordshire, erudite and intelligent, even from a young age, and teased mercilessly because of his acne. Before he ever joined the police, he said he'd started stealing identities as a means of escape, a way to reinvent himself, and people who'd known him at UEL – where he studied English and Psychology, as a man called John Bennik – said he could be strange, and sometimes quite awkward. His final-year dissertation was on the work of Eva Gainridge.

In 2009, the year John Bennik disappeared, Kent joined the Met.

From there, his talent for appropriating identities, his lies and the stories he created, became a sort of addiction. He was able to use the police databases as a way to remake himself, and to target people, sniffing out men like Gavin Roddat. Roddat was in the computers because a fifteen-year-old girl had told her parents that he slept with her. In the end, there wasn't enough evidence for the police to pursue the investigation, and the girl didn't want to press charges, so Roddat got away with it.

But only until Gary Kent turned up on his doorstep.

After that, Kent unearthed a succession of people like Roddat – men and women who had secrets they didn't want outed – dug around, watched them and then threatened to expose them. They never knew who he really was, they just knew he would destroy them. He even leveraged money – small amounts that, collectively, became bigger – which was how he was able to afford the huge renovations at the house in Mountford Road.

In the weeks that followed his arrest, building firms employed by Kent to work on his property at the east wall said in interviews that Kent had told them he was converting

472

the house into two separate homes, which was why he wanted two kitchens, two living rooms and two main entrances. That was a version of the truth, but as Kent swapped so regularly between contractors, and also did a lot of the interior work himself, no one ever realized the true extent of his plans. And because there were never any visitors to the house, except for McMillan – who visited on the rare occasions that Melody Campbell needed a doctor – no one noticed another weird quirk: next to the second entrance at the back of the property, beyond the barbed-wire gate which led to the front door of the duplicate house, Kent had mounted a small sign reading *40 Aintree Drive*. It was why, on that first day, Melody had told Field that she lived with me at my address.

The story Kent told Melody was that someone lived in the other side of the property, although she said in one interview that she'd thought it slightly odd that she never heard them or saw them and could never open one of the doors on their side of the building. That was the door that led through to the rooms with the photos and the Dictaphone recordings in them. Kent kept them permanently sealed off from Melody, and in the end, like so much else, he trained her to go along with his explanation.

In stark contrast to those who knew him at university, detectives at the Met never described him as strange or awkward. In fact, quite the opposite. He was sociable, smart and ambitious, loved to learn, and worked hard. He was a natural choice for CID. In fact, he was so successful in hiding who he was, in hiding what he was doing to Melody Campbell, to Erik McMillan, to Gavin Roddat, to all the others, that Field told me a few of her colleagues were visibly upset, even tearful, when they found out the truth.

'They liked him,' she said. '*Everyone* liked him.' Including her. 'He'd been on my team for two years and, until a few weeks ago, I'd have trusted him with my life.'

Although she'd begun to suspect something was going on with him, she didn't know what, she just had a hunch it might be related to one of their cases somehow. Enlisting my help had been a shot in the dark, a chance for her to see if she was right and not suffer any of the fallout if my search for Melody went south and she wasn't. It was also a reaction to bad tactical choices she thought Carmichael was making, but her position on that was a firm second place to finding out the truth about Kent. The fact was, she'd used me, and had been prepared to abandon me to the Met if it came to that, so, at the start of our phone calls, she often began with a half-hearted apology. I believed she meant what she said, that she was sorry, but she wasn't good at contrition, and it never sounded entirely sincere.

In truth, deep down, I found it hard to forgive her.

Evan Willis, the counsellor at St Augustine's, and the man who'd looked like a good fit for John Bennik, was released by Spanish police within two hours.

In a strange and unintentional piece of timing, he'd flown out to Spain to meet a woman he'd met online, on the same day Gary Kent had returned from Killiger. Willis and the woman had got on so well, he'd ended up staying in Madrid, neglecting to tell his employers what he was doing and why he wasn't at work. He'd come to hate his job at St Augustine's and decided – if he got the sack – it wouldn't matter much to him.

'I see my future in Spain with Gabrielle now,' he told the police after.

In a dark case, it was a rare moment of levity.

A few times, I asked to see Melody, but all my requests were turned down by the police. I understood why. It would have confused her, and scared her, and ultimately affected her

recovery. Field assured me she was safe, receiving counsel-
ling, and already in a deprogramming process aimed at
helping her reclaim her former identity – but it would take
time.

Answers would come, but they would come slowly.

When she was put in touch with extended family, former
friends who had known her and worked with her in Belfast,
Field told me it had been hard: she didn't know any of them,
didn't even recognize the shadow of Melody Campbell, except
in very brief snatches. And Kent's story about Melody having a disease where she couldn't be outside for longer than a
couple of hours also made things harder. Like his lie about
them having neighbours, it had stuck. It scared her, gnawed
at her, and because Kent had repeated it to her over and over,
across the entire time they were together, she came to believe
it wholeheartedly and without hesitation. Field reported back
to me that, as Melody travelled around, or sat outside, she
would often start to panic, repeating the lies that she'd been
taught.

Based on information she'd provided, and interviews with
Kent, detectives came to the conclusion that – after splitting
up with Nora Fray – Kent had moved to a ground-floor flat
in Plumstead, under the name of Carl Mulgrew, until early
2011, which was why he knew the area so well. And while the
police suspected that he wasn't being completely honest with
them about where he kept Melody after he'd abducted her
from the conference in Birmingham, the property he'd lived
in also had a basement flat, which had flooded three years
previously. It had stayed unoccupied in the time he was living in Plumstead, so they assumed that he'd kept Melody
downstairs until he eventually moved to Mountford Road.

In his home, they found a keycard for St Augustine's and
keys for the locks on the security fences around the nature
reserve, which was how he was able to turn up at McMillan's

office uninvited, and take Melody out to the reserve at night. When he came into the hospital, he would always use the south entrance, avoiding cameras. On his instructions, and with the aid of cadaver dogs, they also found a body about fifty feet from the old east wall.

It was Nora Fray, his former girlfriend.

He blamed the murder on his fragile mental state at the time, and on Eva Gainridge, who he said put ideas into his head with the story of Oliver Beaumont, the violent protagonist of *The Man with the Wolf's Head*. When that didn't stick, he switched the blame to Erik McMillan, who was treating him at the time Nora Fray was murdered, saying McMillan encouraged him to kill Nora – but, again, no one placed much stock in it. Eventually, when he failed to alter the axis of the case with any of those things, he tried telling police the truth about Erik McMillan, about how McMillan had been gay and emails sent between him and Bruce Dartford had led to Kelly McMillan killing herself. But that failed to stick either. The emails were gone, I'd torn up the letter McMillan had written to his daughter, Kelly was dead, and so were McMillan and Dartford.

In the end, Caitlin McMillan was devastated by the murder of her father, but at least her pain was a little less than it might have been. In the moments of confusion that had riddled me for a week, I'd been seeing clearly that night in Killiger: ripping up the letter was the right thing to do. If Caitlin had known the truth, if she'd read her father's words, she'd have been overwhelmed by the sense of betrayal, and plagued by it for years.

And if I'd learned anything in the time since Derryn had been gone, it was this: just losing the person you loved the most in the world was sufficient.

Grief was bad enough on its own.

82

In the immediate aftermath of Kent's exposure, I received so many calls from the media, had so many people camped outside my home and the motel I was still sleeping in, that I had to switch hotels entirely and change phones. I always kept a spare one at home, as well as the prepaid, but only a few people knew the number of the spare.

Annabel. Ewan Tasker.

Kennedy.

The call from the media that concerned me the most wasn't any of the ones trying to chase down an angle on the Gary Kent case, it was the one I received from Connor McCaskell at the *Daily Tribune*. When I checked in with my regular phone, I found a message from him on there. He'd only left one, and it had landed two days after the events at the house – way after every other one of his peers had called.

It was because he had something his rivals didn't.

'Mr Raker,' he said, 'it's Connor McCaskell from the *Daily Tribune*. I get that you're not picking up your calls, but it's in your interests that we speak, believe me.'

I called him back.

'Great to talk to you,' he said, like we were old friends.

'What do you want?'

'I want to talk to you about Bryan Kennedy.'

I remained silent but, inside, I was startled and unnerved.

'What about him?'

'He's renting from you, right?'

'He was.'

'He's not any more?'

'No. Why are you so interested in him?'

'I'm not,' McCaskell said, 'I'm interested in you. But when I started digging around, I realized something: you're renting that place to Mr Kennedy, but he doesn't actually have a bank account. In fact, from what I can see here, he pretty much doesn't have anything to his name at all. So you're renting it to him, but he's not paying you – or, at least, not through any banking system. There are no records of him at any of the utility companies, so he's not paying rates either. He has no landline there at that cottage and no Internet. So who is he?'

'What's this got to do with Gary Kent?'

'Nothing,' he said. 'I told you, I'm interested in you.'

'I'm not that interesting, believe me.'

'I disagree. I find you fascinating. I've looked at your cases, I've seen the things you've done, the accounts you've given to the police. You're pretty unique, you know that? You're smart, and you're noble, and you're daring, all the things that the public want to read about. I'm just not sure that's all of it.'

'I don't know what you're talking about.'

'Everyone has secrets.'

'I'm going now.'

'Is Bryan Kennedy yours, Mr Raker? Is he your little secret?'

I hung up.

At the time, I was at Annabel's, so I jumped straight in the car and drove from her house down to the cottage. When I was almost there, I got in touch with Kennedy at the hotel in Newcastle and told him what had happened.

'Shit,' he said.

'Stay where you are until I tell you otherwise.'

'Okay.'

'Did you remember to grab your passport?'

'You want me to go *abroad*?'

'I want us not to go to jail.'

'Yeah,' he said. 'Yeah, I've got it here.'

But there was something else in his voice.

'Kennedy?'

'Are you going to the house to clear my stuff out?'

'That's the general idea, yeah.'

'So I can't go back there?'

'What do you think?'

I heard him go to speak and then stop again.

'What's the matter?' I asked.

'Nothing,' he replied, too quickly. 'Nothing's the matter.'

By then, I was at the cottage. I let myself in and pushed the door shut. It was cold, the heating off.

'Don't screw around,' I said. 'If there's something going on, I need to know about it. McCaskell digging into you is both of our problems, remember that.'

No response.

'Kennedy?'

'Don't call me that. I hate that name.'

'At this point, I couldn't care less. What have you done?'

He went to respond, to come back at me – an instinctive reaction to deny everything, built on years of practice – but then he stopped himself, as if the next lie had evaporated on his tongue.

'I've found something,' he said quietly.

'What are you talking about?'

He hesitated for a moment more, like he was reaching for another lie, and then he seemed to accept that he'd been rumbled, that his lies were pointless. He had been forced to lie to everyone else he met in his life, pretending he was a fisherman called Kennedy. I was the only one he could tell the truth to.

'It's in the living room,' he said.

'What is?'

He chose not to respond again.

I walked across the kitchen and opened the living-room door, staring in at the furniture Dad had spent his last few years using. I wasn't sure what Kennedy was talking about, or what I was supposed to be looking for – but then I saw.

He'd pinned up newspaper cuttings, pages he'd torn out of books, photocopies from encyclopedias, printouts from web pages he must have accessed at the library. He'd stuck it all to the walls with masking tape, and had written all over it, underlining whole passages, words, photographs, titles. I tried to make sense of it, of the headlines and the pictures and the words I saw illuminated with highlighter pen, but I couldn't.

'What the hell is this?' I said.

'It's why I've been asking you so much about your cases,' Kennedy replied, his voice crackling along the phone line. 'I needed to get my rhythm back. I needed to get a feel for this sort of work again.'

'Are you *insane*?'

'It's okay,' he said, cutting me off before I could say anything else. 'No one knows who I am. *No one.* There's no trail. All of this has come from the library. I haven't made any calls. I don't have the Internet. I don't have a phone. The only way anyone ever finds out about the stuff on those walls is if you invite them into the house. Once you take it down and box it up, it'll be forgotten.'

I looked at the walls, feeling livid and panicked, uncertain of what to say. All of this put us at risk. Whatever he thought, however circumspect he'd been, it was dangerous. But there was also something absorbing and impressive about it, even oddly profound. It was like a man had returned from the afterlife. Before his career spiralled out of control, his family disintegrated around him, and he convinced the world he was dead, this was the detective I used to know.

480

'What *is* this?' I said.

'I've found something.'

I tried to make sense of the walls.

'What do you mean, you've found something?'

'I mean, this is big, Raker,' he said. 'What I've found, it's really fucking big.'

83

Whatever Kennedy had found, however big a discovery he thought it might be, in those first four weeks it wasn't big enough. His clothes, his belongings, the printouts and the photocopies, it all went into the attic as soon as I moved back home and, alone again, haunted by the idea of what had happened inside my house, I collapsed in on myself. I was incapable of finding the motivation to work, crestfallen inside the rooms that Gary Kent had corrupted. When I closed my eyes at night, all I saw was him and my wife. I was tortured by images of what might have happened, of Derryn struggling for air and him forcing his way on to the bed, his lips on hers.

I couldn't think of anything else.

But then, one day, Field knocked on the door.

I almost didn't answer, couldn't bring myself to have another conversation about Gary Kent, but then she leaned into the glass on the front door, cupped her hands to it and said, 'Raker, I know you're in there.'

She looked at me when I opened the door and didn't say anything, but I could tell what she thought of how I looked. I was broken, cleaved down the middle, and it showed in every line of my face, in the colour of my skin.

'I've got something that belongs to you,' she said.

She was holding it in her hands.

'I'm sorry we've had it for so long. It's only just been released from evidence. If I'd known it was here, I would have told you at the start, but it totally passed me by.'

'What is it?' I asked, curious.

'They found it in Kent's home.' She paused. I could hear

her trying to find the right words. 'He said he took it from Derryn in the last few weeks of her life. He got into the house five or six times during that period, and the first time, he said he went through the drawers of her bedside cabinet and . . .'

She stopped.

'And what?' I said.

'This is how he knew so much about you both – how he knew about the things you said when you were alone. She was going to leave it for you to find after she was gone.' Her voice wavered a little. 'Eventually, she just became too ill to continue, but before that, she was hiding it from you because she didn't want to upset you. Kent says she hid it inside the covers of an old Eva Gainridge hardback.'

I swallowed.

'I'm so sorry, David. None of us should have got to read this before you.'

'What did she leave me, Field?'

'This.'

She handed it to me.

It was a hardcover A5 diary.

I took it from her and a weight shifted from my body; a heaviness. I held it in my hands and opened it up. And as the pages fanned apart, I realized something: whatever he'd attempted to do, whatever he'd stolen from us, however much he'd tried to destroy me and to alter the narrative of our lives together, Kent wasn't the man Derryn remembered at the end of her life. It didn't matter that he was there in those final few days, it didn't matter that he tried to manoeuvre his way between us, it didn't matter what he said to her or what he didn't. However hard he tried altering it, what I'd been to her, and what I remained, would never change.

I was the person who married her.

I was her husband.

I was the one who had loved her, above all others, for sixteen years.

David,

These opening pages have been blank for a long time. I didn't know how to introduce this diary, really. I started writing it after I found the first lump, two years ago, and then just carried on. I found it helped me clear my head. I found it cathartic. I've wanted to show it to you often, but for some reason it never quite felt like the right time.

But things have changed now.

I can't leave these pages blank any longer.

As I finally sit here and fill up these lines, you're out on the back lawn. I can see you through the bedroom window – on your hands and knees, pulling dead flowers out of the beds – and I can tell you've been crying. I can see it in the redness at the corners of your eyes. That's why you offered to go out there, even though you hate working in the garden, because you're trying to stay strong for me. I love you for that. But today the news was hard for you to hear. I think today was when we looked at each other and we realized how little time we have left.

Because, today, I told you I was stopping the treatment.

I told you I couldn't go through it any more. All the procedures and the medicines and the sickness: it's just too much for me. And because of that, because I've made this decision, it means our journey – everything we've had together – is coming to an end. You and I, we don't have decades any more. We don't even have years.

We have months.

Throughout the rest of this notebook, you will find things we did and said that you remember. You will find things you might have forgotten. You will see things that I've written that you might recall differently. I doubt that there's anything that you'll seriously disagree with, but there might be. Over sixteen years, we would sometimes fall out (mostly about your terrible taste in music, ha ha) but those times were rare and barely register with me now, so I hope they didn't linger long with you either.

I hope you'll look at these pages sometimes and you'll think of me, but I hope – and you need to promise me this, Raker – you won't become stuck. What we had was special, maybe so singular and extraordinary that it's impossible to find again. But isn't that the nature of all relationships, D? They're all singular. They are all unique. Trying to find something exactly the same as what we had will be a fruitless search, and it will only make you unhappy. But trying to find something equally unique – that's much easier. It's as easy as talking to someone. So, in the years to come, don't punish yourself, D. Think of me sometimes, but never punish yourself.

After this, I will go back to writing in this diary, to filling in what I can about the days that pass. At some point over the next few months, I know I will stop, not because I want to, but because my body has given in and I no longer have a choice.

It doesn't matter, though.

Even if I'd never written any of this, you'd know. You'd know that my love for you never faltered, never wandered, never greyed or wilted for a second. Whether these words existed or they didn't, you'd know.

Here at the end, D, you'd just know.

You were my husband, my best friend, the absolute greatest thing that ever happened to me; you were the teller of the worst jokes known to man (and woman), and the guaranteed runner-up when we went jogging; you were always the loser at Trivial Pursuit, and always the winner at obscure movie trivia. You were handsome, and generous, and you could always make me laugh.

I agreed to go out with you because I felt there was something different about you, something special. I married you in the knowledge that I was right and in the absolute belief that it would remain that way for as long as we were together. And now I'm leaving you knowing that all those things remain true. You have been my rock, my strength and my hope. You have become the foundation on which I'm built. Every day, every week, every year, you loved me, and I loved you back.

And nothing will change, even after I'm gone.

I will love you, always.

My precious, wonderful husband.

Derryn x

Author's Note

For the purposes of the story, I've made some small changes to the working practices of UK police forces, in particular the Met. My hope is that anything I've altered or adapted is done with care and is subtle enough not to cause any offence.

Acknowledgements

As with all my books, *You Were Gone* has been a truly collaborative effort, where I've leaned on a collection of brilliant and talented people to make me look loads better than I actually am.

Chief among them are the amazing team at Michael Joseph, starting with my editor Maxine Hitchcock, who helped to craft, streamline and immeasurably improve the early drafts of the book, and who has been an incredible advocate for my writing ever since we began working together. Huge thank-yous are also due to Laura Nicol, Katie Bowden, Tilda McDonald, Chris Turner and the whole of the sales team, Aimie Price and the Production Department, Beatrix McIntyre in Editorial, Jon Kennedy who did such a brilliant job of designing the cover, and James Keyte and everyone in Audio. I'm sure there are people I've missed out (for which I apologize), but please know I'm *so* grateful for everything you do for me. Finally, a Raker book wouldn't be a Raker book without the super-powered eagle eyes of my awesome copy-editor Caroline Pretty.

Camilla Wray was, as she constantly is, an absolute rock when The Panic set in. Not only is she a fantastic agent, she's also a wonderful person, a great friend and she pretends to laugh at my jokes. A Weaver-shaped thank-you is due to the gang at Darley Anderson too, including Mary, Emma, Kristina, Sheila, Rosanna and Roya.

Thank you to Mick Confrey for his insight into being a detective, and for suggesting some of the ideas that formed the beginning of the novel. He pretends never to mind when I adapt (and sometimes just ignore) the actual rules of police work, because I think it serves the story better, so any mistakes in the novel are entirely my own.

To Mum and Dad: I love you both so much. Thank you for everything. To my sister Lucy, creator of 'Libraries' and 'Is it 1-4?': you're amazing, Ken. To the rest of my family and friends, both here and in South Africa: thank you for all your love and support. And to Sharlé, who I couldn't do any of this without, and Erin, who assures me she's old enough to read the books now (she isn't), it's hard to know what to say other than: you two are the best thing that ever happened to me.

Finally, the biggest thank-you of all, as always, goes to my readers. Ten years ago, when I signed a publishing deal with Penguin, I never would have dreamed I'd get to Book Nine – but because of your faith, support and generosity, not only has it actually happened, I get to spend my days dreaming up new and dangerous ways to mess with Raker's head.